Some Say Fire

Gregory Zeigler

RAVEN'S EYE PRESS · DURANGO, COLORADO

Raven's Eye Press
Durango, Colorado
www.ravenseyepress.com

Zeigler, Gregory.
   Some Say Fire/Gregory Zeigler   p. cm.

ISBN   978-0-9907826-5-0
LCCN   2015955315

Cover art by Jane Lavino
Graphic design by Lindsay J. Nyquist, elle jay design

Printed in the United States of America
1 3 5 7 9 10 8 6 4 2

Contact the author: gzeigler@wyom.net
Visit the author's website: gzeiglerbooks.com

Dedication

For Dear French Friends, Dom and Miss B, JN and MP.

And to Jane Lavino—courageous friend and cutting edge artist
without whom we would literally be uncovered.

Also by
Gregory Zeigler

Travels With Max:
In Search of Steinbeck's America Fifty Years Later
2010

The Straw That Broke
2013

If climate change continues unabated one in six species could disappear by the end of the century. Some land and sea creatures are already moving to new habitats because of warming, and scientists warn there will be a dramatic increase in extinctions in species unable to adapt to heat waves, droughts, floods and rising sea levels.

Author Mark Urban on Smithsonian.com.

June 6
Friday

Is revenge sweet? When righting a horrific wrong after a protracted wait—hell yes, revenge is sweet. Susan felt exhilarated and vindicated as short squat Ernie Longbraid, resembling an orange duck, shuffled into the Pinal County Superior Court for sentencing on a plea bargain. His court-appointed lawyer, a tall ruddy man named Patrick Templeton, rose from his table and spoke to the bench. He claimed Ernie's youth in 1986 combined with alcohol and drug addiction had driven him to commit his offense.

His *offense*, Susan remembered with disgust, was no less than crushing the back of her dearest friend's skull with a stick of firewood. Since the age of sixteen, Susan literally had dreamed of—and back then even prayed for—the day she would arrest Ruth Patricio's killer and avenge her senseless death. Today was sweet, all right. And it helped to have Jake there to share it.

The gavel banged and Longbraid was escorted out, eyes on the floor, to begin a sentence of twenty years without parole, right there in Florence, Arizona. The judge retired to her chambers. The lawmen, lawyers, and a few spectators headed out of the courtroom. The air conditioning unit rattled. Late afternoon sun slanted through high windows.

Jake put his arm around Susan's shoulders. "He'll be what, high sixties, when he gets out?"

"Only if he's a very good boy in lockup," Susan said. "Why couldn't he just rob her without killing her? Knowing Old Ruth, she'd have given him her dearest possessions."

"Because clubbing her from behind was easier than looking her in the eye?" Jake squeezed Susan's shoulder.

"I don't feel the anger I had always expected. He's a pitiful loser."

"That's good. That's healthy. You spoke with action. Rage will poison you. It won't hurt him or teach him. Now Longbraid has twenty years to think and maybe even learn something."

"Or not. That's between him and his ... whatever," Susan said

"This calls for a celebration. I checked with Wanda. She'll hang out with Amy at the Airstream until nine. They'll eat some pizza and stow Amy's stuff for the haul back to Boulder tomorrow. I hope 89 north of Flag is back open."

"That's some pretty bad fire up that way. Scary to think of driving through it. With a kid, I mean," Susan said.

"Not as scary as Phoenix traffic," Jake said.

"It's nothing to joke about. I read in this morning's paper six buildings have burned."

"I just hope they catch and string up whoever started it—like that hunter who ignited the Rim Fire. Careless asshole almost cost us Yosemite. We can check ADOT for road openings online tomorrow morning. What do you say to some Mexican?" Jake asked.

Susan pushed her blonde hair behind her ears and blew out a breath of air. "Only if it comes with air conditioning and ice-cold tequila confections."

"You provided the proof for the Longbraid collar, you call the shots."

They stood to go out into the June desert heat.

June 7
Saturday

Morning dawned classic Arizona—clear, dry, and hot. There was no discussion about the route to Boulder, Utah. U.S. 89 north of Flagstaff was still closed due to heavy smoke from forest fires. The online highway report listed visibility as near zero in the vicinity of Sunset Crater. That left one choice if Jake, Susan, and Amy were going to make it home that day.

They headed north across the desert on a circuitous route that at least avoided Phoenix traffic. Jake drove. The Airstream trailer gleamed in the sun. Soon they climbed through forested foothills north of Globe. Susan rode shotgun. Amy snacked and exchanged texts with friends in the back of the Suburban. She was wearing a blue t-shirt with white block letters that Susan had battled with her over and ... compromised—it could never be worn to school. It read WHERE THE HELL IS BOULDER, UTAH (SOMEWHERE UNDER A ROCK)? Amy blamed Jake for the move from Jackson, Wyoming to Boulder and she was staging a private protest.

"The air in this boat sure isn't working great," Susan said, lifting strands of blonde hair off the collar of her teal polo shirt.

"What would you expect from a '97 with over 200k on her?" Jake pushed the brim of his black and yellow Pirates ball cap and glanced in the rearview. "Look how nice the trailer's tracking. I love her brand name. Truly looks like a silver cloud. Always love telling people—'57 Flying Cloud. I've had Majestic since starting college in 1989 and this purple bucket's the best tow vehicle I've ever owned."

"Yes, you've told me, and it's maroon—one of my top five favorite colors. So can we fix the air situation?"

"Sure." Jake lowered the front two windows with the buttons on his armrest. Hot air blasted in. "There you go."

"Very funny."

He grinned at her. "I may have a little problem with gambling but your jones is air conditioning. You're an AC addict. Been a little tougher to get your fix since the massive power outages from the dam bombing, eh?"

Susan shot a look that could chill a room in Yuma in July. "You try growing up in the Arid-*zona* desert with a preacher father who loves to give blistering sermons in the sweltering heat." She smiled. "Hey, it's one of the reasons we went north. If I hadn't moved to Wyoming and joined the Jackson PD, I would've never met you. I don't know what I was thinking—letting you charm me into quitting and moving back south to hot ol' Boulder. You should be damn glad I hate heat. I rest my case."

Jake shook his head and chuckled. "Thank you, counselor."

"I'm getting a headache from all these trees flashing by."

"Spoken like a true Wyoming girl," Jake said, turning to Amy. "Growing up tree deprived." He pointed out the windshield. "This is Tonto National Forest. Every bit as mountainous and forested as the Flagstaff area but, thankfully, not as visited because of the reservation and no interstate."

"Hmm, Tonto—maybe they should call it Johnny Depp National Forest," Susan said.

Jake smiled. "You'd like that, wouldn't you? You'd pay to watch that guy food shop."

"Yesss, sir, I would." Susan pushed her hair behind her ears and looked in the rearview at Amy. "We're having us an adventure, eh kiddo?"

Amy scoffed, rolled her eyes and turned back to her cell phone. She slapped it down on the seat next to her shoulder bag adorned with a multi-colored appliqué of sneakers with real laces and crossed her arms in front of her chest. "An adventure with no cell service. I'm bored."

"Listen Miss Eleven-Year-Old, you're darned lucky to even own a cell phone," Susan said.

"Who needs cell? Look." Jake nodded out the window at the steeply sloped conifer-covered mountains. "Check out that pretty little creek trickling through those huge granite boulders. Adventure begins where cell service ends."

"Why don't you try and sketch the stream, honey?" Susan said.

The road began a corkscrew climb, slowing the rig and working the motor. The temperature dropped a bit with rising elevation. Susan hung her arm out the window and let the current flow over her fingers. She held her hair at the neck with her left hand. Although the forest drooped pale and stressed from prolonged drought and beetle-kill, the faint scent of pine and dry duff filled the car. At the top of the mountain, they passed a sign that read WHITE MOUNTAIN APACHE TRIBE WELCOMES YOU. And then a second that read BREAK A TREATY; BREAK THE LAW.

As they descended, Susan heard a whining engine on her side of the road. A cloud of dust rose through the forest from a gravel track that intersected just ahead. A small blue pickup flashed through the trunks of trees separating the two roads—a cluster of bandana-adorned heads visible in the truck's bed.

"Better close up before that dust drifts over," Jake said, raising the windows.

"Watch out for that truck. It doesn't look like it's going to stop. Probably a bunch of lit-up braves playing weekend warrior," Susan said.

"It damn well better stop. I have the right of way." The pickup was drawing even with Jake's rig. A grim, dark, soot-covered face perched behind the wheel. Three other men crouched in the bed from which a harsh red glare emanated, thick smoke trailing the truck like a flag.

"Jake!" Susan yelled. He stood on the brakes and the rig shuddered to a stop as the truck accelerated out of the side road spitting gravel. A short burly man stood up, braced against the cab, and hurled a lit flare at the Suburban. The flare spun on the hood, spouting flame and smoke, and rolled off. The truck shifted gears and raced around the next bend.

"Christ," Jake said. "Is that flare in a safe spot?"

"Yeah, I can see it on the shoulder. Shouldn't hurt anything. Why?" Susan asked.

Jake gunned his engine, bucking the Flying Cloud to life. "I'm going after them."

"Let it go. We're in the middle of nowhere," Susan said.

Jake banked around a curve. The Flying Cloud leaned but tracked and settled back to level. The trees fell away on the downhill side, revealing a panorama of the rugged wooded gorge below. The blue truck was visible, two tight switchbacks down.

"I'm not letting it go." The Suburban picked up speed.

"Now this is an adventure," Amy shouted. Susan turned to check her daughter's seatbelt. The road-cut rock whizzed by in a blur. Susan braced. She peered thousands of feet to the rocky bottom of the mountain. Jake steered around another turn.

Susan said, "This is insane. We are on a reservation mountain road in pursuit of Indians, with no authority and no back-up."

Jake wrestled the wheel and rounded another curve. Susan's magazines flew off the dash to the floor. "I'm not going to confront the jerks. I just want to find out who they are. Grab the binos out of the glove box. See if you can get the plate." Jake sped up through a straightaway that dipped and rose like a roller coaster.

"Woo hoo!" came from the back seat as the rig crested the hill and leaned into another bend. The vintage Airstream mirrored every move flawlessly.

Susan tried to look through the binoculars while fighting the bouncing of the car. Jake hit another descending curve hard, downshifting to brake. The trailer fishtailed slightly on a patch of gravel but corrected immediately. Just in time. A semi-truck lumbered into view in the uphill lane.

Amy, righting herself in her seat hooted, "Yeah, baby!"

Jake rounded the next bend and encountered a gray Volvo, Kansas plate, cautiously descending. He locked the rig down; the retrofitted electronic brakes on the trailer squealed and grabbed. The rear of the Volvo came up so quickly it was like peering through a film camera while racking the lens. The gray-haired driver glanced with startled eyes at his rear-view and then immediately began to search for a place to pull over. The shoulder was narrow and dropped away just beyond the guardrail. Jake stood on the brakes and rode the Volvo's tail.

"Come on you turkey. Move over."

"He has no place to get over," Susan said. "You should slow down."

The car, the Suburban and the trailer rounded the next right hand turn like a short train, the lead driver frantically looking for a way out. Finally a narrow flat shoulder came up and the Volvo dumped safely off to the right.

"Passing by intimidation. Love it," Jake said, swerving across the middle line and streaking past the Volvo.

The blue truck was on a long straightaway below. Susan was finally able to focus the binos. "Okay, I've got it. Amy put this on your phone."

Amy fumbled for her cell. "Go Mom."

"Arizona JBB … JBB3202." She put the binoculars on the seat between them and squeezed Jake's arm. "Now will you slow down, please?"

"Got it," Amy said.

Jake steered the Suburban over to a passenger-side pull-off perched above the valley. The blue truck had disappeared. The trailer groaned as the rig eased to a halt.

They climbed out of the car. Amy brushed crumbs off her short white shorts. The wind exhaled in the pines; a rivulet of water in a draw beside the road giggled its way down-mountain. A pair of ravens tumbled and soared above them.

"I can't wait to write this What I Did Last Summer," Amy said. "Chased Apaches with my Mom's crazy boyfriend's Airstream."

The gray car from Kansas slowly cruised by. The driver stared at Jake like he was insane. Jake waved, smiled and shrugged.

"What on earth were you thinking? I'm afraid to even look inside the trailer."

"Pissed me off. They could've hit Majestic with that flare."

"I totally get that," Amy said, giggling. Jake laughed.

Susan smiled and shook her head. "What a cowboy." She caught Jake with her glance. "You know who would've loved this?"

"Yeah, I do," said Jake, casting his eyes skyward. "He'd laugh 'til his belly shook."

"Beverly would have loved this."

"To Beverage," Jake said, raising an imaginary glass.

"Yup. To Beverage," Susan said, looking up at the top of the mountain. She noticed a boiling cloud ascending. "Is that smoke up there?"

Jake grabbed the binos off the front seat and studied the pass. "It sure as hell looks like it." He rushed around the front to the driver's side. "Let's go. We need to get to cell service or to Show Low, whichever comes first, and report a fire and four punks in a pickup."

"Yee haw! Let's go catch that guy from Kansas again," Amy shouted, jumping back in the car.

Jake backed the rig a few yards. He turned to Amy and winked. "Just remember. Do as I say, not as I do, Boo Boo."

"If I didn't have to do *as you do, Boo Boo*, I wouldn't have moved from Jackson *with you, Boo Boo*."

"Hush," Susan said. Amy suddenly got very interested in her cell phone.

Jake winced. "Wow. I did not see that coming."

Susan stared at the ground out the side window and murmured. "The women in my family have never been known for telegraphing punches." She turned to him. "Especially when aiming...." She pointed to below her belt.

Jake clamped his knees together and popped his eyes wide, smiled, stretched his neck, and shifted into gear.

Jake drove through the little town of Boulder then headed down the valley into the gloaming toward their place a quarter-mile below. Beyond their access road, Highway 12 crossed Boulder Creek and climbed away through buff-colored buttes—their towering bluffs backlit with the last of the day's sunlight. They turned left off the highway onto an unpaved road and bucketed a few hundred feet to the right turn through the fence onto their leased property. Ahead on the dirt road lay a few other spreads like theirs with pastures abutting willow and cottonwood-lined Boulder Creek. Irrigation water from wheel lines arched over square fields of hay and alfalfa. Amy sighed in her sleep in the back seat.

When Jake climbed back in after opening the gate to their property, Susan put her hand on his muscled arm and whispered, "You did it, cowboy. You got us home in good shape with daylight to spare." As he turned the rig slowly onto the packed sand drive, which led into the locust groves by their cabin, she looked back at her daughter.

"I can't tell you how happy it makes me to see my child so secure and content." She turned back to Jake and squeezed his thigh. "And I do get why you wanted to move to this beautiful small town. It's good to be closer to Matt and Tim and to see our three kids roaming around here when the boys visit. All razzing about Boulder aside, I love our life here. I really do. And I think Amy will too, eventually. I love you."

"I love you too, babe, I love our little … what—extended unit that resembles a family? Like you say, it's especially nice to see Amy and my boys together."

"Yeah, wouldn't it be nice if Rachel valued that too and let them visit a little more often. That woman has more excuses than a recidivist con."

"I've got my fingers crossed she won't pull them out of our camping trip as yet another way to exact her revenge and keep my…" He glanced in the rearview at Amy while braking to a stop on the concrete pad next to the house, "…my family jewels in a vice."

Amy sat up yawning. "What jewels, Jake?"

"Uh … family. Your mom and I were just discussing our little family."

She was suddenly wide-awake. "You two are *not* getting *married*, are you?"

Jake glanced at Susan with a look that said you take this one.

"Don't sound so excited. No immediate plans to register at Bed, Bath and Beyond, sweetheart. We are just enjoying the feeling of closeness and togetherness. Jake is looking forward to Matt and Tim's visit next week."

"Yeah, me too. We make up one fourth of a soccer team."

"Ok, team. Let's get Majestic unhooked, plugged in and back to serving her role as the guesthouse. Amy, you place the wheel chocks and then go close the gate. Susan you get the water hose and shoreline. I'll unhitch."

"Aye, aye, captain." Susan saluted and slid out of the car.

At bedtime, Amy, at her mother's insistence, had apologized to Jake for being rude in the car. She hugged both adults and headed off to bed with her book.

Soon after, Jake and Susan relaxed in the front yard in matching green camp chairs sharing a bottle of rosé. A fire crackled and sparked in a metal basin with a screen dome. Flames lit up the barn wood siding and red metal roof of the house and reflected off the side of the Airstream. Alpenglow still outlined the pinions and junipers topping the buttes to the west.

"Now that we have Ruth's killer behind bars, I want to concentrate on Bev's," Susan said.

"I feel every bit as adamant about solving Beverly's murder as you do. Lest you forget, however, these little vigilante jaunts don't put money in the bank."

"I was very frugal in Arizona. Thank God for friends' couches."

"Let's be honest. You were either damn lucky or damn good in Arizona ... to solve Ruth's murder as quickly as you did?"

"I'd rather be lucky than good. That *was* one for the textbooks wasn't it? I should write it up as something like ... say ... the six degrees of pilfering." She stretched her arms up and then dropped her hands behind her head. "I remember staring at Ruth's antique silver cross as a kid when she brushed my hair. I would know it anywhere. So when I saw it on the checkout girl at the supermarket near the rez and, I admit that was either good fortune or it was meant to be, it was easy to trace it to the girl's mother."

"Right, but in most cases it would have either dead-ended there or at least gotten murky as to where to go next."

"Perhaps, for a less experienced detective. But in my case the mother gave up her ex-boyfriend in a heartbeat. One could even say she was thrilled to burn him."

"I sense you're enjoying this retelling just a little too much," Jake said.

"I'm relishing every sweet moment. Where was I? Oh yes. The deadbeat ex presented a bit of a challenge but *he* finally admitted under intense pressure and interrogation—even though he'd told the mother he bought it new—that he got Ruth's necklace and cross from the pawnshop in Casa Grande."

"And you got lucky a second time, *or* perhaps it was meant to be a second time, that the pawnshop had been in the same family for eons and their records were positively anal."

"There *was* a little luck involved there in addition to more damn fine investigative work."

"And?" Jake prompted dutifully.

"And … when Longbraid's name popped out of that shop owner's ancient box of index cards, my heart almost leaped onto his cluttered and battered old desk. I immediately remembered Ernie as a kid. My brother ran with him occasionally. Bad medicine. I was certain I had my guy—the checkout girl, the mother, the boyfriend, the pawnshop owner, Longbraid and Ruth—six degrees. Maybe I should consider a PhD in pilfer-ology."

"Do you mean PHD as in pretty hot detective, or pretty—hot—detective? If so, I can testify to both. Really fine work, Susan. If I may say so it is a great boon to this little investigative agency to have an investigator who is a former fully sworn law enforcement officer with extensive investigative experience, who knows how to talk cop, and who also happens—and again this is just pure luck—to be as smart as Smart, Maxwell Smart that is, as gorgeous as Gabor—Eva, I always preferred Eva to Zsa Zsa—and as hot as a Hee Haw honey in heat."

Susan jumped onto his lap and pinned his arms down. "A Hee Haw, honey? *A Hee Haw, honey?* YOU are such a *weirdo.*" She leaned in close to his face. "You better be careful or—," she twanged, "*I'll find another, and PFFT, you'll be gone.*" She sat up, poked out her chest and wiggled her butt in his lap. "Ohhhhhh, your thighs feel soooo strong."

Jake laughed and made an exaggerated effort to wipe the moisture from Susan's raspberry off his face. "If you can control yourself, we need to discuss a little more business."

"Yes, sir," Susan said. "Pardon the unprofessional interruption. I didn't realize this was an official all-staff meeting of the Goddard Consulting Group. How could I have mistaken that review of your childhood TV addiction as anything other than serious business?"

She returned to her chair and her wine glass. Bats swooped high above their heads on mosquito patrol. Stars pulsed. A car crossed Boulder Creek on Route 12 and headed up toward town, headlights tracking illumination across their yard.

"We haven't had a paying customer since Judy in Moab hired us in April to find her husband's killer and shortly thereafter fired us after the local cops beat us to the punch. Former handyman goes down in a hail of bullets and they never do find out why he stabbed his employer to death in his garage. But obviously, services by GCG no longer required." Jake got up to add a log to the fire.

"Shame too. I was really interested in that one."

"One thing's been buggin' me about the aftermath of that case. Could you go on living in a house in which I'd been murdered?"

"Depends on whether I was the murderer."

"I see. Thanks for that clarification and rather dark and scary look into a woman's psyche."

"No charge," Susan said.

Jake sat again. The fire caught new life.

"Yes, well, speaking of charges, we need to be submitting some. I've been thinking since our little adventure today, I might pay a visit to the Apache chief and see if he wants some help finding the braves who are setting fires on the rez," Jake said.

"He?"

"Excuse me?"

"You said, he. How do you know the chief's not a woman?"

"Please forgive me. I want to apologize to all the women of the firm—and especially to those who can imagine murdering their partners—for that gender gaff."

"Apology accepted. You live another day," Susan said.

"Anyhow, I want to speak with the chief because he *or she* might desire some help tracking down the flare-throwers, and since we got a pretty good look at them … long-story-short, if we are going to continue to live in this remote corner of paradise we will need to market ourselves aggressively."

"I agree—on the marketing part—not so certain on the paradise part. Hope they got that rez fire out quickly. Now can we talk about our next pro boner job?"

"Uh, I believe the term is pro bono."

"Oh sorry, Freudian slip after sitting on your lap."

Jake grinned, sat up taller and twirled an imaginary moustache. "Well at least you got the pro part right." He touched an index finger to an imaginary brim on an imaginary hat. "In that department, ma'am…" He smugly nodded toward his lap. "Mr. Johnson and I are definitely a professional team."

"Yep. You've got a gun—I know cuz I've seen it—and it will travel," Susan said.

"I assume you're referring to investigating Bev's murder," Jake said.

"Yes, Bev's killer. The flash of green pant leg under the duster the shooter was wearing still has my attention totally focused on the woman I saw at the meeting at Ashland mine."

"I've been thinking about that. We do have to get to that woman. And I have a plan and the name of the plan is Stan. I'm the man with the Stan plan."

"And the Stan plan is?" Susan asked.

"You get close to Stan. He gets me close to the woman who was wearing green."

"How do I get close to Stan?"

"You visit his daughter, Lyndall Burke, in Las Vegas for more anthropology lessons and another hike in the desert or whatever. As for Lyn, we continue to honor her Aunt Lou's wish that she be kept in the dark about her father's ancillary, yet unsavory, involvement in the foiled plot to steal Colorado River water. You make sure Stan a) knows you are visiting b) thinks you are interested in him and c) knows how to get in touch with you."

"Oh shit. Susan as bait again, I really hate—"

"Now stay with me. Stan knows you saved his daughter's life. He is in your debt big time. You can lure him into a situation where we demand he introduce *me* to that woman. She has never laid eyes on me and she has a rep for liking the boys. So, don't flatter yourself, I'm really the bait this time."

"And if Stan doesn't cooperate?"

"We assure him we will reveal every sordid detail of his involvement in the fraud, corruption and murders surrounding the water grab that was foiled by the dam bombing, with emails to the FBI, The Salt Lake and Vegas media, to his daughter, Lyn, to his ex-wife, Florence, to his masseuse, his AA sponsor, his vet, his pool guy—"

"I think I get it."

"I knew you would, Maxwell."

"Call me Zsa Zsa. I liked her more than Eva." Susan stretched and yawned. "We better get to bed. Long drive for you tomorrow to Scipio to meet Rachel and the boys."

Jake yawned and nodded agreement.

Susan gathered the glasses and aligned the chairs while Jake went to get a hose to douse the fire.

June 8
Sunday

Jake waited in his Subaru wagon at a rest area near Scipio for the boys to arrive from Spanish Fork. Rachel had accepted a position in the accounting department at Brigham Young University in Provo and had chosen to leave Salt Lake and reside in Spanish Fork for its affordability. She was also attracted to that area because it was horse country and horses were one of the ways she could flaunt her independence from Jake, or at least that's how he interpreted her sudden infatuation with all things equine. Since growing up on a farm, Jake had always been leery of horses; he thought horses were dangerous and Rachel knew he felt that way.

Rachel rushed in ninety minutes late, spouting lame excuses about church going long. As a result of ancient seismic tension around the subject of her tardiness, the parents' exchange was brief and anything but cordial.

Jake's plan was to camp with the boys on Boulder Mountain and fish nearby Oak Creek. Boulder Mountain has extensive aspen groves, as well as stands of pine, including the mighty ponderosa, spruce, and fir. It rises to 11,000 feet and is a heavily forested island surrounded by desert overlooking Capital Reef National Park. Jake loved Boulder Mountain and had always wanted to camp with his boys in his favorite spot there in a grove of aspens. He had read on Megboard, the town of Boulder's email bulletin board, that the Forest Service was going to temporarily close Boulder Mountain because of high fire danger due to a low snow winter, a dry spring, and recent low humidity and high winds. Since he had no plans for any open flames other than a camp stove, he hoped he and the boys could get in a few safe days before the closure.

Jake also chose Boulder Mountain for its proximity to their town— Boulder sits in a high fertile valley just south of the mountain—and because Boulder Mountain got little summer visitation compared to the many central and southern Utah scenic attractions and national parks.

Jake lay on his back in the dark tent fighting the urge to go out and pee. The forest was silent. He checked the two padded humps next to him. His sons' sleep-induced breathing was reassuring. He remembered with embarrassment how short and irritable he had been with the boys while setting up the tent. It was a lot to ask of an eight and a ten-year-old. His frustration with Rachel for making them so late washed back over him. He checked the time on his cell phone: 3:03.

Unable to ignore the urge any longer, Jake pulled on his headlamp, quietly unzipped his bag and then the door to the tent and crawled out. He stood, stretched, slipped on his Crocs and crunched across the fifty feet of dry meadow grass that he insisted to the boys was a no-pee zone. Aspen trunks stood as gray guards around him. An owl hooted in the distance.

He heard a motor coming from the direction of the highway, and then headlights stabbed into the trees on the two-track that led past the aspen grove and deeper into the forest. These folks made his late arrival seem timely, Jake thought as he finished up. He paused for a few moments and listened unsuccessfully for the owl then crawled back into the tent and his bag. The boys slept on. Close to dozing off, he was aware of headlights briefly illuminating the inside of the tent and heard the whine of an engine departing. Guess the latecomers didn't like the accommodations, was the thought that drifted through his mind as sleep overtook him.

"Here boy. Come here boy. No, don't go in there. Don't you dare go in there! Mom. Mommy."

Jake's eyes popped open. Matthew was talking anxiously in his sleep. The older of the two boys, Matt seemed to be taking his parents' divorce the hardest. One manifestation was chronic bad dreams. Jake considered waking his son when an acrid smell caught his attention. He sat up and turned his face to the tent window. There was no doubt about it. Something nearby was burning. He yanked on shorts and a shirt, crawled out of the tent, and stood searching the forest with his eyes. There was a hint of sunrise to the east but south of him an orange halo encircled the higher ground like a sunset. The forest was on fire.

Jake thrust his head back into the tent. "Matt, Tim, I need you to get up and get out here. We're leaving!"

"Wha ... Dad, it's not even light out," Matthew said, sitting up and rubbing his eyes. Timothy, always the deeper sleeper, rolled over and slept on.

"Tim, now!" Jake said. "Wake up, buddy. We've got to go." Jake grabbed Tim's leg and shook it. Tim opened his eyes but was clearly disoriented.

"Guys, there is a fire nearby. Come out but leave your stuff in the tent." Jake stood up and tried to assess the danger. It was even greater than he had thought. He could see flames dancing on the ridge to the south but now noticed smoke to the north close to the access road they had driven in on. Hair prickled on the back of his neck. All of his attention was now on saving his boys. "Let's go kids. Now! I need you in the car now."

Matthew came out hugging his iPad and soccer ball, Tim his stuffed bear. They looked confused and scared. Jake hurried them into the back seat of his Subaru and started the motor. Fortunately he always left his wallet and keys in the car when car camping.

"Buckle up!" He turned to the back seat and seeing the panic in the boys' faces said, "Just pretend this is an amusement ride."

He backed the car in a half circle and then jammed it in first gear and bucked it over the grass leading out of the grove. Tendrils of smoke were now visible creeping low in the forest. They lurched and bounced down the slender dirt road that led back to the highway. Jake jolted as two deer appeared out of the dark and smoke, sprinted parallel to the driver's side of the car and then disappeared into the trees. The farther down the mountain they got the worse the smoke. After half a mile he could determine that blazes had started, or had been set, on both sides of their campsite and the fires were rushing toward the middle and Jake and his sons.

"Dad, I'm scared," Timothy said.

"I'm scared too, buddy." Jake said wrestling the wheel and squinting out the front through the smoke. "But we are going to be fine. I promise." He dimmed the headlights for better vision, checked that the windows were up all the way and pressed a button to limit external air and smoke entering the interior of the car. Still, the car was suffocating and he could barely see. Smoke found the cracks in the older car and Jake's eyes and throat burned. They plunged blindly in the gloom.

Matthew started to cough uncontrollably. Jake turned back. "Breathe Matthew, breathe and try and relax. I'm going to get us out of this." He missed a turn and with the screech of metal the car sideswiped a pine tree and was thrown back on the track. Jake barely took his foot off the gas. Flames danced on both sides of them. A shimmering curtain of fire rolled behind the car. A small fir in flames fell across the road and Jake made the instantaneous call to drive over it. There was no turning back. All Jake could see in the rearview now was a solid wall of flames. The front of the car lurched over the log like a lion leaping through a flaming hoop. Halfway over, the car ground to a roaring standstill—high-centered—on a burning tree.

"Shit!" He yelled as he slammed the car into reverse and then jammed it forward. The boys jerked back and forth. The back wheels spun in the dirt.

Timothy coughed and whimpered prayers. Matthew, bolstered by his Dad's words, did his best to reassure his little brother. "Hey Timmy, think how impressed your homies at school are going to be when you tell them you rode through a fire in Dad's car."

Sweat was pouring off Jake's forehead and his palms were slick on the steering wheel. The heat in the car was stifling. Fire reflected in all the windows. Jake was afraid that any second the car could ignite. He considered bailing out and taking his chances with his sons on foot. Then he remembered 4wheel drive low, jerked the separate stick and revved the engine to a shrill pitch. The car bumped and rocked as the front tires bit into the packed earth and then clawed over the blazing tree and shot forward. Jake shifted and the Subaru dove down the road skidding into the next turn.

A large tree crown in flames loomed just ahead falling through the fiery limbs of surrounding pines and firs. Jake managed to steer the car under it and watched it crash behind them in the rearview sending up a wave of sparks.

After what felt like ages, Jake could discern ghost images of trees standing back from the road and he noticed the flames around them had abated somewhat. He guessed he had approximately one more mile to the highway and relaxed a little, smiling at his boys in the mirror.

"Hell of an adventure, eh guys?"

"Dad!"

"What, Tim?"

"My new fishing pole was in the tent. Remember I was sleeping with it."

"Well there is an even newer pole in your future. Looks like we might be shopping for camping gear as well."

"Dad!"

"Yes, Matthew."

"What about the birds and animals?"

"That's one of the hardest parts of a forest fire, buddy, the creatures that are driven away from their homes. But the trees, animals, birds and plants will all come back, they always do ... tell you what, we'll check on our camping spot every year to see the progress, okay?"

They hit the pavement and headed south toward Boulder. Jake got on his cell as soon as he had service in case no one had reported the fire. The 911 Operator said Jake was the first and asked his name. In a few miles he pulled over at a paved viewpoint and got the boys out of the car so they could clear their lungs. Dawn was now fully actualized. He checked his car for damage—new latitudinal scars where he had sideswiped the tree and spots of paint on the doors bubbled with heat.

Smoke and flame raged on Boulder Mountain as the two fires converged into one towering conflagration. Jake was watching his favorite mountain burn. He suddenly understood why so many Americans had mourned after the Yellowstone fires of 1988. Boulder Mountain's aspen forest, what with aspens in a grove all being clones, was said to be one of the largest living organisms on earth. Yellowstone is recovering. Natural and even accidental fires are one thing, but arson in forests another altogether. He thought of the vehicle that had driven past in the night. Could have been a pickup. Could have been a *blue* pickup. It was definitely time to meet with the Chief of the White Mountain Apaches.

He loaded the boys and drove toward home with the windows wide open. A helicopter chopped overhead with a huge bucket swinging below its belly. After it passed above, he heard the thrum of diesel engines from down the mountain and saw spouting columns of black exhaust and circling lights. Forest Service trucks from Boulder roared up the road heading in to fight the fire.

June 11
Wednesday

Jake sat looking somewhat professional in his brown uniform polo with the Goddard Consulting Group logo. He was in the office of the Chief, and damned if she wasn't a woman. He wondered if Susan had somehow known that Gloria Fox was the head honcho of the White Mountain Apache Tribe. Gloria was pleasant, if not effusive. She was solidly built, medium height and appeared to be in her mid-fifties. Her long black hair was streaked with silver, which matched her silver and bead rings, earrings, necklace, and bracelets. She was quick to point out that her title was actually Chairwoman, but she insisted on being addressed as Gloria. After exchanging pleasantries, Jake reported he had observed young American Indian males south of Show Low tossing a lit flare and that he suspected them of starting a forest fire.

"I've had a bit too much experience with fire recently, Gloria. First we had that flare thrown at us on your land last week. Three nights ago my boys and I almost got trapped between two fires on Boulder Mountain near Torrey, Utah. Investigators have determined that one was arson, also. My sons could have died or been seriously injured but luckily came out unscathed."

"I'm a parent myself. I know firsthand the gut-wrenching fear when your kids are in danger. I'm glad your boys are fine. Please go on."

"And it's anybody's guess if the recent fires north of Flagstaff are at all related. I'm not being completely altruistic here because my livelihood depends on this sort of work, but I would like to help you catch the young men who are setting these fires."

"Our new casino brings us great gifts, but it comes with many challenges and problems as well, and our new Chief of Police, William Sweetgrass has a full plate right now. I'm afraid looking for suspected arsonists is a low priority. William and I will review your materials and consider your offer."

"I'd think he'd be anxious to stop those who are bringing such shame on your people," Jake said.

"If you mean catch the outsiders who are endangering our people and our forests, then yes, we perhaps could use some expert investigative help with preventing more of these incidents. As I said, I'll discuss it with William."

"I saw something on your website about fire restrictions."

"The Wildland Fire Management folks at the BIA have issued a modified Stage Two Fire Restriction for the entire 1.6 million acres of the Fort Apache Reservation. We can't even enjoy a campfire or barbeque. The danger is very high and I'm concerned. We dodged a bullet with the fire you witnessed. And thank you for reporting it, by the way. There was very little wind that day. Being early in the fire season, and with the fires near Flagstaff nearing containment, there were just enough retardant aircraft and crews available. We held it to several hundred acres. Next time we may not be so lucky."

"Glad to be of service."

"But if I hire you, Mr. Goddard."

"Jake."

"But if I hire you, Jake. It will not be to capture the Apache men setting these fires. It will be to capture the criminals impersonating Apache men setting these fires."

"Excuse me."

"I'm sure you are a fine investigator, but you are leading with an assumption which is false. What makes you think these men are Apache?"

"Based on empirical evidence. They were on Apache land. They were in a truck stolen off the reservation. We ran the plates with the help of my partner's police contacts. They seemed to know the back roads of the reservation. They were carrying a lit flare and using it as a weapon. And ... uh, they had brown skin and black hair. What makes you think they were not Apaches?"

"Culture."

"Forgive me, but—"

"You are seeing the empirical evidence as you say—the trees. You are missing the spiritual evidence—the forest. Our people have lived here in this unique environment for thousands of years. We believe we come from the earth and belong to the earth. Our mountains are sacred. Our trees are sacred. Our young men are taught our culture from a very early age."

"No offense, Chief, sorry, Gloria, but really I don't see—"

"Okay, then there is this. Our young men are all hunters and they love to fish. We hold competitions every year for trophy elk and prize-winning trout. No one wants to hunt and fish in a burned out forest."

"I'm listening. I'm not convinced but I'm listening. If you hire me and my partner Susan, who, as you will see in her bio, grew up on a reservation on the other side of the state, I promise we'll keep an open mind. The goal is to identify and help your police apprehend the people setting these fires, whoever they are. Fair enough?"

"More than fair. But, as you know, we are in the gaming business. How about a little side bet? If the perpetrators turn out to be Apache, I'll buy you dinner. If not, you buy. Agreed?"

"Sounds good."

"That's not all. If you help us apprehend theses arsonists, regardless of who they are, I will put you and a friend of your choice up in our casino for a weekend. All expenses paid including your first two hundred dollars at the gaming tables." Gloria smiled a broad smile for the first time since Jake arrived.

Jake looked down at his hands and then out the window. "Gaming business, gaming tables. Interesting euphemism."

"Sorry?"

"Ah, nothing. Um ... that's a very generous offer, Gloria."

"Now let's discuss fees, shall we."

Jake laid out his standard per diem and expense package. None of the costs seemed to concern the chairwoman. During their chat about logistics, Gloria's cell chimed but she was courteous enough to glance at it and silence it without answering. As Jake spoke she repeatedly nodded her agreement and asked few questions. When Jake had finished, she told him that she would get back to him soon. She gave him her cell number and said, if hired, he should report only to her, and only by cell. Jake got up to leave but turned at the door.

"I've got to ask. Why consider hiring a white guy?"

"Some of my best friends are white guys." Gloria smiled again. "One-on-one you white guys can be pretty decent. It's when you band together that things can get out of hand. But you bring up a good point and you deserve an honest answer. I'm looking beyond skin color and seeing someone who can help my people. We want to resolve this quietly, as in, without involving federal agencies in any way. Things have not gone well recently with the *Inde*—the people—of the Apache Nation, when the federal government has gotten involved. That is, since about 1849."

"The capture of Geronimo in 1886 was thought to be the end of the Indian wars, wasn't it?"

"Yes it was. A sad day for my people. And still to this day, it is best that we fly under the radar of the United States Government and resolve our own issues." Jake nodded his understanding and started to open the door when Gloria spoke again. "And Jake, you must understand from the beginning that if I hire you, I will be paying you out of a slush fund the casino provides for my discretionary use—off the books so to speak. Only the chief of the tribal police will know about you and he will be sworn to secrecy." She fiddled with her teardrop-shaped pendant necklace. "It was no accident I agreed to meet with you after 5:00 when everyone was gone for the day. If asked, I will deny you work for me." She flashed her brilliant smile. "No one around Fort Apache would believe I would hire a white guy anyway." Jake made a gesture with one hand, palm open and smiled back indicating he accepted her conditions. He closed her office door and walked down the empty corridor toward the parking lot and his Suburban.

The room was dark and clammy for the basement of a building in a desert city. Three men wearing blue bandana do-rags sat on wooden stools at a low round table covered in rawhide with a small lamp in the center. Another man squatted on powerful thighs in the corner. His thick black hair in a braid tied with a leather thong. A floor-to-ceiling metal storage cage took up the back wall. Chief Natchez, standing in front of the door to the cage, spoke first.

"I'm pleased with the success of our operations so far. Three actions taken—three actions successful. Good work, warriors."

The three men sitting at the table smiled triumphantly. The man in the corner, his face half obscured by the shadows, prickled with suppressed energy while displaying little emotion. His thick fingers, knuckles singed and blackened, cupped and tapped his knees.

Natchez said, "But there are also three things that concern me. First, our messengers have not been found in the fires. Second, the fires have been extinguished before causing the widespread destruction we envisioned. We need to correct that in the future. And third, may just be a coincidence but the two most recent fires were apparently reported by the same man—this Jake Goddard. And Little Bear you say you followed this meddler Goddard to the office of the chairwoman of the tribe today? Are we certain this is the same man?"

Blood Speak on the Chief's left spoke. "No doubt about it. They said his name on the police scanner on both—"

Little Bear, the tallest yet youngest of the group, sitting on the Chief's right and always anxious to please, cut him off. "And the car he drove to the tribal headquarters was the same car we saw on the rez in the mountains above Carrizo Creek. At that time he was towing a large silver trailer." He nodded at the man squatting in the corner. "Lone Wolf threw a flare as a warning but he chased us down the mountain while pulling that trailer. He's a crazy son-of-a-bitch."

Long Silence, sitting across from the Chief, an ugly man of few words, grunted in agreement.

"Throwing a flare. Good choice. Modern flaming arrow," Natchez said.

Long Silence grunted again.

Little Bear said, "After leaving the Chief's office he headed north toward St John. Unless he plans to drive all night, he has to stop somewhere."

"If the flare didn't convince him, perhaps he needs a stronger message." Natchez turned to the man squatting in the shadows in the corner. "Lone Wolf, I think you know what must happen when a person, especially a white, gets in the way of our sacred actions. God demands a strong response. Remember Apache Chief Lobo Blanco and Wagon Mound."

Lone Wolf stood and approached the other men. The olive skin of his cheek reflected the light. His eyes were filled with excitement like those of a stallion that had just been spurred into a gallop. He was short but powerfully built—his ham hands strong enough to snap metal arrows in two, and then again in four. He nodded and climbed the wooden stairs to the first floor and went out into the night. The exterior door banged shut.

After leaving Gloria Fox's Fort Apache office Jake drove until he tired. When he pulled into The Tomahawk Motel in St. John it was after 8 p.m., and he had already had a long day, having left Boulder at 7 a.m. to make his meeting with the Chiefwoman—he decided he was going to refer to Gloria as the Chiefwoman—he preferred it to Chairwoman. He arranged for a room on the first floor, entered, tossed his ball cap and duffel on the chair, slipped off his Crocs and socks and stretched out on the bed.

He called Susan on his cell and they chatted about the day. The meeting had gone well and he felt confident Gloria was going to hire them. He heard movement on the floor above. Susan reported some ferocious backyard one-on-two soccer skirmishes resulting in yet another ball over the fence and yet another protest from their lanky bachelor neighbor, who they called Mr. Suspenders. Susan mused about the fact that there was no male equivalent to the very descriptive term, spinster. It was that kind of conversation. The boys were good. Amy seemed happy. Susan was fine. Jake said goodnight to each of the three kids, and stripped off his jeans and brown uniform polo. Wearing his boxers he took his toiletry kit from the duffel into the bathroom, and soon came out and hit the sack. He turned the window unit to fan. He climbed in under one sheet. The bed was decent. Soon after closing his eyes, he heard a shoe drop in the room above him. Cool air wafted across the bed. While anticipating the sound of the second shoe, he fell into a deep sleep.

June 12
Thursday

Morning comes in quick and hard in the desert in June. No point in trying to sleep much past six. Even with the blinds closed, light drives through the cracks and penetrates the eyelids. Jake dragged himself out of bed with a plan to catch coffee and breakfast on the road.

He closed his motel room door and, with his cell and car keys in one hand and his duffle in the other, walked the few feet to the Suburban while checking messages. He unlocked the door and slid into the driver's seat still looking at his phone. He tossed his duffle into the back seat, leaned to place his cell in the console cup holder and, poised to put the key in the ignition, looked up. He was staring right down the gaping maw of a wild-eyed animal. The shock drove him back against the headrest. The creature was obviously dead, tongue lolling out against the glass, blood smeared and partially dried on the windshield and hood.

Jake took a few deep breaths to settle his heartbeat and slid out of the car to examine the carnage. Someone had placed the recently severed head of a cow elk on his hood. The elk's eyes were glassy and clouded but still retained a hint of the terror suffered just before dying. A nub of a white bone glistened where the spine had been severed. Blood still seeped a bit out of the serrated flesh of the neck. Flies were circling, abuzz with interest.

Someone, probably an Apache, was trying to scare him off. Jake scanned the parking lot and saw nothing but a few cars. Most, like his, bore out-of-state plates.

Fortunately he had slid his keycard into his jeans' pocket. He went back into the room and came out with a plastic laundry bag and a cup of water. He placed the water on the curb by the car, picked the elk head up by one ear, bagged it and walked across the lot to the motel dumpster. He returned to the car and poured the water on the windshield. No one had come out of the Tomahawk. He was still alone in the lot.

Jake backed out of the parking space, turned out of the motel property and headed north. He found himself checking his rearview more often than normal. He was one farm boy who as a child had learned a deep respect and admiration for animals, and their slaughter had always been a bit unsettling. The thought of breakfast no longer appealed.

Amy was driving toward the goal. The "goal" being Jake blocking a tattered net while squinting into the mid-afternoon sun with Timothy in front of him providing a thin line of defense. Susan split out on the grass to Amy's right, anticipating a pass as Matt rushed the goal on Amy's left. When Timothy challenged her, instead of passing to her mother, Amy juggled the ball up on her instep and chipped it toward Matthew, leading him a little. Jake had the height advantage so the older kids had determined, although outnumbered and playing goalkeeper, he was not allowed to use his hands. He loped out to his right toward his attacking son but miscalculated by half-a-step as the ball arched in perfectly to Matthew's forehead. Timothy was guarding Amy and Susan but the action was now between Matt and his father, both pretty intense competitors. Matt leaped into the air and head-butted the ball into the net and slammed into Jake. They fell to the ground, Matt on top.

Amy yelled, "Goooooaaaaal!"

Tim said, "Darn it, Dad. I thought you had him."

Matt chanted, "USA! USA!" in Jake's face.

"Foul! Foul!" Jake cried, rolling his head back and forth.

"I didn't foul you. I headed the ball before I crashed into you," Matt said, still on his dad's chest.

"No, it's your *breath* that's foul. It deserves a red card."

Matt exhaled hard close to his father's nose.

Jake made exaggerated attempts to pull his face away. "Yuck! Carrion breath—that's what it reminds me of. The only time I've smelled breath so foul is when I woke up at high noon in July in the desert with a vulture sitting on my chest. Just like you." Jake laughed and rolled his son off of him.

"When did that happen, Dad?" Tim asked.

"Let's take a water break and I'll tell you guys all about it." Jake got up, dusted off his shorts, put his arm around his sons' shoulders and walked them toward the hose at the side of the house.

Amy plucked the soccer ball out of the net and rolled her eyes at her mother. "Jake would make up anything to take a break while in denial about the score."

"I don't know, honey. It doesn't surprise me one bit that Jake woke up in the desert at high noon in July with a vulture on his chest." She flashed her eyebrows up and down. "He does some of his best work lying down."

"Mom, please! TMI!" Amy wailed.

"Now, Amy, get your mind off sex. I was, of course, referring to how Jake courageously stopped the truck of my abductor in the Nevada desert by lying down in the road." She pushed her daughter's blond hair behind her ears. "Come on, let's go get a drink of water and learn all about vulture breath."

"Who was at the door?" Jake asked.

"JWs trying to leave a copy of the Watchtower. Get this. The guy's pitch was that the mag included an intriguing article that claimed end times didn't have to be all bad. He was really cheery about it."

"What did you tell him?"

"I handed it back and told him my father was a minister in The Salvation Army, which is true, and that you and I were good Presbyterians."

"Which is not true. Plus, we're living together in sin. You're definitely going to hell." Jake handed her a drinking glass and she toweled it dry.

Their little place came with a rarely used dishwasher. Hand washing was a ritual they enjoyed. It placed them hip-to-hip in front of the sink looking out the window at an expansive view of Boulder Mountain. On this night a few cumulus clouds bumped the summit and the amazing light surrounding them was just becoming adorned with its summer evening gilding. Dishwashing was also a chance to put their heads together while keeping their hands busy. The kids were absorbed in an animated feature on DVD in the living room. As usual, the sound was just a notch too high.

"That was Gloria Fox who called me."

"I figured it was important or you wouldn't have taken it during dinner."

"She hired us. Which is good news."

"And the bad news?" Susan inquired, watching Jake stretch up on tiptoes. He placed a glass in the cabinet on the wall to the right of the windows, allowing her to admire his tan calves below his khaki cargo shorts.

"We've been so busy since I got back from Arizona and the boys dragged me out of the car for the Boulder Cup Soccer Championship, I haven't had a chance to tell you about a little incident early this morning."

While Susan scrubbed the pots, Jake filled her in about the elk head on his hood.

"So the bad news is, someone was warning you off before you were even hired," Susan said.

"Yeah, that's a little disturbing," Jake said.

"What did Gloria have to say about the elk head calling card?"

"It's like she's wearing blinders when it comes to her young Apache men. Even though she had just told me during our meeting that they are great elk hunters, she refused to accept the suggestion that the arsonists, and for that matter my early morning elk decapitators, were tribal members."

Susan turned and called into the living room. "Amy, can you turn down the TV, please?" She blew a strand of hair off her forehead and pushed others behind her ears with her wrist. "Why do you think that's the case?"

"Something about culture ... Apaches are taught the earth is sacred, et cetera, et cetera. All good stuff, mind you, but there are lots of ways culture and religion can become perverted and twisted to murderous ends. I hope we learned that lesson on 9/11/2001."

Susan reached to the stove for another pot. "Let's finish up here and mull this all over." She smiled at him. "If nothing else we are good at mulling."

"We don't have a choice. We need the money. I have to accept this job but it would feel a little better, especially given the already bizarre circumstances, if we were on the same page as our employer."

She handed him a pot. "Dry first, mull later."

Jake and Susan finished the dishes and then sat at the antique wooden kitchen table polishing off their dinner wine. First they discussed Gloria's offer, and her apparent unwillingness to consider all angles. Susan then aired a concern regarding their collective inexperience when it came to arson and forest fire. Finally their mulling shifted to something even more immediate—the Stan Plan, and what the next few days held. Susan reviewed her recent phone conversation with Lyn Burke and Lyn's invitation to visit in Las Vegas for the weekend.

When it came time to put the kids to bed, they decided to let a few of their concerns steep overnight due to their hard fast rule that no cop shoptalk was to occur after kid bedtime.

Of course, rules were meant to be broken and that one was no exception. When Jake and Susan had crawled under the covers, windows open to welcome the cool mountain air, Susan propped herself up on one elbow and said, "Okay, I know I'm breaking our rule, but we're responsible for three children right now. How can you be sure the people who threatened you with the elk head didn't follow you to our home?"

He rolled to her. "Because I've been doing this for over twelve years now, and not to brag, but, as you know, I helped solve that historical Mormon document forgery case with that crackpot whose weapon of choice was the pipe bomb. I gained a sixth sense during that one about being followed. It happened almost daily. So, put it out of your mind. No one tailed me." She looked skeptical. "Sweetheart, I drive with one eye in my rearview. I would know, I promise." He gave her a kiss on the forehead and rolled away.

June 13
Friday

After morning coffee on their sunny deck, Jake and Susan, in their efficient manner, addressed some of their unresolved concerns. They made a few phone calls and plans came together quickly.

Later Susan headed up the sand driveway in her red Toyota pickup. She tried to block the sun with her right hand as she watched for Jake to file in behind her in his newly repaired green Subaru, thinking, yet again, what bad color choices all three of their vehicles were for living in the perpetually sunny and often scorching central Utah desert. She adjusted her air conditioning.

Jake followed with all three kids on board. Amy had refused her mother's offer to ride shotgun with her part way, preferring the company of Jake's sons, and off they sped toward I-15, the vehicular spine of the Intermountain West. They planned to convoy until they hit I-70 near Richfield. Then Susan would turn south toward I-15 and Las Vegas; Jake planned to head north on U.S. 50 and later connect with I-15. Jake would return his sons to their mother in Spanish Fork and had arranged just that morning to drop Amy at the Driggs, Idaho property of Clint, an old ski bum friend who was boarding Cassie, Susan's horse and Cinder, Amy's black lab. Amy was going to spend several days riding and working on recently married Clint and Virginia's twenty-acre spread while Jake drove on to Mammoth Hot Springs to get a primer about fire from a buddy who was an Engine Captain for Yellowstone National Park. After Gloria Fox hired Goddard Consulting Group, Susan had expressed her concern about the two of them lacking expertise, so Jake had called his friend Pete first thing that morning and requested a crash course in investigating suspicious forest fires. Pete had been urging Jake to visit him in the summer for years and immediately agreed. Bags were packed quickly and by mid-morning the troops were on the move.

Friends are great, Susan thought as she led the two-car convoy through town, and interesting development this "friendship" between eleven year-old Amy and ten-year-old Matthew. Matthew was mature for his age especially for a boy, and somewhat typical for children of divorce, he was growing up fast. Amy, also a child of divorce, appeared to be taking a shine to him. Funny how quickly things change. Just before school let out for the summer, Amy had been interviewed for a school newspaper article featuring students who were new that year. When asked the obligatory question about boys she said, "Some of my friends in Wyoming were boy crazy: that's all they ever talked about. I'm trying to concentrate on schoolwork and sports." Yeah, well, that was last month. Matthew had a lot of Jake's charming qualities. He was smart, kind and inquisitive. No female of any age could fail to note he was tall for his years, unselfconsciously handsome and athletic. Like mother like daughter. Although Amy was slow to accept Jake in her mother's life, she did not appear to be having any such problem with Jake's son in her own. Could be a bit complicated if they were ever to become stepsiblings, but Susan had to agree, they would make an amazing couple. Gawd, enough of that, she chastised herself.

As the road began to climb up the now partially burned over and still smoldering Boulder Mountain, Susan concentrated on her assignment. Enjoy a reunion of sorts with Lyndall Burke, who she hadn't seen since the aftermath of their escape from the top of a Nevada butte, and get noticed by Lyn's father, Stanley.

She dreaded the thought of Vegas in June but Lyn had said to be sure and bring her bathing suit and Susan had a new bright yellow Roxy tankini. Jake said it set off her powerful back, shoulders and arms. She had to agree she looked pretty good in it. Hopefully, Stan Burke would think so too.

Susan had given hugs all around before Jake sped off with the kids. She drove under a sky so clear and blue it looked as if you could dive into it. She soon passed Cedar City and St. George, such an easy drive now that the speed limit had been raised to 80 on I-15 through Utah. Her thoughts were pleasant, mostly about her little extended unit that resembled a family, as Jake had called them.

It was south of St. George just before the Arizona Strip and the Nevada line that she slammed into memories of the Lyn Burke case—first as Susan drove down through the convoluted rock faces of the precipitous Virgin River Canyon. When Lyn had been reported missing by her mother, Florence Burke, Susan, who had been assigned the case by the Jackson, Wyoming PD where Lyn had last been seen, and Jake, who had been hired by Lyn's aunt, Lou Cuvier, had inquired at Lifewater, an environmental organization, into Lyn's whereabouts. Forrest White Wolf, Lyn's supervisor, lied to his boss, Professor Noah Skutches, and reported Lyn was happily backpacking and doing scientific research in the wild remote Virgin River area Susan was now driving through.

Next Susan passed though Mesquite, descended a long hill and saw an exit for Overton and Lake Mead National Recreational Area. It was there that the drama had ended when White Wolf had finally been exposed as a murderous mole for the Southern Desert Water Authority and a consortium of Nevada businessmen. White Wolf's covert assignment was to ferret out radical environmentalists who threatened SDWA. Susan had shot and killed him near the mouth of a new tunnel or straw on the shore of Lake Mead, probably saving Jake's life in the process.

As she neared Las Vegas just before the junction of U.S 93 and I-15, she thought of the area to the north where she and Lyn Burke had been dropped by a helicopter on top of a butte by several of White Wolf's corrupt cronies from the Southern Desert Water Authority, including a fat, florid Irishman named O'Connor and an excessively surgically enhanced woman known as the Water Witch. White Wolf had murdered Fernando Diaz, a Lifewater field scientist, by pushing him off a cliff, sexually assaulted and abducted Lyn Burke, and ultimately murdered Noah Skutches. When Susan and her friend Bev Witt had gone sniffing around Ashland mine, owned by Lyn's father Stan Burke, looking for Lyn, White Wolf beat Susan senseless and someone shot and killed Bev. She suspected that someone was the Water Witch. The next thing she remembered after the assault was waking up beside Lyn on top of a desolate and remote butte with very steep cliff faces on all sides.

Her psyche dug into memories of her escape with Lyn off the butte, the consequent run to a nearby spring and ultimate discovery by, and battle to the death (his) with a lackey of O'Connor's. Her heart pounded as her mind raced back over that perilous twenty-four hours and Jake and Lyn's roles in the happy—as in good guys still walking and talking—ending.

Susan had shot and killed White Wolf (*checked that box, she thought*), just before radical enviros had bombed Boulder Dam. O'Connor had eventually taken the fall when the SDWA plot to steal water from the Colorado River for Nevada businesses, including Stan Burke's mine, and sell the excess to a Japanese gang was exposed. He had spent two years in jail, been ruined financially and had disappeared (*check*). Jake and Susan had given Stan Burke a pass because he was Lyn's father and his role appeared to have been relatively benign (*check*). Plus, that was Lou Cuvier's last wish. But the Water Witch was still bobbing up to the surface as a member of a think tank including occasionally giving interviews on national radio and television.

Susan was the one person who was absolutely convinced that woman was a murderer. She wanted more than just about anything else in her life, now that Old Ruth's killer had been brought to justice, to punch the Witch's ticket and *check that box.*

Susan and Lyndall Burke sat on the edge of Stanley's Burke's pool. The water was a brilliant emerald, the lone contrast to the dazzling white of the patio, which included white tile, white waist-high adobe walls, chaise lounges, umbrellas, tables—all white.

As Susan had learned as a kid in the desert: dark colors burn you, light colors blind you. She wore a large-brimmed straw hat and Ray-Bans. Lyn, being a tall, leggy fair-skinned redhead, suggested the usual pre-sunning ritual. They slathered each other's backs and legs with sun block and joked and giggled like a couple of schoolgirls. Lyn wore a bikini with a red bandana motif and thus had more skin for Susan to cover, which resulted in inadvertent tickles and, of course, more giggles. Then they composed themselves on side-by-side chaises.

"How long have you been staying with your father?" Susan asked.

"Had a falling out with a housemate who started out as a housemate and then became a roommate and ended up as a lover. Ended up as an ex-lover, I guess. Shame, because we were pretty good together, as house-mates that is. That was late last fall. I've been bouncing between my parents' places since Christmas."

"How are your parents?" Susan asked.

"Mom, will always be Mom—fearful, paranoid, dependent. Still grieving Aunt Lou's death. Well, so am I for that matter." She took a sip from her glass. "Still amazed at Lou's courage choosing to die at the dam for her environmental beliefs." Another sip. "And Dad, Dad's business took a huge hit after the dam bombing. Ashland mine was really heavily water dependent. I didn't realize how much so until Planet Earth Alliance hit Boulder Dam and Mead emptied out. You know what they say, everybody takes water for granted until the well runs dry, or the reservoir in this case."

"That had to be a blow to your father but it looks like he hung on to this beautiful home."

"Yeah, he had some other investments in local businesses that saw him through until the dam was repaired—gambling, liquor and all the attendant vices, even a pool and fountain maintenance service—all those wonderful inflation-proof and crisis-proof recreational activities. He doesn't talk much about that or the mine for that matter, but I'm not stupid. I feel guilty sometimes taking advantage of his tainted success by living here rent free, but you don't get to choose your parents." Lyn sucked the remains of her Arnold Palmer nosily through her straw and changed the subject. "What's your most vivid memory from our little trek in the desert?"

"Oh God, Lyn. There're so many. Let's see." Susan raised her eyes to the sky. " *Your* courage and how you encouraged me while we climbed down that rock crack, me with a twisted ankle. The feeling of elation when we were finally down off the butte and free, contrasted with the immediate fear that we had to find water or die out there, and our tormentors would know that was the case and right where to look for us. I could go on and on. You?"

"For some reason, my mind always goes back to the desert spring we found. But not just the fact that we could finally drink our fill and soak, but the reverence you had for the sacredness of water, which you learned from Old Ruth and your other Tohono O'odham mentors. I will never forget that." Lyn took Susan's hand. "Course I love remembering how you, Jake and I kicked that asshole's ass who had held a pistol to your temple while bouncing in his truck down that awful road."

"I've told Amy about that so many times. You nailed his head with your foot. You never know how useful a good soccer kick can be. I don't want her ever to be a victim." Susan stared at Lyn. "In fact, I would be thrilled if she turned out to be just like you, my desert angel." She stood, bent over and hugged Lyn.

After the embrace Lyn took the corner of her towel and reached under her large round sunglasses to dab at her eyes. "You should also tell Amy a well-timed bite can come in handy too. I kicked him. You bit him. Like they say, everything you need to know you learned in Kindergarten."

"I suppose we ought to give Jake some credit. Crazy as it was lying down in the middle of the road it caused Sanders just enough momentary confusion behind the wheel for us all to get the jump on him."

"How is Jake?"

"Best thing ever happened to me. He's a great dad and a wonderful companion." She removed her sunglasses, winked and jutted a thumb skyward. "Pretty damn good in the sack, too. No complaints from this girl. Feels good to be able to say that to a gal pal, can't even mention anything remotely like that to Amy."

"And Amy?"

"Pretty upset about the move as you might imagine and, let's just say, less than receptive to Jake's new role in my life. We like her school in Boulder, but high school coming up in two years has us worried. It's thirty miles by bus over a winding narrow hogback to Escalante and I haven't heard great things about that school." Susan glanced toward the house. "Can I go in and refill our glasses?"

"Sure. Dad may be home, he was glad to hear you were visiting."

Susan walked across the white tile and through a door into the cool interior of the house. She paused at a mirror in the hallway, took off her hat, fluffed up her hair and tucked it behind her ears. She tugged down the top of her tankini to conform to her tan line and expose more of her firm chest—one of the benefits of regular weightlifting.

She entered the ultra-modern kitchen. Chrome and marble gleamed on all surfaces. A television was audible from somewhere back in the house. All she could think to do was bang around and hope Stan would hear and respond by coming to the kitchen. Susan refilled their glasses with fresh ice from the dispenser on the front of the Sub-Zero refrigerator and placed them with a clunk on the counter. She studied her reflection in the glass of the floor-to-ceiling wine storage unit next to the fridge, inhaled sharply and tapped her bare right foot on the tile floor.

Jake had said to flirt with Stan Burke, what a joke. Flirting had never been her strong suit. Her way of flirting, which she now saw reflected in her daughter, was to pick out a boy on the playground she liked and crash into him. It rarely worked. Later when her BFFs took her out to bars she was always the last one to be approached by the available men. Her friends often said that she was the hottest chick in the group but was not sending signals. Perhaps she was, signals such as, *beware or I might crash into you.*

Dust motes drifted in the sunlight coming through the windows over a marble counter that was loaded with small appliances. The counter also housed a double sink. There were no sounds of approaching footsteps in the hall.

She opened the refrigerator and relished the rush of cold air on her skin while seeking the pitcher of tea and lemonade. Suddenly she felt a presence behind her. She steadied herself, removed the pitcher, closed the door, and turned. There was Stan by the sink. He had entered as quietly as a hunting cat. He wore pressed beige slacks and a blue tropical shirt open at the neck.

"You must be Susan," he said.

Susan backed against the counter beside the fridge. The edge was cool against her bare, sun-heated lower back. "And you must be Stan."

He was fit and attractive in a creepy sort of way. He had thick salt and pepper hair, a firm jaw, good skin for having spent so much time in the Nevada sun, and was tall like his daughter. He appeared to be in his mid-fifties. Just at the upper end of my range, Susan thought, and being a dozen or so years younger, I'm probably close to the upper end of his.

"It's wonderful to see Lynnie doing so well." Safe subject.

"She is doing very well, thanks to you." Stan approached and extended his hand. "I've never really had a chance to express my gratitude."

Susan shifted the pitcher into her left hand and took his hand in her right. It was strong but the skin was so soft it could blister through leather. His fingers were manicured.

"No thanks, necessary. It was a team effort to survive. She saved me as much as I saved her. I have great admiration for Lyndall." Susan remembered she was supposed to be flirting and smiled up into Stan's eyes holding onto his hand a beat longer before releasing it.

Stan turned and leaned beside her against the counter. Was it her imagination or was he an inch or two closer than decorum dictated? She noticed him admiring her cleavage.

"Well, I've got to take these drinks back out to your beautiful daughter by your beautiful pool. Would you like a glass?" Susan said. She poured the two glasses full.

"No thanks, I've got a beer going with the last innings of the ballgame in my den. I just wanted to meet you and, like I said..."

Susan returned the pitcher to the fridge and turned to face him. "Seeing Lyn doing so well and knowing she's my friend is all the thanks I need. But, Stan, excuse me." She moved close enough to him to smell his expensive cologne and the beer on his breath. She reached up and picked a crumb out of his chest hair at the opening of his shirt and tossed it in the sink. "Are you having snacks with your beer and ballgame?"

He looked embarrassed. "Guilty. I should always dust-bust myself before greeting guests."

Susan gathered up the glasses and flashed him her best and broadest smile. "Great to finally meet you, Stan."

"Likewise. Make yourself at home. Shame I have to travel for business this weekend. Uh ... I would love to get to know you better."

She raised the glasses. "I have made myself at home. This is just the first of many reunions. We'll have to make sure we do get to know each other better in the future."

As she strolled toward the patio she felt his eyes on her back, butt and thighs. She balanced the two glasses in one hand and opened the door. *Crash into you later*, she thought, as she walked back out into the sun.

June 17
Tuesday

Not a bad three-day weekend, Jake thought, as he waited for his grilled chicken sandwich. Three days in Yellowstone with an old ski bum buddy and some pretty decent pix of a mama griz and two new cubs. Many beautiful miles hiked to lakes and geysers and several beers drunk. Oh, and not to mention the crash course in fire investigation. He and Pete had managed to squeeze in a few hours of boots on the forest floor in old Yellowstone burns as a part of Jake's ersatz training.

The Lick Log Inn, a family café in the town of West Yellowstone was situated in an authentic looking log building. The large wrap-around porch offered several rocking chairs in front of a weathered bronze plaque, laying claim to some historic significance for the building. But it was the Lick Log's roadside sign touting great pie and free Wi-Fi that had attracted Jake.

The morning drive through, and out of, Yellowstone National Park had not been too crazy, just a few animal jams where fauna larger than chipmunks had apparently been spotted, but then later in July is when the legions of looky-loos swarm in. Now he anticipated pretty clear sailing down eastern Idaho to Clint's place in Driggs, where he was planning to spend the night and then load up Amy the next day for the eight-hour drive back to Boulder.

After three days of Amy being spoiled by a child-oriented, childless couple with dogs and horses, he wondered if he might have a pre-teen mutiny on his hands. He had high hopes that the time in the car would be good for his on-again, off-again relationship with Amy. Lord that girl had a mind of her own and a tongue to speak it with. Wonder how that happened, Jake mused. Just hope I can achieve detente before she turns fourteen and the adolescent shit hits the parental fan.

Pete had shared a website with Jake that included a very handy guide posted by the American Forest Fire Coordination Group. He took a sip of the ice water he had requested several times of the youngish and roundish Mexican-American waitress, flipped open his iPad, accessed the café's Internet and opened the AFFCG manual. Pete had said, "Typical of government guides it will probably give you more detail than you need." Looks like it does buddy, Jake thought. His Goldilocks-like motto as an investigator called for, not too little, not too much, but just the right amount of research—no one could skim better than Jake.

Listed were over a dozen government member organizations from the Bureau of Indian Affairs to the National Park Service to, of course, the U.S. Forest Service.

Jake read in the introduction about the importance of the role of first responders in determining the cause and origin of fires. He skipped over that, conceding he could never plunge into the hellish heart of a fire in front of the boys and girls who were trained for such work and were a whole lot younger, on average, than his forty-four years.

He read on and noted several places in the introduction printed in bold: **Make sure that you rule out lightning**, or words to that effect. What he ultimately gleaned from his hasty review of the introductory material was that interviews with the first on scene, coupled with fire spread direction, recent weather reports and a study of topography helped work the fire backwards to area of origin, then fine detail work at the area of origin should reveal point of origin and evidence of the cause. Also, crew leaders—such as engine captains like his friend, Pete—crew bosses, fire module leads, hotshot superintendents, etc. were trained to preserve what they believed was the area of origin, even though few were trained as investigators to locate specific point of origin or determine cause.

Jake pushed back from his reading. Shit, he thought with admiration, thinking back on his mad dash out of the burning forest with the boys, talk about remaining calm under fire. These folks have to fight the fire, survive the fire and figure out the fire, all at the same time. He gave himself credit for only one out of three on Boulder Mountain and admitted he had a lot to learn.

The waitress refilled his water glass without prompting. That's progress, he thought. A wild variety of vehicles, visible through windowpanes above a broad painted sill, drove by on the street in a steady summer stream.

He scrolled down to the end of the introduction and stopped on *Common mistakes in wildfire investigation*. Seemed like something he should probably read. The list of twenty-plus bullets included cautions such as *not obtaining on-scene weather data* and *not properly analyzing the ignition source and ignition factors.*

His eyes dropped down to the bottom of the list to read *lack of adequate photographs* (never a problem for him) and the last bullet, *lack of patience* (also never a problem for him—sometimes Susan thought he was too patient—but often a problem for Susan.)

Next he scrolled back up to the contents and chose *Chapter Two: Fire Scene Evidence.* He resumed reading.

Later, his sandwich and sweet potato fries long since devoured and the plates cleared, Jake looked up and saw he was alone in the café. The waitress was glaring at him. He quickly shut down his tablet, left a generous tip on the table, paid his bill at the counter and went out. At his car, he checked his cell for the time and realized he was going to be late getting to Driggs. Also, there was a text from Gloria Fox saying it was urgent that he call as soon as possible. He sent a text to Clint and asked him to please tell Amy he was running late.

Fearing that he might lose cell service once he pulled out of West Yellowstone, he went back to the porch of the café and sat in a rocker just as the waitress was closing the screen door. She had her purse hugged to her chest and appeared to be leaving for the day. The tip must have worked because she flashed him a big smile and nodded as she passed. He looked out at the traffic crawling from tourist trap to tourist trap. There were RVs of every conceivable make: trailers of all sizes, slide-in campers on pickups, huge fat, fifth-wheels with bike racks on the back and canoes on top, and large buses towing cars. Several of the biggest rigs had little yapping dogs on the dashboards that, with a little taxidermy, could fit nicely, and quietly, in the ashtrays. A tour bus went by and Jake remembered what Clint had said early one recent spring, "The robins are back; can the tour buses full of Asians be far behind?" An older Airstream cruised by and Jake stupidly waved, forgetting he was sitting on a porch and was not in his Suburban hauling Majestic.

Within minutes his call to the Apache Chief had concluded and he was on the road with an upgrade on his assignment. Amy would not be happy to learn they had to drive all the way home to Boulder today with an ETA around midnight at the earliest. So much for road trip bonding.

But Gloria had not minced words, nor did she appear overly distressed. She simply said that he was to come immediately. The police chief had gone back to the burn at her request after Jake had raised her suspicions about the cause of the fire and this time he had found a body.

June 18
Wednesday

Gloria Fox had agreed to Jake's request. He asked that she direct the tribal police to cordon off the crime scene in the burn and guard it, but leave it virtually untouched until he had a chance to study it. They had driven from Boulder after arranging for Amy to spend the two days with her new friend, Kristy, from school. While Susan drove, Jake spent the trip absorbed in his digital forest fire manual hoping to complete his crash course before viewing the Apache fire. They arrived in Show Low, the town named for a high stakes poker game, in the early evening and headed straight up to the burn, which—no surprise—was on the same gravel road where they had been accosted on their recent trip through these mountains.

A few miles up the back road and just after dropping over the summit, they saw a recent model SUV parked off to the side. The gravel continued down the draw and right through the surreal terrain blanketed with debris from the extinguished fire. The car, with a Tribal Chief of Police emblem, was sitting in a firebreak, which shot off at ninety degrees in both directions from the road. Jake guessed the firefighters, sawyers, and swampers had cleared a path around the head of the fire to stop its advance uphill.

Jake grabbed his camera and they slid out of the truck just as William Sweetgrass stepped out of his cruiser in his black police uniform. He seemed tall and light-skinned for an Apache. He had high cheekbones, brown hair over the ears, neatly parted, and sported a thick, trimmed moustache. They introduced themselves. Sweetgrass did not smile, nor did he remove his mirror sunglasses.

"Gloria has mentioned you many times, William, she obviously thinks very highly of you. It's nice to finally meet you," Jake said.

"It was out of respect for the Chairwoman that I offered to watch the crime scene rather than delegate it to a deputy."

"We appreciate that," Susan said.

"We haven't spoken because Gloria has asked that I channel all communication through her. Now that we are face-to-face, do you mind me asking what your thoughts are about this crime?"

"Yes."

"Yes?" Jake parroted.

"Yes, I do mind." He turned and walked to his cruiser, popped the trunk and reached inside. He returned and handed them blue paper booties for their feet, white latex gloves and painters' masks.

He pointed down the road. "It's less than ten minutes to the yellow tape around the body." As Jake and Susan started down the road, he called, "Don't screw up the sheriff's crime scene."

They descended in silence, stepping over burned tree trunks and around denuded downed limbs. They were surrounded by blackened earth, standing burned snags and clumps of singed grass, not entirely consumed. Nothing stirred. There was no sound other than the crunch of their feet on ash and their labored breathing through the masks. Evening sunlight stood in columns as thick as liquid between the trees. Fine particles backlit by the sun drifted in the air. The acrid smell of damp, burned, organic material bit through their masks. Deep char-like charcoal scales lined the downhill side of standing tree trunks. Jake remembered what he had learned from the manual, the side with the deepest char is typically the side that faced the oncoming fire.

They walked under crowns of trees totally burned away and Jake noticed dinner plate sized slabs of rock flaked off boulders from the intense heat. Their booties were covered in white ash. Small plumes of it flew up with each step. The burn area was narrowing on both sides. Jake recalled that fires often begin from the head of a V or cup of a U then spread outward and upward pushed by the wind along the flanks and head.

Soon the crowns of trees were more intact than they had been above. Jake remembered that meant they were approaching the point of origin of the fire where the heat had not been as intense as it was at the terminus. Ahead to the right of the gravel road and close to the center of the burn they saw yellow tape draped around four burned aspen trunks. The tape formed a rough square. Jake and Susan exchanged a glance that was intended as a brace against what they were about to witness. Jake lifted the tape and they entered.

Nothing prepares one for viewing a body partially consumed by fire. In the center of the yellow square was an area where burned debris and downed aspens had been cut back exposing a charred black figure roughly shaped like a human lying face up. The heat had caused the connective tissue to shrink pulling the knees and arms up and forcing the hands to contort into clutching talons. It was as if he, she, or it, had been plucked off a ladder. Except for a vague pattern in the patches of fabric, burned clothing and burned flesh looked like one. The eyes and hair had all burned or melted away. The only color other than black was the white of exposed teeth in the hideously disfigured lower jaw, and a short section of white femur visible where burned flesh had sloughed off the right thigh. Taken as a whole it resembled your worst cooking disaster nightmare—charred almost beyond recognition. In the center of the shriveled and blackened chest area was the shaft of a metal arrow, the feathers burned away.

Susan saw something reflecting more light than the surrounding flesh and the black shaft of the arrow. She knelt down by the body and peered into the destroyed thorax. She said the only words spoken between the two of them since leaving the police cruiser. "Bolo. Silver Bolo with some sort of stone inlay. The arrow penetrated the chest right through the center of the jewelry." Jake started snapping pictures.

This was suddenly very serious business. They were dealing with arson and murder. Back up at the truck, with Sweetgrass now gone, Jake opened the glove box, handed Susan her Glock and tucked his Browning 9 mm into the outside-the-waistband holster in the middle of his back.

Susan took her pistol, turned it over in her hands, raised her eyes to Jake and said, "We're good together. It blows me away we found each other."

Jake nodded but did not respond. They put on their matching brown jackets with the gold Goddard Consulting Group logos over the left breast. Jake had said the jackets were handy for concealing weapons and the official looking logo helped open mouths and doors. Susan wasn't convinced of that second assertion but she certainly was in no frame of mind to argue on this occasion.

As daylight drained out of the forest, they drove down the mountain to meet with Gloria Fox.

After parking and walking past the windows with Bet High Café painted in large red letters, Jake pointed to the Chairwoman sitting alone in a booth near the rear. She wore a blue nylon Show Low High School jacket. It was past nine and there were only two other customers. Two swarthy male stragglers sitting apart from each other at the counter leaned over their pie like birds of prey mantling their kill.

The investigators entered and walked back to the booth. Jake introduced Susan; they sat and immediately ordered—a burger for Jake and a salad with grilled chicken for Susan. Gloria said she had eaten earlier. She sipped at a cup of decaf while they engaged in small talk, mostly about kids and her grandkids. Susan noticed Gloria was wearing a feather with a turquoise stone on a leather thong.

"That's a beautiful feather. Do you mind me asking what it is?"

The Chief held it out from her chest. "It's an eagle feather. Pretty, isn't it?"

"Yes. I don't think I've ever seen one."

"It's from my Goddaughter, Bina and her family. Bina's twelve and is going through what Apaches call The Changing Woman. In August my husband Victorio and I are hosting the Sunrise Dance to introduce her to womanhood. Her parents gave me this traditional gift when they asked us to host."

"Is it elaborate? The dance?" Susan asked.

"Very. It lasts from Friday through Monday and follows strict historical and cultural guidelines involving a medicine man. Bina will enjoy many gifts both literal and spiritual." Gloria smiled. "She will even receive a cane to be used in old age as a way of showing the full arc of life. Most importantly she will be made aware of her new strength as an emerging woman."

"How do the traditional Apache religion and Christianity coexist among the White Mountain Apaches?" Jake asked.

"It creates a lot of push-pull, for instance, in the fairly recent past, the local Christian churches taught it was a sin to participate in the Sunrise Dance. Practicing our traditional religion was illegal until the mid-nineteen seventies. Most of us are trying to live within the dominant culture while hanging on to vestiges of our heritage. Our people are free to choose and even blend religions and few members of the tribe are at all fanatical about either."

"Which do you choose, Gloria?" Jake asked.

She met his eyes. "Personally, I lean toward the traditional because I think it's important to retain the culture. And professionally, as a leader, I feel I need to model those traditional beliefs." She fiddled with her eagle feather pendant smoothing out the fluffy white afterfeathers and the more rigid dark barbs.

"Marrying outside the tribe is part of the problem and wouldn't you know, our mind-of-her-own daughter, Lenna is planning to do just that. My family is as subject as any to these pressures."

"Oh, who is Lenna marrying?" Susan asked.

Gloria brightened and smiled. "My younger daughter, always the unconventional one, fell in love with French in high school—even though she had to study it online because it wasn't offered in the curriculum—minored in French in college and spent the last half of her senior year studying in Paris. She goes to Normandy to research Apache soldier involvement in D-Day and meets and falls in love with a handsome French man with a pretty name, Dominique. Dominique loves horses and all things western U.S., now, apparently, including my daughter."

"Wow. Proud mom," Jake said.

"Just think if they have kids they will be French-Apache-American. Now there's a combination," Gloria said.

"Shades of Sacagawea," Susan added.

"Well sort of, things have changed a bit, thank God. Toussaint Charbonneau actually bought Sacagawea from her captors to join his other wives. And he was French-Canadian."

"That's great news, Gloria. Congratulations," Jake said.

"Lenna and Dom are planning a wedding in Normandy next summer. I have one year to learn survival French before my first trip over there. Lenna says the French appreciate it if you at least try. I'm determined to try. Working on a word-a-day."

"I'm kinda into language," Jake said.

"Yeah, red-necky language," Susan teased.

"Pardonne moi, mon amour." Jake feigned great offense before turning to Gloria. "What's today's word?"

"Aimez beaucoup—love abundantly. Might go into my toast at the wedding."

The waitress brought their food; Jake and Susan dug in. Gloria checked her watch. "Guess we better get busy. I'm glad you convinced me to look closer at that fire. It was like William found the body in no time once I insisted he go back over the burn. Did you see him up there?"

"Yes. Briefly. He was, let's just say, less than thrilled to meet us," Jake said.

"Oh, ignore William. Like I mentioned, he's stressed about the new casino, which he vehemently opposed for what he claimed were moral reasons. He's a sad loner with no family and few friends. Plus he's got issues with whites, the biggest being that he is one."

"One what, Gloria?" Susan asked, fork poised in midair.

"White, or half at least. His father. William's never laid eyes on him. Doesn't know where he is and claims he doesn't care. Ever hear any naughty jokes about traveling salesmen? Issues aside, I appointed William because he's well educated, has extensive training and experience, and he has few interests or commitments to distract him from his work. Lenna may never forgive me. Even though he was several years ahead, she claims he constantly teased and bullied her in high school." She adjusted a dangling silver earring. "Pretty grim up there?"

Susan placed her laden fork back on her plate. "It doesn't get much worse than a burned body."

"No and I guess it's not great dinner talk but we don't have much choice, I have meetings early tomorrow morning. Why do you think the body was overlooked initially?"

Jake responded. "It was in the lower middle of the burn in the center of an aspen grove. Firefighters work the edges of fires trying to get containment and ultimately control. The middle really doesn't concern them so much. Especially an aspen grove where fuels are heavy and burn hot, and root systems are shallow which poses the danger of falling widowmakers. Firefighters would chose to work around an area with that profile."

"What are your impressions of the body?" Gloria asked.

"Susan and I discussed it on the way down. We think the arrow was postmortem," Jake said, before taking a bite from his burger.

Susan added. "It was fired at close range through a small hole in a round piece of silver jewelry that was probably a bolo. Even the slightest movement on the part of the victim would have made that extremely difficult to pull off. The sequence must have been death, arrow, fire."

"So the victim didn't die in the fire?" They nodded. "Well, that's a relief. Terrible way to go. Any theories on the identity?"

Jake responded. "They did a thorough job, whoever they are. The burning was so extensive it was almost impossible to determine gender. In fact, the aspen grove might have been chosen because of the nature of the fuel and intensity of the heat. But probably male based on size alone. And he was arranged, so to speak."

"Arranged?" Gloria asked.

"The killers wanted us to find the body," Susan said. "Arson is often used to cover up a murder. In this case it seems to be intended to show-case it."

"The victim's probably not Apache," Gloria said.

"And why do you say that?" Jake said and shot a side-glance at Susan.

"Our men don't wear Navajo necklaces, or bolos as you call them. We prefer beads and pendants which are usually solid and teardrop-shaped to commemorate the deaths of warriors fighting American soldiers in the 1870s."

"It will be interesting to see what the coroner and forensics come up with," Jake said.

"Yes, it will, but don't hold your breath. Deaths on or near Indian land, even when the race of the victim is unknown, have a tendency to become a very low priority. The common assumption being another Indian-on-Indian crime, probably involving alcohol and/or drugs." Gloria shook her head and stared down into her cup. "The good news is, if it can be called that in a case like this, the fire was started off our land, although it burned across the boundary, and the body was dumped just off the reservation also. That means the local sheriff has jurisdiction."

She lowered her voice and leaned in. "Incompetent as Sheriff Biff and his boys, yes, all boys, are, they are far preferable to the FBI. We are re-quired by law to report serious crimes on the reservation to the FBI." She leaned back against the booth. "Just to give you an indicator of how ef-fective that is studies show that one in three American Indian women are raped during their lifetimes. In 2011 the U.S. Justice Department chose to prosecute only thirty-five percent of rape cases reported on reserva-tions."

"Jesus," Susan said.

"Like I said when we first met, Jake, things rarely go well for the Apaches when the Feds get involved. And I guarantee if this one were on the reservation, their agents would come here wearing blinders, looking only at Apache suspects and telling me nothing. The Sheriff is a local boy. He will keep an open mind and share what he learns with me."

"I have to admit, I'm new at this," Susan said. "As you read in my resume, all my training is in police work for police departments. Frankly, if the PD had assigned me this case, I would be looking at Apache perpetrators and an Apache victim. Statistics prove over and over that the people you're looking for are the closest in proximity to the crime. It plays right into motive, means and opportunity."

Gloria made eye contact with Susan. "With all due respect, Ms. Brand, that would be like me assuming that you're dumb because you're blond, and you are clearly not dumb, far from it. You are operating under assumptions and stereotypes. They're false. None of these men will turn out to be White Mountain Apache. I know my people. Now Comanche—maybe—if the fires had been set under a full moon by mounted Indians riding like fury on steroids—I would definitely go with our old enemy the Comanche. I'd be sending you north to Oklahoma as we speak." Gloria smiled at her private joke. "I'm trying to save you a wild goose chase to the wrong tree."

Susan started to respond but Jake reached out and stopped her by squeezing her thigh. He wiped his mouth with his napkin, took a sip of his water and said, "Let's discuss how you would like us to proceed *assuming* we are ruling out Apache perpetrators."

Gloria pulled some notes out of her jacket pocket.

The counter was empty now. The waitress wiped it down with a cloth and green liquid from a spray bottle. Gloria paid their bill and the three walked out to the parking lot.

The Chief thanked them for coming with such short notice, bid them, "Bonsoir," and drove out of the parking lot to the south.

Jake and Susan climbed into her truck. Susan said, while slipping the key into the ignition, "A little sensitive about the Apache profiling?"

"Ya think?"

"So this is how it works, we ignore training, evidence and the obvious to kiss the ass of our employer?"

"No, Susan, how this works is we give the impression we are kissing

the ass of our employer, and continue to cash her checks, while following the leads and evidence—basically our noses—to any damn tree we
feel the urge to bark up. In the end, all our clients care about are results.
Often in the beginning, they feel they know more about the case than
we do, and that's true for a brief period of time while we're getting up
to speed. I consider my clients' recommendations very carefully but I
always treat them as recommendations, not ultimatums."

"So what's next?"

"Let's check out the Boulder Mountain and Flagstaff fires. I have a
nasty hunch about them."

"I have to say, you learned, or at least are giving the impression that
you learned, a lot about forest fires in a very short period of time."

"It's kinda cool, really. You always hear that something like a ne-
glected campfire is suspected as the cause of a forest fire but who knew
how fire investigators determined that. It's like putting a jigsaw puzzle
together. I'm enjoying it."

"Good. And now maybe things have settled enough and you can concentrate long enough for me to tell you about my new boyfriend, Stan."

"Can-*not* wait to hear how that went. Let's just go as far as we can
toward Boulder and when we get too tired grab a room at any motel—a
6, an 8, a National 9, whatever—en route."

"After this day, *whatever* will feel damn good."

Susan started the truck and backed out of the parking lot heading
north. A small blue pickup occupied by the two men who had been sitting at the counter, turned out of the shadows behind the café and headed
south.

June 19
Thursday afternoon

"The monks are here."

"What?" Jake didn't look up from the scribbling he was doing at his desk.

"The monks are here," Susan said, pointing to the iPad on her lap. She sat in their one comfortable leather living room chair.

"Who are the Monks, a new Boulder family?"

She read from her screen. "'The Drepung Loseling monks are here in Boulder. This year they're creating a Green Tara sand mandala, which they will work on in the common room at Boulder Mountain Lodge, Friday, Saturday and Sunday from 9 a.m. until 6 p.m. It is customary to offer a donation of monetary support for this activity. There will be a collection basket there for cash and checks. It is considered very virtuous to offer to the monks, resulting in positive karma.'" She looked up. "You should definitely plan on a major donation."

"What are you reading?"

"Megboard."

"Oh, great. All I ever see on Boulder Megboard is badly spelled requests to, like, have someone stitch up a horse or to borrow a goat emasculator. Or my personal favorites are the riveting reports of Rusty's romps."

"Who's Rusty?"

"You know, Nancy's roaming ram, Rusty. Spends more time sniffing around for woolly butts at large than in lockup. No rust on that horny dude."

"*Ewe!*" Susan winked at Jake.

"Oh, that was baaaaad." Jake grinned, got up, walked to the kitchen and moved their lunch dishes from the table to the sink.

"I saw that one about the goat thingy. Wondered what was the protocol for returning a borrowed device for castrating a goat. Tie a little ribbon around it with a note saying, *Many Thanks. Had a Ball. Thoroughly Sterilized.*"

"That's what I love about this isolated little town. It's like Brigadoon—lost in time, never changes."

"Brigadoon? What the heck is Brigadoon?"

"That's what our little old landlady, Sara calls it. I Googled it. Brigadoon's a play—a musical—and a film. We should check it out on Netflix sometime. And I agree with Sara. Boulder's like living in the past. Folks rely on barter and each other here. It's pretty amazing. Reminds me of the small town of my youth. A youth spent mostly in the company of bovines." He looked out the window at Boulder Mountain. "Smoke is prettier in the morning."

"Huh?"

"I'm looking at the smoke still coming off the mountain ... it's prettier in the morning than it is now."

She came out to the kitchen and stood beside him. "Love the smell of smoke in the morning ... I like that too, even if it is a bit hard to hide in a fishbowl, about Boulder, I mean. If we're still together in a couple of years, I'd like us to buy our own place here."

He turned to her. "What are you saying? Still together? Where's that coming from?"

"I don't have a great track record ... no, wait, actually, I do. I've successfully run away from lots of men. Only one, my ex, ever ran away from me. Took me awhile to get back on my game after the shock of that, I admit."

He put his arms around her. "Unlike Rusty, sweetheart, I will never let you break out or run away. Nor do I intend to ever wander, so... "

"So?"

"So I guess we are just running together."

"Like cheap paint?"

"No. Like a majestic mated pair of wolves cruising around in an Airstream appropriately named Majestic. Let's go check on Amy."

Susan backed him into the living room toward his desk. "First, tell me what you were writing." She reached down and snatched up his small spiral notebook usually reserved for investigative details. Jake grabbed for it and missed. She read, "*Chasing beer bottles rolling down hill* and *Floozies with Uzis under their skirts doling out bursts of just deserts.* What the hell?"

"It's part of my recovery program. Folks with creative outlets have a much higher success rate. I've always wanted to write country lyrics, so ... I guess I'm *gambling* it'll help me."

Susan grinned and looked at his notes. "Oh this is really good: *What did you miss—misogynist? What did you miss—misogynist? Your sister's tips? A kiss on the lips?* This is going straight to the top of the charts. I can hear it now. This goes out to all you boot-scootin', bronc-bustin' women haters. Watch out, Brad Paisley!" She slapped his notebook on her thigh. "These aren't country lyrics. You're ignoring the basic rule of T and B: tractors and trucks—boots, buds and babes. That's your basic country. Back to the drawing board, Brad."

Jake retrieved his notebook from Susan's hand. "Let's focus on a little business. I've been thinking about our next move with the Bad News Braves."

"So have I. Here's what I've come up with. There's going to be an arranged body in each burn."

"Wow. I agree."

"And the body has been overlooked as it was with the Fort Apache Reservation fire."

"Correct, but a technicality, the fire was started just off the reservation."

"Funny how that happened. So we have to find the bodies and somehow identify them without revealing that we are unofficially investigating these fires."

"Ideas how we might do that, Wonder Woman?"

"I'm still adjusting to working in the PI-way, as in, under the radar and only quasi-officially, but I'm learning. We now know where to look in the burns. We look. We find. We report anonymously. The local sheriff takes the credit."

"And?"

"That's not enough?" Susan paced with her hands on her hips. "Okay, I think I've got it then. The local coroner identifies the body; the local paper runs the story. We let those working in an official manner do the heavy lifting for those of us sneaking around feeding off the bottom and plucking the low hanging fruit."

"Ouch. A little harsh, but yes, you have just earned your decoder watch. The dedicated public servants of each jurisdiction will be focusing locally. We'll try and take what they come up with and connect the dots to create the big picture. Let's go see how Amy and Kristy are doing and then head up to the Boulder Mountain burn."

Driving up Boulder Mountain involved climbing a monumental and massive uplift. As they started the ascent in Susan's truck, they could see residual smoke emanating from the opposite side of the mountain, but when they neared the top they saw nothing but verdant forest, blemished somewhat by patches of standing, gray, beetle-kill pine and spruce. Jake regretted not driving because he had nothing to distract him as they headed up toward the burn. The closer they got the more he felt a mixture of grief and anger at the apparently intentional destruction of such a magnificent old forest. A bulldozer and backhoe were parked at the turnoff from Highway 12 into the area of the fire. The flames had thankfully not crossed the highway. A green canopy containing a bubbling stream flowed down to the vermillion rock valley below—a bombed out hellscape loomed above. Red retardant was splashed on boulders and banks on the burned side as if the forest's blood had been spilled.

Susan stopped at the crossbar of a sawhorse barrier with a sign that read DANGER! ROAD CLOSED. Jake jumped out and swung the barrier to the side. After Susan passed he closed the crossbar and hopped back in the truck.

As Susan bucketed up the two-track, Jake noticed with irony that it was somewhat improved by all the heavy firefighting traffic. Burned branches without a leaf or needle on them scraped the sky. Smoke danced up in discrete tendrils. They drove through a charnel hell fully expecting to uncover at least one extinguished life in the incinerated form of what is appropriately referred to as human remains.

"Over there to the left is where the boys and I camped." They passed a maze of down and scorched aspen that looked like a giant's game of pick up sticks. "I don't want to think about what would have happened if I hadn't smelled the fire. Thank God I'm a light sleeper and Matthew was having bad dreams."

"Now that I see this, I'd say you used up one of your nine lives. Gives me the creeps to think that I could've lost my three boys in this ugly mess."

They drove on in silence until they approached what appeared to be the narrowing area of origin of the upper fire. Jake asked Susan to pull over and park. The truck crunched across several down and burned branches.

Jake suggested that they treat the truck as if it was sitting at 6 o'clock. He'd fan out to the right and Susan was to head left and they would meet at 12 o'clock, always keeping each other in view if possible.

Jake had not gone more than seventy yards through stark standing timber when he stepped over a scorched log and noticed a charred shape tucked up against the backside partially covered by several denuded black limbs. He kicked off the cover and exhaled. It was the burned carcass of a doe with one badly broken leg caught in the crook of a limb; no doubt it had happened while fleeing the advancing fire.

After approximately sixty minutes of searching what Susan had come in her mind to think of as Dante's private Hell, she looked up to check on Jake while stepping over a small cracked and scorched boulder embedded in the burned duff. When her boot landed with some force on the other side it penetrated the forest cover and she fell spread-eagled on the rock with her foot jabbing down into a smoldering root system. She yelled for Jake.

Heat and pain enveloped her lower leg as she rolled away from the rock and freed her ankle. By the time Jake reached her she was on her knees slapping at her hot boot with her ball cap. Smoke rose from the cavity by the rock her misstep had created.

Jake squatted and brushed embers off her boot and lifted her pant leg to check for burns.

"You okay?" Jake asked while gently slipping down her singed sock.

"Yeah, just a little shaken I guess. I didn't even notice the weak spot on the other side of that rock."

"Your quick reaction and thick sock appears to have saved your skin."

"I guess that's why they call them Smartwool socks—save the skin of people who do dumb shit."

Jake stood. "Since an hour of working the origin of this burn has turned up nothing, let's take a break and mull."

They sat on the end of the pickup's bed, drank water out of aluminum bottles and snapped down peanut butter energy bars.

Susan beamed at Jake. "One of the reasons I fell through is that I was distracted by you. You looked like a damn bird dog zigzagging back and forth."

"Hey, easy. I learned that technique from my buddy, Dick and his better half, Buster. That's how Buster would search for my keys when Dick tossed them into the tall grass without Buster seeing or hearing. He was a hell of a search and rescue dog. Died recently at the age of 12. Broke Dick's heart. I figured it worked for Buster, so...."

"This is certainly not what I expected to find," Susan said. She blew hair off of her soot-covered face.

"Yup. I was pretty certain our theory was solid. There is no doubt in my mind that this was arson based on the coming and going of that vehicle, what I witnessed first-hand in the fire, and what was reported at the interagency coordination group website. But where's the body?" Jake stared down at his ash covered hiking boots.

"Where is the body, indeed?" Susan said looking deep into the burned part of the forest. Shafts of sunlight illuminated drifting smoke like some sort of cheap theatrical effect. "One thing that's different here from the body dump in the rez fire, excuse me, the near rez fire, is no aspen. The only aspens we've seen were where you camped."

"Right. And we know there can't be a body dumped there because I was there when the fire started."

"Unless… " Susan turned her gaze to Jake. "Unless … they dumped or moved a cadaver into the aspen grove after the burn was extinguished."

He slowly turned his face toward her and grinned. "That's insane, Wonder Woman—wonderfully, brilliantly insane. Let's go check it out."

Susan drove her truck back down the mountain and parked just off the two-track near the destroyed grove. They walked toward the tangle of skeletal aspen trunks. It resembled a barricade piled up and torched by a rebelling populace. As they stood at the foot there was nothing visible in the gloom of the pile but more ghostly trunks.

"I'll climb in, why don't you do your Buster thing around the periphery," Susan said.

Jake headed counterclockwise around the pile. Susan began to scramble up. She had not gotten more than twenty feet when Jake called out.

"Holy shit! There's a body here Susan. It appears to be female with an arrow through a necklace. And she's got *my name* on her."

June 20
Friday

Jake and Susan were doing what aided their best thinking while avoiding curious pre-teen ears; they hiked up the ranch road that traversed from the highway past their driveway and then through a pinion-juniper forest high above Boulder Creek and onto an irrigated plateau. In the distance, sandstone buttes shone white in the early afternoon sun. They had just finished lunch at the cabin and Amy had settled into the hammock in the locust grove with her favorite author, cell phone handy—just in case.

"What blows me away about Gloria is that nothing rattles her. I call last night to report the remains of a middle-aged white woman in business attire pierced by an arrow and posed in the Boulder burn and Gloria takes it in stride and calmly asks me if the body had been burned. When I say only partially, she equally calmly tells me that the first cadaver, the one found near her land, has been identified."

"Who was it?" Susan asked.

The sound of a large bird's wings scraping the air in flight brought their eyes up to the sky. It was a raven and it cast a shadow twin on the road's grassy bank. A gust of wind stirred the limbs on the lush streamside cottonwoods beyond the cultivated fields below.

"Looks like our gorgeous day might be interrupted by afternoon thundershowers," Jake said. He pointed to clouds building towers to the west.

"Hope my daughter knows to get in out of the rain. But I'll take it. Rain's nice in any form except when it brings dry lightning."

"Like everything else in this case, it's a little weird. And score one bull's eye for the Chiefwoman; he's not Apache. Andrew Millar, an art gallery owner from Show Low." Jake dug his notebook out of a front pocket, flipped it open and read. "Millar was white, affluent—his father a successful California developer back in the day when they made big money—and Millar had been battling cancer." He looked at Susan.

"Cancer? What the hell?"

"Pancreatic. Terminal."

"It's like, whoever's doing this wants to kill but not really," Susan said.

"Yup. Makes me wonder what we will learn about vic number two who was wearing my nametag."

"I just hope we didn't make a mistake removing the note before we called the sheriff's office. Read me what it said again."

"I share your concern. We're going to some pretty serious extremes to achieve Gloria's goal of operating off the official grid—flirting with obstruction." Jake flipped some pages. "*Since you show no dread or terror, you can help us spread fear and fire.*" Jake stared at the page as if he felt some explanation would present itself. Then he brought his eyes up to Susan's. "What we got?"

"We've got an *us*. That indicates more than one person and/or a cause. We've got a reference to terror, admittedly a pretty overused term these days but still perhaps significant. Most importantly we have a perverse reference to you helping whoever *they* are. How can they think you could possibly … I'll be damned. We found the body. We called it in. We helped them. Son-of-a-bitch."

"And they have figured out that a) I won't be scared off and b) we don't want to have our relationship to the White Mountain Apaches and Gloria Fox become public knowledge so they could pretty much assume we would call it in anonymously—might have even figured we'd keep the note. That first body being found just off Apache land is suspicious too. They had to know a few hundred yards the other way meant FBI. It all points back to a close relationship with the Apaches."

"But Gloria won't buy it," Susan said.

"No, I'm pretty sure if we're going to get Gloria to buy into any Apache involvement, we're going to have to offer incontrovertible proof. And right now we're still at the crapshoot stage."

"Okay, so we know they've known about you ever since the severed elk head calling card, but what possible long term good do you do them? They can drop bodies all over the region and make the anonymous calls themselves."

Jake shook his head and glanced out at the swarming clouds. "Beats me. Maybe they're paranoid. They think they're being watched or even have their phones tapped." Thunder echoed through the distant buttes. "We better not push our luck regarding Amy getting in out of the rain."

They turned just as a blast of swirling wind stirred up by the encroaching storm pushed them from behind. Shooting out of the darkening thunderheads, lightning licked the flat top of a sandstone butte. Leaves blew horizontally off the streamside trees below.

They were climbing up on the deck to the cabin just as rain began to pelt down in large drops, pinging on the metal roof. Amy was visible through the picture window talking on the landline. That was odd. The only people who called the landline were solicitors and pollsters and Susan had taught her daughter to politely hang up on them.

"Can you hold a sec, she just got back?" Amy walked toward the screen door with the portable as Susan pushed through with Jake behind.

She handed her mother the phone and turned to go back to the living room.

Susan put her hand over the phone. "Who is it?"

Amy said over her shoulder, "Oh, sorry, Mom. Said his name is Stan Burke."

Susan turned to Jake wide-eyed.

"*Ewe*," Jake whispered.

June 21
Saturday

"Know what today is?" Jake asked. He was driving Susan's truck. Red sandstone rushed by in a blur.

"I know it's my first and last date with Stan Burke," Susan said. "Who does he think he is calling on a Friday and asking me out for the next night because he *happens* to be coming to St. George on business?"

"You like a little more lead time?"

"Well, *yeah*. Need time to do my hair and nails, clean and lube my Glock—girly stuff like that."

"Besides your last date with Stan, do you know what today is?"

"Honestly, I've been rushing around so much I'm not even certain what the date is."

"June twenty-first—"

"Ah yes, summer solstice *and* the two-year anniversary of the straw and dam bombings."

"Correct. Also, almost two years ago to the day we were at Stan Burke's mountain home at Brian Head near Cedar City, although Stan was not present, and here you are going back near there to visit Stan at the Hilton in St. George, but as he says, with your own room, of course."

Susan fiddled with the truck's radio. At first she found nothing but Christian music, right-wing talk and static. Finally she found a country station with a song in progress.

"This's for your research and recovery," she said, sitting back. But the station soon faded as they drove around the butt of a red rock butte.

"Bummer, just when I was wondering if the buck in the boots was going to get the babe in the bar," Jake said.

Susan switched it off. "Since there's absolutely no other option and I'm desperate for entertainment, want to try your latest on me?"

Jake turned to search her face. "You sure?"

"I'm sure. *And* I'm desperate."

"You're not going to razz me? Give me honest feedback?"

"Honest. Honest feedback."

"I've been playing with one I think has promise. Last Call in Budville is the working title." Jake cleared his throat, reached for his aluminum water bottle nestled in the cup holder and took a gulp.

"Last night in Budville and the beers are all the same.

One good thing 'bout Budville. No one knows my name. No one knows my shame.

Tumbled into Budville fresh out of weed.

Ah ... let's see, oh yeah.

Tumbled into Budville fresh out of weed.

Blowing out tomorrow like so much bad seed.

Last call in Budville and then I'm done.

Suck down a Bud and it's bed, bathe and be gone."

Jake looked at Susan expectantly.

"Oh my God. Now you're talkin' country. That has serious potential."

"You think?"

"I do. Just the right amount of bad poetry and deep despair capped with a bad pun. Emmy Lou Harris said you can't know country until you've had a broken heart. Sounds like your guy's had that and worse." She shook her head and chuckled. *"Budville—Bed, bathe and be gone—* love it."

"There is a Budville, believe it or not. Off I-40, west of Albuquerque," Jake said.

"Why don't you ever write about Utah?"

"I've tried but Utah has no music in it. John Denver heard the musical quality in West Virginia and Colorado, but he never tried a song about Utah. Even Roy Rodgers sang about having a home in Wyoming. You can hear the music in that but U-tah just doesn't work."

Susan started to do a very bad riff on Roy. "*I had a home in Wyoming 'til my boyfriend drug me away—*"

"Oh, please."

"*—to U-tah, where there's no music—*"

"Thank you. That confirms my theory. Absolutely no music in that," Jake said.

Susan slapped her knees and bent forward in laughter. Jake grinned and made an exaggerated check of the rearview. "I want to be certain we're not getting pulled over for really bad singing."

They rounded a curve through rocky terrain sprouting sporadic pinion and juniper trees and saw the entrance to Zion National Park.

After paying and entering Zion, Jake drove the tree-lined park road that switched down through several layers of sandstone. It was a river of green through every shade of white, tan and red. They traveled beneath sheer walls ascending to towering peaks.

"This is like driving through sculpture," Jake said.

"Some would argue the work of the divine sculptor," Susan said.

"Obviously that's how the early Mormon pioneers saw it, considering all the biblical references, starting with Virgin, as in the town and the river, and Zion. At least they allowed some diversity with the inclusion of the Temple of Sinawava, the Coyote God to the Paiutes. But for my money, water was the artistic element. From seas to streams to trickles; in Zion alone, nine layers of sandstone formed by water, from the Dakota Formation at the top to the Kaibab at the bottom—nine steps out of a couple dozen formations in the Grand Staircase. It all pretty much goes back to water."

"I'll drink to that," Susan said, reaching for her water bottle in the console cup holder.

"Speaking of my Budville musings, just west of there, south of Gallup, is El Morro National Monument. El Morro has nine hundred years of history etched into its soft sandstone starting with petroglyphs from the Puebloan people, followed by the inscriptions of seventeenth century Spanish Conquistadors and finally English-speaking folks from American wagon trains immortalized their passage. Why were they there? One reason—water. There's a reliable pool of water at the base of the butte and as long as there have been humans in that thirsty area, they've been hanging out at that pool."

Jake switched on the headlights and they drove through a tunnel in a sandstone monolith finally emerging at the other end into blinding light reflecting off white sedimentary rock walls.

"Whoa," Susan said, blinking and holding up a hand to shield her eyes. "That's a little bit like coming to the light isn't it? Rebirth."

"Lots to inspire here, both the religious and the environmentalist," Jake said.

"I've never understood why they aren't natural allies," Susan said.

After leaving Zion, Jake and Susan stopped in Springdale for the standard liquid exchange. Pee out, petrol in. Susan purchased a pair of Sockguy socks with the name Zion and a picture of one of the geological features on the ankle. Amy loved wild socks. The Zion socks fit the bill. Then with Susan driving they headed toward Hurricane north of St. George. Jake's cell pinged with a message. He saw it was from Gloria and played it on speaker.

"Hi Jake, Gloria. Have to make this short. Rushing as usual. The female victim placed in the Boulder Mountain fire has been identified by the sheriff from Torrey. Brenda Petersen, lived in Torrey. She was 54, independently wealthy, came out west as a dude to play cowgirl and stayed. She married a cowboy who ran a saw sharpening shop in winter. She had metastasized stage-four breast cancer and was not expected to live long. That's all I've got for now. Check in when you can."

"All business, as usual," Susan said.

"Not all business, actually."

"Oh, yeah what was not all business?"

"I have a text from her came in around the same time saying the French word for the day is potager, means vegetable garden."

"Ah, po-ta-ger," Susan mimicked.

"Veggies for the pot. Think I can remember that. But still, no suggestion of Apache involvement." Jake looked out the side window. "I've got an idea. Let's go home from St. George the long way, through Colorado City to 89A to the Flagstaff burn. Should be a pretty drive through Navajo country. Now that we've got these arsonists' MO, we might just stumble over another body in a burned aspen grove."

Susan said, "Just don't offer to buy me any silver Indian jewelry. I'm kind of off of it right now."

He pointed at her with his index finger and nodded before turning his attention to speeding up through a straightaway.

Jake waited in the dark in the bedroom of the suite Stan Burke had booked for Susan. She had left the door to the room slightly ajar so Jake could slip in when she went down to meet Stan for a drink in the bar. Then, as they had planned, she invited Stan to her suite for a romantic room service dinner. Jake regretted not bringing his iPad. He had nothing but Stanley's awkward attempts at seduction to entertain him, and Beyoncé, who Stan had playing on his iPhone through the room's provided dock and speakers. Susan's assignment was to extract any information she could about the Water Witch and Bev's death without tipping her hand. But she had really gotten nowhere with that. Their mark had proven to be wily and very much of the old school "don't worry your pretty little head" about serious matters of that variety. Which was, Jake mused in the bedroom, pretty fucking stupid considering he was trying to bed an ex-cop. Jake was to emerge from the bedroom when Stan made his move. Considering Don Juan was on his second bottle of wine, Jake expected that to be any minute.

He watched the action through a slight crack in the door. Stan and Susan sat across a small table in an alcove. Susan had made certain her host had his back to the bedroom. Two candles flickered on the small table. There was an open French door onto a west-facing balcony. The floor-length curtains billowed on the gentle breeze. Out the windows, sunset firelight spread across the bottoms of clouds dancing close with the mountains, and ignited a lingering cross from the contrails of passing jets. Jake could hear something about liking your face and that rhyming incongruously with taste. He couldn't make it out but tasting a face seemed outlandish even for Beyoncé.

"Beautiful night out there," Stan said.

"My very favorite day of the year."

"Speaking of beautiful. You're sure pretty and sexy in candlelight," he said.

"Thanks. I need all the compliments I can get but, let's be honest, low light and alcohol consumption are a girl's best friends when it comes to pretty and sexy."

"I just can't resist any longer, Susan. I'm going to kiss you." Stan stood and bent across the table.

Susan smiled seductively and leaned in as if to present her mouth but instead placed her flat palm over Stan's expectant lips as Jake opened the bedroom door and slipped up behind him. Stan's eyes popped open.

She gazed into them. "You men are *so* easy."

Stan's pupils widened as the barrel of Jake's pistol pressed against his temple.

"Oh, where are my manners, have you met my boyfriend, Jake?"

Stan stiffened. "What the hell?"

Jake pulled up a chair and sat beside Susan with his pistol trained on Stan. "Hi, sweetie." He gave Susan a peck on the lips. "You look so pretty and sexy in candlelight, I just can't resist you." He turned to Stan. "Nice to finally meet you, Stan. I've heard so much about you, I feel like I should've wasted you years ago."

Stan's eyes flew back and forth between Jake and Susan. "You set me up. What do you want from me?"

"It's a simple proposition, Stan. You will get Jake an entrée into the life of your friend, the woman known affectionately as the Water Witch, or we will broadcast your involvement in her shit to the universe."

"And beyond," Jake added. "I made a pact with your sister-in-law, Lou, just before she died so heroically. I promised I would not tell your daughter of your involvement in the Water Witch's shenanigans, including I presume, being complicit in Lyn's abduction." He leaned in and bore his eyes into Stan's. "Even though it was a last wish, and Lyn deserves better—she certainly deserves better than you—I will break that deal in a heartbeat if you don't give us the Water Witch."

"I never … I … I was told Lynnie was fine … like she was at a spa or something. At the time I had no idea how much danger she was in."

"And later when you did have an idea, what did you do to see that your friend was punished for her actions?" Susan demanded.

"I … I … "

"You did nothing because you knew accusing her would implicate you," she added. "But now you're going to get Jake close to her or pay a heavy price."

"There's no way I can get you access to her. The director doesn't even work for Southern Desert Water Authority anymore. I've cut off all contact. I have no communication with her because of what she did to my daughter, lying to me the whole time."

"In a heart … beat, Burke." Jake said without taking his eyes off Stan's face.

"I'm not even certain how to reach—"

"This is not, like, a business negotiation." Susan said. "Have you forgotten you hired Ranklin Moody to harass me and my child when it was my job to find your child?"

"And we're not like the business people you associate with, sleazy as they may be," Jake said.

"No, we're much more dangerous. I'm certain what with your Vegas history you're familiar with the term 86, as in to 86 something or someone. That originally meant to take someone out in the desert 8 miles and bury them 6 feet under the sand," Susan said.

Jake got up, walked around the table and placed the pistol against Stan's perfectly styled salt and pepper hair.

"Heck, Susan, we've got miles of empty desert and millions of tons of sand around St. George."

"Right. And it would be days before anyone even figured out Stan had been 86ed."

"Easy peasy, trigger squeezy. Should I use a pillow to muffle the shot or just blast Beyoncé?" Jake pressed the barrel into Stan's skull. He went rigid but didn't respond. Jake started to whistle through his teeth, *Nearer My God to Thee.* Stan, wincing and turning pale, slowly leaned sideways away from the barrel.

"Oh Jesus, Stan, he's whistling. Jake only whistles when he's really tense."

"Okay, okay. I'll get you inside her compound but the rest is up to you."

Jake eased back on the Browning.

"I have a pool cleaning service. We do her pool. I'll get you trained and put you on the crew. That's the best I can do. I don't even know if she's in Nevada these days. If you're caught, I'll deny I knew anything about you."

"Deal." Jake and Susan said simultaneously. Jake dropped his hand, the pistol slack at his side.

"Good call. You just saved us from some really bad Beyoncé," Susan said.

Stan mopped his forehead with his napkin. He slid his wallet out of his back pocket and fished for a card. He rejected several before settling on one. He handed it to Jake. It read Gushers—Reliable Pool and Fountain Maintenance.

"We are scheduled to train new hires at my warehouse in Craig—the address is on … on the card—just after the 4th."

Jake put Stan's card in his breast pocket. He slid the pistol back into the holster in the middle of his back, sat again in the chair next to Susan and grinned at Stan.

Later in bed, in the suite paid for by Stan, Jake and Susan made love. In the afterglow, Susan was on her belly. Jake was lying on his back lifting strands of his lover's hair with his fingers. She smiled and her shoulders shook with laughter.

"Did you see the look on his face when you said, easy peasy trigger squeezy?"

"Yes, but my all-time favorite look was the one after you warned him about me whistling."

"Yeah ... I was like, whatever you do, Stan, don't *make Jake* whistle. What a wuss! As if I would be attracted to him. *Ewe.*"

"I don't know, I think you might have a thing for the manicured entrepreneurial type who hires others to get their hands dirty. Too bad you didn't have a chance to check his toes. Wonder if he has them done too?"

She giggled. "With polish." They both laughed out loud and then Susan shushed Jake and pointed to the connecting door to the next suite.

Susan asked quietly. "So where in the world did easy peasy come from?"

"That's a Flesh-man original. You haven't met Trey Fleischman, have you?"

"No I haven't, all you've told me is he's a buddy from Geology Club in Salt Lake who's into vintage Airstreams."

"I haven't required his help recently but he is also my go-to guy when I need some lab work done. Flesh-man works for CRUP. Generally when I ask him to do a little something for me on the side involving DNA, blood splatter, fiber, hair, whatever, his response is, *easy peasy lemon squeezy*. I love the guy, dinner plate glasses, nerdy laugh and all."

"CRUP. What—?"

"Consortium of Regional and University Pathologists. Actually he has a cred that is even better sounding than CRUP. He got his training on the SPLAT team in the Air Force, investigating crashes."

"What does SPLAT stand for?"

"Nothing really except for the obvious. It's not an officially sanctioned term." Susan wrinkled her nose.

"I know, I know crude, insensitive, but spot on, so to speak."

Susan did her best nerdy, forcing-out-air laugh, "Wha wha wha...is Trey's laugh like that?" She tried to tickle Jake but he rolled away onto his stomach.

"No, it's the closest thing to a yuck-yuck I've heard since I watched a lot of Three Stooges."

"Last week?"

"Oh, yuck, yuck. That's a good one."

Susan ran her hand down Jake's back to his muscular butt. "I remember wishing I could do this at the Howl at the Full Moon Festival when we were searching for Lyn and posing as a married couple sharing a tent."

"Instead you made me get out of the tent while you undressed. Go figure."

"Well gosh, Jake, I had just met you," she said softly. "And you were married." She leaned in to press her lips to his ear and slowly slid her fingers between his butt cheeks. "Besides, I'm a good girl," she whispered.

"Oh, yes." He sighed. "You're very good." He spread his legs slightly and pushed his face into the pillow.

June 23
Monday

Jake and Susan stood beside a table in a shaded pull-off in the roadside picnic area they had chosen for lunch en route back to Boulder from Flagstaff.

"No, no, no. You are not doing that. You're not involving Trey Fleischman in our investigation. No way."

"Susan, what's the problem? Trey has been helping me for years." Jake placed a Ziploc sandwich bag containing a small gray object on the table beside their small cooler.

"He's a civilian with a life," she said. "That's the problem. You'll be placing that life in danger."

"Look, think this through step-by-step. Just as we predicted, we found an incinerated body in the Flagstaff burn. But with no arrow, no note, nothing that assures us it was the same Indian, or whatever, arsonists making the same statement. How can we be certain of a relationship? Even though this was their earliest fire that we are aware of, why alter the MO later? If Flesh-man can determine this cadaver was terminally ill with cancer, we have a confirmed pattern. If not, we might have a coincidence that could lead us down the wrong road for months."

Susan—her hands on her jean-covered hips—looked into the tamarisk, willow and cottonwood that spread downstream. "I'm not comfortable placing another of your friends at risk." Birdsong emanated from the trees.

"Another of my friends? Oh, this is really about Bev, isn't it."

Susan turned to look pleadingly at Jake. "Yes, I guess it really is."

Jake reached over, gripped Susan's shoulders, and caught her eyes. "I promise no one will ever know Trey is involved in any way and that I will not take him into the field or expose him to any danger. Okay?"

Susan lifted the brim of his ball cap and tilted her head playfully. "Okay. That's all I can ask." She pulled Jake into a hug.

They turned to sit side-by-side at the table with a view of the stream meandering through sandy banks.

Susan picked up the baggie and ran her fingers over the outside of the plastic covering the object. It was shaped like the tip of a sword only thicker.

"So you think these bumps and lesions on the xiphoid process are going to indicate some sort of cancer?" Susan asked.

"That's my best guess from the little bit of anatomy and pathology I've picked up in First Aid courses over the years—certifications that seem to be expired more often than not."

"Hope the sheriff's folks aren't well trained enough to miss this part of the body," Susan said. She placed the bag in the cooler and got out the sandwiches they had purchased earlier in Escalante.

"They shouldn't. What's one little bone out of 206?"

Susan probed between her breasts with her first two fingers on her right hand. "Actually from what I remember from my medical certifications, which I never allow to expire by the way, this little sucker is cartilage that ossifies after the age of 40. I hope it tells us what we need to know." She opened the cooler and dropped the plastic bag in. "Let's eat."

They unwrapped their sandwiches and chewed in quiet reflection.

June 25
Wednesday

Forty-eight hours in a holding pattern on a case was enough to make Susan crazy. But there wasn't much to do except wait for Trey Fleishman's response to the sample Jake had sent. There had been no new reported man-caused fires in the region. But that could have been the result of a brief respite from the drought in the form of a widespread two-day gentle soaking rain. A female rain as Old Ruth had called it when the monsoons of Susan's youth came to southwestern Arizona. The sun was out again at last and Susan was suffering from cabin fever. She charged out the door right after an early breakfast. She was wearing a black tank top, matching spandex capris and her brand new neon green New Balance runners.

Susan relished the engine-warming start to a run. Her feet pounded up the packed sand driveway. She leaped over the few remaining damp depressions; the deeper sand beside the two-track looked all the softer from the recent rain. She was a little breathless as usual, starting out in oxygen debt and with heavy legs. By the time she reached the top of the driveway, it was all systems go as her breath and pumping limbs synchronized.

She ran up the edge of the paved road between cultivated fields and was passed by a white delivery van before topping the hill in town where Route 12 takes a ninety-degree to the north. Susan jogged straight ahead at the junction into the sun. She felt a cooling breeze on the Burr Trail

Road as she ran past the wood building housing the Burr Trail Grill.

As the road leveled out her afterburners kicked in with an endorphin blast, which cleared her head. She waved at comely silver-haired, Megan Smith who was leaving the grill and walking to her orange Jeep Wrangler. Seeing Megan reminded Susan she needed to contact her with a posting for Megboard, Megan's invaluable one-woman community service project. Amy had outgrown her bike and wanted help listing it for sale.

Boulder Mesa loomed to Susan's right. The cracked and lined rock reminded her of white elephant skin. She tried to remember what Jake had taught her about the origins of Navajo sandstone. She was pretty sure it was one of the few layer-cake formations in the Grand Staircase that originated as sand dunes. Cleansing sweat dampened the area between her shoulder blades.

She pounded past the brown sign that warned that the Burr Trail to Capital Reef had extreme grades and sharp curves. She started to round one of those bends to the south and saw the sign surrounded by trees that indicated she was about to enter Grand Staircase Escalante National Monument. White sandstone buttes lined the road. Soon she was out of view of town and was reminded just how remote Boulder was when she saw the sign indicating it was 75 miles to the next service. She glanced up over her right shoulder at massive Sugarloaf Mountain to the west. Her breath was even, deep and rhythmic.

It was still early and no cars had passed her on the Burr. She heard the first vehicle approaching from the rear and shifted over as close to the shoulder as she could without getting mired in the deep roadside sand. For a while she ignored the car behind her; she was totally tuned into her breathing and the beautiful scenery. But in time it occurred to her that the car had not passed. She glanced over her shoulder and felt the muscles in her back tense. It was not a car. It was a small blue pickup—two dark-skinned men in the cab, two in the bed. At first the truck hung back a few hundred yards. Then it bore down on her but slowed at the last second to remain just behind her. Susan touched her chest and recalled with a jolt that she didn't have her cell. Scary reports about breast cancer and phones tucked in jog bras had influenced her fateful decision to leave it at home. She was jogging on an isolated stretch of road with no cell and only one escape route and the blue truck was sitting squarely in the middle of it.

The truck accelerated and came so close she thought it might clip her, but it backed off. Adrenaline surged. She kept her eyes forward and just kept running. She didn't know what else to do. The truck advanced again. She could smell the heat of the engine and hear the crunch of the tires. This time the fender bumped her left leg almost buckling it. She staggered and then regained her equilibrium. She felt a painful tear in the flesh on the top of her calf where the grit on the fender had scraped her skin. She set her jaw, forcing air out between her teeth, and just kept pounding, further away from town and safety, heart slamming, sweat flying off her forehead. The truck approached again. Susan gritted her teeth and ran even faster. Finally the truck flew past in a blur and as it brushed by she felt a sharp flick and sting across her buttocks. One of the men in the bed still leaning over the passenger side was pointing and laughing; he held a long cylindrical object in his hand. He wore a bandana on his head. His face was covered in bright war paint. The pickup blasted ahead of Susan.

She turned to sprint for town. In an attempt to head back at her, the driver jerked the wheel and threw the truck into a four-tire slide. But the rear wheels skidded sideways and jacked the truck perpendicular to the road with the bed over the deep sand. Her assailant wasn't holding on and was thrown out of the bed onto his back. The engine roared as the rear wheels spun; sand shot out from under the tires and sprayed the jerk on the ground. He popped up sputtering and yelled something at the driver. The last thing Susan saw over her shoulder as she bolted for town was three men slipping and falling in the sand while struggling to push the truck back onto the road. She eased her pace, glanced back again and saw the little truck digging in deeper and deeper. If she weren't so frightened and her ass weren't so sore she would've been laughing it off.

Once back to the safety of the town, and running much slower, she mulled over what had just happened. She had being harassed and whipped with an arrow by the arsonist Apaches. Their scare tactics hadn't worked on Jake so now they were obviously trying to warn her off the case and get to him through her by assaulting her close to home.

Her fear had been replaced by anger. She was pissed. The Bad News Braves knew where Jake and Susan lived, and now, Goddamnit, it was time to get them where they lived.

Amy had charmed their neighbor, Mike, into hiring her to help with his animals and eventually the first cutting of hay on his five acres. Before leaving the house in Jake's Subaru to go back to the Burr Trail, Susan made sure Amy had reported next door to her job.

Susan and Jake strapped on their pistols and drove to the place where Susan had last seen the pickup. All that was left was the deep divot the stuck truck had dug. Susan noticed something fluttering in the breeze at the sign announcing the National Monument. They stopped to examine it. A green VW camper with out-of-state plates drove by heading away from town; the young male driver waved. A target arrow, possibly the one that Susan had been whipped with, pierced the breast of a barn owl just below its heart-shaped face pinning it to one of the posts supporting the sign. The arrow came away with ease, as if it had been wedged by hand into a hole. The owl's chest cavity, pecked empty by scavengers, crawled with bugs. It appeared to be long dead, probably road kill. They buried the owl in the sand back from the road and headed home.

Jake called Gloria from his desk in the living room and, after bringing her up to speed on the third cadaver and sending the sample to Trey Fleischman for analysis, relayed the details of the morning. Susan sat in a chair behind him carefully holding the arrow by the plastic vane and studying the shaft and metal target tip. It had been easy to check the lacquered shaft for prints. She had found none.

Susan could hear Jake's frustration rising. He rolled his eyes, shook his head and punched speaker. Susan adjusted the fresh bandage on her calf.

"If I had any doubts before, they are completely cleared up now. Susan's attackers are not Apache. They are probably not even Indians."

"Enlighten me, Gloria. Susan is listening, you're on speaker now."

"Hello Susan. Glad you're okay."

"Thanks Gloria. Just a little shaken up. Might have been the best workout I've had in ages. I ran like hell."

"I can imagine. I need to have a few less sit-downs and get out there with you. Okay, Jake you ready to learn about Indians and owls."

"I'm all ears."

"In most tribes, owls symbolize death. Even hearing an owl hoot is considered bad luck, let alone handling a dead one and sticking it to a post. From childhood owls are engrained into our culture as evidence of impending death and disaster—the Indian equivalent of the bogeyman. They are considered to be ghosts who carry messages from the grave or deliver messages to people who have broken taboos. No Apache would kill an owl or handle a dead one—really bad Karma."

"Karma? Is that an Indian term?" Susan asked.

"Yes, actually it is."

"Bad karma—an Indian term?" Susan insisted.

"Yup. Sheet not blanket." Gloria chuckled, causing both Jake and Susan to relax a little. "I suppose if some folks want us to be Native Americans, when Apaches were Native Mexicans before they were Native Americans, they should call those folks over in India, Native Indians."

"Might *curry* their favor."

"Lame, Jake. Don't mind him, Gloria. He writes bad country lyrics full of bad puns." Susan held the arrow up to the floor lamp by Jake's desk.

"Here's an interpretation you might like," Gloria added. "In some tribes owls are portrayed as bumbling bunglers who are banished to the night as punishment for their lazy or bad behavior."

"*Banished bumbling bunglers.* I might be able to use that in a song," Jake said.

"That sounds like our gang of losers," Susan added.

"So, seriously—you can't imagine a single circumstance under which the deeds we are investigating could have been perpetrated by your tribesmen?"

"You'd make a good lawyer, Jake." There was silence. "Hmm. Okay, if these actions had been a one-off, say, the flare thrown at your car, I might think, bad behavior probably fueled by drugs or alcohol. But the way these events have been planned and executed and the numerous cultural taboos—such as handling dead bodies and dead owls—that have been broken, if these guys are Apache they have wandered way off the reservation, so to speak. And if I had four renegades in my community, don't you think I'd be aware of them by now?"

"Point taken, Gloria, but—"

"Why don't you take a look at some of these crazy, white supremacist, anti-government types who shoot without provocation at rangers but never forget to cash their social security check? We had an incident like that in southern Arizona a few years ago."

"Um, because we've seen these bunglers twice close up and they, uh … aren't white," Jake said.

Gloria cut him off. "Iron Eyes Cody, the Hollywood Indian known as the crying chief in the Keep America Beautiful commercials—one hundred percent Italian. And don't get me started about Johnny Depp." She giggled. "But I have to admit he's pretty cute." Susan pointed at Jake and winked. "You know Jake, I served for years on a community council with a local rancher from St. John. He loved to say, if your horse is dead, you probably ought to get off. Oh, sorry, hang on."

They heard a muffled discussion followed by the sound of a door closing. "Sorry folks," Gloria said. "Got to go. Keep in touch. Let me know what you hear from Salt Lake on that third body. Thanks for the update. You both be careful. But get me results."

"Wait, Gloria. What's the French word of the day?" Jake asked.

"La sale de bain—bath room. Might come in handy. Bye." Gloria ended the call abruptly as usual.

Jake turned away from his desk. Susan held the arrow by the two ends; she flashed a huge grin.

"What?" he asked.

"Two things: you just got a smack down from the Chief, and the Bad News Bunglers have just handed us a new lead. Unlike our first two arrows, this one carries a clue. I didn't notice it before because it's very faint but this baby is stamped with a name. It's almost hidden by the plastic feathers." She squinted at the shaft near the vane. "I can make out Desert and then cap A followed by r-c and then cap P followed by h followed by a smudged space and then cap A followed by r-i followed by a space. I'm guessing it's probably Desert Archery, Phoenix, Arizona, a store or something."

"Vanna, tell the pretty lady what she's won on The Wheel." Jake reached to the corner of his desk for his laptop and Googled Desert Archery/Phoenix, Arizona.

June 30
Monday

Susan and Jake sat on their deck in the mid-morning sun watching Amy in her big straw hat riding across Mike's field on the back of his restored red Massey Ferguson tractor. An easy breeze came up off of Boulder Creek, rustling the grass and carrying the sweet smell of the hayfield with it. Jake's cell vibrated with horror movie music, his ring for Trey Fleischman. He picked up and punched speaker.

"How's life, Pi?"

"Flesh-man, great to hear your voice. You're on speaker and Susan is here."

"Hi Trey."

"Hey Susan. How's life with Agent 3.141?" He yucked and Jake and Susan exchanged a glance.

"Never a dull moment. Need to meet you sometime."

"Would like that. Maybe catch you at an Airstream rally. Jake you still thinking about doing Antelope Rally in Medicine Bow, Wyo, next fall?"

"I haven't ruled it out but neither of us is a great white hunter like you so I wonder what's the point?"

Across the dark green field Amy and Mike were off the tractor hand-rolling irrigation pipe on large wheels.

"Not required. We got country living, hiking, thermal pools on the Platte, even golf. We get some good speakers too—authors and such."

"We will def discuss it, Flesh."

"Great, Pi. All I can ask. You going to come to Bob's lecture next week?"

"Help me out, Flesh, I'm a little out of the loop—Bob?"

"Smith, Bob Smith. Geophysicist, U. of U. He's lecturing at the club meeting next week on the plumbing under the Yellowstone caldera. He's speaking just before the big three-day 4th of July weekend kicks off."

"I wish I could but this case has got me really tied down. I can't reveal many details, but..." He glanced at Susan. "We're dealing with some creeps here who're playing for keeps." He didn't want to invite Trey's questions so he jumped to the business at hand. "What you got for us?"

"What I got is a BLT with a big fat ole' kosher pickle."

Jake chuckled. "Too early for lunch so clarify, please. Layman's terms."

"BLT—breast, lung and thyroid. Kosher pickle—kidney and prostate."

"What about them?" Jake asked.

"Those are the five cancers most likely to metastasize to bone and it's not pretty. They manifest on bone, as you suspected, as humps, bumps and fractures."

"Also on ossified cartilage, Trey?" Susan asked.

"Lucky for you two—and your boyfriend is nothing if not damn lucky—yes." Pause for yuck, yuck. "The body from which you rascals purloined this xiphoid process had some form of advanced cancer from the BLT with a kosher pickle menu."

Jake and Susan looked at each other with relief and slapped a high five.

"Bless you my brother. You may have just saved us a hell of a lot of work," Jake said.

"Not a problem, Pi-man. Like I always say, 'Fuck Google. Ask Trey.' Let me know if there's anything else I can do. Looking forward to meeting your gal."

"His gal owes you a big hug, Trey," Susan said.

"When you look like me and do the work I do, you gotta take 'em when you can get 'em. I'll bank that one and look forward to it."

"Thanks again, man. Best to the Geology Club folks. See you soon. Be well," Jake said.

"Have a good 4th. Stay safe, play safe and keep in touch." Trey ended the call.

July 3
Thursday

"Seems like we spend our life in cars." Susan fiddled with the radio trying for NPR without much success. They chose Jake's Subaru to save Gloria gas expenses and, Jake had argued, reduce their carbon footprint. He was driving. The highway followed a sun-sparkled stream below majestic mountains so numerous they weren't all named on the map.

The investigative team was looking very official in their brown with yellow trim caps and brown polo shirts with the Goddard Consulting Group logo. Their jackets were in the back seat. Susan pretty much hated the uniform and was looking forward to some downtime to do a major redesign. Jeans—in Susan's case, tight jeans—and low cut hiking boots finished off the sleuthing ensemble.

"We have to travel for work," Jake said. "Film or novel, every good thriller has at least one car chase in it and here we are chasing around in cars. Just imagine you're a star in a white-knuckle thriller. It's either this or starve in Boulder." He rubbed his belly with his right hand. "And as you can tell, I'm not much for starving."

"True. Not much call in Boulder for gumshoes investigating anything other than a rampaging ram. Think I'll pretend I'm Katee Sackhoff," Susan said.

"Oh yeah, I like her in 'Longmire.' She looks like she could kick my ass and then drag me to bed," Jake said.

"Hmm. There were some interesting shades of gray in that little observation." Jake sucked air through his teeth and shuddered. "You perv, you," Susan added.

Susan gave up on the radio and studied the passing scenery. "I can't believe you talked Mike and Cindy into taking Amy over the holiday."

"It was her idea. She's got them totally charmed."

"Glad she's using her charm on someone."

"Hey, she's a farm hand who loves working with their animals and chickens, and they pretty much pay her chicken feed, they *should* provide room and board," Jake said. "Even though it requires so much driving, I'm glad we've got this job right now, exasperating and narrow-minded as Gloria can be. Pretty frustrating call with her the other day but at least her bias has narrowed our search. Now we know we're looking for Italians in war paint setting forest fires."

"Yuhhh." Susan did her best scratchy and nasal Sopranos. "Hey Tony, I got a offer you can't refuse. We dress up like Indians and torch some Goddamn trees."

Jake smiled. "Gloria drives me nuts but this is a fascinating case and she does have some good points. Interesting contrast if you think about it. American Indians were forced onto reservations carved out of what was originally Indian land, and then later federal land. Shortly thereafter in the early twentieth century copper kings, lumber barons and railroad magnates did everything they could to purchase federal land dirt cheap while fighting it being placed in the public domain. And after losing that battle, they resisted any fees being charged for the use and abuse of federal land; yet some ranchers today believe they are entitled to do anything they please on public domain lands and have the mandate to take up arms to defend their poached grazing rights under the Second Amendment. At least the greedy bastard fat cats tried to buy the western land. Today folks insist they are entitled to use it and abuse it without the inconvenience of owning it, maintaining it, or paying taxes for it."

They had circumnavigated Flagstaff and were in towering Ponderosa pine forest heading south on the long descent to the desert and Phoenix. The snowcapped San Francisco Peaks were visible through breaks in the forest canopy.

"That was a helpful call from Trey. I liked him. He sounds like a good guy."

"Great guy. Loads of fun. A real study in contrasts. Belongs to the NRA and listens to NPR. Quick to tell me he doesn't belong to NPR, though. I say that makes him a poacher on intellectual property."

Susan found the station she had been seeking but kept it on low volume.

Jake continued. "He's a very smart guy. You can ask him anything about Airstreams and cars, new or vintage, but be forewarned, a short question about an engine will result in at least a thirty-minute lecture. I swear he pleasures himself with consumer reports and car mags. He's forever quoting them and always seems to have them immediately at hand."

Susan was fiddling with the radio again. The reception was better and something caught her attention. "Wait, I want to hear this." She turned up the volume. They caught a short report on the unilaterally established Islamic Caliphate or IC. The reporter stated that 1,000 foreign fighters a month were traveling to the Middle East to join IC for a total of 16,000 so far. The report included a quote from an audiotape released on social media purportedly recorded by IC's self-proclaimed leader. He scoffed at the weakness of his adversary, the U.S.-led coalition and urged all Islamic Caliphate fighters to take the battle everywhere and ignite the earth against Satan and all tyrants. The piece included an update on the current status of an American man held hostage by the group. An attempt by the U.S.-led coalition to free him had failed. In the aftermath of the failed rescue attempt, the radical Islamic group announced that unless their demands were met the hostage had three days to live. Another very public—again, thanks to social media—and humiliating beheading was promised.

Susan turned off the radio in disgust. "That poor man and his family. That is the ultimate perversion of religion. Satan must be delighted to witness the Middle East swarming with bloodthirsty, murderous, religious fanatics with more slithering in every day to sign up."

"Oh come on: the underwear bomber, the shoe bomber, the Times Square propane tank bomber, these guys are amateurs, a joke."

"The Boston Marathon bombers, the Charlie Hebdo shooters, if these guys are a joke, you could die laughing. Makes Saddam look like a teddy bear," Susan said.

"But, it's not as if this is a first, historically speaking," Jake said. "Christianity probably has as much blood on its hands as any religion. One of my favorite bumper stickers—I need to get one somewhere—says, *Lord protect me from your followers.*"

"With mass murders, public beheadings and crucifixions, IC is setting new records in brutality against humanity. I've got friends more liberal than you that sound right of Curtis LeMay in what they're saying we should do to IC. Since their adherents are currently living in the Middle Ages we should bomb them back to before the Stone Age," Susan said.

"We enjoy plenty of religious fanaticism right here at home. I worry about Matthew and Tim and the influence of their born-again evangelical mother. Tim was praying the night we were running from the fire."

"My father was an evangelical *minister* and I don't even attend church. Best way to insure a kid never goes in a certain direction is to have the parent push that way big time. Plus, prayer has a great calming effect. Don't worry about him praying. Shit, I was praying when Lyn and I were climbing down off that butte in Nevada two years ago. I was praying you would show up and my prayers were answered." She punched him on the arm and tugged on the hair sprouting out below his ball cap. "And you keep showing up. I have to say you are good at showing up." She squeezed his neck with her hand and then rested it on his shoulder. "Not to worry, you are raising two red-blooded, American, prepubescent males. I caught Tim staring down my shirt the last time he visited and remember the time Matthew tried to convince us Hooters was a family restaurant. Chips off the old block."

Jake grinned. "Ah yes, those good ole' family mammaries." He reached sideways with his right hand for her left breast. She caught his wrist and pushed his hand back. "Just another desperate guy making a grab for the girls. Shall we review?"

"If you won't let me grope, might as well."

"What we got?"

"We got: three bodies found in intentionally set forest fires. Two had metal arrows shot postmortem through expensive pieces of jewelry. At least two were prominent and affluent. We are still waiting on an official ID in the media in response to an anonymous call to Flagstaff authorities regarding cadaver number three. Two were burned post-mortem, one may not have been. Taking the fires in chronological order, the fire in which the last body, the one without an arrow, was found was the first fire that was set. All three victims were ill with terminal cancer before they were murdered."

"And we've got two sightings of four men in a stolen small blue pickup in war paint and looking for all the world like Indians but who our client is certain are not. We know they are onto us. You got a bloody elk head bauble and a sweet note on a body—fingerprints still pending from tribal police. I got a slight scare and one good stroke with a wooden arrow. And we are on our merry way to Phoenix to check on the name in the vane of that arrow," Susan said.

"I just hope our efforts will not be in—"

"Oh, don't even," Susan groaned. "And then we drop you in Las Vegas to begin your training as a cute and irresistible Gushers pool boy."

"We have one thing other than arson linking all three fires."

"Bodies with cancer," Susan said.

"And what does that mean?"

"It's a little bit like Jeopardy—three people with cancer murdered and then placed in forest fires is the answer—now what the hell is the question?"

"Open a button or two and put the girls to work for the good of mankind and of Goddard Consulting Group." Jake prepped Susan for her interview with the presumably male owner of Desert Archery. They were parked in the lot of a small mall, engine and air running.

She removed her ball cap and placed it on the dash, shook out and finger-combed her hair, and opened all the buttons on her polo. "And for all the creatures of the forest, large and small," she said. She exhaled and smiled at Jake, grabbed the arrow off the dash and opened the door.

The heat smacked her in the face forcing her back into her seat. She slammed the door, pressed her hands to the air conditioning vents, stared out the front window and slowly shook her head. "I can NOT believe I'm back in Phoenix in July. I must be out of my freakin' mind." She sighed, looked down and pulled open her shirt top a little more to reveal half-moons of tangerine lace. "Hope you can breathe in there, girls. Let's go to work." She exited the car carrying the arrow.

"We give these away for promotions when parents buy packages like, you know, targets, inexpensive compound bows and such." John Fenstermacher, the storeowner, who had generously offered to assist Susan personally, responded to her query. He looked to be low to mid-fifties, had thick sandy hair that fell over his forehead and a square, some would say, German set to his jaw.

"So, not high end?"

"Hell, you can get Uth Gen Tru-Flight 18' metal tipped target arrows for three bucks online and they cost us less wholesale."

"Good deal for the money?"

He leaned toward Susan across the counter struggling to keep his eyes level—smell of mints on his breath. "Be honest—piece a crap. Tips regularly break off in the targets. Kid's toy really."

"Have any memory of between one and four American Indian men buying archery equipment here and getting these arrows as a part of the package?"

"Indians? Can't imagine a red-blooded Indian worth his stripes using these arrows for anything but pickin' his teeth."

"You've been very sweet, thanks."

Susan grabbed the arrow off the counter and started to leave, but turned. "Just one more question. Do you sell to any anti-government types?"

"God yes. Very popular with parents of a certain bent. Survivalists, Abos—sorry, people into aboriginal survival skills—anti-Fed militia types, anti-immigration, and armed vigilantes living on the fringe. Some of our best customers. And since their interest is more about lifestyle than sport, they like to indoctrinate their kids early. That's where the packages with the free arrows come in."

"Any Italians?"

"Italians?"

"Just kidding. Thanks for your help."

He seemed to want to prevent her from leaving. "Actually, with this selection of camouflage face paint, which could come in handy in your line of work…" He pointed to tubes, sticks and plastic compacts in white plastic bins down the counter. "I could probably make you look like Little Black Sambo. Oops. Okay to say that these days?"

"I'd be the last person to guide you on what's okay to say, John. But I probably would have gone with Little Blond Sambo."

"That's a relief. We live in funny times. Got girls—sorry, women— jumpin' around half naked on the sidelines of pro games, yet a male announcer would be out a job in a heartbeat if he was to mention it."

"Tough time to be a man." Susan flashed her high-beam smile. "Just not right, women using their physical attributes to manipulate boys. Sorry—men."

A crude letter-sized poster taped to the counter caught her eye. "What's this?" She moved back to the counter, tapped the poster with the arrow and then bent down to read it.

John leaned closer and stabbed at it with a finger. "Oh that's Buck Waller's annual July 4th beer and Fed bash. He throws a party at his compound and uses it to seek new recruits. Everyone is welcome as long as anti-government rants and readings from the constitution appeal. No thanks. They hold a archery competition every year and Buck's a very good customer so we agree to advertise the party but my employees are told to offer polite excuses and not attend."

Susan noticed an address on the flyer. "Do you have more copies of this?"

"Christ, do I ever. It's our yearly source of scratch paper. Buck's man Pork drops off least two dozen copies every June."

"Pork?"

"Pork. Skinny as a rail, believe it or not. Grew up poor in the Appalachian Mountains if that tells you anything. You, know, squeal like a pig. Really scary guy."

"Tells me more than I want to know, thanks."

John turned and headed down the counter. Susan shifted to where she could examine the various packages of face paint and muttered to herself. "Makin' bacon." The bell on the store door dinged and a heavyset man entered wearing camo cargo shorts and a sleeveless tan t-shirt.

"Be right with you," John called. He walked past a wall covered with expensive, high tech bows and lethal looking arrows splayed like a turkey gobbler's tail feathers. He ducked through an opening under an Employees Only sign and was back in a second with a copy of the red, white and blue flyer. "I'm going to give you this but I suggest you don't go anywhere near Buck Waller." Susan thanked him again and left with the flyer.

Jake checked his iPhone and found the nearest Starbucks. In his opinion, conditioned air, caffeine, Wi-Fi and that rich coffee odor were required in order to consider their next move before heading to Nevada. They parked in front of a Del Taco, crossed the sweltering pavement and entered. It was cookie-cutter Starbucks but cooler than the car by far, well lit, and somehow reassuring. A large placard just inside advertised a drink called Flat White with the words, "Simplicity is its own artistry." An attractive African-American couple sat at a long brown wooden table. Colorful canisters of teas lined the area in front of a display case bursting with pastries. Bottles of flavorings for drinks lined the back wall and above the coffee grinders and makers were black signs with white letters listing choices and prices.

While Susan lined up an iced latte for him and an iced tea for her, Jake sat at a small table beneath a photo of two cupped hands filled with coffee beans and opened his iPad. He began to build a profile of Buck Waller by first seeking what was easily accessed free online by the mildly inquisitive. He also planned to visit a few of his subscription services available for a fee to the obnoxiously inquisitive.

Susan carried their drinks around waist-high sandwich boards advertising specials and placed Jake's on the table. She leaned over to read by his shoulder. "Googling is a beautiful thing," Jake said. His eyes slid to her lacy cleavage. "You're distracting me."

"Ogling is not a beautiful thing. Sorry, forgot to put these away." She buttoned up.

With his right hand he scratched notes on a legal pad he had placed beside the iPad while his left scrolled the device. Susan made out several phrases on the notepad:

Former bounty hunter, 2 misdemeanor counts carrying a loaded firearm into a national park back when it was illegal, 2 charges domestic violence, 1 charge threatening BLM rangers. Name of his militia is Eagle Guard.

"Wow. Nice guy, ole' Buck," Susan said, sitting across from Jake and taking a sip of her tea.

"Regular sweetheart. Here's a post on the Anti-Defamation League site reporting Buck claims to have personally prevented 2,000-plus illegal immigrants from entering the country. It says he lives on 400 acres of land near Wickenburg, sold to him cheap by a supporter. He has four employees but untold numbers of volunteers. Among many other grievances against the Feds is his belief that Mexico is planning to invade and take back the southwestern United States, and he's pissed the government is doing nothing about it. He also believes that the Feds are behind both the pine-bark beetle infestation *and the forest fires being set around the west.*" Jake looked at Susan. "We need to meet this guy. I'm surprised he doesn't blame the government for drought and climate change. Then again, he probably denies the climate is changing. What a piece of work."

Susan held up the party poster from the archery store. "Really looking forward to spending the holiday with Buck."

The black couple got up, bussed their cups to a bin by the wall, and headed out. A middle-aged white woman carrying a large purse and a thick book held the door for them as they left.

"Waller publishes a right-wing newspaper called the American Bugle. He's used it and social media to organize several citizen militias to perform Operation Border Secure, a coordinated three-day vigilante sweep of the border starting on this July 5th."

Jake shook his head, still reading. "This screwball is a pair shy of a full house."

"Maybe so, but that still leaves him three of a kind. Christ, I hate to think what fate awaits the illegal immigrants caught by Buck's army," Susan said. "Hey, did you notice the new drink Starbucks is advertising? The Flat White—might be the worst corporate brand name where women are concerned since the iPad."

The new arrival now perched behind her book in a nearby leather chair and, obviously eavesdropping, glanced up at Susan and chuckled. Jake hadn't even touched his drink and was too absorbed in his research to offer Susan a rejoinder.

Susan arranged to spend time with her friend Rebecca, left behind when Susan and her ex-husband Keith moved from Phoenix to Jackson, Wyoming nine years ago. Becky worked as an ER nurse at Banner Good Samaritan Medical Center. She was on the late shift but Susan caught her on cell and they made a plan to meet during her break in the medical center cafeteria. Jake dropped Susan at the hospital and found a store nearby advertising Independence Day paraphernalia. He purchased two matching his and her long-sleeved western type shirts with American flag motifs and, worrying a bit about going to Buck's Bash in a Subaru, purchased a Don't Tread On Me bumper sticker for good measure. Later, after catching a fast food burger, Jake picked up Susan and they checked into a Motel 8. After settling in, they heard a few muffled pops in the street, no doubt from folks getting the jump on Independence Day. It was a quiet night for the detectives with a Diamondbacks ballgame playing softly on the flat screen and the air conditioner humming under dancing drapes.

July 4
Friday

After nasty motel coffee and a "free" breakfast that even Louis Burton Lindley, Jr. would have found wanting, Jake and Susan spent the morning in their room catching up on research and email. Around noon they slipped on their matching patriotic shirts and checked out. They loaded their bags in the car, slid their pistols under their respective seats and drove a few blocks to El Abuelito, a Mexican restaurant Jake had noticed the day before. The restaurant was cranking the air, which pleased Susan, and had a colorful décor including walls adorned with garishly painted larger-than-life-sized masks. In short, it filled the bill to kill a few hours swilling iced tea and eating Mexican food—compensating for the slim pickings food-wise that had been on offer at the motel.

The party was advertised to begin at 6 p.m. so at 4:30 they headed west out of Phoenix. Jake insisted on driving as an essential part of the role they were playing, which they had defined as: Fox-News-watching, talk-radio-listening, flag-saluting, constitution-quoting, women-in-the-passenger-seat-and-other-rightful-places, right-wingers. They practiced en route, laughing all the way at the foreign sound of the requisite illiberal rant of the far right.

The flyer indicated that Buck's place was south of Wickenburg in the foothills of the Vulture Mountains off Vulture Peak Road. As Jake and Susan approached Wickenburg on Route 60 the sun was sitting directly above the Vultures, a steeply inclined sparsely covered discrete hogback. Vulture Peak Road turned out to be a well-maintained, well-used, sand and dirt track. They drove past a demolished house foundation surrounded by a short rock wall with a large human-like saguaro behind it, and later an abandoned mine site cluttered with metal tanks and tubs. The road dropped down a sandy slope. In the bottom was a green street sign for Cemetery Wash, a dry arroyo with a few vehicle tracks in it. The road climbed up the other side.

When they finally arrived at Buck's property, the sky above bald and rugged Vulture Peak was already showing a tinge of pink. They stopped at the guard station and Jake lowered his window. An older black SUV was parked behind the small building. An American flag snapped on a pole. Past the entrance, the road wound around a butte. No other buildings were visible from the gate. A hound howled plaintively in the distance. A coyote appeared to be answering. Saguaro, fishhook and prickly pear cacti marched up toward the spare and sere Vulture Mountains. Sparse clusters of catclaw, false indigo, desert thorn and creosote bush clung to the sand channels and slopes. The scene had an oneiric quality with nightmarish overtones. Susan passed Jake the flyer and he held it out the window. An olive green Hummer with tinted windows pulled up behind, dwarfing their car. The burly guard came out and asked Jake to wait a moment. A red light blinked in a box on the post beside the cattle guard and they were waved through the fence.

"It just occurred to me that the word supremacist, as in white supremacist, shares a suffix with the word racist," Jake said as they drove into the compound.

"Really, that just occurred to you? Was that a camera on that post filming your lily-white ass, Mr. Starr?"

"I suspect so, Mrs. Starr. Can't be too careful when you're living under a government that intentionally decimates whole forests with bugs and/or fire and every cactus has two or three invading spics lurking behind it."

"Jesus, Jake!"

"I'm just practicing."

Jake parked in a designated area cordoned off from the main

compound with buck and rail. The fence was covered with posters advertising Operation Border Secure. Susan got out and studied a poster. It invited patriots concerned about the sanctity of the border to meet at 9 a.m., July 5th at the Walmart in Wickenburg.

The lot was not full but was filling fast. The green Hummer pulled into an open slot down the row. As Jake had anticipated, the vehicles of choice at Buck's Bash were gas-guzzlers—from Hummers to large pickups—lots of pickups—to the bigger SUVs. Two large saguaro cactus marked the opening in the fence, which was the access to the central party area. Buck's compound was like an oasis. A green raft on a brown sea. Irrigation had allowed him the luxury of grass the size of a football field in an environment in which it would not have lasted three days without extensive watering.

At the far end of the green field was a bandstand flanked by beer and bar tents. Several people clustered in front of the bars drinking and talking. Jake and Susan had nailed the fashion choice for the day. It was definitely tending toward the red, the white and the blue. Musicians had parked a van behind the open-air bandstand and were unloading instruments. Picnic tables flanked the field on packed sand. Behind them on both sides sat two large propane grills emanating a mouth-watering barbecue bouquet. Behind the grill to the left stood a line of port-a-potties. Red, white and blue bunting, balloons and American flags adorned every surface. The party was just ramping up.

Jake and Susan huddled just inside the grassy area trying to be subtle about their surveillance. Jake spoke quietly, eyes scanning. "I'm guessing that large log building with the big porch straight ahead beyond the bandstand is Waller's house and possibly his office. Those long low buildings set back to our right, the stables. The archery competition is probably held behind them. That way the straw bales used for the targets don't have to be hauled far."

"That all sounds right. Everything else looks like typical ranch outbuildings. We didn't discuss how we're going to make sure we speak with Waller. Or should we meet Pork and let him lead us to Waller's wallow?" She elbowed Jake and winked.

"I thought bad puns were my department." Jake eyed the party scene.

"I'm thinking I might get a country song out of this experience along the lines of the perennial favorite, *Proud to Be U.S.*"

Susan looked around and whispered, "Which of course, we both are, but not to this extreme. I have a feeling if Waller uses these deals to recruit, he'll come to us. He has gone to a lot of trouble and expense. Let's go have a drink on Buck."

The Scrub Oak Boys Band, or so said the lettering on the base drum, was comprised of a lead guitarist, a base guitarist, a keyboardist and a drummer. The drummer got the band on rhythm and off they went into an upbeat gospel tune promising something along the lines of Jesus soon arriving and lots of folks not surviving. A few revelers took to the dance floor but many more turned their faces skyward and clapped or chanted along. The band members were all dressed in what would be described as western, but with less patriotic fervor than the guests. The keyboardist was also the lead vocalist and Jake noticed he had a very pleasant voice. The sun had moved closer to the Vultures with flame beginning in the clouds promising a spectacular sunset. More people poured in and soon a sea of white faces filled the central grassy field. Jake and Susan remained by the back fence nursing their drinks. As alcohol was gulped down the volume of the party ratcheted up. The only dark faces present were Hispanic and they bobbed above white serving jackets and/or stood behind white tablecloths laden with heaps of summer picnic food. Several ravens worked the edges of the crowd, occasionally scoring a treat off a discarded plate in the burgeoning trash bins.

Betty, an initially jovial, button-busting, redheaded woman, got chatting with Jake and Susan while sipping at her drink and snapping at a slathered hotdog in a bun. After she took the last bite of the dog and wiped the mustard from her mouth with a napkin adorned with the American flag, Betty's dogma started to bite hard right. "Demo-commies are trying to destroy this country and rebuild it as a socialist state." Betty's paunchy husband Rob joined them and soon demonstrated how he had both the Constitution and Declaration of Independence on his phone. Rob was in oil wells and at the moment was well into getting oiled. His meaty hands caressed a Jack Daniels and water in a sweating red plastic cup the size of a Slurpee.

"I saw a piece recently on how scrap metal from the twin towers was being reconstituted into a warship. Fox News covered the story. Commie Net News did not. Hell," he said, spiting a little saliva and breathing bourbon breath. "It was recycling; you'd think tree huggers and aluminum luggers would love it. All CNN ever does is the government's bidding and for all we know, Washington and CNN orchestrated 911."

"Don't get me started on Obama-scare and the death panels," Betty said.

Deciding that Betty was absolutely correct in suggesting it would be a huge mistake to get her, or Rob, started on any new subject, Jake said, with a glance at Susan, that they had been thinking about dancing. They broke off and drifted toward the band.

"I have to ask, was that a red, white and blue bra I glimpsed through Betty's gapping buttons?"

"Apparently it was, yes," Susan said. "And I'm sure Rob loves saluting those babies."

"While standing at attention," they said, simultaneously, and cracked up.

Between songs, the Boys introduced themselves to the attendees. The lead singer, Rowdy, mentioned that they had started the band in a Chevy Tahoe on a dream and a prayer. Rowdy offered praise to the Lord for their success (Thanks, as usual, God), and thanked Buck for his support.

Rowdy announced the archery competition would start at the wall of bales beyond the stables in five minutes and then he and the Boys got back at it. They sang about a woman who lives like the Madonna but listens to Merle. Two round and red-faced women in their high fifties stood in front of the band, swayed to the music and waved their hands as if they were at a revival. Several men retrieved their compound bows and target arrows from their cars and headed toward the stables. At last the Boys settled into a standard set of bluegrass. A small portable dance floor had been assembled over the lawn in front of the bandstand and several older couples and one woman with a small child in a long dress were doing a gingerly western swing. Jake took Susan's hand and was pulling her up on the wooden surface when she said, "If you truly want me to try and move around that floor to music, you better find me another wine."

"Be back in a sec with more grape for guts," Jake said.

He moved to the right toward the bar and hit a crush of people yelling at each other over the music. A small lone aerial bomb burst above in a descending red splash and was met with a cheer. After a few minutes of maneuvering, Jake secured two fresh plastic glasses and squeezed back through the throng balancing the drinks. The band was really rocking and the dance floor was filling. Jake searched the crowd around the dance floor, but Susan was gone. He stood on tiptoe and searched the faces nearby. No Susan. Lights were coming on around the compound. He pushed back toward the parking lot thinking she might have gone there for some reason. As he neared the exit through the fence it was immediately obvious she was nowhere near the car. Fear rose in his chest. He went out, put the drinks down on a car hood and scrambled up on the fence. The sun was setting on the Vultures. A large, lone cruciform saguaro, the only object sitting perpendicular to the near perfect ridgeline, was backlit in a blaze. The ridge below was black, the sky above blood red. A few people pointed at the spectacle and the crowd hushed a little. Another lone aerial bomb arched toward the mountains, its trajectory culminating in a white flash and loud boom. Jake started. The crowd roared. He checked the lines for the johns. No Susan. Scanned the areas by the grills. Not there.

"What the hell?" A hand grabbed the back of his belt and tugged him down off the fence turning him. He was face-to-face with a tall sinewy man in a black cowboy hat, flannel shirt and tight jeans held up by a wide leather belt with a large silver belt buckle.

"Hey, I'm Pork." He thrust out his cracked palm and dirty fingernails.

"Uh, D. J. Starr. Nice to meet you, Pork." Jake gripped and immediately thought of hand sanitizer.

"I'll bet yer lookin' for the missus."

Pork pointed to the porch wrapping around the main house. It was in shadow. "Mr. Waller's up there. Pretty wife's talkin' to him. Butch's bustin' to meet you, too."

Jake, Susan and Buck sat on the porch of the main house in rocking chairs in a semi-circle. Pork clomped inside, banging the screen door.

Waller chatted about last night's baseball game and the recent dry weather. He wore a worn suede jacket with a western cut and light brown paramilitary pants with multiple pockets; the one on the right thigh bulging with what appeared to be a handgun. Waller had the look of former military trying to hang on to that memory of fitness and toughness. He spoke with civility and a slight southern accent, but it was obvious that reactionary with a hint of cracker lurked just below the surface.

Buck Waller ran his hand over his blonde flattop hair. "You folks don't appear to be affiliated with any of the local militias. If you have a few days to hang around I can see you meet patriots from several groups during Operation Border Secure. Be doing your patriotic duty where our government has failed miserably."

"We read the poster and it's a great thing you've pulled together. Unfortunately I have to be in Vegas during that time for some training," Jake said.

"Shame. You'd like these folks. They're passionate about a mess of citizens' issues here. Have you read any of the regional press on the subject of ranchers' rights on BLM land? By the way, speaking of rights, it is no accident, if you ask me, that rights, right wing and righteous have so much in common." He nodded his blockish head, knowingly.

"I've followed it a bit in the mainstream press," Jake said.

"I mostly read People magazine," Susan said. "Was it in there?"

"I'm afraid not, Mrs. Starr. And Mr. Starr, the mainstream press is anti-rancher. A more accurate source is Stockman's for print, or White Speaks Network for radio and blogs. Or, my paper, the American Bugle."

"You've met Melinda, I'm D.J.," Jake said. "Please call me D.J."

"D.J., the conservative media is calling the BLM rangers communists and eco-jihadists for using potentially murderous force to deprive ranchers of their rights on federal land. The Second Amendment is our ace and the Feds know it. The founding fathers gave the individual the right to bear arms against the tyranny of government. What's that mean? The bearer can kill someone in government if the reason is justified."

"Do you think burning federal forests is justified to protest the government presence in the West?" Jake asked.

"Do what?" Buck said.

"There've been several recent forest fires intentionally set around the region. I was thinking, hoping really, it might be an anti-government protest."

"Forest fires. Setting forest fires. Hmmm, don't think so. Not our style. We want free access to public land, yes. We need national forest and BLM land for economic and recreational purposes. Hell, we want to feel like we *own* that land, truth be told, and use it for whatever purposes we choose as citizens of a free country, but we don't want to destroy it. Makes no sense. My theory is the Feds are burning their own forests to prevent God-fearing, tax-paying citizens from using them."

A shout went up from the area of the archery competition.

"Someone must a hit the bullshit-eye on the picture of Barack Hussein. It's been our favorite target since 2008."

"Is it possible a small anti-government cell might be setting the fires?" Susan asked.

A sour disdainful look spread across Waller's face. "Now hold on, Melinda. It is Melinda, right?"

Susan nodded.

"Eagle Guard practices military discipline, as do most other militias in the Southwest. Don't you think I would know it if we had some soldiers gone rogue?" A text dinged. Waller dug his phone out of the left thigh of his cargo pants and checked it. His eyes rose slowly as he tucked away his device. "Pork has just informed me that he has the pictures from our last hunt up on the flat screen in my office. I would be honored if you would let me show them to you."

"This is such a great party," Jake said.

"Yes, great band. We were just going to dance," Susan said.

Buck shot a hard look. "I insist. Wait 'til you see the monster I bagged."

"Just curious. Was this a recent hunt?" Jake asked.

"Last week, why?"

"Season?" Jake asked.

"Oh, hell, that's state and federal horseshit. They've no jurisdiction on my property."

Buck held the door. As they rose, Rowdy was calling for a break. He promised to announce the winners of the archery shootout when they returned to the stage. His announcement was met with shouts, hoots and whistles. Susan and Jake entered the cool shadowy cabin, well, testosterone cave really—wood, leather, antlers, firearms, bows, arrows and taxidermy. There was a faint odor of cigar smoke. Buck pointed to a closed door under a bison head to the right of the stone fireplace. Interesting design choice, Susan thought, as she led the way toward the office door—animals and the weapons that destroy them.

Jake and Susan sat side-by-side on a small, light-brown leather couch. They faced Buck who had perched on a high-backed chair behind a massive desk. He had his feet up on the desk and was turned toward the flat screen above his head on the wall. Pork stood back by the door behind the couch.

Buck clicked a remote and a picture of a huge doe mule deer popped up. The dead animal's tongue lolled and its head hung limp off the gate of a black pickup. He clicked again and showed a picture of himself holding up the deer's head with both hands and grinning at the camera. He quickly clicked through a few more pictures of his kill.

"She's a beauty, isn't she, Susan?" Buck said without turning.

"Yes…" Susan realized they had been caught. There was another click but this came from the cocking of the hammer on a Colt .45 revolver, which Pork had pressed against the back of Susan's skull. Susan went rigid.

"And here's another beauty." A picture of Susan in her police uniform flashed onto the screen. "Susan Brand, Jackson Hole Police Department. This guy, not so beautiful."

A headshot of Jake from his consultancy's website clicked onto the screen. "Jake Goddard, private investigator. Good news is, Jake, you're not a Fed. Bad news is you're a PI who is probably working as a government contractor."

"Buck, I can explain—"

Pork shifted the pistol to Jake's head.

"No, no, no, there is nothing to explain. If you already lied about who you are, and why you're here, why would I believe anything you said from this point forward. I photograph everyone who enters my compound. Asking for ID would be rude and it's so easy to fake. The face recognition search application and Google do the rest. Love technology. Reminds me of that old Spy vs. Spy cartoon in Mad Magazine. The Feds spy on us, we spy on the Feds. And you are Feds, or at least you're working for them. There's no other reason you'd be here."

Buck pulled a Sig Sauer P210 Legend with a custom wood grip out of his cargo pants pocket and aimed it between Jake and Susan. "Sportsman's Warehouse had a special on these recently. Nice little pistol." He addressed his sidekick. "Pork, I've got these two. The archery competition should be over, go set us up a private party on the backside of the bales. We'll need a six-pack of beer, propane lantern and two shovels." He turned back to his captives. "You're a detective, right Jake?"

"Yes. Susan is retired from the police force, she works for me."

"Oh, she *works* for you when she's not suckin' your dick, Dick Tracy?"

Susan tensed. Buck shifted the pistol to her.

"I'll bet that's workin' great. So, if you're both detectives then you must've visited my website."

Shit, Jake thought, I can't believe I didn't do that.

"And if you visited my website you saw it states in very plain terms that anyone entering my property without an invitation, and especially if they're federal employees, will be terminated with extreme prejudice." He typed a few keys on his computer, displayed his blog post on the flat screen and read aloud. "Any Fed comes on my land uninvited will be shot. The U.S. Government has no jurisdiction on my land! The founding fathers gave the individual a gun to fight the tyranny of government. The bearer can kill someone in government if the reason is justified. You tread on my rights as a citizen, I'll kill you as mandated by the Second Amendment."

Susan stood as if to leave. "Well then, we're done here, because we had an invitation and we don't work for the federal government."

"Oh, that's funny, bitch. Sit down." Buck waved the handgun.

"But it's true. We're working for the Chief of the White Mountain Apache Tribe," Jake said.

"Trying to determine who's setting forest fires around the west and leaving dead bodies in them," Susan said. "Doing our job eliminating the militias as suspects."

"Like I said, too late for your new version of the truth, time for consequences." He gestured with the pistol toward the back door to his office.

Jake and Susan, with Buck trailing, crossed a sand parking lot at the rear of the log house and headed toward the area behind the stables. The music was ripping again and boots stomping the wooden dance floor echoed above the din of excited chatter. The air had cooled and the stars were blinking on. They passed a broken down saguaro in the throes of death and an old front loader with a rusted bucket. There was a loud boom; Jake and Susan both ducked. Stars burst above bathing them in blue light. Buck chuckled as the two uncoiled.

"That was embarrassing," Susan said. She felt the pistol pressed into her back.

"Scared you didn't it? Looks like the fireworks are about to begin. That's good because none of the folks at the party are going to notice loud noises."

Jake wheeled toward Buck and was suddenly facing the Sig.

"Don't try to be a hero, Jake. You'll go first and fast and your little pig bitch will go last and slow like a suckling on a spit with Pork manning the barbecue." He cupped Susan's ass with his left hand.

Susan said through gritted teeth, "Do that again I'll see you lose every finger on that hand."

"Not likely, sweetheart, not likely." Buck squeezed again hard, slid his fingers up to her bra strap, snapped it, and then shoved her. "Over there behind that wall of bales festooned with Old Glory." He was indicating a large pile of straw bales covered with targets below, flags above. He sang, "*Let's start this party pronto, uh huh.* Isn't that what a little wanna-be-jigaboo blond girl like you sings? I figure that singer picked the name, Stink, cuz white, nig, spic, or chink, all y'all's pussy's stink like week old gut piles. What say, Jake, does the little lady make your fingers stink?"

"Hey Buck, you're really talking ignorant trash while you're holding the pistol. How about you put it down and we settle this man-to-man," Jake said.

"Or hell, man-to-woman. I think even I could kick your fat ass," Susan said.

"Move!" Buck shouted, just as more aerial bombs thumped out of their tubes. The simultaneous explosions created an arc of multicolored rain above and below a curving white curtain descended to the ground as fine as lace.

Behind the straw wall and totally out of sight of the party beside a bench fashioned out of two bales, Pork had lit a propane lantern connected by a black rubber hose to a large portable propane tank. Pork and Buck settled onto the two bales near the lantern. Buck tossed two shovels at the straw bale wall indicating to Jake and Susan that they should begin digging just behind it. Two pistols were trained on the captives. The fireworks gathered momentum. Booms overlapped booms as bursts blossomed in the night sky illuminating the Vultures.

"Don't worry, this won't take long and it doesn't have to be very deep. We'll just slide the bale wall back a few feet over your graves tomorrow," Buck said.

He yanked two beers out of the six-pack on the sand and handed one to Pork. Then Buck pulled two cigars out of the inner chest pocket of his jacket. Pork leaned back and scrambled in his jeans for his lighter. He lit his boss's cigar then licked and sucked on his while eyeing Susan lasciviously.

Buck said. "Let's go, two graves. What are you waiting for?"

Jake and Susan started digging. Bombs continued bursting above.

Pork lit and took great pleasure in his cigar—puffing, blowing rings, pulling it out of his brown teeth and examining it sideways in admiration. "Love these Cubans. That's one good thing the head monkey-in-charge in Washington is doing, opening up Cuba for better cigars." He examined his pistol.

"Love this Colt too. I carry it to remember, huh Buck?"

"That's right, buddy, white man never wants to forget what Samuel Colt did for us."

Pork said, "No one wanted the Colt revolver at first, Colt was bankrupt after a few years. Then a dozen or so years later the army ordered a thousand. Colt was bust but he got partners and he filled the bill. The rest is history; history changed in the white man's favor by this little beauty." He patted the revolver. "The Single Action Army, the gun that won the west for the white man over the red man. Changed history like Buck and me's gonna change history and preserve the white man's God-given superiority."

Jake stopped digging and removed his ball cap to push back his sweaty hair and mop at his forehead with his forearm. "Thanks for the history lesson, Pork. Case you forgot, that pistol was also called the Peacemaker."

"It was good enough for Pat Garrett and George Patton, it's good enough for me. Packs a punch. Bet you lunch, Buck I line 'em two up over their graves head-to-head, I can drop 'em both with one bullet."

Buck took a suck at his beer and wiped his mouth with his sleeve. "Yer on. But the lunch has to be in Vegas, all expenses paid by the loser." Pork dug a sparkler out of his breast pocket and twirled it unlit between his fingers.

For a time the only sound behind the bales was Jake and Susan stabbing and shifting sand. The party carried on as guests applauded the fireworks. Soon Susan's shirt was soaked with sweat revealing her cleavage and bra. Pork gulped his beer and entertained himself by lighting his sparkler with his cigar. While eying Susan, he made figure eights with the spark in the air.

"Buck, you the boss, but I think we wastin' a fine piece of ass here." He cupped his left hand and pushed down hard on the bulge in the front of his jeans. "Maybe Miss Piggy should go down on us before she goes down for good." He pointed at his crotch with the Colt and then back at Susan.

"Pork, you're one hound dog it's hard to keep on the porch."

Pork howled like a hound. "Hard is right. Ask my mama. Told me I entered this world with a hard-on as big as a grown man's thumb." He jumped up and, swinging his sparkler in a full circle, started a sort of staggering, foot stomping twirling dance. "EEEEEEE. That's how a pig sounds when stuck." He grabbed at his crotch, held his fist with thumb extended in front of it and added hip thrusts and ass slaps to his gyrations.

"If we didn't have pressing social obligations, we would try on this pig for size, for sure. But we've got to get this done and get back. Plus I don't relish sitting here and watching your skinny white ass bounce up and down even if it does mean seeing Miss Piggy get porked." Buck laughed, chugged his beer and tossed the can, sucked on his cigar and sneered at Jake and Susan. "Hell at the rate yer going, I'm glad as hell we aren't trying to get down six feet. I'm missing my fireworks because of you two. You're taking all night. Dig Goddamnit!"

Still holding the sparkler, Pork lurched up to Jake and pointed his Colt at his chest. "Y'all know what 86 means?"

"86, Pork?" Jake stopped digging and angled the shovel handle in his right hand like a choked down baseball bat. He looked at Susan. She stopped. It was time. "Yeah, we know what 86 means don't we, Susan."

He took a deep breath and twisted his body and shovel back to the hole.

"Let's see, I believe it means eight out of ten times, sixty percent of people threatened at gunpoint while digging their grave attack with their shovel."

Jake swung the shovel with both hands, whanging the blade into the side of Pork's face and slamming him backwards onto the bale bench. The force knocked the revolver away; the sparkler sputtered loose on the straw bale. Buck swung his pistol toward Jake just as Susan shoveled sand into his eyes and stabbed the blade of her shovel into his windpipe, causing him to snap back then buckle forward. Jake chopped with his shovel and sliced the rubber hose, causing propane to spew toward the two men. Susan wielded her shovel like a sledge and clobbered Buck flat on the top of his head, forcing him to drop his pistol. She swung again for the fences, connecting with his ear. The sparkler caused a fireball to erupt in Buck and Pork's faces and ignited the bale bench. Buck dropped down on his knees. Flames danced around him. He blindly searched the ground with his hands for his Sig Sauer. Pork was cooking and screaming in pain. Buck found the butt of his gun. Susan whacked the shovel blade's edge down on his fingers with the sound of a butcher's cleaver cracking bone. Buck hugged his hand into his body and howled like a gut-shot beast. Leaning back from the flames, Jake reached a foot in and kicked Buck's pistol toward Susan. Then he snatched up the four beers left in the holder. Susan grabbed Buck's pistol and removed the clip. She tossed the clip and the gun onto the roof of the stables. Jake scooped up Pork's revolver and did the same.

They ran toward the central field and the party, but as they rounded the front of the main house slowed to a brisk walk. The noise from the fireworks was deafening. All eyes were on the sky. No one seemed to notice the smoke rising from behind the bale wall. The fireworks reached a crescendo with staccato strobe concussions that felt to Susan like punches to her chest that competed with the pounding of her heart.

Jake ripped off a beer and handed it to her. He pulled one off for himself. They worked through the crowd sipping, smiling and nodding. The last boom echoed off the buttes to wild applause. As the cheering faded, the band cranked up again.

"Wait!" A large man stopped Jake cold with two huge hands to his chest, almost spilling his beer. Susan waited beside her partner, smiling anxiously.

"Don't I know you?" he shouted over the music.

"Happens all the time. Don't think so," Jake said, trying to pass.

One hand remained while the other wagged an index finger in Jake's face. "I do, I know who you are." The inebriated hulk leered down into Jake's face.

"I don't—" Jake started.

"Yur the coach of the Norland Saints."

Jake shook his head. "Buddy, I'm lucky I can find time to coach my kid's soccer."

Jake tried to brush by but got blocked again, "Sean, Sean, oh shit, yur Sean whasisname." He leaned in to study Jake's face and looked very serious. "Hey, I totally got it when you offered bonus bucks for fuckin' up other players." He tried to chest bump but Jake ducked under and past.

"Football's the game that bleeds red, white and blue." The big man sang thrusting a thumb skyward and dancing a little jig. "I've been waitin' all week for Sunday night."

Susan tried to squeeze past.

He grabbed her in a bear hug. "I'd like to get to know you."

Susan shot a hard smile up at him. "Oh, sweetie, if only I had the time." She latched onto his leather belt with both hands in case she needed the extra leverage. "You got a big pair, big boy?"

"Huge." He said, grinning.

"Great. Then there's no way I can miss with my knee."

His grin dissolved as quickly as his grip.

Susan waved at the jolly drunk giant and pushed further into the crowd.

They slid by one observant faux cowboy reveler who was pointing to the burning pile of straw topped by American flags, which were now beginning to smolder. "Would you look at that? Damn Buck will stop at nothin' to make a display of protest and patriotism."

"God bless, Buck. God Bless, America!" said the faux cowgirl, holding herself up on the faux cowboy's arm.

Jake and Susan had just reached their car when the propane tank by the bales exploded. It sounded like a grenade going off in a culvert and trumped all booms that night. Flames rose fifty feet into the air. When the burning straw bale wall toppled and threatened to ignite the end of the nearby stables, folks began to look a little alarmed and a few shouted that this might not be part of the show. A few others even had the presence of mind to fish for their cell phones.

Jake and Susan jumped in the car, backed out and headed for the entrance road, Jake keeping his speed low. They groped around under their seats and pulled their pistols into their laps. The security guard's SUV from the entrance station raced by as they slipped away into the dark of the Arizona night. When they turned back onto the pavement of Route 60, emergency vehicles in full-on response mode passed them heading toward Buck Waller's ranch.

For the first few miles they could still see the flames from the fire and the pulsing emergency lights out by the mountains now bathed in moonlight. They turned left on Route 93 in Wickenburg heading for Vegas. Eyes darting to the rearview mirrors, they quickly put thirty-plus miles between them and the Vulture Peak Road. When Jake felt they had traveled a safe distance, he pulled off the highway. They got out and met in front of the car; hugged, laughed nervously, high-fived and hugged again. Jake sucked air in through pursed lips and slumped back against the car's hood. Susan put her hands on her hips to stop her fingers from shaking, blinked her eyes and shook her head several times.

She uttered the first word spoken to Jake since they left Buck. "Mother—*fuck*."

Jake and Susan were tired when they pulled into Kingman for gas but still too wired to stop for the night.

Susan drove across the desert of northwestern Arizona. Jake stared out the window. "I feel like shit for taking you into that situation."

"Last I heard your crystal ball was on the blink, so how could you possibly know what we were getting into."

Jake turned to look at her. "Nice to say but, for starters, I should have checked his website. I visited just about every other website that had information about Buck Waller but failed to turn up his website. It might have tipped me off to his homicidal hatred of anything remotely related to government intrusion, and the grave danger I was placing you in."

"While you're Monday morning quarterbacking you can shoot a little blame this way. The guy at the archery store tried to warn me about Buck and I blew it off." She flashed a weary smile at him across the dimly lit car. "So, *I* shouldn't place *you* in that sort of danger." Susan reached over and squeezed Jake's bicep and attempted to change the subject. "What we got?"

"I'd say enough information from Buck before Pork busted us with that text message to assume the militias are not setting the fires. They are gleefully breaking just about every other law, but do not appear to be our arsonists. Do you agree we look elsewhere?"

"I do. And Buck, bless his heart, gave me an idea of where to look. He mentioned the Feds starting these fires, which of course, is more of his particular brand of crazy. However, I remember hearing on the news a few years back that a firefighter was caught setting fires seemingly to keep the adrenaline and money flowing. Maybe while you're in Vegas in your Speedo becoming a poster-boy for Gushers I'll pursue that angle."

"Wouldn't explain the bodies," Jake said.

"No it wouldn't unless the bodies are a decoy to deflect blame. I've got a woman friend in Salt Lake who is a smoke jumper. I'll start by asking Jen what she thinks are the chances that one of her colleagues is setting fires to remain gainfully employed."

"Sounds like a plan," Jake said, trying to sound enthusiastic. He sucked in a long slow breath and then released it. "Are you okay?"

"Yes, rattled for sure, but okay." She lifted her right hand from the wheel to inspect it. "My hands have finally stopped shaking. How're you doing?"

"Seeing those two men burn, evil as they were, reached a whole new low in my short career as an investigator. Hell, I got into this as a researcher of historical documents. A job any librarian could have done. But yeah, I'm ok. The pool thing should be a good distraction—assuming things go according to plan."

"The old *according to plan* thing. That's the challenge, isn't it? Avoiding train wrecks like tonight."

"Yup. That should become our mantra, train on tracks." He rubbed his eyes with his fingers, pinched the bridge of his nose and yawned. "Oh. Sorry." He shook his head to clear it. "You should still probably head back tomorrow if you're up for it. You can drop me at a car rental in the morning."

"I'll be up for it. I'll miss you but I learned long ago in this insane business called policing that after a traumatic experience there is nothing like a night snuggled up with Amy to calm my rattled nerves and get me grounded again."

"Think she'll still agree to that when she's fourteen?"

"Seriously doubt it, so I'm maximizing it now. Like Flesh says, putting hugs in the bank."

Susan yawned. Jake yawned again. To the northwest an arc of artificial light illuminated the cloudless sky above Vegas. They drove on—lit by a partial moon tracking above—in exhausted silence.

July 7
Monday

Jake stood in the shade of a narrow overhang in an industrial park built on hardpan on the edge of Craig, Nevada. The sun baked on the exterior metal of Gushers' warehouse and glinted off the windshields of the company vans parked in a long white line in the lot. He was on a break from the first day of pool service training and finally able to check email on his iPhone. He had one from Susan mentioning that after a prolonged and therapeutic snuggle she had enrolled Amy last minute in a two-week field science camp in Grand Teton National Park. Annabell, one of Amy's friends from Jackson, had called and asked if Amy could join her in the program. Susan had immediately agreed. She wrote of her plan to drive to Wyoming and drop Amy at the school in Jackson and then shoot back to Salt Lake to meet with her friend Jen to inquire into the history of firefighters committing arson.

Jake hurriedly tapped a reply: *sounds good/local news this am—two dead in ranch fire near wick, az./said accident due to alcohol, fireworks and faulty propane tank. Invite Flesh to go for coffee in Salt Lake. Thank him again for me. Love you. Amy too.*

"Yo, Jake." A head popped out of the entrance door. Jake hit send and looked up.

"Yeah, Vern."

"Back at it, buddy. Stan ain't paying you to dick around with your phone."

Jake followed Vern into the florescent hum of the metal and concrete cave. The door slammed shut. Cold air washed over them. They picked their way around and over colorful hoses and pool vacuums of various sizes.

Vern was on the short side but wiry and wound tight. He said over his shoulder, "How you know the boss, anyhow?"

"What makes you think I know him?"

Vern turned and tapped his white ball cap brim stained with gray finger-length streaks. Long strands of ginger hair sprouted out beneath. "I'm no dummy. I figured by the way he said I should keep my eye on you." He flapped a bent arm. "Take you under the ole' Vernon wing. Give you this one-on-one treatment."

"Oh, I appreciate the concern, Vern, but I'm not looking for any special favors, just cuz I'm Stan's second cousin."

"Second cousin?"

"Yup. Once removed."

"What the hell?" Vern pulled a rag out of his rear pants pocket and wiped his hands. He wore the standard Gushers uniform, white shorts, polo and brimmed ball cap. The latter two embroidered with the blue Gushers logo.

"Same great-grandparents, Stan and me. You ever heard of six degrees of separation?"

"Sounds sorta familiar," Vern said, now looking very confused.

"That's me and the boss, six steps removed."

"Six steps?" He grinned, showing yellow teeth. "Guess I don't have to treat you so special."

"What's on the agenda for the rest of the day?" Jake asked.

"We finish up the overview of the equipment. Break for lunch. Spend the afternoon on water chemistry. How you at chemistry?"

"I did okay in high school when I wasn't trying to blow the lab up. You?"

"Sucked worse than this vacuum." Vern kicked at a red hose. "Funny what you end up doing."

"I hear you. I was glad my school didn't offer sex ed cuz if they turned me off to sex way they did to poetry I wouldn't a had near as much fun in high school."

Vern rocked back on his heels. "Ha. That's good." He walked over to a bank of metal shelves and selected a flat plastic apparatus on wheels. "Tomorrow morning we do three pools together then you're on your own, buddy."

"Stan say anything about the houses I'll be servicing?"

"Oh, he sure did." Vern's look twisted toward diabolical. "Once-removed cousins gets the pick of the litter."

He moved to the end of a hose and bent down to attach the vacuum.

July 8
Tuesday

Vern had demonstrated and remonstrated. The woman who owned the large stucco house they were now servicing, the third and last on Jake's day of shadowing Vern and which was to become Jake's alone, was extremely fussy about the condition of her pool.

"One leaf on the bottom, buddy, and you'll be hearing from the boss cuz *Ma—dame* knows him personally and she will call him day or night." Vern snagged a small green leaf in the pole basket he was skimming across the surface.

Jake found that interesting since Stan had claimed he had no contact with the woman. He squinted up at the sky and adjusted his Gushers cap. "This patio is surrounded by Palo Verde trees. How you supposed to keep every little leaf out?"

"Pray one didn't blow in within an hour of your visit."

Jake wondered what else Vern knew about the proprietor. "Who is this woman, anyway?"

"Used to be a big deal with the water authority. Don't know much else, except…"

Vern leaned in, glanced over his shoulder toward the shuttered house and said sotto voce, "She parades round here less on than a decent set of underwear." He rolled one hand in front of his chest and whistled. "Nice." Vern straightened and resumed his authoritative posture for the benefit of his trainee. "But as Mr. Burke says, 'We see nothin'. We hear nothin'. And we damn sure don't say nothin'.'"

"If she worked for the water authority she should know a pool cover could save thousands of gallons from evaporation and keep shit out of the water."

"Buddy, that's thinkin'. Ain't nothin' in Vegas get you in trouble faster. Grab the test kit."

Jake reached into a white bucket, pulled out a blue plastic container about the size of a shoebox and handed it to Vern. "Here you go."

Vern opened the box, selected a small bottle with a yellow cap and stooped to collect a sample. Jake handed him a multi-colored test strip from a separate cylindrical container in the bucket. Vern held up the bottle, shook it and let it settle, examining the contents. "Madame likes her water pure and readily available." He opened the bottle, dipped the strip and handed it to Jake. "She does not *wish* to deal with pool covers." Vern squinted up at him. "You're just lucky she's out of town right now. It will give you several service visits to up your game." He pointed to the test strip. "How's she look?"

Jake studied it. "Looks good. Out of town? Any idea how long."

"Turns out I do but why you so interested?"

Jake rolled his hand in front of his chest and leered at Vern. "Can't wait to see 'em, that's all."

Vern smirked, nodded his understanding and grabbed a long aluminum pole attached to a vacuum head trailing red hose and dropped it in the pool. "Since I'm the only pool technician's lasted more than two weeks with her, we got sort of close, in a strictly professional way. Told me last service she would be gone for a while to Idaho on a wolf hunt."

"Wolf hunt?"

"Yeah, she's a big time hunter and shooter. You'll see some of her taxidermy trophies when you service the pool equipment in the basement. She said wolf is one a the big ones she never bagged and in parts of Idaho, like near … Cascade I think she said, you can hunt 'em year-round."

"Wolf hunt, shit."

Vern straightened. "Any final pool questions?"

"No, Vern. Think I got it. I'll tell Mr. Burke you're a hell of a teacher."

"I'd appreciate that." Verb grinned and touched his hat brim with an index finger. He handed the aluminum pole to Jake.

"Okay, you got keys to the basement and all the gear you need to finish the job here today. I'm cutting you loose, cadet."

"What no patch or diploma?"

"You last a month with this woman I'm sure Cousin Stan will pin a medal on you. See you back at the hose barn."

Vern gathered up his personal equipment, slapped Jake on the shoulder and left around the side of the house.

July 13
Sunday

Six riders wearing hunter-orange vests picked their way up the sun-streaked evergreen-lined trail in the River of No Return Wilderness. Brown leather scabbards laden with rifles swayed on the horses' flanks. Susan, astride Claude, led two horses packing camp gear and food. While preparing for the trip, the weathered outfitter-wrangler, Kipp, had quickly sized up Susan as a tenderfoot and recommended Claude because he was "just dumb and slow enough to be idiot proof." Having made the strategic decision to only reveal enough riding experience to get hired, she thanked the sexist jerk with feigned relief while filing a mental note to kick him in the balls later.

Kipp also gave her a crash course in horse packing. "I recommend you have the Senator double check everything you do with Whitey and Brownie. Even packers worth a damn has lost pack animals, rolled a pack animal down steep hills, had pack saddles slip to the side, or had horses step off trails and wreck in steep terrain."

"I'll have Mr. Stark look at everything."

He glared at her. "You better." He turned and spat a tobacco stream. It splatted in the brown dust. "Whitey probably wouldn't spark if you fired a gun by his ear, but Brownie will rodeo at the drop of a hat. Always keep Brownie at the back with a break-a-way lead."

"I'll remember that, Kipp, thanks," Susan said.

"And don't surprise Brownie when you start Claude and Whitey or he will sure hell break his lead. Or worse."

"Got it, Kipp. I'm sure grateful for the kind advice."

Claiming limited horse experience was intended to help preserve her cover story: she had just stumbled into Cascade after a nasty break-up and had seen the ad for a camp cook placed by Dead Aim Outfitters. An experienced camp cook for a horse packer outfit would normally be an expert rider, but someone who just blew into town, not necessarily. The small matter of actually doing some camp cooking—Jake and Amy would both have a good laugh at that prevarication. What the hell, she thought; I'll worry about that one later. Jake always says, in the business of private investigation it's best to live one lie at a time.

She glanced back at the two packhorses with some pride in how well they were behaving and performing. Whitey, dirty white with brown feet, followed by Brownie, all brown except for a white forehead blaze, huffed and snorted and plodded along behind. Fortunately, Kipp had had just enough patronizing forbearance to show Susan how to tie up the string. "Take a doubled piece of nylon baling twine and tie it in a loop around Whitey's pack hitch ropes." He had demonstrated while talking. "Tie Brownie's lead rope to that loop. Lead Whitey off at a slow pace, verbally cueing Brownie to come on up, too. The twine will break easily under strain but if you're careful and lucky they won't lean on it and snap it. And careful where you take them too—a bunch of purty grass is going to cause all hell to break loose." So far, no breaking hell, Susan thought.

She was happy to be last in the line of riders. That created a safe distance from her person of interest, the Water Witch, who, having immediately established her place in the hierarchy of the pack-trip pack as the alpha female, led the group up the trail, lifting her skinny tight-jean-clad ass in time with each torpid step her horse took as if she were competing in some sort of slow motion equestrian event.

A sudden clattering step over a large rock caused Claude to dance sideways in the trail. Susan did a little spontaneous acting and appeared to narrowly avoid being thrown. Brownie in the rear aided the effect by bucking a few little quarter turns. The riders ahead, except for the self-absorbed Witch of course, stopped and turned in their saddles to look back at her. She caught herself, straightened, waved that she was fine, adjusted her cowboy hat low on her face, cued Brownie to come up and put Claude and the string forward again while smiling secretly at her charade. Brownie quickly gave up on his half-hearted protest and settled into line. One concern had already pretty much vanished. The Water Witch was apparently not in the habit of showing any interest in the help and as yet had not even glanced at Susan, let alone recognized her.

The group slowly angled up a tree-covered ridge carved with steep switchbacks. Susan looked down through the trees to a wide rushing stream descending a narrow rocky cut. She found the sound of the pounding water soothing even from several hundred feet above. That and the rhythmic creaking of saddle leather. She reviewed the unexpected series of events that had landed her as a camp cook on a wolf hunt in Idaho.

Jake had been successful beyond their wildest hopes in determining the Witch's whereabouts but rather than being suitable bait for the lecherous old bitch as planned, it had turned out Susan was much closer to her actual location. Having just dropped Amy off in Wyoming for a two-week field science course she was only a day's drive away from Cascade, north of Boise. Jake said that he would come as soon as he could untangle himself from Gushers without creating suspicion and that Susan should wait for him in Cascade. He added that he hoped she would do nothing but observe until he got there.

Susan rushed over to Cascade without any plan other than what Jake had suggested. But then with the same kind of luck that had led to the arrest of Old Ruth's killer, the morning of her first day in town she glanced at a cluttered community bulletin board outside a café and saw the ad. Dead Aim Outfitters was seeking an experienced camp cook for a wolf hunt scheduled to depart two days hence. She figured that would be more than enough time for Jake to get to Cascade and for them to plan how he would shadow her in the mountains. She walked into the outfitter's office that same morning and was hired on the spot. Didn't seem to be too much competition for the job and they certainly had not taken any time to do a background check. Sid Busser, Dead Aim's owner, had also lowered the bar on the experience requirement, accepting Susan's claim that she was a great cook in general and had done extensive cooking for her large family on extended camping and pack-trips.

Busser gave her several lists of supplies and informed her she had less than forty-eight hours to plan and prepare for the three-day outing. He cautioned her that the food had to be good and plentiful because the group was going to be made up primarily of prominent local ranchers, organized and led by Zack Stark who was also a State Senator. When Susan inquired if any women would be in the party, Busser's response was, "One—some woman from Nevada—friend of Stark's." Before she left, Busser showed her where the stables were at the edge of town and told her to meet with Kipp, his head wrangler, two hours before they were scheduled to trailer the horses and head out. Between trips to various stores securing supplies on Dead Aim accounts, Susan left Jake a few hasty updates on his cell voicemail. It worried her that she had never received a response and even more so, that he had not yet arrived when the trip's scheduled departure neared. But then cell sucked in that isolated little mountain town in the central Idaho wilderness, she hoped he had called and she had simply missed it and that he was on his way.

When the day of the trip arrived and she had still not heard from Jake, she decided bailing was not an option. It would have eliminated any hope of getting close to their target. Letting her slip through their fingers was not an option.

The slow climb on Claude was causing a little weariness. Susan was out of saddle shape what with Cassie, her horse, being boarded by Clint in Driggs, Idaho. She stood in her stirrups to stretch her legs and give her butt a break.

Sunlight angled through the pines and gleamed intermittently on Claude's dark chocolate shoulders. He was sweating. The air was pungent with pine and horse scent. A slight breeze cooled the riders. The packhorses huffed and snorted their way up hill; their shoes clicking and clattering over rocks. It was the sort of summer mountain day that reminded transplants like Susan why they moved to the Rocky Mountains and natives why they stayed. Susan glanced over the orange backs of the guests at the trip organizer and leader, Zack Stark, riding just behind the Water Witch. Stark was a native who had stayed and had immediately appeared to Susan to be a decent sort. At least he spoke to her rather than ignoring her or speaking down to her.

Camp was a copse of conifers beside a green flower-filled meadow. On the other side of the meadow past where the horses were hobbled, a stream meandered through aspen and willows. Snowcapped gunmetal gray humps of distant peaks formed the backdrop. While Susan set up the camp kitchen, each rancher pitched his own white canvas tent forming a rough semi-circle. Stark helped the Witch erect hers, slightly apart from the men. Rifle scabbards were hung from stumps of sawed off tree limbs.

After a passable dinner of burgers and beans, Susan offered coffee. Zack Stark had uncapped the Jack Daniels, poured shots in mugs all around and stood sipping. A fire snapped and sparked in a circle of rocks. A hermit thrush trilled its solitary call from deep in the trees.

The three cattle ranchers perched on log rounds. The Water Witch had insisted on bringing a folding camp chair and she lounged close to the fire in it, right leg tossed provocatively over the arm. Although it was already high mountain chilly, her form-fitting red plaid shirt was wide open to the forth button and bolstered and enhanced flesh pushed up and out. She looked exhausted from the ride.

"Nothing like a snort by the fire after a good mountain feed," Butch Watson said, resting his boots on a rock and pushing his sweat-stained Stetson back on his forehead. He was long and taut as barbed wire.

"Hush, Butch, I suspect ole' Zack is about to get on his soapbox and tell us why we're here," said Lucas Wright. He eased his belly out over his massive silver belt buckle while chewing on a sliver of wood framed by his droopy white mustache.

Phil Wells stared into the fire. He looked like a T.V. cowboy—handsome, neatly attired, blue bandana tied perfectly around his neck, his black cowboy hat like new.

"You know me too darn well, Luke. Can't sneak up on you," Zack Stark said.

"Hell you ain't snuck up on anybody since you tricked Mary into marrying you. And to think she coulda had me," Watson said.

"I'm sure there's been times when she wished she had, Butch. Turns out it was Mary recommended I bring you three up here this weekend. She's as concerned as I am about how we're treating our new neighbors."

"If it's those dot-commer, newcomer, rich dudes she's worried about, much as I love Mary too, she won't get much sympathy from me," Lucas said.

"It's the wolves, Lucas. We're concerned about the slaughter of the wolves. Thought you all might be open to a discussion about the delisting."

Susan poured the dishwater into the edge of the fire and began to dry the pots and pans. Zack eased over and splashed an inch of whiskey into her cup.

He turned back to the fire. "Folks, gimmie a guess at how many wolves were killed illegally since reintroduction."

"Not near enough," grumbled Phil Wells, speaking for the first time since dinner.

Stark ignored that crack. "Ten wolves killed right here in our back yard in the last six months, twenty-one in New Mexico and Arizona. A dozen in Wyoming. Hell, toss in the eleven grizzly deliberately killed in Montana last year and you have a slaughter of threatened and endangered species that is giving us western ranchers a black eye. BBC was just here covering it. The media loves these stories, but that's not my chief concern. A healthy ecosystem requires healthy predators. You all saw the damage to Yellowstone from overpopulation of elk before wolf reintroduction, yet Butch, you sport a bumper sticker on your pickup, 'Save an elk herd-kill a wolf.'"

"Look out boys, it's tree huggin' time," Butch said, "Stark, we don't want to kill all the wolves, just the ones killing our cattle."

The Water Witch interjected. "Anything that makes these handsome gentlemen's lives more difficult probably needs to be controlled, Zack."

"Controlled, yes, but not slaughtered," Stark responded.

Lucas Wright said, "Shoot, I like wolves much as any wild animal, but you know very well that the cattleman's way of life's getting squeezed from all sides, wolf predation just might be the straw that breaks the rancher's back."

"Okay, I'm sorry," Zack Stark said, sitting on a log round. "I get worked up about this." He looked at each of them in turn. "But we'll only stop this carnage if we enlist the help of livestock ranchers. That's what I want to talk to you boys about."

Susan hung on the perimeter as the debate raged, noting both the comments and behavior of the guests. Watson and Wright did most of the talking. Wells said little, but his demeanor darkened with each sip of whiskey. Might mean something, might not, Susan thought. She brewed a second pot of coffee and kept a close watch on Wells and The Water Witch.

Away from the circle of fire, the stars shimmered like quartz pebbles in a black-bottomed stream; a luminescent ring formed around the moon.

July 14
Monday

Mountain morning light crept in soft and gray. Susan rose first. She pulled on jeans and a sleek black down jacket, crawled out of the tent, brushed her hair and teeth, splashed water on her face and quietly started the coffee water on the stove. Soon Zack unzipped his tent, tucked his tan suede shirt into his jeans, ran three fingers through his graying brown hair and joined her by the camp stove. When it was ready, he suggested they carry their coffee across the meadow to the bank.

The stream rushed noisily over boulders, greeting them as they sat.

"High cirrus clouds," Zack said, looking up. "Could mean a summer storm." He smiled at Susan. "All this extreme weather from sea to shining sea and yet, I guarantee you every person in this party will deny that the climate is changing."

He looked to the western horizon and then directly at Susan. This was the first time she'd been this close to him. He reminded her a little bit of Paul Newman in his later years. Stark's blue eyes were every bit as unsettling. "You're obviously new to Cascade. Where you from?"

Wheels spun. Someone had taught her to keep as close to the truth as possible. "Near Phoenix originally. Father was a preacher on the reservation. I was not exactly what he had in mind in a daughter. Hate the desert and I hate preaching."

"Married?"

"Yes." She glanced at her Swiss Army watch. "If things go according to plan, for exactly thirteen more days."

"Sorry to hear it. Always tough. Kids?"

"Fortunately not. Custody battle will center around one fat spoiled black Lab." Susan tried to shift the focus off her. "I'm just curious, are you and our female guest ... close?"

Zack looked a little taken aback at her question.

Susan tilted her head and smiled. "A gal just likes to know these things."

Zack sipped at his coffee. "You could say we have something more than an acquaintance—and something less than a friendship—born of political necessity. As you know, Idaho and Nevada share a border. She is a very influential person in Nevada, used to head the Southern Desert Water Authority based in Vegas. We like to keep our relations with officials from Nevada neighborly." He winked at her. "Never know when you might need to borrow a cup of sugar." He cleared his throat. "Politically speaking, it has been fairly easy for Idaho and Nevada to remain on amicable terms. Can you guess why?"

"I would say it would probably have something to do with water."

"And you would be smarter than the average bear if you did." Zack continued, "we've got it; Nevada has an insatiable need for it. And that rather innocuous looking woman was a regular mama grizzly when it came to procuring water for Las Vegas. But Idaho is blessed with plumbing that in no major way connects with Nevada. We are not, and I thank my lucky stars just about every day for this, even members of the Colorado River Compact—the outdated, unscientific and often ignored agreement that slices up the overtaxed Colorado River among seven states and Mexico."

Susan had sized up Stark as a talker and thought it might be beneficial to encourage that. "She seems like a fish out of water, pardon the pun, among your rancher friends."

"Frankly, I invited her because she's been badgering me for years to go on a wolf hunt and because I felt she'd make the male guests feel less guarded and put on the spot by me. I'm happily married but my buddies here are all bachelors or widowers and, though I've never known her to date a man even close to her age, I'm not above trying a little matchmaking."

"Zack, let's be honest. You stand out in this crowd too, in a good way. Mind if I ask what your background is?"

"I'm a dude rancher and a Republican State Senator but my degree is in wildlife and conservation ecology. As you could tell last night, I put this trip together to lobby my rancher friends about wolves. They have influence. They can make a difference."

"No offense, but how is shooting wolves going to help wolves?"

He looked over his shoulder toward the tents and then leaned toward her. "I know these men well enough that I felt getting them close to wolves, but hopefully not close enough to actually kill one, could ultimately benefit the local conservation of the species." He sipped at his coffee. "Are you aware of the wolf's current status as a game animal?"

"No, sorry."

"The federal government has just removed the wolf from protection by the Endangered Species Act. It's called delisting. The new Idaho management plan permits wolves to be killed by any means without a license in most of the state. Several were shot in the first few days. Since reintroduction of the wolf to the Yellowstone Ecosystem in the mid-nineties, I have cheered their robust return but my buddies here would argue that's because my livelihood is dudes not livestock. Wolves don't prey on rich folks from Chicago. Thank God. But they do occasionally prey on cattle and the like. Canis lupus occupies an important niche ecologically and I don't want to see them lose ground, or possibly be eradicated again like in the 1930s."

"I see where you're coming from."

"You like murder mysteries, Susan?"

"I live and breathe murder. Can't get enough of it."

"I'm wrestling with one. In recent months, even before delisting, many wolves around the region were deliberately killed—decimating some packs. Most incidents have occurred on or near the grazing allotments of the men I've invited on this trip. Idaho ranchers are notoriously tight-knit. I'm not saying these guys are personally slaughtering and poisoning wolves but someone in this party knows who's doing it. I intend to find out."

Susan wanted to hear more but was feeling pressed to get breakfast started. "What are your plans for the group today?" she asked.

"Wildlife viewing, of course, but I really hope our guests will get to witness one of the local wolf packs socializing and perhaps even hunting, but at a safe distance, for the wolves that is. It just might sway these hard cases." He chucked a stick into the stream and watched it dance away.

"Let me cut to the chase, Zack. Do you suspect any of your friends of killing wolves illegally?"

"I've known them forever. Our dads rode, hayed and raised barns together, but—"

"It's none of my business. I'm just Dead Aim's hired hand, but if there's anything I can do while I'm here at camp today." Stark looked skeptical. He stroked his three-day growth and bit his lower lip. "My soon-to-be-ex was … is a cop. I know a thing or two about sleuthing. Plus, I'm an animal lover myself."

He held her gaze. "Hmm." He glanced off toward the mountains and considered. "Why don't you see if you can secure a cartridge and something for finger prints from each of them." Stark tossed the remainder of his coffee into the grass. "Except the lady from Nevada, of course. I doubt if they're wolf killers, but … as they say on the cop shows, just for elimination."

He stood up and brushed off his pants. "Oh, and if you hear shots come on out. Just my luck one of them will bag a wolf and then we'll need help. Make lots of noise, though; hunter's orange is only sort of a deterrent. Plus, you know bears and their appetites. They're always hungry and can smell gut piles for miles. Some folks believe a gunshot is a dinner bell for bears. Carry your bear spray."

After breakfast, the hunters saddled and rode off. When the sounds of their coffee-fueled conversation, creaking leather, and clicking horseshoes died away on the trail, Susan was left with the hypnotic rhythm of the stream and the occasional birdcall. After a brief wait, she bagged and labeled the hunters' coffee cups for prints and searched their duffels for shells. She spent extra time rifling through the Witch's belongings, not because she expected to find anything to confirm her suspicions that she was in fact Beverly Witt's killer, but simply because it felt good to violate the bitch's privacy.

Detective work done, she spent the remainder of the morning on camp chores and dinner preparation. The weather deteriorated rapidly. By noon the skies had darkened and the temperature had plummeted. By mid-afternoon large fat flakes coated the trees—by 5 p.m. six inches of snow blanketed the landscape.

Susan had donned a woolen cap and mittens. She was bending over building the evening's fire, when she felt a presence behind her. She straightened and turned and looked into the gaze of a commanding wolf.

Her eyes were dark, wary and wise, her gray coat thick and lush. A pinkish tinge at the ruff of her powerful neck signified a recent meal. She panted short bursts of steaming breath. As quickly as their eyes locked, the wolf dissolved into the falling snow leaving huge canine prints to slowly fill with flakes.

Susan started to prepare salad for dinner still excited about encountering her first wolf when a loud noise startled her. Shots boomed from the forested hills above camp and echoed down the valley.

She clicked off the propane stove, grabbed her pistol, hunter's orange vest, bear spray and headlamp and headed out.

It was still hours before sundown but the light was dim and flat in the storm creating a dreamscape of blurred images. White flakes coated flowers and scrubs and the branches of evergreens and leaves of deciduous trees, creating a landscape seen only in fairytales and snow globes.

She called out when approaching a clearing near the source of the shots. As she emerged from the trees she saw movement. Her wolf was down. She ran to her, pistol drawn. A bullet sizzled past her head. She dove behind the animal and struggled out of her orange vest, jamming it under her chest. Several shots followed in rapid succession. It was getting dark and Susan prayed she would blend into the snow as it continued to fall. Her only other cover was the wolf. A shot thumped nearby sending up a puff of snow—Susan burrowed deeper behind the animal—then another shot. Even if she knew where in the distant spruces the bullets were coming from, her Glock would be useless at this range. She wondered if the shooter could see her rapid breath. Hear her heart. Smell her fear.

She lay flattened in the snow behind the wolf for what felt like a lifetime. At such close range the wolf's coat was rich, dense and multi-colored containing white, gray, brown and red hairs. Susan had an almost irrepressible desire to bury her fingers in it. Blood trickled out of a bullet hole in the animal's massive neck, staining the snow red. She panted and flopped her head, tongue lolling, in an attempt to rise, spouting gouts of blood. Susan shushed her and patted her flanks. Her forepaws paddled feebly at the snow; her large black footpads caked with white.

The gusting wind blew the wolf's coarse gray hair against Susan's chin. Still she lay flattened in the snow behind the belly of the dying animal, afraid to move.

The shots had stopped. Snow continued to fall softly as the animal panted her final ragged breaths. At last, the wolf was still. All was white and still.

A human scream erupted from the spruces. Susan jumped up and sprinted fifteen yards to shrubs that led to the cover of the forest. She crouched and circled toward the sound—Glock at the ready. The trees, dim light and falling snow provided good cover. She swiped at her snow-flecked eyelids with her sleeve and felt her way forward.

She entered a small opening in the trees and noticed irregularities in the surface of the snow. She circled to a broken and gnarled spruce. From the tree it was a clear shot to the wolf. She took a chance and switched on her headlamp. The irregularities were tracks and they were everywhere: human, horse and ... large, dinner plate-sized impressions. The hair stood on the back of her neck—grizzly. She switched off her light and listened—not a sound. She was alone. She took a breath and switched on her headlamp again.

She mumbled to herself, "The shooter stood behind this tree." She picked a rifle out of the snow. "Winchester, 30-06 bolt action. The Witch was the only one who brought that rifle." With her light she traced bear prints and bloody drag marks leading up into the dark of the thickening forest. "Whoa!"

Something shiny caught her eye at the base of the tree. She picked it up and tapped it against her leg. It was the Lucas Wright's silver belt buckle.

She sucked in three deep breaths and tried to concentrate. What we got? She thought: someone shooting and killing a wolf; someone shooting at me; signs of both the Water Witch and Wright, and signs of a grizzly bear attack. It looked like the trophy hunters had received an unexpected invitation to be dinner.

It was getting late and she was cold. She was not inclined to track a hungry grizzly at dusk. She decided to leave this one for the rangers and the sheriff.

Back at camp snow continued to fall. Susan stuffed a few belongings into her saddlebag and prepared one pannier on the white packhorse for emergency supplies. She left a note in case Zack Stark returned, but guessed she would find him at the trailhead. Susan was certain she had Zack's wolf killer, or the bear did anyway, but she was anxious to hear Zack's version of the day's events and determine, if possible, exactly what had happened to the Witch.

Susan led the string back up to the clearing to check for any new signs of the hunters or the bear. She reined in Claude and dismounted, holding her bear spray. The unseasonal snowstorm continued unabated—the she-wolf now just a mound of white. No new tracks were visible. Susan was preparing to mount when a figure emerged out of the trees on her right. She turned to see the Water Witch, poorly dressed for the weather in just a flannel shirt and hunter-orange vest stumbling toward her on foot, a Remington 700 model rifle with a Swarovski scope at her waist. Susan's Glock was out of reach in Claude's saddlebag. She tensed and waited.

The Witch had insisted Susan return to the camp and build up the fire. She hunched under a blanket in her chair near the rising flames holding the rifle casually aimed in Susan's direction. Although the Witch was shivering and close to incoherent, Susan knew she was no less dangerous than a rattlesnake after a cold night slithering slowly toward the sun. The Witch demanded that Susan heat water. Susan nodded. She switched on her headlamp and worked at the stove, her mind buzzing with strategies. Regardless of how distracted and disoriented the Witch seemed, the rifle, safety off, followed Susan's every move. Susan assumed, although it was Lukas Wright's weapon and some of the maximum of five shots had been fired, that it was still loaded. It was night now and calm but the snow continued to fall, casting an eerie gray light. Susan was cold, yet sweat formed under her hat and in her gloved palms. While waiting for the water to boil, she dug out two mugs from a camp box and opened a plastic baggie full of tea bags.

"So what happened out there?" Susan asked.

The Witch jerked as if awakening, "Wha happened?" She blinked and focused on Susan. "Tree-hugger Stark had no interest killing wolves. But Lucas did." She shifted closer to the heat from the fire. The wood, mostly dead dry limbs collected from the ground, popped and crackled as it burned. "He 'vited me to join 'im and 'gainst Zack's wishes we split off." She shivered and hunched her shoulders. "We gave ... gave up and headed back here when we saw that wolf. Lucas gave me first shot."

"You intentionally shot a healthy female wolf that was causing no harm?"

"Lucas said ... a bonus kill a breeding female. Nits become lice, he said."

"Oh that's great! Why the hell did you shoot at me?" Susan demanded.

The Witch shifted the barrel so it was pointing right at Susan's chest. "Saw you, uh ... run up to the wolf with your pistol and knew you were no camp cook. Hadn't really looked at you but knew you then. Scope helped in this shit weather." She glanced up at the sky but quickly back at Susan. "It was same ... distance shot as your fat friend at the mine. Can't believe I missed you—fired last cartridges in my rifle."

Susan drew air in through her nose. She felt oddly relaxed and focused after hearing what she had needed to for so long. This despicable woman *was* Bev Witt's killer.

The Witch babbled on. "Horses bolted. Bear charged ... Lucas tried to shoot but it knocked down his rifle. I grabbed it." Her artificially stretched face cracked with a blue-lipped grin. "You know old joke; all I had to do was outrun the fat old rancher ... and I did." The smile faded as flesh snapped back into its recently reassigned alignment. She shook her head. "I looked back once. Bear was dragging him. Then got lost finally circled back here."

"You picked up Lucas's rifle but didn't try to save him?"

"Grabbed it and ran."

"Maybe you wanted the bear to have something to keep its mind off you." Susan realized she was in an unusual position of power, considering she wasn't armed. If the Witch had planned to kill her, she would have done so by now. A person accustomed to the desert spending a night out alone in a mountain blizzard surrounded by wild animals is in serious danger. Or at least she would think she was. The Witch needed her and that bought Susan critical time.

"Now get me your pistol. Don't try anything. You know what a good shot I am."

"It's in my pack on Claude."

"Get me a hot drink, then do it," the Witch ordered. "And make sure those horses are tied well … might need them to get me out of this white hell." Susan brought her a cup of hot water with a tea bag in it. A few sips seemed to revive her. "I'll blow a hole in you sbig as your cowboy hat if you fuck with me." She aimed at Susan's face. "Get that Goddamn pistol now."

It was getting dark and Jake was in the zone of the cone of headlights rushing to Cascade, Idaho as fast as he dared, his stomach clenched with the fear that he was too late to help Susan snare the Witch. He knew from a message that he retrieved from his cellphone, after the security goons had returned it to him, that Susan had gone into the mountains as a camp cook with a party of people, which included the evil woman. Although he agreed that it had been an opportunity Susan shouldn't pass up, he regretted not being there to assist. He knew the witch was as dangerous as a loaded pistol and just hoped Susan was being cautious, was not in danger and was not doing anything rash. He called and left her a return message just in case she got in cell range in the mountains so that she would be aware that he had been delayed, knew that he had received her message, and that he was finally on the way.

He was driving through northern Nevada, nothing visible but yellow lines and rabbitbrush lining the roads, having the occasional brush with rabbits when they darted across in the headlights of his Ford Focus rental. He was thinking back on the time at the Howl at The Full Moon Festival near Ely when he, Susan, and Lyn Burke's aunt, Lou Cuvier were searching for Lyn. That led to sad and angry thoughts of the brutal way his friend Beverly, who was just doing him a favor, had been murdered by the Water Witch or one of her flunkies.

While Jake and Lou had stayed at the Howl to monitor things there, Susan had left to case Stan Burke's mine in Beverly's semi truck with Bev driving. It was to be his last drive. Bev's violent and untimely death had inspired Jake's first writing—lines that felt more like poetry to him than country. *Grief begins as a glowing coal burning your palm but eventually becomes a cinder you can carry in your pocket.* There was a sweet irony to that. In life, Bev had been an old gambling buddy of Jake's. In death, Bev inspired Jake to write which later became an important part of his rehabilitation and recovery as a compulsive gambler.

Of course, Susan had played a critical role in his recovery. Susan. Shit. Susan, who was currently in the wilderness with Bev's killer. He slammed the steering wheel with his palm. *I should be there!*

When nothing else worked to take his mind off his partner. Jake puzzled over lyrics to a new country song he had been working on. He was too self-conscious to call himself a poet; country felt accessible and comfortable. He loved country music because country told the best stories and he thought *Fire*, had the potential of telling a pretty good story.

Fire!
A rarely welcome word.
Fire!
Jump from fryer into flame.
Fire!
A command to execute.
Ready now to shame.

But whose bullet is to blame?
Shoot! Ready? Aim.
Fire!

Jake was whistling the first line of Johnny Cash's "Burning Ring of Fire" when his phone trilled and he saw Gloria's name on the screen. He answered. She had information regarding one deceased Skip Denton, the body in the Flagstaff burn.

"It follows the pattern. An independently wealthy advanced-stage cancer sufferer," Gloria reported. "What do you make of that?"

"I'm convinced it is the key to solving this mystery. Susan and I are going to focus on the similarities between the victims—especially the cancer. There has to be a connection, through the cancer, leading to our killer arsonists."

Gloria kept the call short as usual. Jake was alone with his thoughts again in the hurtling car. He eased through a four-way stop with no sign of settlement or other vehicles. Getting back up to speed, he considered the all-business Chiefwoman. He knew Gloria had to run a lot of meetings but he'd bet, if he were a gambling man—which, of course, he was not—her meetings rarely wasted time or lasted long.

Jake drummed his fingers on the wheel. Yawned long and loud. And played with a new line he had been teasing out, not certain where it might fit in any of his songs in progress.

Can't lose for winning.
Can't lose my winnings.

A low sleek convertible came up behind on a straightway and immediately passed, blasting the rabbitbrush with wind. Large bugs smacked his windshield. He thought of the line from the U2 song, "Every Breaking Wave" he had heard it for the first time recently, "*Every gambler knows that to lose is what you're really there for.*"

He found it and played it on his iPhone wondering if that was why he had, until recently, gambled so obsessively. Was it really to lose? If so, he was damn good at it. Also, listening to Paul David Hewson singing about breaking waves gave him an idea. He would see to it that Susan got a well-deserved break after her one-woman witch-hunt.

He smiled knowing Susan would razz him for not being available to go after the Water Witch but he would counter that by claiming he had sacrificed greatly by breathing pool chemicals for several days while gathering valuable intel regarding the woman's whereabouts.

Both breathing steam, Whitey stood patiently while Brownie huffed and bobbed his massive head. The snowfall had slowed a little.

"What's taking you so long?" The witch held the crosshairs of the Remington squarely on Susan's chest.

"I'm checking on the horses like you said."

"You're taking too damn long. Give me that gun now."

Susan had hopes of digging out her knife and partially cutting Brownie's lead, but the Witch had never taken the scope off of her. She searched around in her saddlebag and pulled out her Glock. She walked toward the woman with the handle of her pistol forward.

"Stop there. Toss it over here by my feet." Susan underhanded the Glock to the spot indicated. The pistol slid in the snow. She lowered the rifle. "Good girl. Sit."

Susan brushed the snow off a log round and sat. "Why did you kill Beverly and strand Lyn and me on that godforsaken butte?"

"Isn't it obvious? If White Wolf was reported by you for being at that meeting at the mine with me—the enemy of the environmental organization that employed him—his cover was blown and it was game over for our water grab."

"But why kill Beverly but not me?" Susan bent cautiously and tossed another limb into the flames.

"He was dispensable. No use to us. We thought you might still have some value. And Lyn was spared because she was family to Stanley. Obviously it was a mistake to leave you alive but I must thank you for this opportunity to tie up that loose end. I can occasionally forgive, believe it or not, but I never forget. You, your cronies and those fucking eco-terrorists put us all out of business."

"I prefer to call them radical environmentalists but we weren't working with them. Even Lyn's Aunt Lou wasn't working for Planet Earth Alliance at the time of the dam bombing. Her concern for her niece's welfare caused her to dig into their plans and they ostracized her. We were all just trying to rescue Lyn, an innocent young woman."

"I believe the military term is collateral damage."

This discussion was going nowhere and it sure as hell wasn't increasing Susan's chances. She realized it was time to make her move.

"Look, I've got the horses loaded and ready to travel down to the trailhead. Why don't you just let me slip the pack off the last horse and you climb on and I'll lead you out of this storm."

"What makes you think you can do that?" The Witch glared over her steaming mug, the rifle resting on her lap.

"I'm actually very good with horses—used to be a mounted police woman. I can get you out of here."

The Witch's eyes searched the surrounding forest for another solution.

"I'm your best option," Susan said. "No one is coming back up here tonight in this storm, believe me."

"Maybe I'll just shoot you and go out on your horse. I'll say I caught you going through our stuff and that you threatened me with your gun."

"You could try that but then you're not familiar with mountains and horses under the best of circumstances." She kicked at the snow. "And these circumstances are far from the best. In fact, you can easily die in these conditions."

"Maybe we just spend the night here."

"Oh, and you'll what, sleep with one eye open?"

The Witch sipped silently at her tea then drained the last bit. "You lead me out of the mountains and I'll think about letting you live. Now get the horses ready."

Susan got up, brushed off her pants and walked to the pack string while the Witch followed her with the rifle.

The unseasonal weather had cleared; the moonlight turned the snow-covered forest to dull silver. Three horses, with silhouetted riders on the first and last, passed slowly in and out of moon shadows. Susan, on Claude, led down the mountain with her headlamp adding additional illumination to the trail. Whitey, heavily laden with packs—Susan had convinced the Witch they might need the supplies—was second in the string, and the Witch brought up the rear. She was clinging awkwardly to the frame of a hastily padded packsaddle strapped to Brownie. She had Susan's Glock sticking out of her vest pocket and held Lucas Wright's rifle in her right hand pinned under her elbow. The Remington bobbed up and down with the horse's steps but still covered Susan's back. Brownie occasionally sidestepped, tossed his head, and snorted his displeasure with the unaccustomed shifting weight of a rider.

Susan's headlamp beam stabbed back and forth among the trees. Tree trunks were plastered with fresh snow and branches bent under the weight, forming arbors just over the trail in some places and in others arching all the way to the ground. She was relieved to have bought some time and to be heading down out of the mountains, but she didn't believe the Witch would let her live a minute beyond the point she no longer needed Susan for her survival.

They rounded a rocky bend in the trail and began to slowly pick their way down the steep switches above the stream. The horses hooves occasionally slipped but the snow was already melting and the footing, although muddy, was not icy. Susan leaned out of her saddle and looked straight down the incline to the rushing water. She turned Claude at a switchback; he tossed his head and sidestepped a little. While the string descended the next several switchbacks, she surreptitiously studied the Witch, searching for weakness. Her adversary was obviously tired and uncomfortable but in terms of firepower and the ability and willingness to use it, she was still very much in control. Susan figured she had one shot at escape.

As the horses rounded the last steep switchback before the trail bottomed out in the valley beside the stream, a snow-laden spruce branch arched low over the trail ahead. Susan lay down, hugged Claude's neck and brushed under. On the downhill side she turned, reached back and shoved the branch; it uncoiled spraying a screen of snow. She simultaneously spurred Claude with a shout while leaning into the cover of his downhill side. Whitey followed with a head-throwing lurch, catching Brownie off-guard.

The rodeo began. Brownie reared, snapping his lead, and the Witch flipped back above him like a rag doll. Susan moved Claude and Whitey further away on the trail. The Witch jerked off a shot at Susan but it went high, ripping through tree branches. The retort caused her horse to spin and buck all the more. Susan calmed Claude and moved again, seeking to put distance and the cover of trees between her and her attacker. Whitey followed nervously but passively.

On one abrupt turn from the bucking horse the rifle barrel hit a tree trunk and spun out of the Witch's hand to the ground. She gamely stayed on for the full eight seconds but there was no buzzer and there were no clowns coming to her rescue. She even managed to get the pistol out of her pocket but the bumping and jerking combined with a snow-slippery grip caused the Glock to flip out of her hand and bounce to the rocky path.

Brownie appeared to have no intention of quitting until he unseated his load. He turned and bucked again and this time landed with only two feet on the trail. As he slid down the hill backwards on his haunches the Witch clung onto the saddle—the horror of her situation etched on her face. Brownie tried frantically to regain his footing, slid further and then rolled sideways, his entire bulk pinning the Witch with a sickening crunch as the packsaddle tree crushed her abdomen. Together they skidded toward the rushing river. The horse landed on a small spit of rocky beach, broken bone exposed in his bleeding front right foreleg. The Witch wasn't so lucky. Obviously unconscious, she slipped into the freezing plunging water, came to the surface, rolled slowly in the rapids, flowed over a partially submerged boulder and was swept away.

Susan dismounted and tied Claude. She patted Whitey and spoke softly and reassuringly. She walked back up the trail above the injured horse. The animal bellowed in pain and tried to get up, panic in his eyes. Susan picked up the Remington, pulled back the bolt with her right hand, kicked out the empty and saw the rifle was out of cartridges. She returned to the horses with the rifle shaking in her hands, rummaged in Whitey's panniers and came up with a .243 caliber cartridge taken from Lucas's tent. She loaded the cartridge and gently slid the bolt forward, pushing the new round into the chamber. She brushed snow and pine duff off the scope while she walked back to the place on the trail above Brownie. She leaned against a tree trunk to steady her aim and inhaled several times to regain control of her heartbeat. After a sharp intake of breath she fired and put one merciful bullet through the animal's brain. A grouse clattered out of a pine below her as the shot echoed down the valley.

July 15
Tuesday

Susan walked past giant sagebrush, pulling leaves off, off to smell the pungent odor to get centered and focused and try and remember the desert is not the enemy. There were small rocks and sand in her shoes. She walks through a desert stream now and the water is so cold in contrast to the heat emanating off the sun baked rocks. She comes to a waterfall. Spring water pours at her feet like an open faucet and then washes back away from her in refluent waves like a film reversed. Vegetation lines the stream—tamarisk with wispy branches and pink flowers. Sand and dust gets into everything. It is twenty degrees hotter in the sun within fifteen yards of the streambed. She is in the shade now. Shade is so cool by contrast. All plants have defenses, thorns and spines. Spanish olive tree has huge thorns. Horseflies. The feel of warm gritty sandstone. Almost looks soft. Watching your feet and where you place them. Loose sand slides back. Anasazi ruin up in rock bowl. Moki steps carved on boulder at bottom. Vast, empty, wall of rock emitting heat, sustaining little life. Constant reminders that the desert sustains little life. Like in the shadows, or just underground. Visual overwhelms auditory but there are sounds if you listen. Wind in cottonwoods. Birds. Echoing raven mimics cries of ancestors. The scale-descending trill of the canyon wren. She is back in the shallow water. A horse is bellowing somewhere nearby. There is a flash of light followed by a rush of heat from above in the streambed.

Suddenly flame is coursing toward her on top of the water; it bursts over the edge of the waterfall and pools at her feet swirling up her legs burning her flesh as high as her waist...

Susan blinked twice and awoke, heart racing, in a strange bedroom with blue walls. It took her a few moments to remember where she was. Not in the desert as she had been dreaming but based on the view out her bedroom window still in the mountains. Then she recalled meeting Zack Stark on the trail near the trailhead. He and the other two ranchers had followed a hunting pack of wolves for hours through the snow and ended up close to the trucks and trailers. Because of the weather, Watson and Wells had suggested packing up their horses and heading home. Stark had promised to bring their gear out.

He was heading back up to camp when he ran into Susan. She told him about the wolf being shot. He looked disgusted. But that look turned to one of utter incredulity when she relayed the events of the apparent bear attack and the truly unfortunate horse accident when she was leading the woman from Nevada out of the mountains to safety.

They rode to the trailhead, quickly unsaddled the horses and loaded them in the Dead Aim trailer already attached to Zack's White Dodge Ram truck. As they neared town, cell service resumed and Zack called in the accidents and then later he stopped at the sheriff's office. A deputy who was rushing because he was needed at the trailhead interviewed Susan briefly. He said the sheriff wanted to schedule her for more intensive questioning in the morning after she got some rest. Back in Stark's truck she checked her phone but found the battery was dead and would need to be charged.

Stark had invited her to spend the night at his mountain cabin in the hills above the reservoir on the edge of Cascade. His wife, Mary, had been kind and solicitous—a lovely woman with gorgeous gray hair.

Susan reached to the bedside table and unplugged her iPhone. It displayed, 9:14 a.m.—9:14: *Jesus opened his eyes.* Her phone indicated she had several voicemail messages from Jake and one from Amy. It was great to hear his voice. He had made it to Boise and would drive up Route 55 and should be in Cascade by mid-afternoon. It will be a welcome relief to see him, she thought. Now if she could just reach Amy. But that would have to wait. She responded with a text to Jake telling him she couldn't go into details but she was fine. It would be best if he waited in Boise for her.

She flopped back against the pillows and threw her arm over her eyes, thinking she could sleep for a week.

July 16
Wednesday

A huge promontory jutting straight out into the breakers dwarfed Jake and Susan as they walked along the wide beach that ended at the base of the headland's cliffs. Thin morning mist hung over the waves angling into the shore. Gulls cried and lifted into the wind. A battalion of six pelicans skimmed above the breakers. The couple, both garbed in brown Goddard jackets and ball caps, khaki shorts and running shoes, walked hand-in-hand on the firm sand just above the reach of the waves, their eyes searching for sand dollars and agates.

After a cup of coffee each, they had wandered down the winding road to the shore from their cabin high up on the bluffs overlooking the town of Oceanside, the beach, and the peninsula that prevented through traffic in the town. They were staying in a rental that belonged to a friend of a friend of Jake's. He had arranged it while driving to Idaho from Las Vegas. Fortunately the cabin had been available for the five days he hoped to get Susan away for some much needed R&R. Jake had checked with Gloria and told her they would use the brief vacation to plan next steps in the arson case. The desert was out because of Susan's antipathy for it, and he was just intuitive enough to guess she was going to be ready for a break from the mountains as well.

He was right; as soon as he had called from Boise and suggested it, Susan resigned from Dead Aim, claiming she had been traumatized, which was not entirely a fabrication; she convinced the sheriff to let her travel by promising to be back early next week for any final inquires, and said goodbye to Zack and Mary Stark.

After meeting Jake at the Best Western in Boise, he drove her truck while she curled up in the passenger seat. In a rush she relayed the details of the pack trip and the witch's demise and then slept all the rest of the way across Oregon. They had arrived at midnight.

This was their first beach walk and she was dead tired but already feeling a little better. It always helped to be with Jake. The moisture on her face and briny smell of the sea air helped as well.

"Gloria sounded good," Jake said. "As usual she stressed the need to have this thing solved before leaks reach the federal agencies, but she gets that we need this break to mull and plan."

"All I care about is what the French word of the day is," Susan said sleepily.

"Word of the day."

"Huh?"

"Mot du jour. The French word of the day, according to Gloria, is word of the day. Mot du jour."

Susan stopped, turned, and stared at him with mouth half open and eyes heavily lidded. "The word of the day is word of the day? Who's on first?" she said, echoing the Abbott and Costello routine.

Jake grinned, nodded and then turned to walk shoulder-to-shoulder again. "You're a regular Calamity Jane."

"What's that supposed to mean? I cause catastrophes wherever I go?"

"You apparently don't know the true history of Calamity Jane."

"I'm sure you're going to set me straight."

"Yes, Ma'am." Jake touched his cap brim and bowed slightly. "Calamity Jane, I read recently online—"

"Between porn sites?"

"Oh, now that was below the belt."

"Oh, I'm sure it was."

"Ah-hem," he cleared his throat. "Where was ... ah yes, Calamity Jane, aka Mrs. Martha Burke, no relation to Stan, was a memorable western frontier character who claimed she got her name because she carried two guns, and any man, and in your case I would add any woman, who trifled with her was inviting calamity."

"Then I'm honored."

The ocean breeze kicked up. Susan fought her hair back behind her ears. She bent to inspect a sand dollar. It was broken and she rejected it.

They walked awhile in silence. "So, Calamity Jake. What happened down there that caused your three-day delay?"

"That is a classic story of overreaching, I'm afraid. We had what we needed. We knew where she was. Wonder Woman was on the scent. All good. But I just couldn't resist a little snooping beyond the basement, which was the only area I had permission to go for Gushers' work. I know what security cameras look like. I didn't see any. Must have been hidden. Lost close to forty-eight hours locked up in the warehouse of her security firm answering some intense questions and waiting while they tried to reach her. Some sort of security firm with a hell of a lot of clout, considering they were not official members of any law enforcement group, state or federal, that I could find in a web search—very weird. It was torture, I tell you. Food and bunk were okay but TV reception sucked—no Wi-Fi. Finally had to use Stan's influence to get sprung. I hate the thought of owing him anything, but I knew you were pretty vulnerable and exposed without your boss at your side, so Stan begrudgingly vouched for me and I rushed to Idaho. There you have it."

"Not really sure what you could have done, *boss*. I mean, I had to go for the camp cook thing, it was just too good to pass up, and what were you going to do?"

"Wait a minute. I obviously have a much more heroic image of myself than you do. I imagine me lurking around in the woods keeping an eye on you—"

"Fighting with your horse and ultimately getting lost in the snowstorm. That's not exactly providing the best in back-up."

"Not exactly, no." He studied the dark bags under her eyes and slipped around and started working on her shoulders. "But I can, however, offer the best in back rubs." She leaned into his hands and felt her muscles release.

He whispered in her ear, "And it just so happens I know of a little shop on Ocean Street that specializes in homemade chocolates and since it's also a coffee shop, they are open as we speak."

"Bless you, bless you, bless you. I am chocolate."

"Is that literal or metaphorical?"

"It's *choclical*." She turned to face him. "Let's go to Ocean Street for a chocolate breakfast."

After Susan sucked down a large mocha coffee and devoured three chocolate croissants, the two of them had slowly climbed the hill back to their cabin. They were sitting on the wooden deck outside the master bedroom overlooking the long wide beach below. To their right, up the shore lay the flat verdant top of the jutting peninsula. Sitka spruce, much taller than the cabin, shaded the deck.

"First and foremost, this break is about rest and recuperation. Back rubs, beach walks, chocolate—"

"Ugh."

"Assuming you are ever able to look at a piece of chocolate again."

"Never."

And it's about sleep—lots of sleep with the doors to the deck open and the breakers singing us lullabies."

"Ahhh, that makes me miss, my Amers." Susan yawned. "She sounded so good on the phone. Never thought I would hear my daughter excited about drawing moose poop and studying beaver dams."

"She's with her best friend from Jackson and that's a powerful incentive. I'm really glad to hear she's doing so well. Did she … uh … mention me?"

"Look at that osprey hovering above the waves, hope she catches a fish for breakfast." Drifting brown wings reflected sunlight. "Did Amy mention you? Oh yeah, she asked all about how you were doing."

Jake always knew when Susan was being untruthful but appreciated her for this little white lie all the same. "My point is," he said, "we can perhaps accomplish a few things while we're here relaxing. We've got the

Wi-Fi and the small portable printer I bought at Staples in Boise. Unless you have a better idea, let's plan to do three things. I will check Flagstaff, Torrey and Show Low papers for any information about the bodies found in the fires if you will track down the friends and families of Andrew Millar, Brenda Petersen and Skip Denton for anything important connecting them that might not have been in the press coverage. After my research, I will build an attractive, comprehensible timeline and flow chart with the Sharpies, poster board and art supplies I also got in Boise."

"I'm glad you volunteered for the art project. Frankly, I would rather draw moose poop." She looked out over the swells to the blue horizon. The osprey dove at the water but came up empty-taloned. "There'll be no pressure and no schedule other than to complete these tasks before we depart, right?"

"Promise. No pressure. No schedule."

"Then I agree." Her eyes went to the horizon again. They sat without speaking for several minutes. "She *was* a witch, you know."

"Why makes you say that?"

"I read as a teenager during my all-things-weird-and-bizarre period that an old English test for a witch was to tie her hands and feet and toss her in a lake. If she drowned she was a witch. If she didn't drown she wasn't a witch. I watched her go under the water. She never came up for air. And I didn't even have to tie her hands and feet."

She got up, bent over, kissed Jake on the lips and looked into his eyes. "Thank you for booking this beautiful place." She uncoiled and yawned. "Now I believe it is time for my morning nap."

She dragged herself into the room, yawned again and slid under the duvet with a contented sigh.

July 19
Saturday

Three glorious indulgent beach days in and Susan was finally beginning to recover. Jake had obviously chosen her work assignment carefully, knowing that, first and foremost, she needed rest and pampering, but at the same time would be pissed if given something trivial to do. He had cooked pancakes for breakfast and while cleaning up afterward announced a meeting for that afternoon during which he would unveil his schematic and they would share what they had learned.

Susan finished up her cell calls on the deck, organized her notes, and read magazines on a chaise lounge the rest of the morning while Jake busied himself in the living room with his white poster boards. At noon Susan came in to made lunch. Jake finished and theatrically draped a beach towel over his creation, leaving it propped up on a small rectangular brown wooden table against the white paneled interior wall—the only wall without windows and an ocean view.

They sat on the deck off the living room at a round glass table with iced tea, and peanut butter and orange marmalade sandwiches with carrot slices. Jake was wearing his usual tan cargo shorts with his sun-browned legs propped up on a chair across from him. At a shop in town, Susan had found a scooped-neck, cotton beach dress with a rainbow-on-white theme. She was looking tan, freckled, relaxed, and, if you asked Jake, sexy as hell. The dress hugged two points on her chest, revealing she was wearing nothing underneath. They had become accustomed to the sound of the breakers below and spoke a little louder than usual in order to be heard above the music of the surf.

"Let me just say, Mr. Goddard, I love you very much. I really, really appreciate your thoughtfulness in arranging this vacation and…" She turned toward the sea and shouted, "I LOVE THIS GORGEOUS OCEAN." Gliding gulls called back from above the jutting peninsula. Waves tossed white foam high on the rocks at its base. Wind swished in the spruces.

Jake gently pulled on the hairs at Susan's neck. "What's your favorite memory? Apart from the amazing sex acts I performed," he asked, feigning earnestness.

"Oh my God. If the sex is eliminated—it would, of course, have been the very first thing to come to mind—I guess I would have to say the deep, deep relaxation that is possible here combining beach walking, sitting on the decks and watching the waves break below and just … just chilling by the sea."

"Sweet, huh?"

"Very sweet, my sweet. I have not spent this much time at the ocean in my life. I'm hooked. You are going to have to promise we will come back."

He stared at her for a moment, leaned across the table and kissed her on the lips. "I'm so glad you weren't hurt or … worse in Idaho, and I solemnly swear we will be back. Next time for at least a week."

Afternoon sun filled the living room. The sea was calmer now; the sound of the waves muted and spaced further apart. A gentle breeze filled the house with moist air. Jake stood by his covered display holding a capped black Sharpie. He had insisted Susan pull over a chair from the dining area and she sat as if she was at a recital. He whipped off the towel. Susan whipped up enthusiasm.

"Wow, Jake. All those newspaper clippings and photos of our victims all lined up in neat rows and the map of the western United States in the center. You didn't rip that out of my road atlas, did you?" She gave him her pursed-lipped, Church Lady look. "Oh, and the lines of yellow yarn connecting the headshots to the locations of the fires on the map. I mean with so many victims, three, right, how would we ever have remembered where the bodies were found?"

"You like it? Or are you just being sarcastic?"

"Oh, I love it. But where does my information go?"

Jake pointed to three lined spaces below the pictures of Andrew Millar, Brenda Peterson and Skip Denton and to that day's date, which was left blank at the bottom.

"The newspaper articles reinforce what we already knew or learned from Gloria. Andrew, Brenda and Skip: all well-off, all middle-aged, all suffering from advanced stages of cancer, and all living in small western towns at the end of their lives. Andrew and Brenda were transplants. Skip grew up in Flagstaff. And then the obvious, all ended up in man-caused fires under suspicious circumstances. As we suspected none of the articles mentions any of the other similar events. No connection was noted, at least not in the newspapers."

"And the timeline to the right. You write so damn small I can barely read it."

"May I share it with you?"

"That would be nice."

Jake pointed with the Sharpie and began to read aloud:

"6/4—Flagstaff fire

6/7—flare throwers/4 dark-skinned, sooty, "non-Apache" men in a stolen blue pickup on same day as Fort Apache rez fire

6/8—Boulder Mountain fire

6/12—Elk ornament for Jake's hood

6/17—Andrew Millar from Show Low found in Fort Apache rez fire/ metal arrow through bolo

6/19—Brenda Petersen from Torrey found in Boulder Mountain fire/ metal arrow through squash blossom necklace incl. sweet note to Jake

6/22—Skip Denton from Flagstaff found in Flag fire/no arrow/no jewelry

6/25—Susan harassed by apparently same 4 "non-Apache, "dark-skinned men/target arrow provides clue that leads to dead-end (literally for B. and P.) in Phoenix."

"RIP, B&P." Susan couldn't resist.

Jake added an editorial comment. "It is noteworthy that the Bad News Bunglers have apparently gone to ground. There have been no sightings and no activity we can tie to them in over three weeks."

"Because we can't tie something to them doesn't mean they haven't continued bungling and spreading the bad news."

"Very true." Jake tapped the bottom of the timeline with the Sharpie.

"And finally today, 7/19, followed by a handy blank space to add anything new you learned from your phone calls to family and friends. Neat huh?"

"Way neat. Great work. I'm certain it will help us connect the dots."

"Thank you."

Susan glowed with anticipation. "It's good you left extra space because I think I have some information that should definitely be added to your very cool timeline."

"What's that?"

She made an exaggerated study of several pages of notes. "Let's see, I know it's here somewhere. Now what did I ... ah, here it is. According to Andrew's surviving spouse, Linda, Brenda's daughter, Bertha—can you imagine naming a child, Bertha—and Skip's very dear and discrete friend and neighbor, Ralph, all three victims were receiving treatment at Lifebridge Cancer Center in ... Phoenix, Arizona."

"Oh, my God!"

"Yup."

"So we really were on to something with that target arrow. Looks like it's back to Phoenix, Wonder Woman."

"And that would be the bad news." Susan's expression went flat; she stood, turned slowly, glided like a specter to the open French doors and looked out over the ocean. Her dress luffed gently around her legs. She couldn't even muster the energy to push her hair behind her ears.

"Phoenix, Jake? You know how I feel about Phoenix," Susan said in a quiescent little girl voice. "I'll ... I'll just stay here by the pretty ocean enjoying the cool sea breezes and you can call me when you learn something important and I'll immediately add it to your very impressive poster. You know, sort of like your girl Friday. I'd even be willing to add

Monday through Thursday, just as long as I have the weekends to walk on the beach. Okay, Jake? Jake?"

She turned. He was gone. He was in the bedroom packing.

Jake came back out twenty minutes later. Susan had not moved from the doors. He slipped his arms around her waist and pressed up against her back. Each advancing swell below formed an expanding white line, then a crashing waterfall, then a tumbling, foaming, noisy rush that splashed into the rocks and dissipated on the shore.

"You okay?"

She turned, moisture in her eyes, unusual for Susan. "Oh, God Jake, I can't remember being so exhausted. Not when Amy was born, not when Keith left ... it is so peaceful here. I just want you, my daughter, this ocean and peace."

He held her shoulders and put his cheek beside hers and then pulled back and looked into her eyes.

"In high school I had a shop teacher, Wesley Drew. Every kid was engaged in Mr. Drew's classroom. One reason, shop is hands on. Another reason, students chose their own projects. And when a kid hit a snag and, for example, couldn't figure out the geometry to get the pieces to fit right as I so often did with say, a bench or a rack for baseball bats, I, just like every one of his kids in the forty-plus years he taught there, would call Wes over and say, 'Mr. Drew I've got a problem.' He couldn't have been nicer. He'd smile and walk around my work table, look at the pieces of my chaos from several different angles, ask me a few leading questions, pat me on the back and say 'Wow, Jake you do have a problem. How're you going to solve it?'"

Jake dropped his arms to his side. "Used to piss me off. Once I fired back, 'Mr. Drew, you're the teacher.' He said, 'that's correct, Jake, I'm the teacher—but it's your problem on your project. Now how're you going to solve it?' After a few months of that bullshit if I hit an impasse, I wouldn't even bother asking him for help, I'd just go to the resource materials in his classroom and figure the damn thing out."

"I think I get what Mr. Drew was doing."

"I sure didn't at the time, being somewhat clueless and always seeking the easy way out. It was when Rachel and I were on the rocks and I was desperately seeking solutions to our marital problems while trying to protect my sanity as well as my relationship with my boys when I remembered Wes's lessons and I thought, son-of-a-bitch, he wasn't just teaching us how to build shit, he was teaching us about life." He stepped beside Susan, slipped his left arm around her waist and they looked out at the horizon. "He died recently. I never got to tell him. I put a post on Facebook, 'Mr. Drew has passed—with an A+.'"

Susan collapsed into herself a little. "Jake, I'm just tired."

"Susan, we've got...." he pointed over his shoulder to the poster board, "...four bunglers ending decent people's lives prematurely and endangering our already drought-stressed forests. They have to be stopped. No one I know is better at this work than you. Even Stan Burke worships you for saving his daughter's life. Didn't stop him from coming on to you. Can't say as I blame him for that. I get that. I came on to you too, sort of."

"I just need time at home and—"

"I know and rightfully so." He turned to her. "You witnessed three pretty horrible deaths in less than two weeks. But like I said, you are one of the best people I know at solving problems. You're like a bulldog with your jaws locked on the pant-leg of the bad guy. And rest assured, Buck, Pork and the Witch were as bad as they come. I knew, *knew* if the Witch went up against you then the bitch was going down—somehow. Investigation is about solving problems and Goddard Consulting requires your help to solve this problem. I can't do it without you."

She turned, held his face in her hands and spoke softly. "Just let me sleep on the deck tonight. Let me be rocked by these waves one more night and I should be fine." She turned back to face the ocean. "Hopefully things will get wrapped up quickly in Cascade and then we can be on our merry way back to infernal Phoenix."

Jake hugged her from behind. "Tell you what. We'll spend a day or two in Salt Lake before we dive back into it in Phoenix. Maybe you can finally talk to Smokejumper Jen, and we can take Flesh-man to lunch. Sound good?"

"Anything to postpone Phoenix. Based on your inspiring lyrics I think I might even like Budville more than Phoenix."

"Thank you, my love. Thank you, my partner." The waves pulsed. The wind gusted in the spruces dropping a few brown needles on the deck.

"Bless you, Wes." Susan turned her face up to the sky. "Bless you for guiding Jake Goddard on the path of problem solving, for if he had not learned to solve his problems, I would not have him today. And for the beautiful and sturdy benches he is going to make me now that I know that he acquired the skills under your watchful eye."

"Got any use for a bat rack?" Jake asked before resting his chin on her sun-warmed shoulder.

Susan and Jake gazed out over the heaving ocean, a few soft clouds on the horizon, and felt themselves drifting inexorably closer together.

July 22
Tuesday

The freeway cut across a pale green sagebrush steppe, which gently ramped up to distant and sparsely wooded mountains. Jake was driving while Susan slept in the passenger seat. They crossed the state line into northern Utah and were heading toward the Wasatch Front and Salt Lake City.

The day before, Susan had dropped Jake at a motel in Boise and driven back up to Cascade. Her time there had been relatively brief, and the questioning related to the hunting accidents thankfully light, no doubt because Zack Stark had vouched for her.

And it didn't hurt that all the physical evidence the sheriff's deputies had investigated at the two scenes: the signs of a bear attack—including the bloody drag trail—shot wolf, and position of the euthanized horse, bore out what Susan had reported.

The only time the questioning got intense and Susan began to feel moisture on her neck was the sheriff's confusion over what rifles were fired when. That was understandable, Susan had answered, considering that the woman from Nevada had discharged Wright's rifle *accidentally* when Brownie, startled by a random branch dropping its snow load, tried to buck her off. It was all a blur, Susan said, but she was pretty sure the rifle blast caused Brownie to buck harder and ultimately lose his footing. Shortly thereafter, after she saw there was nothing she could do to help the unfortunate woman, Susan had fired the same rifle at the horse.

The sheriff wanted to know how she had come to have the correct cartridge to euthanize the horse with that particular rifle. She told him to check with Zack Stark and that is when Stark verified she had collected it at his request. Considering Stark had enlisted Susan's aid to spy on his fellow ranchers, his choice in the aftermath was to support her or appear rash and foolish. He supported her. Stark was a good man. He even thanked her later for helping him solve the mystery surrounding the rampant wolf killings. He probably would have stood up for Susan regardless, but it never hurt to have leverage, especially with politicians.

After the sheriff concluded his interview, he was more than happy to answer Susan's questions. Neither Lucas Wright nor his female hunting partner had been found, but both were presumed dead. If the bear and river hadn't gotten them, the weather certainly had. Susan learned that apart from her, there were only two other survivors from the vicinity of the camp; the horses Lucas and the woman rode were found in full tack by an outfitter at the trailhead the morning after Susan was picked up. Busser had been notified that he was responsible for moving the dead horse to a location well away from hikers' and horse packers' eyes and noses. Idaho Fish and Game and USFS rangers were looking to trap and destroy the man-eating bear. Susan felt the griz should be located and awarded a medal but she didn't mention that to the sheriff. She thanked him and left his office.

And either the deputies were still really pissed about the initial search and investigation that had kept them out all night in bad weather or Lucas Wright had been extremely unpopular. As Susan was gathering her things and leaving, she overheard part of a conversation coming from the coffee break room. One of the men quipped, "Does a bear poop Wright in the woods?" Followed by muffled snickers.

Using her jacket for a pillow, Susan had napped across most of Idaho. She was awake now and Jake broke the silence.

"You okay?"

"I'm okay. Oregon helped. Getting Cascade in our rearview helps." She yawned.

"You think they're really done with you?"

"I didn't sense that there would be any follow-up, amazing as that may sound. Sheriff was all—let's wrap this baby up and go to lunch. Small towns; gotta love 'em."

"It would appear, my friend, that you have once again dodged a bullet, both literally and figuratively. You totally lucked out in Cascade. Wish I'd had you by my side back in my rambling and gambling days. You're one lucky babe." Jake pulled out to pass a semi lumbering up a long hill.

"Blessed," Susan muttered at her truck's side window. She noticed a hawk perched on a roadside fence post but she was too tired to mention it.

"Huh?"

"Any time I told my father I was lucky he'd say, 'you're not lucky, you're blessed.'"

"You believe that?" Jake asked.

She turned to him, exhaustion still evident in her face. "Not really."

"You had me wondering for a second."

"Hard for me to believe God would worry any more about my shenanigans than he would fret over the outcome of a cracker college football game, regardless of how much genuflecting and praying she observed on both sidelines."

"Wow. You covered your gender bases there."

She smiled at Jake wearily. "Just want to do everything possible to ensure my blessed luck doesn't suddenly run out."

"We could use some gas. Feel up to a late lunch?"

"As long as it's an Arby's sandwich or Carl's Jr. burrito."

"I'm very familiar with your fast food preferences." Jake peered out the window at signs advertising a truck stop. "I'm officially on the hunt for lunch."

Susan slanted her seat back, adjusted her jacket under her head and closed her eyes.

Jake called Trey Fleishman and told him they were en route to Salt Lake. Trey suggested they meet for dinner at Lamb's Grill on Main.

Susan had long wanted to meet Trey. Jake was looking forward to hanging out with his buddy, but he confessed to Susan he had an ulterior motive. He was betting Trey could offer valuable insights into the Lifebridge Cancer Center in Phoenix and how to best set up surveillance there.

The partners discussed Trey's potential involvement and agreed they would only share that they had recently connected three separate bodies in three separate fires with treatment at Lifebridge. Susan insisted they reveal no other details from the case and ask nothing of Trey that could in any way place him in danger.

Evening traffic during the approach to Salt Lake was heavy but mostly going in the opposite direction. Jake exited I-15, negotiated the downtown grid and pulled into a parking garage near Lamb's Grill.

They found the big man outside the restaurant wearing an old tropical shirt with a faded hibiscus pattern and jeans. Curly brown hair sprouted at the neck. Jake introduced him to Susan and Trey stuck out his hand but she brushed it off and gave him a huge hug, knocking his large-lensed glasses askew. He grinned and adjusted his specs, his face flushing medium-rare.

Trey had predictably forgotten to make a reservation so they sat in a row in plush leather chairs facing a polished wooden counter. Waitresses, waiters and bartenders dressed in whites scurried around the room. Although other diners could be heard in quiet conversations most of the sounds were those of clattering cutlery and contented eating.

Jake mopped at his mouth with his cloth napkin. "So, Flesh, I gotta ask. How do you do what you do, all day ... with the stuff that you do it with ... and then come to Lamb's Grill and order the lamb?"

"Rare," Susan added.

Trey grinned to his left at Jake and then winked to his right at Susan, speared a dripping piece of bloody lamb and shoveled it into his mouth, chewed and began speaking between swallows.

"So glad you asked me that, Pi-man." He burped silently and chewed on. "Oh, sorry, Susan." He took a sip of his red wine. "Ah, let's see. Generally it doesn't start until 2, or maybe on a good day when I've had a big lunch, 3 o'clock. But around that time it's pretty predictable. I'll slap a sample on my table and while sliding over the microscope or reaching for a scalpel, I'll study the odiferous and discolored tissue considering different etiologies."

Jake knitted his brows in confusion.

"Oh sorry, in layman's terms, I'll consider different origins and causes of the nasty malignancy in front of me. And then, inexplicably I'll find myself thinking about what I'm going to have for dinner."

Jake put his fork down and puffed out his cheeks as if ill. Trey's shoulder's started to dance and out burst the infectious yuck, yuck.

Susan laughed, took a bite of her trout and rice and surveyed the restaurant in the wall-length mirror. "I really like this place, Trey. Food's still great even after that explanation of your twisted appetites. Love the classic decor."

"This sweet old place is one of my favorites. Lamb's has remained essentially unchanged since 1939. The booths, tables, bar, counter, these great leather counter stools caressing our butts, even the light fixtures, came from a restaurant previously located on Main Street known as Gunn's Cafe."

"Well, son-of-a-gun, Flesh-man, you wow me, once again, with your uncanny knowledge."

Trey flashed his eyebrows Groucho style. "Just call me Barney Google with the goo-goo-googely eyes." He fished his iPhone out of his breast pocket and shook it at Jake. "Long term memory right here in my pocket." He turned to Susan; she could see her reflection in his giant glasses. "Think we can lose him later?"

Susan shook her head and spoke in a stage whisper, "He's a tough one to shake, Trey. As I've told Jake he's really good at showing up and hanging around." She winked conspiratorially. "The only time I've noticed him making himself scarce..." She leaned forward to look at Jake and raised her voice, "is when the going gets really rough."

"I heard that," Jake said, concentrating on his meatloaf and mashed potatoes.

Trey turned and beamed at Jake, "Oh, you mean when the going gets tough, Jake gets going—*the other direction?*"

Jake put down his fork and knife and took a drink of water. "O—kay. Let's talk about why we're here, shall we? I mean we all know it's not because of Trey's sparkling dinner conversation or your rapier-sharp wit, Susan. But first, do you two rascals want more wine?" Trey held his glass out. Jake poured.

"Not for me, thanks." She turned to Trey. "Got an early jog with my college friend Jen tomorrow."

"All right, then." Jake put down the wine bottle and dabbed his mouth with his napkin. "Trey, thanks so much for that glimpse into a day in your life and for providing that wonderful segue because, buddy, we need to talk about cancer and one cancer treatment center in particular. You good with that?"

"Oh I'm good all right, but the meter is running and I'm beginning to wonder if in this lifetime you'll ever be able to square your debt to me. However, one vintage Flying Cloud in excellent condition could just about settle the score."

"Rather you take my first-born," Jake said

"Love Matthew, but no thanks. You're doing a fine job of screwing him up. You don't need my help."

"Might have to be paid off in the next life, Trey," Susan said.

Trey glanced in the mirror behind the counter. He clamped his teeth together, stuck out his chin and nodded his head up and down. "Celestial rewards? Before I come back as a breeding bull. What the hell, I'll take it—especially if you toss in a few heavenly virgins—or heifers as the case may be. Fire away, Jake." And then in a southern belle accent, "I just dearly *loooovve* to talk about *can*-cer."

July 23
Wednesday

Susan fell behind Jen as they charged by a group of walkers climbing a steep hill. Cresting the rise, Susan glanced up at the early morning sunlight shooting through gaps in the Wasatch Range. The paved loop road around Sugarhouse Park offered one of the best mountain views in Salt Lake.

Although the day was clear and promised heat, it was still relatively cool. Susan noticed, however, that Jen had started to sweat. She studied the beautiful musculature in Jen's tanned back and the tattoo of flames peeking out of her gray spandex top at the bra line. Jen was one of the most confident and powerful women Susan had ever met. Yet, it would be a stretch for Jen to reach the 5-foot-7 mark on her tiptoes. Her lustrous, brown, shoulder-length hair was tied back in a braid.

On the downhill now, and charged with endorphins, Susan pulled back up beside her friend. Jen turned her head and smiled. She had full sensual lips and green eyes like pools of forest light. Susan had long ago realized that she was attracted to approximately one out of every one hundred women. Jennifer Wise was one.

Susan and Jen first met in the weight room of Northern Arizona University when, as a student there, Susan discovered the pain and joy of lifting. They had immediately hit it off and agreed that being two of the few women at the college who pursued weight training they should team up to push each other and at the same time deflect unwanted male attention while working out. They eventually grew very close and their adventures included mountain hikes, mountain bikes, and even sharing a tent on one short all-women backpack in the San Francisco Peaks.

After graduating, it had been fairly easy to keep in touch and meet up occasionally for a therapeutic hike, ambling girl-chat, and requisite glass of wine at Rubio's Wine Bar—a quiet, rustic neighborhood place they had discovered near the college when they were students. On one such occasion—both women having confessed to recently going through a rough patch involving errant boyfriends—one glass of wine flowed into two, bottles that is, and later while waiting outside for separate taxis, Susan, nearly overwhelmed with affection, touched Jen's cheek, looked into her amazing eyes and somehow found the crazy courage to kiss her, as in *kiss*-kiss her, goodnight. Jen kissed back.

At lunch the next day, again at Rubio's because they had to pick up their cars, they were hung over, a little embarrassed, and giggly. Eventually they agreed that the kiss was a sweet surprise, even erotic, but still just didn't feel right. Their bond, if anything, was deepened by the brief experimentation.

Susan had joined the Phoenix PD soon after college and Jen worked at various jobs around the state. She did a semester at the National Outdoor Leadership School in Wyoming, became a wilderness first responder, and was later hired as an EMT in Jerome and ultimately a seasonal firefighter for Grand Canyon National Park. Susan had always admired Jen, but she was really impressed when she learned her friend had parlayed all her wilderness experience and medical training into becoming one of only a handful of female smokejumpers compared with close to five hundred male smokejumpers for the entire United States Forest Service.

When Jen had called her all excited from the Aerial Fire Depot in Missoula, Montana and said she had just qualified as a Zulie, that she had passed the rigorous four-week training, which included carrying a one-hundred-and-ten pound pack over three miles, and successfully finishing a timed obstacle course, not to mention the many practice jumps from planes hitting ever smaller targets, Jen's status in Susan's estimation jumped to something near heroic. Zulies parachute into remote and inaccessible wilderness areas threatened by fire. And, as Jen had explained, dropping in where trucks couldn't go was only the beginning. After jettisoning their chutes, smokejumpers hand dig miles-long firebreaks—building line as smokejumpers called it—and chainsaw hundreds of trees in the path of the fire.

Continuing down the hill, their shoes slapped the pavement simultaneously, their arms pumped in rhythm and their breathing formed a perfect cadence. Jens's right elbow was wrapped in neoprene and Susan noticed she was favoring it a bit. She had regained just enough breath to ask a question.

"What's up with the brace?"

"Pulaski's elbow. I've got tendonitis from the impact of slamming a Pulaski into roots and rocks. Puts me on the disabled list but, the good news is, it only hurts when I chop or chainsaw. Can still get my fix jumping recreationally."

"Fires getting worse?"

"Oh you bet." Jen turned her head away and spat on the grass. "More standing dead beetle kill trees among other factors means hotter and larger burns. Fires are way up."

"Climate change a factor?" Susan asked.

"For sure. Winters not cold enough to kill beetles. Summers are hotter and drier. Less humidity and moisture. Alaska is heating up at twice the rate of the rest of the country. Fires up there are starting one month earlier than before and this summer is likely to be one of the biggest fire seasons ever recorded."

"What are the general indicators?"

"Twice the acreage burned in the recent decade compared to the decade before. Twice! This summer may break all records for total acreage burned across the West. USFS is burning through money faster than trees are burning—two hundred million a week."

"What's that mean for you?" The two women had leveled out on the flat and ran past two teenage boys on the grass tossing a ball back and forth with their lacrosse sticks.

"Beginning of this season, we received an inter-agency study telling us to be prepared for catastrophic fires, especially in Arizona and California. So it means more work, more money, but much more danger. Couple days leave at home like this, even when on the DL, is increasingly rare." She glanced at Susan. "We both look damn good ... but neither of us is a college kid. Might be near time for Jen to retire from jumping fire."

"Where are the worst areas right now? Other than the two you mentioned."

"Nevada and New Mexico also. Utah is pretty bad too."

Susan made a mental note. She and Jake had investigated fires in two of those five states.

They had reached their three-mile mark and began a fast warm-down walk. A Senior Citizens van crept by in the car lane, several low round heads visible in profile. Susan and Jen crossed a bridge over a tree-covered stream that fed the park's lake.

"Jake and I have been hired to find the arsonists responsible for several fires in some of the states you just mentioned." Susan though it better to not mention the Apache connection or the bodies. "What are the odds they were started by government employees?"

"There have been such cases in the past, but that was usually during long stretches of idleness. There were times some of my action-starved alpha colleagues would pace around the ready room checking and rechecking chutes like caged tigers. I remember thinking if a fire doesn't start someone's going to start a fire. It does happen. I heard one such miscreant was even a firefighter for the Air Force. But to my knowledge in this new, hotter, drier normal, no one is complaining about lack of work."

"Can you think of anyone that might fit that profile?"

Jen stopped, put her hands on her hips and sucked in air. Susan hadn't noticed they were back at their vehicles. "There was this kinda weird guy—smokejumper." They walked over and stood by Susan's truck letting the sun warm their bodies and dry their sweat. "I got a strange vibe from him. He was very strong and always helpful, offered to carry the chainsaw and stuff. But he rarely smiled or joked around and something just wasn't right." Jen grabbed the top of the truck's bed wall and bent over to stretch her powerful thighs and back.

"Remember his name?" Susan asked. Jen pushed back up and picked up a foot for a quad stretch. Susan could barely keep her eyes off Jen's flexed thigh.

"Bill something, Indian sounding. Around the campfire after a good sixteen hour fight he would talk shit about how we should start burns ourselves and not only make good money but exact revenge on the government." Jen switched legs. Susan placed her hands on her hips and twisted back and forth at the waist.

"What was his issue with the government?"

"He was a member of some tribe. Didn't look very Indian but claimed that was his heritage. You know, hundreds of years of oppression, Wounded Knee, et cetera. Firefighters' pay sucked while politicians and lumber barons got rich. All pretty much true, mind you."

Two women strolled by deep in conversation. One pushed a jogger-stroller with a sleeping infant. The other walked a chocolate colored Newfoundland that, tongue dragging, looked like it just wanted to stretch out in the shade. Jen approached the dog, let him sniff her hand and rubbed his ears. The dog snaked its huge pink tongue out and covered her wrist. She looked longingly as the women passed and the dog shuffled off.

"What a cutie, huh?" Her eyes followed the Newfie. "Bill's pleasant demeanor hid a mean streak. He loved to bully rookies. One time a rook, a guy, accused Bill of getting his job through affirmative action and it took four of us to restrain Bill and prevent him from killing the kid. He was always trying to impress me and I thought his posturing was all beer infused macho anti-government bullshit but then—"

"What?"

"We jumped into a fire in northwestern Montana and after we worked our butts off racking up overtime for four days and were packing up to walk out to the trailhead—I will never forget the look on his face. He had this shit-eating grin. I remember it because his face was covered in soot and he was like, all teeth, and because I had never seen him smile before. He just leered at me and whispered 'Zulies 1, Uncle Sam 0. You owe me one, Jenny girl.'"

"Wow. Very strange comment."

"I remember thinking that it was crap. But later the fire was proven, although very remote, to be man-caused. And then I remembered he had taken a few days off just prior to the jump and nobody knew where he went—all admittedly circumstantial. The mind plays such tricks. They never caught the perpetrators. What really struck me. A thought I just couldn't shake. I knew if he was involved, he was the sort of needy man who could never keep it to himself. Couple seasons ago he didn't show up for spring training and fitness testing. I was relieved, really."

"Have any idea what tribe?"

"If he mentioned it, I don't remember. He was always trying to get me to do a sweat lodge with him. Pretty sure he had something other than purification in mind."

"Sexual healing, maybe. Sure you can't remember his last name?"

"No, but I might be able to get it from the files at the base in Missoula."

"I would really appreciate that, and an old address if there is one. You've got my cell number. Anything else you remember? What about his looks?"

"He wasn't bad looking. He had one eye, the left, with a sort of scar, v-shaped, in the lower lid."

"What about interests, hobbies…?"

"Oh, hunting and fishing for sure. Christ, that and *revolution* were all he talked about. He was constantly talking up bow hunting. He claimed his injury was from an arrowhead flint knapping accident. A shard flew up and struck him just below the eye. He talked like it was the only true way to hunt. If we saw any wildlife he would comment on whether it was a good distance for a shot with an arrow. He had this irritating habit— constantly taking aim with an imaginary bow and shooting imaginary arrows. Crap like that."

Talk of bows and arrows got Susan's total focus. Jen looked out across the park remembering.

"One of those really weird guys who never does anything overt but who just makes you uneasy. Know the type?"

"I do indeed, Jen. I would appreciate anything else you remember or can learn about this Bill guy. Anything would be appreciated. It sounds like he fits the passive-aggressive profile of the arsonist, too."

"Yeah, sneaky fucks," Jen said, turning back to Susan.

"Give me overt anytime," Susan said. "At least you can see 'em to smack 'em."

Jen untied her car key from her shoelace and unlocked the door of her white Jeep Cherokee; she reached in and grabbed a thin green jacket, slipped it on and dug into one of the side pockets to pull out her smart phone.

"Can I show you something cool on YouTube?"

She accessed the website, typed a quick title, skipped over an ad and thumbed the arrow for play. Susan shifted and shaded the phone with her hand. There was dramatic music accompanying the clip. The point of view was that of a skydiver shooting video from a helmet cam. The skydiver came over the roof of a house descended to the level of a back-yard pool on the edge of a slope, dropped in to skim the water with both shoes, before lifting just in time to clear the far end of the pool and patio and land in a field beyond. The clip ended.

"That's unreal."

"That's me," Jen said.

"No way. You skimmed across a pool and lived to tell about it?"

"I fell in love with jumping fires and then in the off-season started skydiving recreationally and then in competition. First I did accuracy."

"Landing on a dime?"

"No, actually landing on a quarter. Then I got into canopy piloting." She pointed at her phone. "It's also called swooping."

"I can see why. You look like a graceful bird swooping down and landing on water."

"There's a great airfield for practicing just a few hours east of Salt Lake. That works in the summer when I have a little free time here at home. In the winter I like to jump in Arizona. Got great pilots who have become friends in both locations. Earlier this spring near Flagstaff, I sustained seventy miles an hour for a few hundred horizontal yards and at times my feet actually skimmed the grass. It was a trip."

"That's awesome—what an accomplishment. And I didn't think you could possibly top being a Zuliegirl. I want my daughter to grow up as confident and fearless as her honorary Aunt Jennifer. Maybe without the flying, swooping, and burning trees part."

Jen grinned. "How is Amy?"

"Growing like a weed. Talking trash. When Jake's two boys visit she loves playing big sister-in-charge, even though she is only one year older than Matthew. She just had a great experience at a science camp in Wyoming. She's spending a couple nights at the home of a friend in Jackson, the girl she attended camp with. I'm due to shoot up there soon and get her."

Jen leaned against the side of her car. "Jake good?"

"Jake ... the best, Jen."

"Ah, family. Traded adventure for that. Might really regret it one day. Quickest way to get called to a fire jump is to make a dinner reservation with a date."

"Family has whole new meanings these days, girlfriend. I'm sure you will have a family of your own someday—maybe with a half dozen Newfies."

"Hmm. One big hairy guy and one big hairy dog would probably do the trick." She smiled. "Take care, Susan. Great to see you." She turned to her car.

"You be careful out there."

Jen turned back to face her friend. "This from the woman who leaps off tall buttes to rescue the girl and save the day. Nobody's shooting at me. Don't worry. We have a mantra before we jump. Man up! Mann Gulch! I take it as meaning; be brave but don't be stupid. You may know the Maclean book *Young Men and Fire*, about twelve smokejumpers died in the late forties in the Mann Gulch Fire in Montana. That book has been passed around our camps so much it's covered in sooty fingerprints and singed around the edges."

"How many firefighters total dead this season?"

"Thirteen ... so far. And yes, we're all counting. We allow development in drought-stricken, high fuel areas and then sacrifice blood and treasure protecting the structures. Vicious cycle in a warming climate."

"Just ... take care of yourself. The Newfies of the world need you."

The two women hugged, promised to talk soon and went their separate ways.

Trey took the morning off work to be with Jake. They had agreed to meet Susan for lunch at twelve-thirty at The Dodo restaurant just off 21st South. It was close to Jake and Susan's motel in the neighborhood called Sugarhouse, like the park.

When Susan arrived the two men were under an umbrella at a black metal table on a patio that was surrounded by a low brick wall.

Susan sat. A tall waiter wearing a black Dodo t-shirt came over with three waters. They all ordered iced tea and light lunches.

"Still full from that amazing dinner last night. Too hot to eat much." Susan fanned herself with her folded napkin. "So what have you two buds been up to?"

"Extreme mammals. The rare. The amazing. The spectacular. Special exhibit at the Natural History Museum up above the U," Trey said.

"Flesh scored discount tix through his work. We've got to bring the kids there. It's really kid-friendly. Very educational." Jake gipped his ice water glass with both hands then touched them to the back of his neck to cool it. "How was Jen? Good run?"

"She's good—buff and gorgeous as always. Barely kept up. It was great to see her and I got some interesting information." She glanced at Trey. "Maybe later."

"Did she say anything about firefighters starting fires?" Trey asked.

Susan stared at Jake.

"I have a confession. The Museum was incredible, especially the geology and anthropology, and we even got a short walk in the lovely shaded Red Butte Gardens right next door to it, but after we exhausted the subjects of rocks, airstreams and extreme mammals ole' Flesh here just kept picking my brains about our case like a damned carrion eating bird."

Trey smiled and pushed his glasses up at the nose bridge. "It's what I do all day. Pick at bones. Professional bone picker."

"So he's ... pretty much up to speed," Jake said apologetically.

"And extremely interested," Trey leaned in and whispered. "Arrows through jewelry on burned bodies with cancer. Damn! Now that's extreme."

Susan sat back in her chair and stared with cold eyes at passing traffic. The waiter brought their salads and drinks.

Trey scratched at the stubble on his cheek. "This is awkward I know, but you had already sort of deputized me with the xiphoid process path workup."

"Nothing personal, Flesh. Susan just worries about involving friends."

Susan sighed and concentrated on dressing her salad. "I really appreciated your help with that, Trey. And your insights last night about cancer center personnel and protocols. You've already saved us weeks of work. Jake's right, it's nothing personal. I was really looking forward to meeting you and I'm glad I did, so...."

"Susan also comes out of the Police Department tradition in which you don't discuss work with anyone. Might explain the high alcoholism and divorce rate," Jake said.

Susan stopped her fork in midair and said, "Might also explain the domestic abuse. Let's change the subject before I get arrested for assault with a deadly eating utensil."

Jake grinned, tilted his head and peered at her from under the bill of his ball cap. Susan glared at him and shoved her hair behind her ears.

"That's fine. I totally get it and the last thing I want is to interfere or cause a spat. But just so you know, I got vacation coming and no plans or obligations. Not since my last rat died that is—unless you count my cacti and they're pretty low maintenance. So I'm totally available and anxious to help."

"Have scalpel. Will travel?" Jake's joke fell flat with Susan. Trey chuckled, quietly.

His offer to help had been so earnest it was all Susan could do to not jump up and hug him. Maybe at the same time she could smack Jake.

And that admiration only grew when Trey, obviously not that experienced in relationships, intuited that it might be a good time to change the subject. She saw him glance at Jake's Pittsburgh Pirates cap.

"How 'bout those Pittsburgh Pirates? Coming on strong mid-season."

Jake brightened. "Bats have warmed up. Pitching is peaking. Manager is finally…" He scratched the back of his head. "You told me once you hated baseball."

Trey unfurled his innocent look. "I did? Yeah, I guess I did. Too slow." Trey yucked, causing Susan to giggle and Jake to laugh out loud.

Susan said, "I've heard of dog people and cat people and I've even known a few edgy bird and snake people, but getting to know you, Flesh, I'm learning to admire a whole new category. People who prefer the company of rats and cacti."

"That's me. And I'm a trendsetter. Watch for a run on rats." He nodded authoritatively, picked up his fork and stabbed a generous portion of greens. "Got Wi-Fi at your motel room?"

"It's a suite and it's got it all." Jake being sarcastic.

"Sweet. I've got an idea that involves a little online time to learn all we can about your cancer center of interest. That's what they say on the cop shows, right—person of interest?" He waggled his eyebrows. "I've got my laptop in the car. Let's go there right after lunch before my nap."

From that point on, it was a full-on assault on their salads.

Their room, posing as a suite, was really little more than the typical motel room decorated typically. But just past the closet with cheap metal shelves, queen bed and low dresser with flat screen was a kitchenette with a stove, full fridge, sink and L-shaped counter covered in vinyl. That gave Trey a place to set up his laptop and connect to the Internet. With Susan sitting beside him on a stool and Jake watching over his shoulder, Trey Googled Lifebridge Cancer Treatment Center, Phoenix Arizona.

The website was attractive if a bit typical and bland—a desperate attempt to make treating cancer seem appealing.

"Let's see now," Flesh flipped through the site. "Pic of the building circa mid-80s-institutional, still shot of middle-aged couple hugging—hopefully not hugging goodbye forever, oh, here's a nice touch." He looked at Susan. "A still shot of a rainbow hitting desert terrain complete with saguaro. One of my favorite cacti in one of your favorite environments."

"So Jake has told you about my love of the great wasteland." Susan took over as tour guide. "Open Monday through Saturday, 9 to 5. Guess people don't have cancer on Sunday. Link to request an appointment, link to pay your bill. That's seems kind of premature, I haven't even made an appointment yet. Support groups, classes, special programs, stuff about insurance, better hope you got that. Bless you Barack. Oh, of course, Find Us On Facebook. Like I'm going to *friend* my cancer treatment center." She turned and shot Jake an incredulous look. "And check this out. They got five of the top docs for 2015 in one magazine and were voted one of the top ten out of all the Arizona Cancer Treatment Centers in another. That means they could be number ten out of what, twenty? How many cancer treatment centers can there be in Arizona? Oh and here's my personal favorite, one huge shit-brown button labeled Become A Patient. All benign but scary as hell."

"Everyone hates cancer treatment centers until they need one," Jake said. They heard the yap of a small dog passing on the terrace outside their room.

"Okay, now let's go to Google Earth. I bet I can even teach you two Pi-dogs a new trick with Google Earth. Trey jotted down the address for Lifebridge, brought up the Google Earth globe, typed in the address and hit search. The world began to turn, the view zoomed and blurred and then resolved itself into what appeared to be a mall-like setting with a narrow golf course running behind it. There were pins for Ironwood Mall, Lifebridge, a nearby condominium complex and several businesses and hotels.

"Now here comes the fancy finger work. Almost as fun as playing video games."

Trey switched the angle to street view and suddenly they were panning across a parking lot in the center of Ironwood Mall and over to the cancer center which they recognized from the website photo. Then Trey panned past a chain grocery store with a pharmacy, a Paradise Juice, and a Staples store.

"Whoa, stop there."

Flesh stopped and after a few seconds the image revealed a brightly dressed middle-aged couple walking hand-in-hand toward their car.

"Can you back it up?"

"No prob."

"Yes. I knew it." Jake pointed to the monitor. "There it is—the ubiquitous Starbucks right across from Lifebridge. Susan, sweetie, you can set up your binos right beside your iced latte and spy all day in air conditioned comfort."

"Flesh I love this view. This is so cool. Too bad it's not real time. We could stakeout Lifebridge from the comfort of our home," Susan said.

"These images are from 2011, so...."

"You'd make a good 007 spy." Susan hugged him from the side. "You can be our Q. That's short for Q'ute." Flesh's face flared.

"I feel more like I'm going into this with my eyes open now. I've used Google Earth a lot but, you were right, I wasn't familiar with the street view option. Thanks, man," Jake said.

"For your eyes only, brother. Glad to help. If you get down there and decide you just have to leave the comfort of your coffee shop and go inside, call me first. I've got some ideas of how you could execute a fake pick-up for pathology samples."

"Will do, Q," Jake said.

Susan added, "Plus, it's pretty easy to be incognito in libraries, hotels and hospitals. Staff are usually focused on their jobs and accustomed to unfamiliar faces coming and going in the background. I've always wondered how long you could sit in a patient waiting area drinking coffee and catching up on germ-infested magazines before someone actually noticed you and asked if you needed help. Might make an interesting study."

"Yeah, particularly if, when finally asked, you smiled, said no thanks I'm just waiting, and sat there for another five or six hours with no apparent purpose," Jake said. The little dog yapped back in the opposite direction. "Course the only problem with that scenario as far as trying to make an ID is the small percentage of employees who ever go near the reception area."

"I would be cautious about any of this," Trey said. "And very well-rehearsed if you try the path pick-up ruse. Everyone is on edge these days post 9/11. I'm sure even more so in Phoenix since those two homegrown, self-radicalized, jihadists were gunned down in Texas while trying to massacre people because of their taste in cartoons."

"Yeah, I saw that on the news. Good advice, man. I get it. Try not to look suspicious or like we are casing the center for any reason. Use the pathology ruse judiciously."

"And only if absolutely necessary," Trey said.

"Right. We'll save it like a get-out-of-jail-free card," Jake added.

"That I cannot provide." Trey shut down his computer and started to pack it away in its case.

"You've already provided so much, Trey. Really, really grateful and so very glad to meet you."

"Same, Susan. And remember my offer. I appreciate your concern for my safety but I can take care of myself. I speak the same language as those folks at the cancer center."

"Yeah, that's right. Flesh can take care of himself. Show her your NRA card, Flesh."

He rummaged around in his beat-up black Victorinox backpack. "Don't think I have that, but let's see, just so you know what a good influence you are on me, Jake. Now where is it? Maybe this outside ... here we go." He beamed and held up a card with large letters printed on it. "Official member of Utah NPR."

"I'm stunned," Jake said.

"Got the complimentary mug and five CD set."

"An intellectual to boot. Well, I declare you could turn a girl's head." Susan hugged him and added, "You've got to come visit us in Boulder. It's a hotbed of closet NPR listeners."

"You'll fit right in, buddy."

Trey shook Jake's hand, suffered through an awkward bro hug and slap on the back, and departed.

July 24
Thursday

Jake and Susan did what people do in the Intermountain West due to the paucity of public transportation, yet another marathon car trip. They left early (*The butt-crack of dawn*, Jake cracked as they pulled out) in Jake's Subaru, and drove the five hours from Salt Lake to Jackson. They picked up Amy and her gear and then headed straight south to Boulder, bypassing Salt Lake and going down Provo Canyon. It was a total of thirteen hours on the road but they arrived home safely just before dark.

The time in the car on the way up to Jackson provided a chance to plot next moves in Phoenix, catch Jake up on Susan's conversation with Smokejumper Jen, and touch base with Gloria by cell. They discussed it and decided to say nothing to their employer about Jen's strange colleague who she suspected of setting forest fires until they knew more about him.

An hour south of Jackson Hole, heading north through Star Valley, Jake called Gloria. When he concluded his call, Susan, who was driving at that point, spoke. "So I got distracted by those jerks in the red sports car trying to pass me back there. I only caught some of your conversation with the Chief. Didn't sound good. What's up?"

"As I suspected would happen, she's starting to question our meager progress."

"Yeah, well, given her resistance to any suggestion of Apache perpetrators and her fear of any Fed involvement, I sometimes wonder if she isn't afraid of the fallout if the case is solved."

"I guess that would depend on what the solution is. She does seem to protest a little too much."

"Maybe her worst nightmare is that someone proves that her tribesmen are involved in this felonious activity on her watch. Could make getting reelected difficult," Susan said.

"And make reporting the Apache suspects to the FBI mandatory," Jake added. "Said she finally received forensic results from the sheriff on Andrew Millar's burned body but didn't learn anything new: terminal cancer, dead before being placed in the fire, arrow through silver jewelry and thorax postmortem but also pre-fire."

"God this is frustrating. Gloria's impatient for results? I'm impatient for results! Ever occur to you that Gloria hired us because she sees *us* as bunglers?"

"Hoot-hoo," Jake chortled at his rather feeble impersonation of a bungling owl. As usual his lame humor caused Susan to smile, shake her head and relax. She steered around a curve and through a small roadside wetland with blackbirds clinging to every cattail.

They had come up with a plan for covering Amy during their time in Phoenix. It was Jake's idea but Susan made the phone call. Their landlady, Sara, was a jewel. She had been wonderful to them from the start. She obviously loved her place in Boulder although her work as a beloved elementary teacher in Salt Lake kept her preoccupied most months of the year.

Sara was single, childless and in her early sixties. She looked like a woman who would be right at home on a farm—sturdy, bosomy, German stock with a ruddy round face and a shock of short-cropped white hair. Sara was a warm, handsome woman and kids gravitated to her. She often spoke of retirement and living full time in Boulder but it kept getting pushed forward. Jake and Susan sometimes speculated that was in part because she didn't have the heart to kick them out. She had sought, and said she believed she had found in the Goddard/Brand crew, people who cared for her place as much as she did.

In time, she had become a good friend and, being a kid-person, had connected with Amy.

Sara had mentioned on several occasions that if Jake and Susan were ever called away for work, especially in the summer, she would love to come and stay with Amy. It was the perfect solution and somewhat eased Susan's guilt from the anticipation of leaving her daughter so soon after getting home from camp. But then, her little girl was no longer so little, she had a job after all, and Sara would make a great companion for walks and talks in the evenings. Sara was thrilled and said she could be there by Sunday morning.

On the way home, near Evanston, Wyoming, after Amy had relayed all her camp adventures and hilarious mishaps and had finally talked herself out, Susan informed her of the Sara plan. Amy shrugged a sort of *whatever*. But in the vernacular of pre-teen affected indifference, Susan took the lack of a vehement negative as a strong positive.

Their risk analysis as far as the Bad News Bunglers having come so close to their home came down to this: if the BNBs had wanted to seriously hurt Susan instead of just scare her, they could have. They decided to give neighbors, Mike and Cindy and little old landlady, Sara—it was Sara who had first referred to herself as their little old landlady from Salt Lake City—a vague warning to be on the alert for strange men, possibly in a blue pickup truck.

That night they were all tired but relieved to be back in Boulder. The two adults tucked Amy in bed, each hugging her and telling her they loved her. Too exhausted to even drink a glass of wine, they turned in themselves, happy to be in their own bed. Jake reached up and switched off the light.

A glorious summer night enveloped the little mountain-desert hamlet of Boulder. A few neighbors' porch lights and the stars above were all that were visible from their open bedroom window. Jake reflected on what they had discussed during the drive. Most importantly, Amy was going to be well cared for. Also, they had plotted out next steps. It was all settled—all planned. They had worked out the details with the usual excellent teamwork. A few much-needed days at home and then Goddard Consulting Group would be off to Phoenix for the second time in three weeks. Susan was completely still lying on her back. Jake thought she was asleep until she turned away onto her side. He rolled toward her and rested his hand on her arm. "Night, sweetheart."

"Fucking Phoenix," Susan muttered.

A breeze stirred the bamboo wind chime on the deck outside their bedroom. Coyotes barked and yipped in a distant field.

July 27
Sunday

The two investigators had stripped off their light outer layers and sat beside the pool in chaise lounges in the shade of a canvas awning. They were in the rear courtyard of the two-story Ironwood Marriott, which they had discovered online was a short distance from the Lifebridge Center. There was not much tourist action in Phoenix in the dead of summer but the off-season prices were very reasonable and that had lured them into choosing Marriott—a bit more upscale than their usual.

Susan declared on the way down that if she was going back to Phoenix in July she intended to maximize her time inside with AC, or outside poolside. She had dragged Jake down to the pool minutes after they returned from a spicy dinner at the neighborhood Thai joint.

Susan was wearing her yellow Roxy tankini. Jake had purchased a baggy dark green Patagonia swimsuit for the trip. He had agreed to join her at the pool if they could discuss a little business. An email from Trey had arrived while they were taking care of final details for the trip and settling Amy in with Sara, and he had not had a chance to do much more than print it and throw it in his backpack.

Jake and Susan had the pool to themselves. They wore sandals because the white concrete patio was still blazing. Within minutes sweat glistened on their bodies. Jake read in low tones in case they could be overheard from the rooms above.

> *Dear Pi-man and Pi-woman,*
>
> *If I can't join you in the field, I would be honored to be your "Q" at HQ. That is as long as the puns end with "Q'ute" and thanks again for that, Susie Q. (I know how Jake likes to play with words, often leaving them tattered and bloody like a mouse after "playing" with a cat.)*
>
> *I can't make exploding martini olives or equip your Subaru with special hidden gun ports (wish I could) but I've been considering what you're hoping to accomplish in Phoenix and I predict that "going in" is inevitable.*
>
> *Here's what I've come up with:*
>
> *Option #1: Lifebridge Cancer Treatment Center performs biopsies. All cancer treatment centers do. Lifebridge uses an outside lab (similar to my lab, CRUP) for all of their anatomic pathology testing. That laboratory, wherever it is, requires a daily courier service to pick up specimens at Lifebridge. Lucky for you, courier services generally don't pay much so they have high turnover. I'm pretty certain Lifebridge doesn't have much of an opportunity to get to know the couriers—they are probably used to new faces from the courier service coming and going. In fact, I can pretty much guarantee they hardly pay attention anymore when someone new walks in and says they are there to pick up the pathology specimens. So here's what I propose, after determining who the courier is and what sort of vehicles they drive, you go in impersonating the usual service. Obviously, you do this an hour or so before the regular couriers typically arrive. Jake tells anyone who asks that he is training Susan to cover the route so you are both granted access. You also say that, as the supervisor, you have actually never set foot in Lifebridge before. Or that it has*

been years since you have. This will provide a cover for the inevitable cluelessness you will feel and no doubt demonstrate when you enter. The good part about the cover that your ignorance (both unfamiliar with the layout) provides is that you can snoop around a bit and open a few doors using being new and clueless as a reason for not knowing how to go directly to the pick-up point. If anyone accosts you simply act as if the whole thing was a miscommunication and mix-up. "I'll check back after I call my dispatcher," etc. Brilliant.

Option #2: There's big money in cancer. Vendors want to do business with Lifebridge. They will often set up a noon meeting and provide lunch for staff. Often times, companies like Lifebridge may not even check out the vendor beforehand, having been blinded by the free lunch offer. I could see you two concocting a fake business scheme. One does the sales pitch and distracts a large portion of the staff for an hour with Subway sandwiches while the other roams around in the facility virtually unobstructed. This not only gets you a chance to look closely at most personnel (stuffing their faces), it gets you access to the building. Genius.

Option #3: Lifebridge contracts with a janitorial service. These people almost always come in after hours and have the place to themselves. You two, as janitors, would have unlimited access to offices, paperwork and maybe even computers, if you set everything up properly. Christ, after we leave CRUP for the night we get all kinds of unsavory characters in our office. We've never had anything stolen, but it would be easy to do so. Our janitorial company is supposed to control night access, but you know how that goes. I've seen friends, boyfriends, girlfriends, spouses and children of our cleaning crew in our offices. Yes, they could get fired, but normally who is there to catch them and turn them in? Cleaning folks don't make much money. I'm sure you could join the crew and gain access by tossing out a few

Benjamins. What the hell, it would probably double their pay for the week. Although day staff would obviously not be around, these places all have their warm and fuzzy displays with photos of personnel on the wall somewhere. You could look for your suspect(s) there. Like it.

I could probably come up with more options but right now I have to listen to "All Things Considered" on NPR.

Your man at HQ

"Can you believe this guy?" Jake asked.

"Love him more every day."

"All right then, let's get busy considering his suggestions."

"Yes, of course, right away. But first, I just have to make one little adjustment."

Susan got up, stretched her arms high, slipped off her sandals, hopped a few quick steps to avoid burning her soles and slid into the water. She came up to the surface, pulled her wet hair out of her face, and motioned for Jake to join her. "Now this is the way to consider options while in Phoenix."

Jake shook his head and chuckled, pushed off his chaise lounge and sat beside her on the wet edge of the pool with his sandaled feet in the water.

"As you know, unless I'm really, really hot I'm more of a beside-the-pool guy than an in-the-pool guy. Even though I am a fully trained technician. Oh look, there's an area over there that could use a little more vacuuming."

"You are such an expert when it comes to pools." Susan slid her cool wet hand up the inside leg of his bathing suit. "Perhaps you should see what could be done with your hose."

"Not fair. This is a business meeting. We're considering options here *in view of the whole motel.*"

"What, the three other people who are staying here?" Susan squeezed his upper thigh. "Maybe I'll consider my options later in our room."

She placed her other wet hand on his chest. "Screwing your business associate is highly underrated. It has its advantages. Saves time, travel and room expense."

"Can we concentrate, please?" Susan slowly dragged her nails down his thigh to his knee. "Thank you. Now, Q option #1."

"Just a preliminary thought. Assuming we decide to ignore the risk of being recognized and go in. I would go with #1 first because odds are our guy is in the main group of Lifebridge personnel who work there during the day. If that doesn't produce a hit, I suggest we go second with Q's third option because we are then also covering the smaller subset of folks who work there only at night."

"Wow, you actually were paying attention."

"Jumping in the pool helped. Otherwise, somewhere north of ninety-five degrees my brain shuts down faster than a maxed-out credit card."

They sat that way conferring quietly, Susan soaking in the water, until the sun dropped behind the building and the pool was in shade.

July 29
Tuesday

Oh, the crushing tedium of surveillance. It was only the second day of staking out Lifebridge Cancer Treatment Center and Susan was going out of her gourd. She and Jake had decided that, even in a coffee chain known for slackers, loungers, Internet surfers and the occasional homeless person seeking refuge, it would be too obvious to lurk more than four hours a day. Although they read online that office hours at Lifebridge began at 9, they realized their male suspect of color in his mid-twenties to early thirties could be a janitor, or he could be a doctor, or he might be anything in between. Jake knew that personnel at cancer treatment centers come and go at all hours. He had learned that while accompanying his father to a similar center in Pennsylvania. He didn't feel showing up at or just before 9 a.m. would necessarily increase their odds. They settled on the busy lunch hours, 10 in the morning until 2 in the afternoon.

The PIs observed dozens of patients, as if facing execution, shuffling hesitantly into the brick and glass utilitarian building. They quickly became familiar with the Lifebridge uniform—dark blue top over white pants—as they watched staff exit the center and cross the parking lot to the shop for pastries, sandwiches and coffees to go. And the employees rarely remembered to remove their nametags, which momentarily excited Susan. There was hope of nailing a twofer—bagging a face *and* a name. She was initially optimistic she would get a positive make on the mug that had leered at her from the bed of the blue pickup after putting a pink stripe across her ass.

But two days of recon in, after dozens of cancer center employees had streamed in and out of Starbucks and an equal number were scrutinized in the parking lot coming and going from the staff entrance of Lifebridge—and even after eliminating the women, the males with pale skin, and the older dark-skinned males—they were left with at least a dozen possibles and so far none that she had seen either close-up or from a distance had so much as nudged her memory.

It had been unproductive and frustrating and Susan had never done either well. She was not a patient person. Hours of sitting while under-exercised and over-caffeinated did not help. She had called and texted Amy so often that the last two emphatic text responses had been, "*Hey, I'm trying to work here.*" And then simply and decisively, "*MOM!!! CHILL!!!*"

Susan normally would have at least jumped up and done a few laps around the parking lot but she was the one who had been closest to the perpetrators and she didn't want to miss making a positive ID. Plus it was too damn hot to consider going out for even a brief break. Somewhat exacerbated by being confined in it, she found the shop depressing. It was corporate clone Starbucks and she was already sick of the cloying skunk-like coffee aroma and the boring barista banter.

Jake, on the other hand, was in his element. He was *totally* chill. He had even established a warm rapport with a cute counter chick sporting a short black bob with bangs and low-cut white blouse under her green apron. The young woman's scooped neckline, among other things, revealed a line of small black letters riding the swell of her perfectly tanned and apparently perky left breast. Susan wondered how many more congenial trips to the counter it would take before Jake could accurately report what that tat for tit said.

Jake swung over with his latest coffee and she could tell he sensed her discomfort. He was always good at reading her. Plus, unlike him, she sucked at poker. He sat across the table at his opened laptop with his back to the window, concern dripping off his face. "Got an email a few minutes ago from Rachel saying Timothy got in a fight at Bible Camp."

"Uh-oh. Not good. Over what?"

"Had something to do with not being Mormon."

"Good reason to fight."

"Apparently he was crying at home during the retelling of the brawl and she tried to cheer him up by changing the subject and asking what he learned at camp. He, of course, answered, 'Nothing.' Rachel pushed and inquired if they had talked about God or Jesus. Timothy thought about it and said, 'It didn't come up.'"

"Oh that's hilarious."

"Yeah. I think Bible Camp admin should be expecting a sermon from my ex."

"Go get 'em, Rach. Take no prisoners. Only converts."

"You doing okay?"

"You know the expression watching paint dry? As a kid, living in the desert isolated on the reservation, we grew up watching water evaporate for entertainment. This is even more boring." Susan sighed and tapped some papers on the table. "I've read this magazine backwards and forwards. Think anyone would notice if I read it upside down?"

"Try reading it while standing on your head."

"Now that just might attract unwanted attention." She lowered her voice. "Isn't the secret to a successful stakeout maintaining an element of incognito?"

"Haven't you noticed how men look at you? Flying under the radar you ain't."

"Must be thinking, look at that fat woman sucking down those high-fat drinks."

Jake wasn't sure where to even begin to respond to a statement like that.

Susan saw a man crossing the parking lot. There was something about his face. "Don't turn around. Large man of color approaching the door to the shop."

"Suggest you get in line behind him. Don't let him see your fat face."

Susan froze. If looks were lasers, Jake's face would be in flames.

The man dressed in the Lifebridge uniform was about 5'10", stocky and powerfully built. He walked with confidence, a big smile on his comely face. He entered the shop, closed the door and got in the queue behind three female customers. Susan flipped Jake both middle fingers from just below the table edge, slid off her chair, crossed the shop and lined up behind the man. She noticed he didn't even look at the signs advertising food and drink options. At one point he rocked back, almost stepping on her foot.

Susan turned and saw that Jake was watching her over the copy of The Week magazine she had left on the table. It had a generic cartoon of the Grim Reaper on the cover. She shrugged at Jake, uncertain this was their guy, and pivoted back around, immediately noticing sweat at the neckline of the man's uniform. His black hair appeared to be shaved at the neck. Not the braid she had observed on the arrow wielding asshole in the truck, but anyone can change his appearance. She inched forward as he approached the counter and ordered.

He paid, dropped change in the tip jar, and abruptly turned. His eyes bore straight into Susan's. She jolted back. He smiled, excused himself in the lilting modulation of the native born Indian, and slid past. She noticed his nametag. Susan pretended she had forgotten her money, which in fact in her haste to get in line she had, and returned to their table. The man picked up his iced tea from a side counter, clicked on a top, poked in a straw and left to cross the parking lot.

"Well?" Jake asked.

"He's Indian alright, but not our guy."

"How can you be so sure, particularly if he's an Indian?"

"I said he's Indian not an Indian. To quote Gloria, sheet not blanket. Vejoy Singh, I believe his nametag read—damn good looking, and a smile and voice that could make a nun hot under the habit. But not our guy."

"Since your Oscar winning performance in line, I've noticed the baristas looking our way and talking among themselves. Might be time to pack it up. I'm thinking we give this one more day and during that time seriously consider Q's proposals for going over the wall."

"Yesssss. I need a run on a treadmill with a blasting fan in an air-conditioned fitness room and a dip in a cool pool."

"I just need a shower and a sweaty, cold bottle of beer in front of a ball game. Let's call it a day."

Exaggerated for effect, Susan sniffed the coffee shop air. "Call it another day of getting skunked."

The somewhat desultory principals of Goddard Consulting Group packed up their gear and departed.

July 30
Wednesday

The investigators were back on Starbucks' surveillance, but only sort of. Yes, Susan and Jake were once again stationed at the table by the door of the shop with an unobstructed view across the parking lot to the entrance of Lifebridge, but their overriding purpose on this third day was to work out how they were going to put Q option #1 into play and morph into a plausible courier service.

Susan was excited to have a plan to plan. Any promise of a reprieve from the passivity of observing was exciting news to her. She casually watched the parade in and out of the cancer center while Jake chatted with the barista and purchased their drinks. A large woman carrying a huge shoulder bag, and with long brown curls sprouting out from under a battered tan golf hat entered. She was a regular that Susan was now accustomed to seeing. She greeted everyone in the shop and settled groaning into a deep leather chair in the corner without ordering.

Jake returned to the table with two iced coffees and sat across from Susan at his already booted up computer, "'All mimsy were the borogoves.'" He tapped at his keyboard.

"Excuse me," Susan said.

He read from his monitor. "From Jabberwocky. It's the third line from Lewis Carroll's Jabberwocky—a poem in his novel *Through the Looking Glass*." He glanced up at Susan, "'All mimsy were the borogoves,' that's what Karen has tattooed on her chest."

"But that makes no sense."

"You're right, it doesn't; that was pretty much the idea. He was writing a nonsensical poem."

"No, I mean a young woman permanently tattooing a line from a nonsense poem on her chest makes no sense." A FedEx driver wearing blue shorts and pulling a dolly full of packages backed through the door. He went behind the counter to drop his packages and get a signature.

"If you were a member of her generation—the generation of environmental degradation, religious wars, a disappearing middle class, limited job prospects, wall street fat cats getting fatter—"

"Okay, okay, I get it," Susan said. A coffee grinder whirred from behind the counter.

"I'm just saying nonsense might make the most sense. Explains why it took me three days to figure out what it says. Plus, the last half of borogoves was always hidden by her blouse."

"So did she give you a little peek at her goves?"

"Well, yeah sort of, it was driving me crazy, the tat that is, so I asked her and she explained it and revealed the rest of the line. Cute lacy black bra strap to boot."

"All right, you old perv, let's buckle down here."

"Tally-ho, Alice."

"As I see it, we need to photograph the courier van sometime soon. Considering that we have not seen a single such vehicle in three days park at the front, we can assume they do pick-ups at the back. We also need to photograph the uniforms of the courier service."

"And at the same time, we can get a sense of their schedule. Might be good to have an official looking pad like that FedEx guy for signatures."

"Right," Susan said. "Then once we have done all that and matched the vehicle, presumably with a magnetic sign on a similar looking rental, and somehow produced shirts with the logo—"

"We step through the looking glass."

"Brilliant."

"You mean, 'brillig,' don't you?" He glanced down at his monitor. "'Twas brillig, and the slithy toves.'"

"Oh you smarty-pants, you. You and Google sure know how to impress a girl." She held his gaze for a beat. "A woman, not so much."

Jake flashed her a Cheshire cat grin and closed his laptop. "Let's run this by Flesh in case we've overlooked something important, or he has thought of anything else."

"Sounds like a plan," Susan said, relieved. "I'll take it." She eased back in her chair.

There was surveillance with no follow-up plan and then there was surveillance with a follow-up plan. Susan found the latter much more to her liking. She settled in for the remainder of the shift.

July 31
Thursday

Jake was most decidedly taking a hot one for the team. He had agreed to do the courier stakeout behind the Lifebridge building. After burning his thighs on the driver's seat when he slid into his Subaru outside the motel, he had driven, air blasting, the few minutes to the mall. A quick preliminary drive-through behind Lifebridge revealed the expected dumpsters, loading docks, and freight and service entrances. It was all concrete pads, ramps and large metal doors. It was still early and the docks were empty. He noted one gray standard-size metal door with a shiny brass doorknob and a sign above that read, "Ring Bell to Enter." To his left, he saw two white golf carts driving up the obviously heavily irrigated, extremely green—given the climate—fairway of the contiguous golf course.

If accosted, he was planning to be all, "Oh, snap, I made a wrong turn into here. My damn GPS told me this was the way to the golf course."

There was no one behind Lifebridge; still he didn't want to be too obvious. He stopped briefly, took a quick iPhone panorama shot and then drove on around the side of the building through an alley bordering Paradise Juice.

He sat in the mall parking lot, windows down, sweltering. He took off his ball cap and wiped the sweat on his brow back through his hair. The air in the car was stifling. You could fry a tortilla on the dashboard but he was too principled, or stubborn, to sit and idle with the air on.

He envied Susan who he guessed was up to her nose in the hotel pool by now. Over breakfast she had coyly demurred to Jake's proposal for the day, saying he owed her one but without elaborating. He pretty much had to agree that he did. In fact, truth be told, he owed her many.

He placed his ball cap on the passenger seat thinking that might cool his head a little. What we got, he asked himself, staring at the front of Lifebridge—a concrete delivery and pick-up area backing up to, and fenced off from, the fairway of a golf course. The drive is one-way but at least it's continuous, which cuts down on the chances of getting trapped back there. There are surveillance cameras, but he knew very well, having cameras and actually keeping security tapes that were of any help in an investigation were two very different things. Still the wise course would be to not be caught out of his car in-frame on either camera prior to showing up in full courier costume.

Then there was the dilemma of the door. Ringing a bell for entrance meant getting face-to-face at least over closed circuit TV with someone who allowed couriers and other service people in daily. They could also deny entrance to a strange face. That he had to give some serious thought to.

He unlocked his iPhone and studied the panorama shot. He was about to put the phone down when something at the edge of the digital photo caught his eye. At the back of Paradise Juice he saw the corner of a small wooden deck surrounded by a railing. He pinched the shot out and saw part of a table with a collapsed red umbrella. The deck must be for customers to enjoy the green space of the golf course, no doubt in cooler seasons, but it would also offer a view of the docking area behind Lifebridge.

The large woman regular from the coffee shop resolutely puffed by his car window and approached the entrance to the cancer center. Jake wondered if the hair under the golf hat was a wig. It struck him that all the shops around Lifebridge were extended waiting rooms—the anterooms of hope and despair. He thought of his father's terminal battle with renal cancer and how he was as equally ravaged and discouraged by the treatments on offer as he was by the disease.

Best not to go there. Got a job to do. Looks like my drink of choice just went from coffee to juice, Jake thought as he tugged on his hat, packed his gear in his daypack that served as a briefcase, including his camera with various lenses, and prepared to begin a vigil on the back deck of Paradise.

By the time he hit the door of the juice store and felt the blast of cold air he had figured out his play. He was a photographer hired to film golf courses around the country for Golf Magazine. That was what he would tell the cute Hispanic juice-ista if she needed a reason to let him go out on the deck when the shop was empty and cool, with his—he studied a blackboard advertising specials—with his icy Mango Madness. Hell, the job had to have some cold refreshing perks on an asphalt bubbling day. Only mad dogs and PIs go out in the Phoenix sun. He approached the counter contemplating deranged dogs and private investigators and all the other insane shit they had in common.

Jake hadn't let Susan totally off the hook. They agreed that if he braved the heat of the day hunting the right shots, she would go out in the relative cool of evening and gather the required material to impersonate the courier service. Jake had returned just after 5:30, changed and prepared to head straight for the pool anticipating total emersion, including the bottle of cold beer he had dug out of the mini-fridge and immediately swiped across his forehead. Susan was cooling her heels, literally, her heels and all the terrain south of her waist; she was sitting reading in the nude, in the office chair with her feet propped up on the vibrating, under-the-window air conditioner. Jake quickly informed her that he had photographed a lot of very hot, very bad golfers as well as two pick-ups by Danon Laboratory Systems of America and then he headed out.

While he was at the pool, Susan pulled on some underwear, shorts and a sports bra, picked up his camera and moved to the overstuffed chair in the corner. She scrolled through his shots. The pictures showed a small white panel van with DLSA on the sides and a bespectacled courier who looked to be youngish, scraggly and skinny. He had a hooked nose that reminded her of Wile E. Coyote. Same guy, same van, arrived twice according to the time stamp of the photos, once at 10:26 and again at 4:33.

In the sequence of shots from the morning, Wile E. was buzzed into Lifebridge empty-handed except for a clipboard, and twenty minutes later came out with official looking containers balanced in his arms. In the case of the afternoon run, he came out after eighteen minutes carrying the clipboard, a few official looking boxes and a small ice chest cooler.

He was wearing nondescript khaki shorts. That's easy. His shirt was brown with dim vanilla stripes. Jake had caught a nice close-up of the breast pocket logo. It had block forest green letters in a light tan oval. Simple. The shirts could be found at any uniform store. The patches could be made up at any trophy store that also did embroidering, the sign a one-hour job at any self-respecting sign store. Thank God for lack of imagination, Susan thought. She was glad Jake had had the foresight to buy a printer in Boise. They were going to need it.

She glanced up at the faces of the three victims on the poster board schematic they had transported from Oregon and taped up on their motel room wall. She prayed, in her way, that this would lead to the breakthrough they sought and the justice those three innocent victims deserved.

Jake returned in a little over an hour looking far less frazzled. Susan, dressed now to go out to dinner in the cotton sundress she had purchased in Oregon, had been watching Jeopardy to pass the time. She clicked off the flat screen.

Jake threw his wet towel on the floor of the bathroom and grabbed a dry one off the rack to spread on the bed. He sat on it, still in his green bathing suit and wearing a blue and orange Denver Broncos t-shirt.

"You were right the other day. Pool does help you think. I've been doing some deep thinking in the deep end."

"That explains your prune-like appearance."

He locked his eyes on the schematic on the wall. "We've been curious about why no incidents of forest fires with bodies recently. That's as far as we know, right? What if there have been other attempts, successful or unsuccessful, by the perps we are pursuing and we just aren't aware of them?"

"Such as?" Susan sat on the bed beside him.

"Do you still have that copy of The Week magazine?"

"The one we read the ink off of while watching Lifebridge?"

"Yes."

She stood. "Somewhere, yeah. Why?"

"Just have a hunch. Can you find it?"

Susan shuffled through several menus and miscellaneous magazines on their desk, found the mag he had requested and brought it over. He opened it to the page entitled "The U.S. at a Glance."

"I remember reading this page in Starbucks the other day. They have this nice map of the U.S. in the center and lines from their short articles to the geographical areas on the map where the reported incident occurred. I figure that's a good way to teach geography-impaired Americans the lay of their land. Here's one top center about transgender women being admitted to a women's college in Massachusetts and another upper left about gun control in Oregon. They do the same for the rest of the world on the following pages."

"Okay, so…?"

"Look at these two. There was a fire reported in the Cibola National Forest east of Albuquerque in the center bottom, which the article says was suspected to be man-caused. And this in the lower left is about a fire near San Diego. No mention of cause. No mention of cadavers or loss of life, if any, in either case. Interesting."

"Yup," Susan said. "But it's fire season and California and New Mexico are two of the drought-stricken states. Man-caused can mean accidentally caused by man. Stupid, yes. But, arson, no. Plus those fires are pretty far from where we've been operating. Where're you going with this?"

"You've got a point. That's why even though these articles were about fires, I pretty much ignored them." Jake studied the magazine page. "This blurb about the New Mexico fire is interesting. 'The warming climate is creating a threat to global forests unlike any in recorded history, said Nathan Grant of Los Alamos' Planet and Natural Sciences Department.' It goes on to say 'Historic forests and irreplaceable ancient trees may be increasingly at risk from hotter droughts and catastrophic fires if the global climate warms as projected.'"

His glance shifted from the magazine to Susan's face and back. "It mentions that drought-stressed trees are less able to store carbon." He looked up. "I mean this is just a vicious cycle and our bunglers seem to be inadvertently or possibly intentionally taking advantage of it—so far at least, on a small scale."

"Which is why we have to stop them before they cause a catastrophic fire. Like the Big Burn—summer of 1910—a blow up that incinerated forests over an area as large as Connecticut. It spread from northern Idaho into Montana and destroyed several towns and killed hundreds."

"How do you know about that?" Jake asked.

"Jen sent me a link to an article about it yesterday."

"Any progress on Bill Something-Indian-Sounding, the revolutionary smokejumper?"

"She's still digging for intel on Bill."

Jake got up, crossed to the map on the wall of the western U.S., and studied it. He reached down, opened the desk drawer, pulled out a blue Marriott pen, and held it up flat to the map. "If you look where we've marked the Boulder Mountain Fire, the Flagstaff Fire, and the Fort Apache Fire they are not in a straight line." He moved the pen in several directions but could never get it to touch all three locations at once. He rested the pen on the map vertically from the Boulder fire through the Flagstaff fire. The Apache fire was off to the right. "Grab a second pen, okay."

Susan searched in her daypack and produced one. "Now hold yours from San Diego to Albuquerque perpendicular to mine."

Susan moved beside Jake and placed one end of her pen on San Diego and the other on Albuquerque, crossing his pen and the marked spot of the Apache fire. "Oh my God."

The two pens formed a cross with all five fires touched by one of the two arms. Phoenix was dead center where the vertical and the horizontal lines intersected.

"Coincidence? I don't think so," Jake said.

"So we're back to looking at Christian fanatics," Susan said.

"This burning cross bumps that demographic back up to the top of the list, but bend the arms of a cross and you have a swastika, cross bones under a skull and you have the pirate's Jolly Roger. As one of our oldest symbols, the cross has been perverted repeatedly to serve the needs of the fringes of society. So, yes, we're looking for fanatics but it's still anybody's guess whether they're Christian."

"But it is a step."

"It's a step, partner. Now we just have to determine in which direction. While you're out creating our courier camouflage, I'll spend some time learning all I can online about these two fires and the history of the burning cross."

"What about telling Gloria all this."

"I think we should cross that bridge when we are ready to burn it."

"Funny. Meaning?"

"Lately, as you know, our employer has become more strident and impatient for results. My fear is that once she sees we have a strong lead in a direction that points definitively away from her tribal members, there will be no going back."

"I get it. I can imagine her telling us, although many are Christians, her folks are as likely to take actions governed by a burning cross as they are to prepare owl omelets for breakfast."

Jake nodded, managed a grim smile and then sat at the desk and opened his laptop. Susan collected her things, grabbed his car keys and headed out in search of shirts, signs and logos. Dinner had been forgotten.

August 1
Friday

Gauzy curtains floated up on drafts of chilled air like Marilyn Monroe's dress in the iconic photo. Susan was alone in the room. She was wearing her bathing suit under her cotton sundress—ready to take the plunge when her work was done—if she were to be honest, her mind more at the pool than on her tasks.

She was placing the objects gathered the night before on the bed and suddenly had the urge to check them off her shopping list one-by-one. Might keep her more focused on the job. She searched for a pen. Jake had forgotten to return hers after the startling discovery of the burning cross the previous evening.

The cross was a shocker. And remained an enigma. They had agreed to mull it over and eventually compare thoughts and Susan eagerly anticipated mulling time on the treadmill later because she did her best thinking while moving. Jake was off confirming the timing of the morning DLSA pick-up, ostensibly to avoid an awkward situation involving a meet-up with a doppelgänger, and probably taking notes right now with her pen.

She rummaged through all the scattered papers, menus, sightseeing flyers, magazines and receipts on the desk, wondering for the thousandth time why Jake was not better organized. Finding nothing to write with, she pushed her hair behind her ears and yanked open the desk drawer. Nothing in the front but postcards (*people still send those?*) and stationery (*people still write letters?*) She felt around in the back and a fingernail caught a small, stiff, cardboard-like square. She dug it out. It was a recently purchased Arizona Lottery Powerball ticket. Oh no, she thought. Not this. Not now. Jake, Goddamnit!

Jake unpacked his camera gear on the bed and was about to tell Susan what he had learned at Lifebridge when he noticed the lottery ticket on his pillow. He sat on the bed facing her.

She was sitting cross-legged in the overstuffed chair by the window attaching a patch to a brown uniform shirt.

"Where'd you get the sewing kit?"

"Begged it off the front desk."

"How's our new uniform progressing?"

"Mine's done. Yours is close." She lifted the shirt she was working on without meeting his eyes. "Magnetic signs should be ready by 2 p.m. You still need to go online and check the rental companies and arrange for the van pickup this evening. What did you learn?"

"Based on a sample of two days observation DLSA hits the center like clockwork, on or about 10:30 a.m. I'm thinking we go in at 9:30 and I tell whoever we're early because it's taking longer for you to shadow me and learn the route. Sound good."

"That sounds great, Jake." Her tone not reflecting her words. She dropped her hands and sewing on her lap and glowered. "Now can we talk about the crocodile that's in the boat with us?"

"The croc ... ah, interesting metaphor. Would you by chance be referring to the object you placed on my pillow?" He nodded toward the ticket but did not touch it.

"Yes, I would. Not only the purchase of a lottery ticket, but the fact that you *hid* it from me."

"Which bothers you more, the fact—"

She stood and dropped her sewing at her feet. "Don't you dare start that psychoanalytical bullshit with me. You know damn well this is like finding a bottle hidden by a recovering alcoholic." She turned to the window. "Why, Jake?"

"You need to stop treating me like a teenager. I can handle this." Jake's volume rose a notch.

That turned her around. "You can handle it? That *sounds* like a teenager who has no clue, NO CLUE what he can handle and no awareness of what he can't control."

Jake took a beat. "Susan, please sit down. Let's both breathe." She waited for his explanation, hands on hips. "Part of my twelve steps for gambling addiction was to ask forgiveness and admit to the mistakes I made. Do you feel I have done that with you?"

"Yes."

"Thank you. Then you know I'm very capable of accounting for my actions, even those driven by my problem." He finally picked the ticket off his pillow. "This ... this is not what gambling addiction is about. This is about the money, pure and simple. We win; we're on easy street, maybe living in a house on the beach in Oregon. I know your mind is back there and not on this gritty job right now."

"Don't make this about me." Susan picked up her sewing and sat again stitching with a fury.

"I'm not, I'm not, truly. My point is, the lottery is about easy money, gambling addiction is about a different need altogether."

"If it's not about winning money, then what is it about?"

"When I'm sitting at the felt and the dealer's showing an ace, I know Blackjack for Idiots would probably say I should play like he has a face in the hole. But that's not what gets ... gets—well for lack of a better word—gets me off. What gets me off is knowing; knowing for certain that I can bust him."

"Maybe it's about losing money. As you've said, you're damn good at that."

"No really, I've thought about it. It's not about winning or losing money. When my chips are being pushed toward me it doesn't matter if it's twenty dollars or twenty thousand; what matters is that I beat the dealer with a crap hand because I *knew* I could."

"Control."

"You got it. Power and control. Same in roulette. I lust for the feeling of controlling the wheel. When the other suckers are placing wide, I lay the action numbers and against all the odds, I have the power to will the ball to land a winner.

"If you think about it, that's when addiction sunk its talons in deep, when my life was out of control. And when did I start my recovery? When you and I got together." Jake plucked the ticket off his pillow and stood. "This was not like finding a recovering alcoholic's hidden bottle, Susan, unless maybe if it was an O'Doul's. Playing the lottery gives me no feeling of control and no kick. It's too random." He flicked the ticket into the trash by the desk.

"Then please explain why you hid it."

"I hid it because I was afraid you might overreact."

"And I'm sure you think I did." Her voice ratcheted up in volume, causing Jake to take his down.

"I'm certain beyond any doubt that anything you do that involves me comes out of caring and commitment. I've never been surer of anything than that—and of us. And that is the kind of healthy control I genuinely need in my life—my life, which has become our life. Now let me look into that rental, okay?"

"Knock yourself out."

Susan went back to her sewing, her needle now somewhat less lethal. Jake sat at the desk and opened his laptop. After a few minutes of searching and comparing prices and locations, he reached down to unlace his runners and slip off his shoes and socks. While bent over, he retrieved the ticket from the mess in the trashcan and slid it into his left shoe.

"The burning cross or Crann Tara originated in Scotland and was used in the 18th and early 19th centuries as a declaration of war. It was intended to be a gathering call for common defense of the clan. It was sometimes ignited on a hilltop, visible for miles around, or a small version was carried through town on horseback. It was kind of like Paul Revere's lantern."

"How do you go from that to the more recent usage here?" Susan asked.

"Who knows why the KKK adapted it as a racially motivated means of intimidating."

"And it's anybody's guess if our bunglers are using it in one of those two historical contexts or for some new and improved depraved reason," Susan said.

Sunlight on a bias reflected off the windows of the cars in the lot. They were sitting in their rental panel van outside Staples but within view of Lifebridge. The last patients had left for the day. This was to be their dry run for the next morning. Although palm trees in dirt strips provided a little sparse shade, Susan had insisted on idling the engine and blasting the AC.

"What did you learn about the new fires on our cross?"

"Not much on the Albuquerque fire. Either authorities on that case are clueless as to actual cause and nothing bizarre like a discarded body has been discovered, or they are keeping all that under wraps while they investigate."

"This is when I miss the police network. You could always pick up the phone and wheedle information out of someone on the job somewhere. You know, just cop-to-cop."

"I'm sure you do miss it. But not having that easy peasy route, or for that matter the legal use of deadly force that sworn officers often use and sometimes abuse, makes PI work a whole lot more challenging and fun."

"Oh, that's right, I forgot. This is fun in the sun we're having here. I think I'd rather have a manicure—total nail removal with pliers included. What about the San Diego fire?"

"Now that's interesting. An elderly rancher was found in the fire presumably burned to death in his truck, which was pulling a horse trailer that also burned. In that case the authorities are assuming he got confused and trapped and he freed his horses to fend for themselves. No horses in the trailer. None dead in the fire."

"Gee. I'm thinking that may not be as innocent as they want to believe."

"No offense, but my experience has been that often your colleagues on the job, as you put it, are all over the obvious and easy assumption like flies on cow pies."

"I wish I could disagree."

A white convertible pulled up and parked a few spaces over. A woman and a young girl, both with ginger hair, got out and placed beach towels from the back over their seats, came around the hood and walked into Staples holding hands.

"So let's see, we got our official outfits, we got our official van, as soon as we slap on the signs, we got our clipboard—"

Jake was cut off by a text pinging in. He removed his sunglasses and lifted his phone off the console. "Who might this ... what the fuck?" His eyes bore up at Susan. "Gloria is missing. No one knows where she is."

"Missing? Where was she last seen?"

"I read you the whole text. You know what I know."

"Who's it from?"

He looked at the unfamiliar number on the screen. "That, I don't know."

"You must know the number."

"All my communication has been with the Chief. I'm not even sure who, if anybody, she shared my number with."

"Text back. Ask for more details and the identity of the sender."

Jake started thumbing his iPhone while Susan looked on, concern in her eyes.

Q Option #1 was drifting up and away with the heat waves shimmering just above the parking lot surface.

A thought crept in low and lurid under Susan's normally unassailable standards. One she didn't dare mention to Jake. How could Gloria be upset with them for not making progress if she was not around to check on their progress? Of course, Susan was concerned about Gloria's well-being, and needless to say, wished for the happy ending that is usually the case with missing adults. She truly hoped they would eventually learn Gloria had been fine all along, but only after Goddard Consulting enjoyed a brief respite from her constantly demanding their agency identify non-Apache perpetrators for these bizarre crimes—which they were convinced were being committed by Apaches. And did that thought make her feel shitty? A little, yeah.

August 2
Saturday

Their room was once again under assault from the blazing Phoenix sun. After learning Gloria Fox was missing, Jake and Susan did a hasty retreat and regroup. Except for a few hours of sleep and a quick early morning run to Starbucks for coffee and breakfast to go, they had been holed up in their Marriott command unit since receiving the news. The overriding question—what the hell to do now?

Obviously lacking specific orders from his client, Jake couldn't come up with a better plan than to head for the Fort Apache Reservation to learn what he could about her status. Being of any use at all was going to be complicated by the fact that he'd been working for the tribe under the table, allowing the Chief plausible deniability. The only other person of authority he'd met, Tribal Police Chief William Sweetgrass, had dismissed him outright.

Jake was certain Sweetgrass would never contact him for any reason, and therefore was not the person who notified him of Gloria's disappearance. So the good news was he had at least one ally who was close to the Chairwoman. If only he could determine the identity of that person. Unfortunately, he had not received a reply to his request for more details and the name of the sender.

One very puzzling thing was that he was dealing with two different area codes; Gloria's was 928, and the anonymous texts were coming from 520. He could probably spend some time and money and find out what name was associated with the number, but who had time? (Hell, who had money?) He decided to try one more thing. He wrote a text and ran it by Susan before hitting send. *How do I know you're for real and can be trusted? If you won't tell me who you are, tell me something only someone close to Gloria would know.* If he got no response, at least he had the cell number and that might come in handy later.

Susan then suggested that, if indeed Gloria had been taken against her will, the sender of the text could be one of her abductors. But after closer consideration, they rejected that idea. There was no rational reason why a kidnapper would do that, plus the language of the text didn't fit the profile. A person who knew where Gloria was would have to be very cagey to text, "No one knows where she is." What would be the point? Jake had tried Gloria's cell several times but it went straight to voicemail.

They were loath to give up on the courier strategy but couldn't come up with a safe alternative to the trainer-trainee charade. Susan going in alone was simply not wise and was not something she relished in the aftermath of her solo witch-hunt.

She had been sitting at the computer for some time looking for online buzz about Gloria's disappearance. There was none. She tossed off a startling suggestion.

"I think we should ask Trey Fleishman if he would come down and stand in for you."

"That was the sound of my jaw dropping."

"Is that what I heard?" She swiveled her seat to face him.

"In many ways, as a person who speaks the language of Lifebridge and the architect of Q Option #1, Trey might be better."

"I don't know about better and the whole thing makes me very nervous, but I don't think we have a choice."

"It should come from you. He'll need to hear that you want him and trust him."

Susan called Trey immediately and caught him just before he left home for breakfast with some buds; he was thrilled. He said he would notify his boss that he was taking the week off, get a coworker to cover his current specimens and head down first thing the next morning—ETA, cocktail hour.

Then they agreed Jake would call The Tribal Police Headquarters and try to speak to William Sweetgrass, both to confirm that Gloria was really missing, and if so, to see if he would collaborate with Jake on the search.

On his second try and after intensive persuasion, the receptionist agreed to patch him through to the police chief at home. Jake hit speaker so Susan could listen. She sat beside him on the bed.

"Chief," Sweetgrass answered, sounding pissed.

Jake widened his eyes at Susan. Too many chiefs ... or was that chefs, he thought.

"Mr. Sweetgrass, this is Jake Goddard. We met—"

"I know when we met."

"I received a text informing me that Mrs. Fox has been missing since yesterday afternoon."

"Who sent the text?"

"It was anonymous."

Silence.

"Can you confirm it?" Jake asked.

"Anything that involves the Chairwoman is strictly tribal business."

"Please tell me if it's true that Gloria has been missing overnight."

Silence.

"Look, Sweetgrass, I can get this information from you, or I can get it from like fifty other sources. Save me some time. Is it true?"

"Uh-huh."

"I would like to help."

"Like I said, this is tribal business. Which makes it none of yours. I have no idea why Mrs. Fox hired you in the first place. Now if you will—"

"Wait. Chief Sweetgrass. Hear me out. If the Chairwoman's disappearance has anything to do with our ongoing investigation in the arson cases, and it's hard to imagine it doesn't, then we have information that can help you find her and bring her home." Jake got up and paced while holding the phone. "If anything happens to your leader, you do not want the local papers reporting that you had access to information that could have led to her safe return and you chose to ignore it."

Nothing but breathing on the other end. Jake, stopped, licked his lips and stared at Susan.

"What sort of information?"

Jake's shoulders relaxed a bit.

"Uh … just last night my partner identified one of the four men who almost certainly committed murder in Show Low and then lit your world on fire. He is definitely one of the four men we saw in the truck on the reservation and she has positively identified him as the man who whipped her with an arrow from the bed of the same truck near our home."

The astonished look on Susan's face was clearly saying *you've got to be shitting me*. She should have been in silent movies, Jake thought, and winked at her.

"If you meet with me, and work with me, I will share what I know."

"Where are you?"

"Uh, close. I could be there tomorrow morning."

"Meet me at the Bet High Café, Monday morning at 10:00 a.m."

"Chief Sweetgrass, with all due respect, I think it's a mistake to wait two—"

Sweetgrass hung up. Jake tossed his phone on the bed. Susan looked stunned.

"What?" Jake asked.

"You mean who, don't you? I positively identified *who*?"

"Oh, yeah, that. You and Flesh better work fast. I'm not going to be able to stall "Sweat-ass" on that ID for long."

Jake's phone pinged on the bed. He reached for it, read a text from 520 and held it up for Susan. *Gloria is trying to learn French.*

August 3
Sunday

Trey Fleishman pulled in at beer-thirty just as promised. Jake had him set up in a room on the first floor and they all gathered by Jake and Susan's mini fridge, cold beers for the guys and cold white wine for the gal. Susan had suggested the pool but Jake talked her out of it. Flesh in the flesh was not his idea of a good accompaniment to cocktails. Plus, he argued, they might need the schematic and laptop for their strategy session.

Although Trey was not a swimsuit model, he was quick. Halfway through the second beer he had mastered most of the details of the case that the PIs hadn't mentioned in Salt Lake, was up to speed on the plan to poke around inside Lifebridge, and was even offering hypotheticals on the Gloria mystery.

Everything went well until it came time to try on the costume. Susan watched from the overstuffed chair by the window while Jake, standing in the middle of the room, held up the replica DLSA uniform shirt for Trey. He pulled off his baggy brown Army-style t-shirt and slipped his arms into the short-sleeved shirt. Buttoning up presented a problem. "Come on buddy, suck it in," Jake said.

"I am sucking." Trey had his chin wedged down and his belly pulled back but still after wrestling the buttons, the shirt purchased for the slimmer Jake gaped in three places. Brown hair poked out little windows all the way to his belt.

"You sure you can't suck it in more?" Jake asked.

Trey released his breath in a burst and the shirt stretched across his expanded midsection approaching maximum button-pop. "Gotta back off those burritos at The Red Iguana," he said.

Jake looked at Susan with desperation. "We don't have time to do another shirt run what with the weekend, sewing and everything. What do you recommend?"

"I've got an idea. You guys finish your beers, I'll be right back." She grabbed her daypack and was out the door.

And she was right back—in the time it took the boys to consume three-quarters of a fresh brew—with a black and blue neoprene truss she found at the pharmacy in the mall grocery store. Trey lifted his shirt; Susan wrapped the device around his middle, resisting the urge to put her knee against him as she might while saddling Cassie, and pulled the Velcro tight.

When he tugged his shirt down over the new apparatus, he looked fine, only a little black material visible through the noticeably relaxed buttonholes.

Trey turned in profile and admired himself in the wall mirror. Jake patted his friend's belly. "Slimmed down by about half dozen burritos, I'd say."

Trey pounded his belly with both hands. "New man."

Susan added. "And the black showing through the shirt, not a problem. Lots of folks who lift for a living are required to wear back support. OSHA."

"Goddard Consulting Group is definitely all about OSHA," Jake said. "Okay, team. Any last questions, concerns, suggestions?"

Susan and Trey looked at each other and shook their heads.

But then Susan said, "Not to kick a dead horse, Trey, I love you, hon, and I don't want to offend you, but I'm going to keep you on a very short leash to be certain you're safe at all times."

Jake added, "Play your cards right, you can use the leash she keeps me on, maybe my spiked dog collar as well."

"I appreciate the concern, Susan. And I'm damn proud to be your sidekick." He snapped to attention. "T-R-E-Y. Drop the E, whataya got? Try. On my honor, I'll *try* to do my best." He raised his right hand in the three-finger Scout sign. "I promise to place caution above all. Which should not be a problem considering what a coward I am." He dropped his hand and grabbed his beer bottle.

Jake said. "Okay scouts, if we're set, I'm going to throw together a bag for a three-day stay, more or less, over near the rez. And then we can go get some Mexican." He started pulling things out of drawers and stuffing them into his red duffel on the bed.

"Sounds good," Trey said, glancing in the mirror again. "Now that I've lost some weight, I could definitely go for Mexican."

"You're getting a salad, big guy," Susan said. Trey looked deflated. "With a burrito supremo on the side."

"Right, buddy. Cuz you worked so hard getting into my shirt," Jake said, bending over his bag.

"Almost as hard as Jake worked getting into my pants." Susan slapped Jake's ass. Trey grinned and blushed.

Jake straightened. "Susan played very hard to get. I got so lathered, I lost fifteen pounds during that rather strenuous rut."

"Get a room, you two." Trey looked around the room. "Oh sorry, guess you already have. Well then, the only way your gonna get me out of your room is to buy me dinner. Let's go."

Trey unbuttoned his DLSA shirt, ripped open the truss, tossed it on the bed and pulled on his brown t-shirt. The three amigos polished off drinks, grabbed gear and headed out into the evening glare with Mexican in their crosshairs.

August 4
Monday

A white panel van with a Danon Laboratory Systems of America logo on both front doors slowly entered the loading area behind the Lifebridge Center. The golf course fairway was unoccupied. Trey maneuvered around the front of a white Sprinter delivery van advertising oxygen, pharmaceuticals and other medical supplies, and nosed into an open bay, just as Jake's photos had suggested. The metal rollup door behind the Sprinter was open. No one was around.

Trey turned off the engine, took a deep breath, pushed his glasses up his nose and turned to Susan. "Ready, Frederica?"

"Frederica?"

"Yeah well, under the circumstances Ready Freddy didn't seem appropriate. Plus Frederica means "peaceful ruler" and you are definitely in charge."

"Thanks for that, Flesh, but the 'peaceful' part remains to be seen." She checked her watch. "9:30 right now. We've got approximately one hour before someone dressed exactly like us in a brown DLSA uniform is going to want this parking space."

Trey tapped his fingers on the steering wheel and jiggled his knees. "That should be plenty of time to get in and get out as well as have a good look around." His eyes darted around the area. "Guess I'm a little nervous."

"I was feeling a little nervous myself until you came up with our bail-out option. I was wondering how we were going to dispose of the pathology specimens and worried about the poor people who would be told their biopsies would have to be repeated and their path reports were going to be delayed."

"Oh that, yeah, thanks, came to me in the middle of last night. Simple, really—to review one more time, just after you get back from your trip to the ladies room, aka snooping around, I pretend my phone has vibrated in my pocket. I take a fake call. I tell whomever we are dealing with at the moment that I was just informed this is meant to be a dry run, and there will be a later pick-up by the regular guy. Then we book. I've even got an idea up my short sleeve of how to persuade them to not mention our earlier visit to Guy Regular when he shows up on schedule. Easy peasy lemon squeezy."

"Those are words I've been waiting to hear."

"Huh?"

"Oh, nothing—just that Jake mentioned that was one of your favorite expressions. I started to use it, and now Amy has picked it up."

Trey beamed. "Hand me that official looking DLSA clipboard from off the dash and let's do this thing."

"Let's go squeeze them easy lemons, Q."

They slid out of the van and headed up the ramp toward the door with the bell.

Jake sat in his Subaru on the gravel lot outside the Bet High in Show Low. A green neon sign touted the best breakfast in town. He saw a waitress moving around behind a smaller sign for the state lottery and one advertising an ATM. He was staring at the tailgate of a muddy red pickup with a fading bumper sticker that read Ditch the Bitch and Go Huntin'. He smiled and thought it would actually be funny, rather than simply obnoxious, if it read, "Ditch the Bitch and Go Antiquing."

He had timed his arrival to be early, so he could gather his thoughts and plan his strategy. There was no doubt Sweetgrass was going to be a tough sell. The only thing that had secured Jake this meeting was the promise to share recent developments in the arson/murder case that might possibly lead to Gloria's return. Which brought up the small matter of the lie Jake told about Susan's positive ID.

He glanced at his watch, 9:45. Hopefully Trey and Susan were inside Lifebridge doing their courier thing and with any luck, sniffing out bad guys and making the promised ID retroactively. They were instructed to text him with any new information as soon as they were out safely.

A tribal police cruiser rolled in and parked at the far end of the lot. The Police Chief got out, looking very much the part in his black uniform and heavily loaded belt. He ambled toward the café. He was wearing the same mirror sunglasses as when Jake first met him. Yes, the high dry Arizona air was clear and it was a bright mountain day but still, those sunglasses were like an insult, a provocation. Jake's phone pinged with a text. It was from Cool Hand Sweat-ass: *Café too crowded to talk. Pull around back, I'll bring coffee.*

Susan followed Trey as he approached the door with the buzzer. He reached out to push the button when she placed a hand on his arm.

"Wait, uh … Tim. Why not just walk in the open bay?"

He dropped his arm and turned. "Why the hell not?"

The loading dock curved around behind the Sprinter. They walked over and entered a concrete shipping and receiving area lined with painted pipes and silver conduit.

A man in a gray uniform passed, pushing an empty dolly toward the delivery van at the dock. He ignored them. Susan took that to be a good sign.

Trey eased through two swinging doors, Susan on his heels. They were in a fluorescent-lit linoleum corridor that ran perpendicular to the doors closing behind them. To their left was an alarmed fire exit. The hallway to the right was vacant and quiet, although muffled noise could be heard from deeper in the building; it smelled of disinfectant. A metal sign on the wall straight ahead indicated that pick-ups and deliveries were down that hall through the next set of doors. They walked past several locked and dark metal cages with chairs, tables, beds and miscellaneous medical paraphernalia stored inside. As agreed, Trey continued to lead. He was, after all, the guy with the command of the appropriate professional jargon, as well, as the "supervisor" in their pretense. Also they had agreed Trey in the lead would provide Susan more opportunity to surreptitiously study faces.

He was about to push through the next doors when a short Hispanic man burst through and almost knocked him over. The man appeared to be an orderly.

Trey started to explain who they were but the orderly looked blank, pointed over his shoulder at the next set of doors, smiled and nodded and headed down the hall past them. Trey looked at Susan. She shook her head. He was not their man.

Trey turned and walked through and they were suddenly in the middle of a cacophony of activity. Personnel in the now familiar Lifebridge uniform bustled about, stopping to chat briefly as they pushed carts full of meds, supplies and snacks to and fro. Susan took in the scene and studied faces simultaneously. People in street clothes, presumably patients, entered and exited what must have been treatment rooms lining the far end of the hall. A man and a woman, doctors perhaps, both in white coats, conferred over a chart near a nurse's station. Susan instantaneously ruled them out—gender wrong in one case, skin color wrong in the other.

Jake had cautioned Trey that appearing at all uncertain would be a dead give-away. He had been paying attention. He strode up to the open window of the nurses' station with Susan following and spoke to a boxy woman with punk blue hair straight to the shoulders sitting behind the desk.

"Morning. Tim Middley, Danon Laboratory Systems. This's our new courier, Betty Wilt. We could sure use your help."

Cream and sugar, Jake responded to Sweetgrass.

He drove to the back of the Bet High Café, steering around several large depressions in the gravel, and parked near two bins and a dumpster. He pushed his Ray-Bans on under his GCG ball cap, prepping for the inevitable hide-your-eyes-to-intimidate pissing match with Sweetgrass. He got out and leaned against the hood of his Subaru. There had been only three cars plus the muddy truck in the front lot not counting him and the police chief. How crowded could it be inside? Just to continue leveling the playing field, he opened his door, slipped his pistol out from under the passenger seat, holstered it in the middle of his back and pulled his brown Goddard Group polo over it. He went back up to the hood, trying his best for nonchalance.

The police cruiser crept around the side of the building looking every bit as sinister with its tinted windows as its occupant in his mirrored glasses. It headed for Jake.

Sweetgrass parked and got out, bent down and retrieved two coffees, and kneed the door shut.

"Two creams, two sugars."

"Thanks. Need this after the drive."

Sweetgrass took up a place beside him leaning on the hood. Jake recognized his holstered grip as that of a Sig Sauer nine—the choice of Navy Seals.

"Where'd you say you were staying?"

"Close. I said I was close." They sipped in silence staring off in the distance.

Jake went first. "So, I want to help find Gloria."

"How can you help when, as far as the reservation goes, you don't exist?"

"I've given it a lot of thought. I can help by going along on your interviews related to Gloria's disappearance. As a second pair of eyes, I might catch something you missed."

"Why the hell would I take some white guy with me on my interviews?"

"Thought about that, too. Because the white guy is a sociology prof writing a book about policing on American Indian reservations, and you have invited him to ride along."

Sweetgrass blew out air, studied his coffee cup and worked his jaw in thought.

"Tell me about this positive identification of one of the arsonists your partner supposedly made."

Jake looked across to the stacks of lumber in the lumberyard that abutted the back of the café's lot. "That's a long story."

"I got time for a long story—especially if it can help the Chief. She's not getting any more gone."

Sweetgrass pushed off the fender, underhanded his partially full cup into the dumpster and turned to Jake, feet spread, hands on police belt at the hips.

Jake had to smile, not only at the body language but also at the reflection of his Ray-Bans in Sweetgrass's dual mirrors. This was all beginning to feel like a swan dive down a rabbit hole after a stroll through a fun house. "'Twas brillig and the slithy toves' came to mind.

"What can I do for you?" Boxy Blue in the nurses' box asked.

"I'm Betty's supervisor. She's in training to take over this assignment. DLSA wants to always insure the best and safest handling of pathology specimens in the perioperative setting. We routinely do these training runs with new hires to insure they understand AST Standards of Practice for Handling and Care of Surgical Specimens."

"What happened to Cody?"

"Oh, um, Cody will be here several more weeks. This's just a dry run for Betty. He'll be by later today." Trey moved in and lowered his voice. "I'd really appreciate it if you didn't say anything. Cody wants to keep everything about his departure from DLSA confidential. In fact, it'd be better for ole' Code if you didn't even mention we were here." He glanced up and down the hall to make sure he couldn't be overheard.

"Since you're obviously a good friend, I feel like I can share with you. Cody's leaving to have a sex change operation."

Her eyes widened.

"And to become a nail technician. Cody today, Cathy tomorrow. We're all wishing him, uh, her, well."

"Wow. That's a lot of change," Blue said, reddening.

Trey bobbed his head in sympathy. "Whole new world."

"Sorry to hear. I mean, not about … I mean, about him … her changing … uh … jobs and all." Desperately seeking a safe way out, she brightened. "But, welcome to you Betty. We'll be seeing a lot of each other. I'm on the doorbell most days. Shine or shine, as we say in Phoenix."

Susan—having narrowly avoided a total crack up at Trey's creativity—turned her eyes back from scanning the hallway, smiled and nodded.

"Yeah, that's for sure. Shine or killer-shine. Refresh my memory, you've had Cody how many years now?" Trey asked.

"Two-and-a-half. I always remember he started when I left to have my third and Sally will be three next December."

Susan cleared her throat and shifted her weight. She needed to move Flesh along before this woman had him gawking at kid pictures.

"So, I'm really embarrassed. Betty's on the espresso express and needs a bathroom and I want to go over the ropes with her on the specimen pick up." He pushed his glasses up and looked down the corridor searching. "And it's been so many years since I've been in the center, in fact I think it was before you started." He studied her nametag. "Teresa?"

"Yeah, Teresa." She tapped her chest. "Must a been. You don't look familiar."

"Can you bail me out and point us in the right directions?"

"Sure. It's Tim, right?"

"Tim Middely."

"Tim, you need to take that first left down the hall there—lab is clearly marked on the left. Betty, you need to go all the way past the treatment rooms and through the doors into the reception area. Look for a sign that says restrooms. It will be the first right and down beyond three offices."

Teresa looked pleased with herself. "Anything else I can do for you?"

"Thanks, Teresa. You're a lifesaver," Susan said, puffing out her cheeks, suddenly realizing she probably could use a bathroom.

"Meet you at the lab, Betty." They started down the hall. Trey tossed over his shoulder.

"Love the hair, Teresa."

"We've connected the deaths and subsequent incineration of Andrew Millar, Brenda Petersen and Skip Denton to the Lifebridge Cancer Center in Phoenix," Jake said. "All three had treatment there."

The cop's stance grew more rigid. "That's old news. Gloria told me that the last time we met. Tell me something I don't know, or I walk."

Traffic noise on the other side of the café was faint but constant. Jake noticed two frontend loaders working the lumberyard behind the posturing Chief of Police.

"We have seen a pattern in the fires that appears to be a cross or a burning cross which might indicate the involvement of a radical Christian group and probably points away from Apache involvement. Gloria assured us you have Christians but few if any of what you would call radical Christians."

He uncoiled a little. "That rises to the level of mildly interesting but purely speculative, Goddard." He shook his head. "A burning cross?" He checked his watch. "You've got thirty seconds to give me something."

"All right. My partner, Susan and a friend who is a pathologist are inside Lifebridge as we speak posing as couriers in an attempt to make a positive ID of one of the murderer-arsonists."

"In an attempt?" Sweetgrass chuckled ruefully. "What you told me Saturday was bullshit. You haven't positively identified anyone associated with these crimes."

"Not as yet, no. But we feel we are very close—"

"Jesus Christ, Goddard!" Sweetgrass shot a look up at the sky and then leveled on Jake again. "That's what you've got after what, two months on the payroll?" He walked around to the driver's side of the cruiser. "Get in, professor." He pointed at him over the roof of the car.

"The first damn time you open your mouth, you're history."

Jake climbed in behind his wheel, grabbed his notebook and pen, cracked two windows, got out and locked his car. He walked to the passenger side of the cruiser, resigned to taking the plunge.

He slid into the cruiser, waited for Sweetgrass to finish sending a text on his cell and they pulled out of the lot—an odd couple of crime solvers if there ever was one.

Trey went around the corner as directed, stopped short of the door to the lab and leaned against the wall suddenly fascinated by his clipboard. He checked the time on his cell. It was 9:51. They were twenty-one minutes into their scope-out and still well ahead of the usually scheduled pick up by DLSA—so far, so good.

Fifteen minutes later after several people had passed him in the hall, Trey was beginning to feel as noticeable as if he were addressing a crowd of thousands in his not so tidy whiteys. The truss under his shirt was chaffing and hot as hell. He started to worry. It was now 10:06 and getting very close to the normal pick up.

"Can I help you find something?"

He jarred at the voice behind him. It was the attractive, olive-skinned female doc in the white coat he had noticed coming in.

"Uh, no I'm good, thanks. Just waiting for my trainee. She's using the restroom."

"Oh, okay. You looked a little lost." She glanced at the logo on his shirt. "But I'm sure you know your way around. My office is just down the hall past the lab if you need any assistance finding your associate in the ladies room."

"Thanks, Doctor...?"

"Raut. Meeta Raut." She didn't offer her hand but flashed a smile that brightened the rather dark corridor.

Trey almost blew his cover. "Tr—," But recovered quickly, "Tim, Tim Middely at your service, courier-wise."

"Nice to meet you, Tim. We appreciate your company. We'd be lost without you." She turned and walked to her office.

"Oh, Doctor, uh, Meeta."

She turned at her door and smiled. "Yes."

"I have an old college acquaintance told me years ago over a beer he got hired here."

"What's his name?"

He shook his head. "It was a long time ago. I'm terrible with names but would know his face."

"Check the far end of the reception area just as you go out the door on the left. All the usual suspects are up there on the wall."

"Will do, thanks again, Doc." Meeta fired one more smile and struck a direct hit, turned, and walked into her office.

The police car cruised down the center of two rows of well-maintained middleclass homes on a tree-lined street in Show Low. Sweetgrass pulled up in front of a small brick and wood bungalow with a fenced front yard and covered porch. He put the cruiser in Park and pivoted toward Jake. "You armed?"

"Yes."

"It goes in the trunk." Sweetgrass reached below the steering wheel, pulled a lever to pop the trunk, got out and went to the rear. Jake slid out, pulled his pistol out of his holster and joined him. There was a bow in the trunk that had enough wheels and pulleys to be a Rube Goldberg invention.

"What the hell do you do with that thing?" Jake asked while slipping his pistol inside.

He slammed the trunk and leaned so close Jake could smell his coffee breath. "Hunt white guys."

The retort that popped into Jake's mind was that, if that was the case, Sweetgrass should shoot himself in the foot—whichever one is white, that is, but instead he ignored the taunt and followed him through the wooden gate, up the grass-lined flagstone walk and onto the porch. He was about to knock when Jake stopped him.

"Wait, what's my name?"

"Hmm. Had a college prof named Steiner. Let's go with Dr. Steiner." Sweetgrass turned and knocked on the screen.

A middle-aged man opened the door. He was wearing tan suspenders over a blue short-sleeved polo shirt. Jake was introduced as Dr. Steiner to Gloria's husband, Victorio Fox. He had reddish-brown skin and wide cheeks with prominent cheekbones. He was slightly taller and a little more round than Gloria and had a thick mop of gray hair. Sweetgrass referred to him as Uncle Victor. Jake surmised that was an honorary title of respect.

Victorio invited them to sit on the porch in three of the four padded wicker armchairs and offered ice tea—both declined. Jake removed his hat and dark glasses out of respect; he noticed Sweetgrass did not. The briefest of pleasantries were exchanged but it was clear that Victorio was agitated, so the Police Chief proceeded to ask his questions.

"When did you last see your wife?"

"Gloria went on a shopping trip to Phoenix on Friday morning, three days ago. She left at 8 a.m." Victorio stared intently into Sweetgrass's face as if the answer to his wife's whereabouts might be found there.

"Why Phoenix?"

"She was gathering supplies for our Goddaughter Bina's Sunrise Dance. You know how complicated and expensive that can get if you try to shop local."

Across the street, two little boys and a taller girl, all with sun-bleached hair and wearing bathing suits, ran out of a brick house and across the lawn to the mini-van in the driveway. An adult, presumably their mother, closed the front door and followed. On the way to the car, she waved at Victorio. He slowly lifted his hand in response.

"When were you expecting her back?"

"She wanted to be back mid-afternoon Friday to get a few work hours in here in her home office before the weekend."

Sweetgrass leaned in and lowered his voice. "Uncle Victor, why didn't you accompany your wife?"

This brought Jake's head up from his note taking. Across the street the van backed out of the driveway.

"How I wish I had." He looked away, embarrassed. "We have a deal, my wife does the driving in Phoenix—I hate Phoenix—and in exchange I do the yard work, which is not her favorite thing."

"When did you start to worry?"

"At first I assumed she had been delayed by traffic, as you know it can be hell Friday afternoons, but began to wonder a few hours after she was due home because she would normally call. Her cell phone went to voicemail every time I tried her. At 6:30 I called you."

"Do you know what stores she was going to visit or what exactly she was planning to purchase?"

Victorio stared at his feet and shook his head.

"I have to ask, how have you and Gloria been getting along?"

"What do you mean?"

"Do you fight a lot?"

"We've gotten along great since our kids left home," he said plaintively. "Different parenting style was all we ever argued about, really. Gloria was really tough on our kids."

"Not money?"

"No, especially since she was elected Chairwoman. We were doing fine. Until this."

Sweetgrass was almost gentle with this next statement. He leaned in and placed his arms on his knees. "Uncle, you understand why I've not been out here before now. We have to wait forty-eight hours after receiving the report even for a prominent person like your wife."

"I understand." He rubbed his palms on his jeans. "But I'm very concerned now that it's gone over forty-eight hours and I have no idea where to even begin to look. This isn't like Gloria. She must be in trouble. There has to be something wrong."

"Does Gloria have any enemies?"

"All politicians make enemies. Just like police chiefs. Comes with the territory."

"Any that might want to hurt her."

"Not to my knowledge. No."

Victorio reported that when his wife was overdue, he had immediately checked with all his family members. Their daughter, Ela, who lived near-by in Whiteriver, said she had received a text around noon, Friday. Gloria wrote she had stopped to grab a quick bite. She asked Ela if she needed anything from Phoenix. Ela had texted back, no thanks. That was about all he could offer.

Jake had played the role of silent observer as promised. He jotted a final note in his notebook, "Sweet, sincere man, wouldn't hurt a fly." He also wrote, "Gloria's LKP was a fast-food restaurant in Phoenix. Check credit card records."

Sweetgrass asked Victorio's permission to search the home and Gloria's computer. The house was tidy, if a little messy in the kitchen and living room from Victorio's weekend vigil. There was no evidence of a struggle or foul play.

The upstairs had that slightly musty, lived-in smell but everything was in order: bathroom clean, towels hanging on racks, bedroom straightened up, queen bed made. Two toothbrushes and toothpaste in their rightful places reinforced the impression that Gloria had not packed in anticipation of several days away. The home provided no clues.

The house phone rang. Victorio pointed the two men toward Gloria's office in a spare room down the hall from the master bedroom and left to answer the phone. They entered. It too, was in order. The paneled walls were lined with pictures of kids and grandkids. There were several taken at official occasions. In those that included Victorio the couple seemed to be happy and comfortable in each other's presence.

Jake noticed a MacBook open on a wooden desk. He hoped that the Chairwoman's meticulousness did not extend automatically to browsing history. With Sweetgrass looking on, he woke up the computer, searched her history and found the websites of stores in Phoenix where presumably she had searched for supplies for the dance. Also the site for Lifebridge Cancer Treatment Center was listed. Jake jotted in his notebook the names and addresses of the stores Gloria had searched. He suggested Sweetgrass ask Victorio to check for credit card purchases in Phoenix that could help them track her movements. Sweetgrass grunted in reply and said they needed to leave for Ela's house in Whiteriver.

10:20 a.m. Ten minutes until doppelgänger time. Trey was about to leave the hallway by the lab to search for Susan when she turned the corner.

He looked at her wide-eyed. "Hey Betty, that took a long time." He pointed at his phone and added in case anyone was listening. "We're due at our next stop *in ten minutes*. Let's save this lab for later now that you know your way around."

"Sounds good, boss," Susan said. She headed for the exit with Trey right behind. They waved and smiled at Teresa but hurried past the nurses' station, through the doors and down the storage hall, and out into the stifling cavernous delivery area. They jumped into their vehicle.

Trey fired up the van, backed out around the front of a Sysco food truck and headed for the corner by Paradise Juice. Just as he made the turn he glanced to the right and saw an identical van pull around the food truck and nose into their parking spot. Seconds later, when they were out of view, he let out a whoop. Susan slapped a resounding high five.

"You see that? That son-a-bitch Cody is punctual. Damn."

"Glad we didn't get to meet him. Could've been a little awkward. Let's get this freakin' van stripped and out of sight behind the hotel and I'll fill you in on my explorations. Had the hardest time locating the restroom. They've got a real signage problem. I kept opening the wrong doors."

They left the mall parking lot and drove the short distance to the Marriott, passing a bank with a digital display that read 103 degrees. Midmorning traffic was light.

As they approached their hotel, Trey spoke. "Can't wait any longer. Make my day, Suzy-Q. What did the amazing PI-woman learn?"

"I never got face-to-face with my most wanted but I did have a weird experience." She stared out the window. "I think he's there. When I was scoping out the three offices before the restroom, just as I opened door number two, I saw a stocky man, tanned or naturally dark, wearing street clothes, quickly turn his back and disappear into the inner office. It was eerie. I called out about being lost and looking for the women's room, etc. But he didn't answer. I tried the interior door but it was locked. I knocked. No answer. His actions could be normal in most cases but the timing and the tempo were off. Like he somehow knew who I was and why I was there. No sign of him when I came back past that door either. Office looked like accounting or some other similar function."

"Shit," Trey offered by way of elucidation. "Might be time to join the suffering masses. A very exotic doctor of the female persuasion told me there are pictures of all employees in the foyer to the reception area."

"Well done. Great what you contribute when we get you away from HQ, Q. You were nothing short of amazing in there. Let's discuss it by the pool in twenty. I'll see if I can reach Jake and get any news of Gloria."

They parked behind the Marriott and each jumped out and removed the magnetic sign on their door. Trey opened the back and they tossed their signs inside. They hugged and headed to their rooms past the pool, which glistened and beckoned.

Observing Sweetgrass chat amicably with Victorio as well as the Apache cop's causal look around the house put Jake on alert. Something wasn't right. Was it a cultural difference in his approach to police work? Jake's instincts told him it was more than that. He suspected Sweetgrass knew something he wasn't sharing.

The Police Chief drove out of Show Low toward the town of Whiteriver. Jake's phone played default marimba and indicated a call from Susan. He chatted briefly and quietly on his cell, revealing as little of what they were discussing as possible. She relayed the strange experience of the man who quickly turned his back and disappeared in the Lifebridge office. She mentioned her decision to next go in disguised as a patient to check the wall of staff photos. Soon he lost service outside of town.

Sweetgrass demanded. "Did your girl make her ID?"

"No such luck. I'm afraid our little courier ruse was a total bust." Jake looked out the window thinking; this's a two way street, bud. You give—you get. You ain't giving. You ain't getting.

Jake reached for the radio and powered it on. A Christian rock group was wailing for Jesus.

Sweetgrass switched it off. "No music." He glanced out his side window, cleared his throat, looked forward and adjusted his cap. "I just like to think."

They entered the Fort Apache Reservation and drove south through the towering forests of the White Apache tribal lands toward Whiteriver. Gloria's older daughter Ela's log home was tucked in the pines above the riffles in the north fork of the White River. Sweetgrass interviewed her on the deck with Jake looking on while she dealt with constant interruptions from a diapered toddler and his four-year-old sister. Goddard's take, she was genuinely concerned about her mother.

Sweetgrass asked a few questions and then asked to see the Friday text exchange that Ela had with her mother. He remarked that it was exactly as her father had reported it. He thanked Ela and asked her to contact him if she heard anything from or about her Mom.

They continued south to Fort Apache and the tribal headquarters. The cracked pavement ran past dirt drives with few trees leading to small rectangular houses thirsting for paint surrounded by brown lawns thirsting for water. The almost identical dwellings held similar collections of beater cars and pickups, their running days a distant memory.

Sweetgrass had arranged a meeting with several friends of Gloria and Victorio in the conference room of the main structure of the brick military complex, ironically once used to house the U.S. military forces charged with bringing Cochise, Natchez, Geronimo and their people to heel. Jake was told to sit at the back of the room and keep his mouth shut.

Later that afternoon Sweetgrass held individual interviews with several of Gloria's staff in the same conference room. Again with Jake observing from the back of the room.

By the end of a long day during which they had learned virtually nothing new, Jake had begun to wonder if Sweetgrass intended to take the search off the reservation to Phoenix where Gloria had last been heard from. He had found Sweetgrass's interviewing technique to be totally lame, and when they parked in the back lot of the Bet High Café by

Jake's car, evening light beginning to cast an orange wash that made even the dumpster look pretty, he told him it was lame.

"Look, I get that these are friends, relatives, honorary uncles, politically sensitive contacts, et cetera, but a woman's life could be at stake here, and I've got to say I found your approach at best, to be interrogation-light."

"Why don't you tell me how a private dick would do it."

"OK." He swung round on him. "I would have eventually asked the hard questions: specifically who are her enemies, both personal and political; specifically who benefits from her removal from power? Who wants to hurt her? Are there any problems with family or neighbors? You don't crosscheck stories. You take each person at their word."

"You know I'm certain this will come as a shock to an *indaa* like you, but Apaches have a much more civilized way of dealing with each other than you Anglos. We treat each other with respect and take what is said at face value. Even your John Wayne said in a film, 'Apaches have no word for lie.'"

"Let me tell it to your straight, then. No lie. This is a waste of my time and Gloria's money. I'll continue the search in Phoenix with what I learned from Gloria's computer. If Victorio has anything from her credit cards that might help, I would like to receive that information. Otherwise, I'll let you know when I find her."

He got out; Sweetgrass popped the trunk without exiting the cruiser. Jake holstered his pistol, walked the few feet to his car and unlocked it on the remote. Sweetgrass pulled out of the lot without looking back.

When Jake opened his car door he found an envelope on the driver's seat that had been slipped through the window left cracked for airflow. He slid in the car, searched the lot to be certain no one was watching, and ripped open the envelope. A note had been typed on a computer and printed on plain white paper.

8/3
Jake Goddard, private investigator
Dear Mr. Goddard,
Aside from our leader Gloria Fox and Police Chief William

Sweetgrass, I am the only White Apache that knows you are working for the tribe. I sent you the text that informed you of Gloria's disappearance and I appreciate how quickly you responded. The risk is too great for me to tell you who I am but I wanted to warn you that all is not as it appears here. Be on your guard. It could be a mistake to trust W.S. I don't dare reveal more now but just wanted you to know you have a friend in me and that I will contact you if I learn anything that will help you find Gloria.

The note was not signed. Could Jake trust the writer? Could he trust Sweetgrass? So far, it was all nonsense. Jake had to make some sense of it. His mind churned—basic investigation technique—go back to what you know for certain and start over from there. What do we absolutely know? We are reasonably certain Gloria went to Phoenix, shopped at several stores and ate at a fast food restaurant. Ela confirmed that she received a text from her Mom verifying that fact. Jake lowered his windows to let in some air and pondered that further. But that's the thing about texts, they can claim to be sent from anywhere and without the ability to tell what towers pinged from Gloria's cell, there was no way to verify that.

An Apache teenage boy in a white apron and hairnet came out of the backdoor to the café and tossed a large black bag of garbage at the dumpster, glanced briefly at Jake, and went back inside.

Jake fired up his Subaru and backed out, his mind spinning right along with the car's fan belt. All we know for certain is that, missing or not, Gloria is not where she's supposed to be, that her family members seem genuinely worried, and that we have several renegades running around, probably based in Phoenix, who are almost certainly involved. Yet no one has received a call about ransom or any other demands. That leads us back to Lifebridge and the fundamental imperative. Catch the Goddamn bunglers. This is no longer about premature death of the terminally ill and scorched earth policies, bad as those are. It's about sprinting against the clock to stop the perpetrators before more damage can be done and a healthy and prominent Apache leader is harmed or killed.

But at the same time he was nagged by the urge to keep eyes on Sweet-grass. The note left in his car, and his PI's nose, were telling him that there was something rotten there. But a white guy, on Indian turf, tailing a tribal chief of police? A priest conducting mass in the nude would be less noticeable.

Those thoughts tumbled over and over in Jake's mind as he raced south under Bear Mountain and down the tree-lined switchbacks of the White Mountains toward Globe and Phoenix.

Underneath it all yapped the thought that Susan would have chastised him for even entertaining. Goddard Consulting Group had a stellar record. Most cases had ended in a solution and a satisfied client. But no one bats a thousand. What if this time, the client is—not only not satisfied—but dead?

Jake was so preoccupied with Gloria's safety, his suspicions about Sweetgrass, and all that was at stake for Goddard Consulting—making him wish he could be in several places at once—he almost drove through Globe without noticing it. Then an idea struck. He braked and slid off the highway into the gravel parking lot of a feed store on the outskirts of town.

It was a Hail Mary at best, but who knew, someone with great hands just might be in the right place at the right time. He had nothing to lose by launching the ball.

Jake thumbed a text to the anonymous note writer's number.

> *Dear Friend,*
>
> *Chief needs your help. U r a White Mt. Apache. You belong on the rez. I stick out like sore white thumb. You warned me about WS. I have doubts 2. But I can't observe him. 2 obvious. You can. Please watch from a safe distance. If actions are "normal" send me that word at end of each day. If not, text me details. Do not approach. Be careful. Help me bring Gloria home.*

Jake hit "send" and felt a little weight lift. Must be the way quarter-backs feel when they unleash a desperate bomb toward the end zone, he thought. Regardless of what happened in the next little while his part in the play was done. The outcome was out of his hands and in the hands of another. He just wished he knew who "another" was. He prayed, which felt like the right thing to do in any situation requiring a Hail Mary, that "anonymous another" was legit.

August 5
Tuesday

Monday had been frustrating. They had made zero progress on Gloria's disappearance. And time for Gloria could be running out. Jake had wasted most of the day playing grab-ass with Sweat-ass and Susan and Trey still lacked a definitive bungler ID. For an entire day invested, the team had enjoyed only one minor breakthrough—Susan's mysterious encounter with one Lifebridge employee.

So Monday night for Goddard and company turned into a general debriefing and group commiseration requiring excessive poolside beer consumption. Jake postponed checking the list of Gloria's stores—looking for the same folks on Monday evening that might have seen Gloria on Friday during the day could be a total waste of effort. Except for Susan slipping out to do some cancer patient costume gathering, Monday night was for the most part an unproductive end to an unproductive day.

There had, however, been one very bright and encouraging note. While feeling sorry for himself Jake had all but forgotten to expect it, so when the three amigos were perched by the pool close to 9 p.m. polishing off a six of Pacifico, and he received a text alert he was immediately elated. The message contained two words, *normal tonight.*

His Hail Mary from earlier that day had apparently been caught in the end zone. Jake shouted and displayed the screen to hugs and high fives all around. "Anonymous another" was officially deputized. Relying on someone he had never spoken to or laid eyes on was an entirely new experience. They all had a good laugh at Jake's expense when Susan made a crack about the fact that his new anonymous deputy had been working hard shadowing his good bud Sweat-ass while Jake had been lying around the pool, drinking beer and feeling sorry for himself.

But now it was Tuesday morning and Jake and crew were back at it. He was out casing the stores he had gleaned from Gloria's computer history equipped with a recent photo of her he scored while Sweetgrass wasted time at the tribal headquarters. Jake hoped the pic would help him confirm Gloria had actually been in Phoenix on Friday.

Trey and Susan were together again on a separate assignment—find *the* face on the Lifebridge staff wall. Trey drove Susan's truck and dropped her in front of the center. He parked and took up the customary GCG post at Starbucks. As Susan slowly approached the glass doors she saw the reflection of a wizened, bent figure in baggy shorts wearing a sunhat with a large visor over a cheap black wig. She had taken a chapter out of Trey's playbook and was determined to give a convincing performance. She slowly eased in the outer doors; a young man in street clothes held the inner door for her as he departed. She emerged into a pleasantly decorated waiting room with chairs lining every wall and arranged in neat rows down the middle.

Several people marked time; some stared at magazines, others stared at the floor. A receptionist's counter abutted the far wall and beyond that was the single door to the interior space she had come through in her earlier reconnaissance. Off to the left of reception was the corridor with the three offices and the restrooms.

She turned to her right and saw the wall display. It was a large array of headshots of determinedly smiling doctors, nurses, and staff members. How could she have missed it on her earlier visit? She studied the wall, pointing and muttered to herself, portraying a new patient anxious to familiarize herself with the people who would soon control her fate. It was a matter of minutes before she determined that her suspect's photo was not there. Then she noticed a blank space in the lower left corner. One picture, and the name associated with it, was missing. The darker paint in the gap compared to the lighter sun-bleached surrounding wall indicated there had been a photo removed recently. She glanced around the room. No one seemed to notice her.

Susan patted her side, as if she had forgotten her purse, muttered some more and tottered back out.

Later in their room after a no-shop-talk-allowed dinner of burgers and beers at a busy nearby burger joint—Susan perched on the bed, Jake in the big chair, Trey in the office chair, the air humming and a ballgame muted on the TV—they discussed what Jake and Susan had learned.

"It would be easy peasy to remove that picture," Susan said. "You could say that you wanted to replace it with a more recent pic or use any number of excuses like you needed a copy for your mother. Hell, for that matter, how soon would it be before someone missed one face out of fifty-plus? I felt invisible in that place. I guess you don't exist until you wake someone up at the counter."

Jake threw his leg over the left arm of the chair. "It's a bummer you couldn't get a look at a picture of your guy but truthfully, this is almost as good. There've been too many coincidences around the Lifebridge connection to not be on the right track. At least one of them works there. The weird thing is they know we know that."

"How was your shopping trip, Jake?" Trey asked, putting his hands behind his head, which accidentally tipped his chair back, throwing up his knees.

"Easy, big boy. I got a hit at Costco over on Elm for 11 a.m. Friday. Young clerk helped her out to the car with her supplies and remembers thinking how cool to be chatting with a real Indian Chief. So we know for sure she was in Phoenix. I tried two other stores with no luck but that doesn't mean she wasn't there. Wherever she is, she's well supplied after hitting Costco. That place was unbelievable."

"Would help to have the name of the restaurant she texted from," Trey said.

"It would. But I doubt Sweetgrass even asked Victorio Fox to check credit card records. That would smack of doing genuine police work. Most importantly, we know Gloria drove here to Phoenix and we know she came to do what she had planned. Having the restaurant would give us a LKP but not much else. Whoever nabbed her almost certainly did so in an isolated location where they couldn't be seen and where they could stash or commandeer her car. God knows there is plenty of isolated terrain between here and Show Low."

Jake's phone plinked and he broke out in a wide grin while checking the text. "Second day, second *normal* from anonymous another."

"You go, AA," Trey said.

"Come on Sweetgrass, come on buddy. Give us some abnormal," Susan added.

"I know he's got it in him," Jake said. He thumbed a reply, *Be patient and keep up the good work. Be careful.*

"You still have no clue who AA is?" Susan asked.

"No idea. I just need about thirty minutes online and I could probably figure it out based on the cell number. I was thinking I might do that later tonight, but truth be told, it doesn't really matter as long as Double A's on our side."

"AA is bringing the ole' A game to the A-team," Trey said. "There's no I in team but there is an A."

"Wrong, Flesh. There is an I, it's hidden in the A-hole."

"Will you two grown boys give it a rest?"

Susan turned to the computer on the desk to check an email that had just chimed in. "Sweet. Sara reports all is well with our little farmhand. She said they had a bit of a set-to over bedtime the other night but that was easily resolved by letting Amy win."

"Don't I know it," Jake said, looking up from his phone.

Trey added, "Like I told you in Salt Lake—rats and cacti. I've never had a single battle over bedtime."

Susan continued reading. "Amy told Sara to tell Jake "hi" from Matt and Tim. Sara says Amy talked to Matt for forty-five minutes on the phone the other night." Susan looked up stunned. "Uh-oh."

"Three quarters of an hour? Amy got my son to string sentences together for three-quarters of an hour? I called a couple nights ago; I doubt

I got a good ten minutes out of him."

"Might be time for Amy's Sunrise Dance," Trey said.

"I doubt it required whole sentences; the occasional 'uh huh' is more than enough to keep Amy going. Oh, and Sara forwarded a Megboard message in case we're missing out on the Boulder excitement." She read from her computer. "Free rooster. Beautiful buff Orpington. Gentle with the ladies and non-aggressive to people. He's got plenty of cock-a-doo-dle-doos left in him."

"God I love Megboard. Reminds you what's important—a non-aggressive rooster that's gentle with the ladies. Now that's what's important." Jake glanced at Trey. "No nasty cock jokes, now."

"What the hell is Megboard?" Trey asked.

Susan and Jake looked at each other and laughed.

"So, fellow investigators, tomorrow it's back to the Lifebridge stake-out."

Susan groaned. "I'd rather eat glass."

"I know, I hear you but what else can we do? We know our guy works there, unless he's on special kidnapper's leave, he's going to trip up and we're going to spot him."

"What's so hard about sitting around drinking coffee?" Trey asked.

"Trey, you're going to love the little cutie with the tattoos behind the counter," Susan said.

"Not that big on tattoos."

"Trust me, you're going to love Karen. She has a perfect pair of tats on her, right Jake?"

Jake took a prudent pass on that little poke. "Oh, I almost forgot. I picked up a surprise for you two at Costco today. I'll be right back." He slipped a keycard into the back pocket of his shorts and headed out.

Jake enjoyed this time of day in the desert city. A cooling evening breeze had kicked up. As he walked in and out of shadows crossing the parking lot, sparkling columns of particles danced in the remaining sunlight. He heard a morning dove and wondered why one was calling in the evening. Then he remembered it was mourning, not morning, and surmised that was due to the sorrowful song.

He opened the rear of his car, grabbed the pool toys and headed back toward the hotel.

The colorful collection of thick noodles held together with two wide strips of plastic wrap had caught his eye at Costco. He suspected Susan would appreciate some floatation while soaking. The package included a robin's-egg blue noodle, a bright yellow noodle, a dark red, a violet, an orange and a purple. It seemed like nothing was sold in quantities of less than six at Costco.

Excessive time in their rooms was driving them all a little nuts. Especially Susan. Jake hoped the toys would provide some diversion. And his purchase was not completely unselfish. He and his boys had enjoyed many foam sword fights in pools. The prospect of slapping his buddy Flesh with a wet noodle was enough to get Jake in the water more and could help them all pass the down time.

Going from the parking lot through the gate by the pool cut off several steps. Jake used his keycard, entered the swimming area, skirted around the edge of the sparkling pool now lit by a ring of underwater lights and headed toward the hotel door by the hot tub. He was passing a small brown building housing the pool mechanicals when out of the shadows rushed two figures. Before he could react defensively, a shoulder caught him in the noodles, tripping him backwards, and flattening the foot of a chaise lounge. Jake, his tackler and the broken chair all pitched toward the edge. A second body smashed into him on the fly and he slammed into the water still clutching the package. That was a stroke of luck because his assailants immediately attacked, while trying to hold him under.

One powerful punch thankfully blocked by the noodles rolled him over. He opened his eyes and noticed the chair sinking; the light on the bottom of the pool was a latticework of shimmering diamonds. He turned to the side and saw a blur of bubbles and thrashing legs. Were there only two men? It was like watching an underwater shot of several people dog paddling in fast motion but these particular arms and legs were aiming blows at his head and body. He'd fend off a kick from attacker number one and attacker number two would land a numbing punch to the head only slightly cushioned by the water. Then while he tried to free himself from one man who was preventing him from surfacing for a breath, he saw the other guy pull back, reach into the waistband of his shorts and produce a long flat piece of metal. He fumbled with the object with both hands while kicking hard to keep his head above water and soon the knife was unfolded into a two-edged blade reflecting wavering light. He pulled back the weapon and thrust it underhand at Jake.

Jake whipped his body back and forth, hugging the pool toys and blocking the blows from the unarmed attacker while absorbing the knife thrusts from the other. He landed a lucky kick in the gut of the man with the knife, bending him over. The knife slipped out of his hand and fluttered to the bottom. But he quickly recovered, delivered a vicious shot from the heel of his right hand, caught Jake under the chin knocking out what little breath he had left, then kicked toward the bottom to retrieve his weapon. Jake maneuvered above, wrapped his legs around his head and held on tight while the pinned man thrashed back and forth and pried at Jake's legs. Jake wanted to rip his ears off but didn't dare let go of the noodles. So he rode him like a bucking sea serpent, hoping his antagonist would pass out from lack of air. Finally, desperate, the trapped man twisted free and abandoned his weapon on the bottom in favor of air at the surface.

Still the other man held Jake so that the water was over his head—not much, thanks to the flotation. Jake repeatedly tried to kick to the surface with his feet while continuing to swing his arms and the noodles back and forth to protect his core. Twice he got close to the surface but both times four powerful arms pulled him down and held him under. After a heel kick at the groin of one of his attackers landed on its targets, he drove his face to the surface and briefly broke through for a life-saving breath when he was once again ripped down. This time his flotation was torn away and he was driven almost to the bottom with kicks. The pressure and pain in his chest were explosive. Four feet jabbed and kicked down at him from above. His head, neck and shoulders endured powerful heel blows. The one short breath had helped, but only a little, and he knew he was close to taking the involuntary drowning breath, the reflexive intake of water that fills the lungs with fluid often beyond recovery. He felt one last blow to his right ear when suddenly his assailants swam for the side.

Jake thrust up, broke the surface and gulped at the air. But in his desperation he hadn't completely cleared the splashing water and he aspirated a little. He rolled on his back and coughed violently. The darkening city sky dotted with first pale stars loomed above. The noodle package floated nearby. He flailed his way to it and hung on. His arms were like water, limp with fatigue. His ragged breath whistled wetly against the foam toys. He turned his gaze toward the edge but the men were gone. Doors slammed and a car started and hurried away. He was alone. He was alive. But why? The floatation had helped but he was absolutely certain if those two whack-jobs had wanted him dead, he would be a corpse floating with the pool toys right now. More painful coughs racked his chest. There was a distant train's horn, or was that the mourning dove's call again? He wasn't certain. A dark liquid like a stream in a lava lamp flowed out from his body and mixed with pool water. He hadn't felt the knife cut him. He worked his way to the edge, slowly pulled up the steps, collapsed in a chair, held his wound and gasped for air. Bright drops of blood seeped through his fingers, flowed down his side and dripped on the concrete deck.

The knife sat on the dresser under the flat screen TV—a RUKO WWII Paratrooper knife with a 5-3/8th inch blade that anybody could find on Amazon. When Jake hadn't returned, Trey and Susan got worried and went down to search for him. They found him by the pool, groggy and holding the bloody gash in his side. After they got him up and were helping him toward the door he stopped and pointed to the object on the bottom. Trey removed his shirt and sandals and managed to retrieve the knife.

In the corner by the bathroom door, with a few nicks and battle scars, was the colorful package of toys. One plastic strip had been severed; the noodles were splayed like a hydra-head.

"They could've killed me. I was totally caught by surprise and immediately overpowered," Jake said.

Susan had insisted he lie down on the bed while she grabbed their first aid kit stored in the bathroom throughout their stay. She examined his side. Thankfully the wound was shallow and superficial. She dabbed on disinfectant, pulled the raw edges together with butterflies, covered them with gauze pads and taped it all down with adhesive tape. Trey sat in the big chair, pale from the realization that he could have lost his best friend.

"This deal is suddenly, like more real than reality TV," Trey said.

"They didn't kill you, thank God. But what does that mean in light of their pattern of only killing the terminally ill?" Susan asked.

Jake coughed several times and then caught his breath. "Ironically, it's like stabbing someone but not deeply or mortally." His hand went to the fresh bandage on his side. "A forensic psychiatrist would probably say their actions are mostly symbolic. Like they are playing at something, trying to send a message but are not totally committed. I'm no expert myself, but the guy was obviously not experienced with a knife; the way he fumbled to open it, the way he held it, the fact that he dropped it, all screamed amateur."

Trey tired for humor. "You shouldn't bring a knife to a pool fight. Should bring a water pistol."

"What did they look like?" Susan asked.

Jake eased himself up and went in the bathroom and blew his nose. He came back and carefully sat on the bed. "It was getting dark, not that I could get a good look when they hit me like a frickin' freight train. The noodles blocked my view of them. Underwater there was way too much agitation. I never saw their faces but judging by their legs they were either very tan or naturally dark."

"Who knew a person's life could be saved by noodles," Trey said.

"Not sure they did, but they certainly helped keep me close to the surface and prevent the knife from doing more damage. I'll never look at those stupid things the same way again."

Susan walked over to the toys.

"Might want to put it above your mantel like a special sword back from a war," Trey said.

"The knife?" Jake asked.

"No, a noodle," Trey said.

Susan grasped the noodles one by one, briefly examining each. "The hard thing will be choosing just the right color."

Jake started to laugh but immediately grabbed his side and grimaced. Susan and Trey got big-eyed and rigid-jawed, like kids in class trying desperately to stifle guffaws.

Jake's phone dinged. Susan reached for it on the desk by the laptop expecting to see a final report of the day from Sara. She didn't.

She read the message to herself. "Maybe this day isn't ending so normal for the police chief after all." She paraphrased for the boys. "Sweetgrass is off the reservation. Your friend is following him."

"Might be nothing, but find out what he's driving, okay?" Jake said while carefully stretching out on the bed.

Susan typed, hit send and had barely put the phone down when she heard a reply. She read it aloud. "*Older Toyota, Corolla. Brown. AZ SMW1925.*" She lowered the phone. "AA is good. Might have a future in the investigative arts."

"I don't deputize just anybody, you know. I was very impressed with how well AA could spell. I require that," Jake said, his arm thrown over his eyes.

Trey passed the time playing online Scrabble on his iPhone. Susan paced and looked out the window, reflexively checking the locks on the door and occasionally insuring that Jake was resting comfortably.

The text they had all been hoping for finally pinged into Jake's phone. Susan picked it up off the desk.

Followed WS to P-nix. Just went in side door of mosque on Florence tween Florence and State.

"Son-of-a-bitch." She handed the cell to Jake. "I think we just hit the jackpot."

Jake took the phone and, still lying on his back, texted back. *Fantastic work. Please return home. We will take it from here.*

"Guys, I need you to watch his car and call me if he moves or if you see anything suspicious."

"You mean more suspicious than an Apache Police Chief visiting an Islamic Mosque at 10:30 at night?" Susan asked.

Jake eased up awkwardly on an elbow. "Susan, you cover now until 2:00. Trey, Susan will stay until you relieve her. Get coffee. Red Bull. Whatever you need, but stay awake. Do not confront Sweetgrass and don't let him see that you're watching him. I should be able to take over tomorrow morning. Make sure you keep your phones charged."

Susan kissed Jake on the lips, packed her daypack, armed herself, and was out the door.

Trey settled into the overstuffed chair wanting to stay near his wounded buddy and yet close his eyes for a little nap before his shift.

The mosque was a dark and sinister combination of brown block and dirty beige stucco. High, steeply pitched, and angular rooflines came down low over small windows, imbuing the building with a hooded and watchful appearance. A tall windowless column shaped like a pencil, point up, was capped with a crescent moon on a short metal staff. The lighted sign, a carved stone monolith, had both English and Arabic lettering. Susan read it—EAST PHOENIX ISLAMIC MOSQUE.

Susan made one pass to be certain she spotted Sweetgrass's car and then parked on the street on the opposite side in the middle of the next block, in full view of the building.

The mosque was in the center of the block where Florence Street curved to the right. Off a driveway on the far side of the building that ended at an enclosed compound for dumpsters she noticed a railing and steps descending to the basement, a single light shining down on the steps from above. The mosque sat in a quiet neighborhood close to a community college campus. Traffic was light. She opened her windows, shut off the engine, leaned her seat back, and settled in for the vigil.

Gloria was locked behind the door of a large metal cage obviously intended for storage in a cool windowless basement room. She sat on a bunk under a floor lamp and flipped through magazines supplied to her by her captors. Her tray from dinner had not been picked up. It held an empty glass and a plate full of picked over scraps and sat on a small round leather side table.

The four Islamic men taking shifts guarding her had treated her, if not with kindness, then certainly with deference. They had provided various essentials, and one, the youngest, had offered a recently purchased hairbrush.

They ignored her questions and refused to speak to her, but their demeanor was never threatening. Each day they had supplied her with toilet paper, a scrubbed out bucket with a lid and the privacy required to use it.

Gloria was tired, a little nervous and very lonely, but oddly, not afraid. Although the purpose of her capture had not been made clear to her, and she could not fathom what these men wanted from her, she felt relatively certain they intended no physical harm.

She heard voices in the next larger room that adjoined hers but couldn't make out what was being said. Then the door to her chamber slowly creaked open and closed and a man stood across from her cell in the shadows. He spoke in Apache and referred to her as Aunt Gloria.

Susan was at it again, doing her least favorite thing. Nothing. Nothing but watching and worrying—about Jake. Although he seemed to be recovering from the shock of his underwater tussle, she worried because he was worried. She knew how important it was to him to find Gloria and get her home safely. She wanted that too, but as the guy whose name was on the shingle, he had more at stake.

No one had come or gone from the side door of the mosque. Traffic had pretty much trickled down to zero.

She checked the street for the hundredth time, scanned the alley and sighed with exasperation. She regretted her haste in running out the door. She would kill for a cup of coffee, some chocolate, and Trey's Scrabble to pass the time.

Just after midnight, an elderly man walked by with a graying Golden, who, if dog's could talk, Susan would swear was saying, "Finally, you get your ass out of that chair and out that door."

Later Susan checked the time on her phone—12:57. Thirty minutes had passed without any activity on the street. All was deathly quiet.

The crash of breaking glass sat her up straight. She grabbed her Glock from between her feet. There was laughter. It was a mixed-gender gaggle of giggling college students, gassed to the gills, experiencing the illicit and hilarious thrill known only to novice drinkers of smashing a beer bottle on the curb. Susan eased back in her seat and watched them stagger off.

To pass a little time she typed a text to Jen, something she had been intending to do for days. She said she was in Phoenix with Jake following leads and asked if Jen had learned anything more about that suspicious smokejumper. She added a few pleasantries illustrated with emoticons, hit send, and immediately worried that perhaps Jen didn't mute her phone at night. She didn't want to disturb her. No one wants to hear a phone beep at one in the morning.

Gloria stood behind the cell door. "I assume you've come to take me home, William," Gloria said cautiously in English. "Unlock this door right now, please."

"It's not that easy, Aunt. Where is our home? How can any of us say this country is our home?" Sweetgrass pulled a cane chair away from a desk by the door, carried it to near her cell, and sat, the metal grid separating them.

"Who are these men? They won't speak to me. What do they want?"

"They are my brothers and my braves. They look to me for leadership. I instructed them to not harm you in any way, but told them to say nothing until I could reason with you."

"Reason with me, William? About what? I want to go home to Fort Apache. My people and my family need me; they must be very worried."

Sweetgrass ignored her plea. "I suspect deep down you hate our subservient lifestyle and our slavish dependence on the casino as much as I do."

She laced her fingers through the grid on the metal door. "What does that have to do with these men?"

"We met in college here in Phoenix. We were taking a history class taught by a Dr. Steiner. He was different in that he taught the history of this country without lies and delusions. Whitewashing, I believe is the very appropriate word for it. We learned that America is one long bloody path of oppression and exploitation by whites—the slaves, other minorities, our people, now the Muslims. These men are Muslims and first became friends and then fellow warriors, jihadi in their terms—"

"Don't tell me you've joined their immoral cause?"

"I've joined their *immortal* cause and they've joined mine. I've converted to Islam and they have been schooled by me in the ways of the Apache."

"Oh, William, as your leader and friend, that breaks my heart."

"But Aunt, it is not two causes but one cause, one justified religious war against the corruption and depravity of western culture. We learned in Steiner's class that it was the bloodthirsty white soldiers who tortured and murdered our people and stole our land in the time of Goyathlay, then went to the Philippine Islands, tortured and slaughtered Catholics and Muslims and stole their land in what was called the Spanish American War.

He leaned in toward her. "Why was the war fought in the Philippines against natives called a war against the Spanish? It was called the Spanish American War because the American government lied to the Filipino people just as they lied to American Indians time after time after time. They promised the Filipino people that they would liberate them from Spanish colonial rule and then tricked them and after brutally squashing any resistance, including Muslim resistance, occupied their country for decades."

"Why are you telling me this? What do you want from me?"

"We've been training for lesser jihad online. Our teachings tell us this war is our duty. The Prophet wrote, 'Whoever dies in a state whereby he never participated in jihad has died on one of the branches of hypocrisy.' Our leader of the Islamic Caliphate has urged all mujahideen to take the battle everywhere and ignite the earth against Satan and all tyrants. The West is at war with Muslims. We wanted to send a message to the tyrant America by setting fires we hoped would cover a huge amount of the sacred country which once belonged to our native ancestors but which was stolen from them. We chose an area in the shape of a burning arrow on an unstrung bow from Central Utah to Phoenix and San Diego to Albuquerque. Think about it, Aunt. God put us on this land first and yet American Indians have the highest suicide rate and lowest high school graduation rate of any minority in the country. One third of our people live in poverty. Our legacy was once noble, now it is drug abuse, alcoholism, domestic violence and incarceration. Then out of sheer economic desperation we turn to gambling. How much further can we as a people be driven down before we rise up? If there can be an Islamic State, is it too much to believe there could be a sovereign country for American Indians?"

She felt herself getting angry. "You're deluded. Why the murders? Why the bodies in forest fires?"

"Lone Wolf ... Mohammed works for the Lifebridge Cancer Center, one of the few things your private investigator has figured out. We chose our rich victims from there because they were terminally ill. We gave them an honorable native death—a chance to live last moments in the beauty of a forest and then be purified with a funeral pyre. It was merciful—morphine from Lifebridge to put them under, plastic bags to stop their breathing—a symbolic message about the white cancer and white materialism that has been devouring this continent since the arrival of the infidel Christians."

"You had no right to kill those people. If you deprived their loved ones of even one day with them you are as bad as those you purport to hate. Violence begets violence. You are murderers, arsonists and vandals.

Nothing more noble than that."

"Our efforts have been diminished by your hiring Goddard and by firefighters that we did not anticipate would be so successful in this time of the larger hotter fires we have been warned about by the BIA. So now we turn to you to insure our holy efforts for Allah command the attention and deplete the resources of the United States Government."

"What are you asking of me?"

"Just two things, Aunt. Agree to these two things and I will free you. You have my word."

"What are they?"

"Goddard works for you. He's getting very close. We have tried to scare him away but that doesn't seem to be working. I want you to stop him."

"And if I agree, then what?"

"Then I ask that you give me just seventy-two hours to introduce you to the ways of Muhammad, peace be upon him, and convince you of the justness of our cause."

"And if I'm not convinced."

"I will set you free and you will never see me again. Knowing how you feel about the federal government intervening in Indian affairs, I'm pretty sure you won't turn us in."

Gloria felt it unwise to contradict that statement. "And let's say I am convinced. What then?"

"You are the Chief of the White Mountain Apache people and a former AIM activist. If you convince the *Inde* to join you, other tribes will follow."

"Cheis once said, 'you must speak straight so that your words may go as sunlight into our hearts.' Speak straight, what exactly are you suggesting?" She demanded.

"I'm urging you to awaken the drums of our warrior ancestors and rise up against the tyranny of white oppression. Take the Apache back on the warpath against the U.S. government."

Gloria glared at Sweetgrass in stunned disbelief.

Trey pulled up beside Susan in his silver Nissan Xterra, nodded and drove around the block. When he returned she was gone; he pulled into her spot.

He had stocked up for the duty. On the floor of the passenger side was a plastic bag from a local convenience store full of sugar and caffeine-laced confections.

He reached down and pulled out a Red Bull and a large bag of Cheetos.

A few slurps and crunches later, he inspected his fingers in the dim light from the street and realized that if he ever committed a felony, he could easily be identified by traces of yellow cheese dye. He wiped his hands on his shorts, burped and searched the area with his eyes. The brown Corolla had not moved. The street was dead.

Suddenly he heard a deep-throated engine as headlights stabbed into his rearview and lit up his interior. He instinctively slid down in his seat. The angle of the lights shifted and a beater pickup crawled by. The cowboy driver cast a glassy-eyed grin at Trey, reminding him just how invisible he wasn't. The truck, now rumbling away at a snail's pace, put him in mind of a college buddy who used to say while driving under the influence, "The drunker we get, the slower we go." The pickup had a bumper sticker by its one working taillight that read *If it ain't country. It ain't music.*

Trey sat up. He made a mental note to find that sticker for Jake's Subaru. He picked up his phone and selected the Scrabble app. He was kicking the computer's butt for a change and couldn't wait to deliver the coup de gras in the saved game.

William left for a few minutes and returned with a short dark man dressed in a black t-shirt and blue nylon sweat pants. The man pulled a second chair over but remained standing back in the shadows behind Sweetgrass. Gloria sat on her bunk.

"Aunt Gloria, this is Mohammed, known in our group as Lone Wolf."

The man spoke softly. "I'm honored to meet you, Mrs. Fox. May I call you sheik?"

"You may call me Gloria, Mohammed. And if you really wish to honor me you can unlock this door and free me."

Mohammed approached the cell, reached in a pants pocket and passed a blue silk scarf through the grid. "Here is a gift from the four of us who have been caring for you. You may cover your hair if you wish."

She took it, turned it over in her hands. "I will, but only because I haven't had a shower in days." He went to his chair and sat as Gloria pulled the scarf over her head, reversed the ends around her neck and adjusted it on her forehead.

"You must have some questions for us, Aunt," Sweetgrass said.

"I have a thousand questions for you, but it's the middle of the night. However, I don't think I will be able to sleep until I ask this one. How can you justify the terror and brutality that the IC is becoming infamous for?"

"Oh, that. Our advisor in Syria, with whom we Skype regularly, assures us that those reports of atrocities are exaggerated by the pro-Israel U.S. media. Anything can be faked these days," William said.

"The *khilafah*, the caliphate is helping people find food, jobs and shelter, as well as a spiritual home. Why else would so many Westerners be traveling to Syria to join in jihad?" Mohammed asked.

"That is what is so unbelievable to most Americans like me. Millions of your fellow Muslims abhor and reject the bloody extremism of your actions, purportedly taken in the name of their ancient and peaceful religion. You are obviously intelligent people flocking to an ideology that is based on slavery, rape, and murdering women and children. Civilized nations will not tolerate your institutionalized cruelty for long. Your caliphate is on a suicide mission."

"When you are on the *deen*—living your faith with body and soul—and you die, it is a death that promises great rewards in heaven. *Allahu Akbar*," Mohammed said.

"God is great, Aunt. To Allah we belong and to him we shall return. Now, we will let you get some sleep but first I need you to send a message to Jake Goddard."

Sweetgrass went over to the table by the door and unplugged her cell phone from a charger.

He spoke quietly by the door to Mohammed. "After the *adhan* for *fajr* get us all some breakfast." Mohammed nodded and went out.

He crossed to the cell. "I've asked Mohammed to get you breakfast after the call to morning prayers." He handed her phone through the door. "Write the text to Goddard and let me see it and then you can sleep. Be sure and include something so he'll know it's from you."

Gloria sat thinking with the phone in her lap for a few moments and then began to type.

It was now 5:30 and although all the windows in the mosque remained dark, Trey discerned a dim light in the sky to the east. He yawned, shook his head, and reached for his Red Bull can in the cup holder. It was empty. He chucked the dead soldier on the floor of the passenger side with the rest of his stakeout trash and dragged his tongue across the top of his mouth, stirring up a sour Red Bull residue. He decided against opening a fresh can and grabbed his phone instead for another round of Scrabble against the computer.

Quietly, the faithful began approaching the mosque for morning prayers. Most walked, some drove and parked along the street, some arrived on motor scooters and a few rode bicycles. They were all male and most wore beards. He glanced out the window and slammed back against his seat when a burly, clean-shaven man came up the side steps of the building and walked down the street away from the mosque. Trey immediately switched his device to text message mode.

August 6
Wednesday

J ake was awakened from troubled waterlogged dreams by a text. He glanced at the hotel clock—5:46 a.m. He rolled to the bedside table. His aching head, neck, and shoulders a reminder of the underwater beating. The text was from Trey, reporting that a short, powerful, dark-skinned man had come out of the basement and walked around the corner. Jake woke Susan and told her. Then he switched the screen to check for other messages and saw he had missed one during the night that had come in sometime after Susan had crawled into bed.

When Jake realized what he was reading, he threw the sheet off and swung his feet to the carpet—abruptly remembering the wound in his side. The bandage above his gray boxer briefs had soaked through. Dried blood caked the white gauze and tape.

He read the text again from the top. *Hello Jake. I know you are worried about me but I'm fine. I was involved in the movement as a young woman because I didn't like how my people were treated. This is a natural return to that activism. I'm being treated very well. Great food, comfortable bed, several sheets and one blanket. Please don't look for me. I'm doing what I love. Just so you know this is from me—the French word of the day is "malherbe."* —Gloria

Susan had jolted up and read over his shoulder. No amount of coffee could have brought them to wakefulness faster. Jake checked the number.

It was Gloria's.

Susan jumped out of bed and paced in her white t-shirt and briefs. Jake shifted to the overstuffed chair being careful to avoid opening his still fresh wound. He rubbed sleep out of his eyes.

"What we got?" He asked.

"We know Gloria is alive. No one could have faked that text. Not and know the whole French word thing."

"Do we believe the text? That she is fine and joining some activist group?" Jake asked.

"Gloria an activist as a kid just out of college. Totally plausible. But leave her family and position to return to that life? No way."

"I agree. So then if this text was done under duress and is not true—"

"Gloria is smart enough to send us a clue." She stopped in front of the window. The rising sun was blood orange. "Can you read it aloud?"

He did. Then followed with, "The first few lines probably don't hold any special meaning. Let me read the last half again starting with 'I'm being treated very well.'" He did.

Susan turned from the window. "Okay, okay, right there is a contradiction. If I've joined someone or something voluntarily, they don't treat me well or otherwise, right? I'm one of them. I'm there of my own free will. I would talk about being accepted, welcomed, returned, reunited, any number of words implying belonging but not 'treated.' It doesn't fit."

"Then I'm guessing that is where our hidden message begins. The next line is food, beds, sheets, blankets."

"A blanket in Arizona in August? Assuming she's still in Arizona. Plus who talks about how many sheets and blankets they have?" Susan asked.

"No one talks about it unless it's code."

Susan was pacing again. "Sheets, blankets, sheets, blankets, sheets and blankets, sheet not blanket—what the hell?" She ran both hands through her hair.

"You mull that while I go online and translate 'malherbe.'" Jake eased his body up and slowly walked to the desk chair. He sat carefully and brought his computer to life.

Susan grabbed Jake's phone and read, paraphrasing, "I'm fine. I'm doing what I love. Bullshit, you are. Where are you, Gloria?"

Jake looked up from his screen. "Francois Malherbe was a French poet and a critic. He died in 1628. How does that help us?"

"What else does it say?"

"Just that Malherbe advocated the classical concepts of clarity and concision of meaning."

"There's no other definition for Malherbe?"

"No. Just the guy. It's a proper noun according to this website."

"Okay, let's Malherbe it. Let's be precise. Break it down."

Jake tapped away at the computer. "Mal—translates as bad, wrong, abnormal." He typed a few more strokes. "Herbe—grass."

"Bad grass. As opposed to?"

"Sweetgrass!" Jake pushed back in the desk chair. "That son-of-a-bitch is involved. I knew it."

"Last I heard Sweetgrass was Apache. Looks like Gloria owes you dinner."

Jake was up holding his side and searching for his shorts. "We should go over there to the mosque and confront the bastard."

"Not so fast, Kemosabe. I had a mystery too remember? And with your help, I think I've solved it."

She whipped off her t-shirt, strapped a black bra across her back and pulled on a violet sleeveless tank top. "If Gloria has several sheets and one blanket, then according to her expression in which blanket refers to her people and sheet refers to India Indians, then Sweetgrass is the blanket and there are also "sheets" or Middle Easterners somehow involved. I think Sweetgrass and several Muslims might be holding her in that mosque. Maybe you're going to that dinner, Dutch."

"How is that possible?"

"How is anything possible today? How was 9/11 possible? It's the new abnormal normal and the impossible possible. Are you strong enough to come with me or am I going over to that mosque alone?"

Jake got his shorts buttoned and was searching for his shoes.

Jake drove. Susan dialed Trey several times, each with greater frustration. How could he not be answering? Jake suggested that when they arrived she jump in with Trey and instruct him to stay in his car and watch for anyone suspicious leaving the mosque while they were inside looking for Sweetgrass.

Jake slowed as they approached the building. Light emanated from the main sanctuary. All legal street parking was taken.

He pulled up beside the Nissan. Trey jolted with surprise and waved tentatively.

Jake lowered the passenger window and shot Trey the silent, shoulders' shrugged, palms up, what-the-fuck-dude look. Just as Susan was exiting Jake's car, she noticed a man carrying two white bags approaching the side steps of the mosque. He stopped and stared at Susan. She stuck her head through the window at Jake.

"That's him."

The man turned and walked hurriedly up the drive by the building, talking into a phone he had fished out of the pocket of his sweatpants.

"Tell Trey what's up. I'm going to see what the bungler has planned. I think he recognized you."

Jake drove toward the mosque and stopped by a fire hydrant across from the driveway. Susan slid in beside Trey, crushing snack bags and clattering empty cans with her feet. "Why the hell aren't you answering your phone?"

He plucked it out of the trash-filled console. The screen was blank. "Scrabble killed the battery and I forgot the frigging car charger."

She peered at the floor and loaded console cup holders. "You remembered all this crap food but forgot your phone charger. Great work, Colombo."

"My bad. Sorry." He studied his hands on the wheel. "So what's going on? Why you guys here?"

Susan was beginning to fill him in when the familiar blue pickup squealed down the driveway with the man she had just recognized behind the wheel. He stood on the brakes by the steps. Susan quickly surmised the truck had been hidden behind the metal doors she had thought were for concealing dumpsters. Three men ran up and out of the mosque's basement. Two leaped into the bed and the third hopped into the passenger seat and slammed the door. The truck turned out of the driveway and sped up the street—Jake gave chase.

Susan's phone rang. It was Jake. She hit speaker. Traffic noise on his end competed with his voice.

"I'll continue tailing the four faux Indians."

"Use extreme caution, Jake. No clue how Sweetgrass fits in but this has got to be a jihadi cell and those lone wolves are typically lowlifes looking to be martyrs."

"They're for sure radicalized Muslims but they're still bunglers playing freshman ball."

"And Sweetgrass's role?"

"I'm hoping we'll have solved that stunner by end of business today. You should stay in the car and watch for him. Don't engage without me there—surveillance only."

A few men began to trickle out of the mosque. Susan punched up the volume on her phone. "What if he tries to leave?" Silence. "Jake, there is no way I'm letting Sweetgrass just drive away, especially if he has Gloria."

"Okay, I get that. If Sweetgrass comes out with Gloria, and only if he comes out with Gloria, shadow him from a safe distance. Keep me posted by cell. It's critical you have a working phone and we keep in touch." Susan shot Trey a look. "Be advised, it's possible my guys are a diversion intended to create cover for Sweetgrass to escape with Gloria. Gotta go. Keep in touch."

Susan ended the call. Her first order of business was to tidy Trey's car by gathering his garbage into a convenience store bag. She pulled a car charger out of a pocket in her shorts and shoved it into his outlet while nailing him with a loaded look. He pushed his glasses up his nose, smiled sheepishly, and yawned.

They had just settled in for the continued stakeout when a knot of men walked out of morning prayers. That jarred Susan to maximum attentiveness. She studied every face that left the mosque. For once her search was rather simple. Just about every man old enough to do so was wearing a beard. Obviously that was not the case with either Sweetgrass or Gloria. Unless...

Her eye selected, rejected and then selected again, a pair of bearded men in the center of the crowd. There was something odd about the way the taller of the two held the arm of the shorter man, and something else bothered her as well.

"See those two arm-in-arm in the center? Look how they're dressed in ankle-length tunics in this heat. Wish I could get a closer look."

"Got binos in the glove box." Trey brightened, thinking this could be the first step on the path to redemption.

Susan snapped open the box, pulled out the binoculars and focused. The pair had separated from the crowd and was angling toward the brown Corolla parked one block up and on the opposite side of the street.

"You have got to be kidding me," Susan said from behind the binos. "This gets weirder by the minute. First we got Middle Easterners playing American Indians and now we got American Indians impersonating Middle Easterners." She worked the focus. "I'm pretty sure that's Sweetgrass and Gloria with her hair covered by a cap, both with fake beards."

Just as she said it, the taller man jerked the shorter person toward the Toyota, dragged him around the back of the car and shoved him into the passenger side. He hurried around the hood looking furtively up and down the street. Susan panned with the binos and saw a bump in the man's cloak where his hand disappeared into the cloth.

"Well, well, well. Is that a pistol in your jubba, Bubba, or are you just happy to see me?" The driver got in, whipped off his beard and tossed it in the back, and started the car. It was Sweetgrass and he didn't seem to know he was being observed. Susan searched with the binos. She was still having difficulty making out the person in the passenger seat but it had to be Gloria and she was clearly there against her will. Sweetgrass gunned it into the street, threw a U-turn and drove away.

Susan pulled the binoculars down. "Q, follow that car."

"Will do, Susie Q." Trey fired up his Nissan. "I've always fanaticized someone would say that to me."

"You watch too many cop shows. It never happens. There's a good chance Sweetgrass doesn't know he's being watched but I'd still stay well back."

Trey eased out and got into step with the Toyota, now three cars ahead, while Susan autodialed Jake.

Just beyond the community college four blocks from the mosque, the driver of the blue truck sped up and ran a yellow light. Jake caught the red, but it was still early and traffic was light. He stopped, looked and went through, eliciting an angry beep from an approaching scooter but causing no damage and attracting no attention from members of the local constabulary who no doubt were still knee-deep in Daylight Donuts. He got close enough to study the two men in the bed. Neither wore a beard. The one kneeling on the driver's side appeared to be fit and in his early twenties. He was basketball tall, dark and Bollywood handsome. He was also scared. Jake watched his eyes dart back and forth like a trapped animal and made a mental note: trapped animals are dangerous. Bollywood was wearing a white strap t-shirt and baggy orange canvas shorts.

The Bad News Bungler bouncing around on a spare tire on the passenger side was older, maybe thirty, and uglier. He had a thick jaw and a long nose. He was dressed in western clothes also: gray Nike shirt and long black athletic shorts. He looked mean and was apparently unhappy about being followed—as if he would like nothing better than to stop the truck, jump out, tear the bumper off Jake's car and beat him senseless with it. Mental note: men who look mean often are.

The pickup with Jake directly behind was passing a railroad yard rife with graffiti covered boxcars in neat rows. Jake did not know Phoenix well, but he sensed they were near the neighborhood with the golf course, mall and cancer center. Except for running yellow lights, the driver didn't seem all that concerned about losing Jake. Such is the plight of the lowly PI, he thought. Speak loudly while carrying a small stick.

The passenger handed a white bag out of the side window of the truck to Mr. Mean. Mean reached in the bag and extracted a paper-covered item for his companion and then dug one out for himself. They settled in to eat breakfast. Jake found that amusing—eating breakfast in the middle of a car chase. Apparently he was not being taken very seriously. Hell, the odds were only four-to-one. Bollywood let the wrapper from his breakfast sandwich slip out of his fingers and it blew across Jake's windshield and tumbled into the street. Litterers, too, Jake thought. These bad boys have got to be stopped.

Judging by Sweetgrass's unhurried pace driving the city streets, Susan assumed the man who had recognized her had either not noticed Trey's car or in his rush had failed to alert Sweetgrass about it. Unless it was a ploy, their quarry still appeared to be unaware of them. It also helped that Trey was being cagey, carefully following Susan's directives and staying well back from the Corolla.

"Any idea what he might be doing?" Trey asked as they passed a brick and glass public school abutted by several fields and a stadium. Sweetgrass was five cars ahead.

"I'm looking at our current location on my fully charged iPhone's GPS and I think he's heading for the beltway out of the city."

"Ouch. My penitence is obviously not over." Trey mimed a right-handed flogging motion over each shoulder. "I guess we'll know soon," he said.

"Hope Gloria's okay. I'm glad Sweat-ass hasn't noticed we're on his tail but I wish I could tell Gloria telepathically the cavalry is back here and has her back."

"I don't know Gloria at all. But 'cavalry' might not be the best analogy."

"Very sensitive, Flesh," she said.

He grinned at the praise.

"Damn good point," Susan added. "I wonder what the American Indian expression is for 'help is on the way.'"

"No clue. But it's damn sure not likely to involve any reference to the cavalry. Who knows, maybe they've never experienced it." He followed the Toyota, now four cars ahead, around a right turn while whistling the theme song from the Mighty Mouse cartoon.

Jake had been correct in his assumption. The truck was heading toward the Ironwood Mall and the Lifebridge Center. He had to drop back when a red light caught him and this time running it would have been suicide. Fortunately, cross traffic cleared quickly. From the street, he saw the blue truck turn into the mall and head for the Lifebridge building. He checked his cell. 7:22—still well before Lifebridge opened for business.

He swung into the mall parking lot. There were several cars parked by Starbucks but little other activity. The truck was gone.

There was no way they could have exited the mall without Jake noticing so he assumed the truck had gone behind the building.

Fearing a trap, he reached for his Browning nine under his seat while easing the car around the back corner. Nothing at the loading dock. He crept around the next corner by the Paradise Juicery. No truck. He sped around to the front of the building. They had disappeared.

He drove back around to the loading dock, parked, got out and indulged in a good old ball-cap-off head scratcher while wondering where the hell the Bungler-mobile could possibly have gone. He looked at the building. The loading docks had huge doors but each had truck-deck high walls in front of them. No vehicle could climb that steep waist-high concrete and drive inside.

He studied the golf course beyond the chain link fence. It was their only escape. But how? Starting at the edge of the fence at the far left of the loading area he pushed on each section. The third section, approximately in the middle of the loading area, gave a little when he shook it. He noticed faint tire marks just on the other side of the chain link where irrigation water had softened the grass. Of course, he thought. Four men running around a golf course in a small pickup in the early morning or late evening would resemble a grounds crew. Maybe one of them worked for the golf course. This had to be how the bunglers smuggled victims and possibly drugs out of the center. He studied the metal pole on the right and found small hinges. He ran to the left side, found two small latches, flipped them down, and the section of fence eased open. He pushed the slack section of fencing out of the way and drove through, jumped out, and closed the fence. He did so to avoid causing alarm as people arrived at the center. There were no golfers out yet. The fairway stretched away to Jake's right into a dogleg left wrapping around a small grove. The flag was just visible beyond the trees. Jake estimated that on a good day it was about a fairway wood to the hole. He could not see the truck but he had the intermittent tracks and he began to follow them toward the green. The truck was probably blending right in, he thought, but a Subaru driving around a golf course? Now that was as obvious as body hair on a swimsuit model.

Sweetgrass had driven onto the beltway as Susan had predicted. She called Jake on speaker.

"He's heading out on 202 toward Mesa. I'm going to guess that at Apache Junction he'll head south to Florence Junction and then over to Globe and back up into the mountains."

"Take him on down to Florence and drop him off at the state pen," Jake said.

"Will do. Can hang out with Ernie Longbraid. How's your chase going?"

"Just enjoying a round of golf. Had a good drive down 6, a par 4, and heading to 7, an easy 7-iron, par 3."

"What the hell."

"I think my guys slipped through the fence behind Lifebridge and are driving around the golf course trying to shake me. Wait—hold on a minute. I see the truck near the clubhouse. Have to hang up. Be careful and keep in touch."

"You be care…shit he's gone." She put down her phone and pushed hair behind her ears.

"This day sure isn't turning out at all as I expected," Trey said.

"In the world of GCG few do, Flesh, few do. He's turning off. Follow but stay back. If he stops at a gas station go past it."

Trey put on his right blinker.

The bunglers must have been planning a long trip. The truck was parked at the back of the clubhouse and the mean and ugly dude had jumped out of the bed to fill a large white water jug. The others waited in the pickup. Jake could tell they thought they had lost him. As he drove around the edge of a scummy pond near the first tee and got within one hundred yards, Jake saw Mean look up startled.

He leaped into the pickup bed, pounded on the roof of the cab and shouted at the driver to go, leaving the water running and the bottle on the ground. With Jake closing the gap, the truck swung around the corner of the building and slammed into a row of beige golf carts, tossing them together like a pile-up of bumper cars. The truck lurched back away from the carts, flattened the water bottle and snapped off the standpipe; a gusher arched above soaking the men in the bed. Jake was thirty yards away and closing. The truck's rear wheels spun in the mud near the broken pipe. The driver downshifted and the truck bounced forward and swerved around the outside of the wrecked carts, tearing dual grooves of turf out of a practice green.

Two elderly golfers in a green cart turned the front corner of the pro shop. The pickup was heading right for them. The driver of the cart veered at the last minute, collided with a Coke machine by the building, and slammed both men up against the Plexiglas windshield of the cart. Another man rushed out the side door of the pro shop, shouted, waved his arms and ran toward the Subaru.

Jake didn't have time to stop and chat, the blue truck was flying out the golf course entrance road. Water poured out from under the gate of the bed, the soggy men squatted and clung to the sides of the truck. Jake swerved around the guy from the shop and bucketed over the curb in pursuit.

In a few seconds, gears screaming, he was hot on the pickup's tail. No more breakfast and water breaks, he thought, it's on.

At the Pilot Truck Stop in the busy commercial area just off the highway, passenger cars and semis maneuvered toward their respective fuel islands. On their approach, Susan searched for the brown Toyota and saw it parked by a pump. She directed Trey to a Gulf Station just beyond the Pilot and suggested he choose a vantage point that gave them a good view of the Corolla. After they parked by a pump, Susan saw Sweetgrass about one hundred and fifty yards away by the passenger door of the car filling his tank. Cars entered and exited the fuel islands. Travelers crossed into and out of the building.

Trey got out, busied himself at the card reader, inserted the hose without starting the pump and leaned by the passenger door. Susan opened her window and heat poured in. She dug the binos out of the glove box and trained them on their target. He was wearing the mirrored sunglasses again. They must have been in the car overnight.

All appeared normal for a while until Sweetgrass started to pull his tunic over his head to remove it. He had slipped out his left arm when the passenger door was slammed open against his knee, forcing him to stagger back tangled in the garment. Susan sat up in her seat to get a better view and saw Gloria charge out of the car and around her captor. She had removed the beard and cap but still wore the long tunic and it slowed her. Sweetgrass ran her down, his half-removed garment flapping behind, grabbed her right arm and, limping, dragged her back to the car. He shoved her in, slammed the door, reached into his right pocket and glared at her. He quickly finished removing the heavy garment with his left hand and tossed it through the back door of the car. He disconnected the hose, banged into the vehicle, started it and exited the truck stop, driving back toward the freeway.

Trey replaced his hose, slid back in and pursued.

"Oh man, I was rooting for her," Trey said as he followed up the access ramp several cars back.

"You and me both, bud. If she'd gotten a little distance on him, I was ready to yell, *drive over there and flatten the fucker*. At least now we know for absolute certain it's Gloria and she's being held against her will."

"Blows me away nobody tried to help her." He had merged and was getting up to speed in the right-hand lane. The Toyota was in view ahead.

"We live in funny times—people afraid to get involved. Especially with Muslims—liberals afraid to offend and conservatives paranoid they're all wearing suicide vests under their jubbas."

"Guess so."

"Think about it, though, if a Good Samaritan does intercede, the person they confront could be an armed lunatic. And in this case—"

"They'd be right."

"Yeah."

"Plus it could put the hostage in even greater danger."

"You're a fast learner, Flesh."

"Jeez, Gloria didn't even get a chance to use the restroom."

Susan slammed her knees together. "Thanks a lot for reminding me."

Jake made no attempt to conceal his intention to stay right on the pickup's tail, his audacity bolstered by the sense that the men had not armed themselves before their hasty departure from the mosque. At least, so far, they hadn't fired arrows at him or brandished other weapons. But then anything, a stick, a brick, a rock can make a weapon.

When the truck ran yellow lights, Jake came through right behind without hesitation.

Wednesday morning traffic had begun to build a little and on several occasions the driver of the pickup tried to use the congestion and presence of other vehicles to shake Jake. But without success—he would not be moved.

Soon the pickup approached a railroad crossing with the caution lights just beginning to signal an oncoming train. Instead of slowing, the driver accelerated in a crazy attempt to cross before the arms were lowered. Jake heard the familiar four blasts of the train's horn warning of an approach to a crossing. He could see the train now a block away and quickly observed that there were two lanes across the tracks and the outside lane was open. He swerved out and shot up beside the truck and they flew over the tracks side by side, narrowly clearing the descending arms of the gate. The train whizzed by in his rearview, horn screaming with indignation.

For a few blocks, adrenaline pumping, Jake made no attempt to drop back. He continued along neck-and-neck, occasionally grinning and waving at the driver of the pickup as if they had just shared an adventure.

Jake had no clue where they were or where they were heading but he began to see signs for I-10. As the two vehicles approached a red light, he decided it was a good time to drop behind again and touch base with Susan. He slowed and swerved into the right lane behind the little truck.

With his head down to type a text at the red light, Jake suddenly sensed motion. He looked up just in time to see the two men from the bed rushing his car. Just as Bollywood reached for his door he hit the button, locking all four. He turned to see Mr. Mean with a roadside rock in his hand prepared to break the glass. Jake whipped his pistol up and aimed it at his forehead. Mean was suddenly freeze frame in the window. His hand slowly released the rock; it dropped out of Jake's view and chunked on the asphalt. The light changed and horns started honking. The two men abandoned their foolish plan, ran back empty-handed and leapt into the back of the truck. The driver sped away, Jake again tailing.

Jake's wheels were turning as well. *I really need to end this game and join Susan*, he thought. *These ill-prepared would-be jihadists don't appear to have weapons in the back but that doesn't mean they don't have them in the cab. And there are four of them with a proven history of violence, arson and abduction. What to do? What to do? What the fuck to do?* Then it struck him.

As the little pickup accelerated up the onramp for I-10 east, he texted Susan with one hand: *Heading S on 10 2ward Chand. BNBs Might b try to join WS at Florence Junction? Will stop them first.*

It was now mid-morning and so far Sweetgrass had done exactly as Susan predicted. Still apparently clueless, he had turned at Florence Junction—a crossroads and little else—and headed east toward Globe. Most puzzling to Susan was that he appeared to be taking Gloria back up into the White Mountains in the direction of the reservation. Trey followed the Corolla into Superior, a small town on the road to Globe.

Susan picked up her phone to respond to Jake's recent text with an update when Sweetgrass surprised them by veering south in Superior on Route 177 toward Winkleman, away from Fort Apache. "I didn't see that coming," Susan said, as Trey turned to pursue. "This is a small untraveled road. I would hang way back as we get near the edge of town."

"Which, judging by the size of this metropolis, will be any second now," Trey said.

"Not even big enough for a Walmart. Oh, but look, there's the Dollar Store. That and brisk lottery ticket sales are usually the best indicators of local poverty," Susan said.

"Kinda sad, folks trying to escape the reservation and landing in a place like this."

"Moving to the suburbs is rarely what it's cracked up to be."

In a few moments, a dilapidated antique/junk emporium next to a small engine repair shop surrounded by enough parked projects for two mechanics' lifetimes gave way to burned-out fields and irrigation ditches.

The Toyota, now well ahead but the only other car on the road, rounded a curve beside a grove of dead snags and scraggly cottonwoods. Susan's phone showed a long text from Jen: *Still riding the DL. Damn elbow! In Flagstaff for conference tomorrow about Dept. of Interior Wildland Fire Resilient Landscapes Program—major bucks thrown at uniting Feds, tribes, states and other groups to create fire-proof landscapes. Promise to get to Phoenix and connect ASAP. Got that info you wanted.*

Jake's plan was nothing special but he prided himself on how it qualified as a PI using cunning over extensive resources and deadly force. He waited for a bright red McDonald's semi to pass and for the space around the blue truck to clear of other vehicles before getting right on the pickup's bumper. He was close enough to notice the driver jerk several looks up at his rearview mirror. Jake inched closer. The pickup driver sped up. Jake shadowed him near enough to stare into the wind-stung eyes of the two passengers bouncing and swaying in the bed. Lucky they hadn't hung onto that rock. He swerved, accelerated, passed and pulled in front of the truck and dropped his speed, causing the driver to brake hard.

When Jake had the bungler slowed to forty-five miles an hour, the truck veered out and tried to pass. Jake responded by moving with him to block. The truck swung back in and passed on the right. Jake continued to fly around the pickup like a raven on road-kill. He kept up this roller derby-like harassment for several minutes, alternating front and back, first pushing and then blocking until he achieved the desired effect. On the final pass he glanced over and saw fury contorting the driver's face. After Jake dropped into the lead in the right-hand lane and began to slow, the driver swung out around Jake's car and sped away in a rage.

Jake dialed the short number he had noted on a sign a few miles back and put the phone on speaker.

"Arizona Highway Patrol."

"Oh, hi, I'm only calling as a concerned citizen."

"What's your concern, sir?" the woman asked.

"I'm watching a blue pickup on I-10 east near exit 152 speeding and driving erratically with two dark-skinned men in the cab and two in the bed. Is that even legal? Driving the freeway with passengers in the back, I mean? I'm not prejudice or trying to profile or anything, but I'm guessing these desperados are Mexican."

"Were you able to get the plate, sir?"

"Turns out I was, AZ-JBB3202."

"Thank you, I'll alert one of our officers."

"Appreciate it. How long do you think it'll be?"

"Shouldn't be long. We have a unit in that area. May I have your name, sir?"

"Sure, no problem, it's—" He hung up.

Jake sped after the truck, wanting to be certain it would attract the desired response when the officer arrived on the scene.

Susan called Jake and left a message about the recent change in direction. She urged him to be careful in whatever he had planned to stop the Muslims and asked what he thought of her doing the same with Sweetgrass. He responded a few minutes later with a brief voicemail message. Susan played it for Trey: "Your guy is armed and has a hostage. My guys don't appear to have weapons. Act only if Gloria is in danger. And be careful."

Susan held the phone in her lap after the message concluded. "I can't believe I missed his call back." She stared at the phone and then at Trey. "God, this drives me nuts! If I had any authority and jurisdiction I would've pulled this bastard over hours ago." She looked out the window. They were passing a ranch dotted with black cows. "Instead we're out here counting freakin' cows and playing alphabet." She pushed blond stands behind both ears. "I've got an A for the *asshole* we're following."

"I believe you covered B for bastard, too. This is a kidnapping—a serious felony. Why don't we just call it in?"

"Well, for starters, that's Gloria's police chief holding her hostage and for all we know the rest of his department is just as corrupt. That leaves the Feds and Gloria hates involving the FBI in her tribal business."

"Makes about as much sense as anything today."

"Needless to say, regardless of her feelings, the Feds will be my second call after Jake if this shit goes seriously south."

"I thought it already had when we made a right turn in Superior."

"Ha. That was only slightly south. You'll know immediately if it goes seriously south, by the bat shit I'll be spewing around the car."

"I'm your wingman, Batwoman. You can count on me."

"Thank you, Robin. If only I had Batwoman's bucks, Jake and I could solve crimes when we wanted to, not when we needed to."

They lost sight of the Toyota for a moment but then the road dropped down a natural break in a sandstone butte to the wooded Gila River Valley. They passed a sign shared by Winkleman's Burger King and Motel 6 and then another sign for the Copper Basin Chamber of Commerce. Sweetgrass was again in view and still in no apparent hurry.

The blue truck sped under an overpass. Sitting just off the on-ramp was a white cruiser. It lit up like the night sky on the 4th of July. Jake dropped back to enjoy the fireworks. Having added his siren to the excitement, the patrolman fell in behind the pickup. The driver behind the wheel of the overloaded, underpowered truck made one of only two truly stupid decisions available to him—the one Jake had hoped for—he made a run for it.

Jake picked up his speed and hung close enough to enjoy the little truck's feeble efforts to get away. Jake guessed the attempted escape had continued just long enough for the patrolman to assume a resisting arrest was in progress. When they passed the next exit, the parade got a little longer. A second cruiser flew down the on-ramp, lights rotating furiously, and fell into line.

Jake couldn't stop chuckling. Guess you *can* find a cop or two when you need them, he thought. This was playing out in a manner that was far beyond his wildest dreams. The second patrol car dropped in behind the truck while the first pulled up beside it—standard procedure to send the message that the car being pursued was outnumbered and outgunned and this should stop before someone got seriously hurt or killed.

The two men in the bed were lying out of sight. Perhaps they had watched too many cowboy and Indian movies and assumed it was only a matter of seconds before bullets sizzled through the air.

Then the driver made the second and final dumb decision; he bailed off the highway onto a gravel strip and bumped and slid to a halt by the fence. One cruiser stopped several yards in front of the truck and the other stopped some distance behind. Jake slowed and pulled onto a paved shoulder about a quarter mile from the action. The doors of the pickup flew open and the bed emptied. All four men were trying to climb the fence when a bullhorn blared those infamous words, *Stop immediately or we will shoot!*

The two patrolmen quickly got out of their vehicles, guns drawn and shouted other commands that Jake couldn't hear over the highway noise. Several passing cars slowed to a speed suitable for gawking. The patrolmen advanced in a crouch. One by one the fugitives dropped to their knees. Soon the cops had them all on the ground face down, with their hands behind their backs secured with plastic zip ties.

Jake started up the shoulder unarmed with hands raised, PI badge visible in the right. He felt a pinch of pain in the area of his knife wound and realized it had completely slipped his mind during the chase. As he cautiously approached the scene of the arrest, he felt a surge of excitement. He could hardly wait to introduce himself to these two law enforcement officers and share what he knew of the four men they had just collared.

Beyond Winkleman, which Trey joked was just a little "winkle" on the map, Sweetgrass and his hostage continued south. For a time the

Toyota dropped out of view but it wasn't the first time it had happened and it didn't really worry Susan. Perhaps under different circumstances it would have. She was tired after so little sleep and was being lulled by the car's motion and the monotony of a slow-motion chase. They drove in unconcerned silence for a time even after passing the turnoff up Aravaipa Canyon. Then she glanced at the clock on the dash and jolted realizing it had been at least ten minutes since they'd seen the Toyota.

"It's been too long. I'm worried we lost them."

"What should I do?"

She checked the clock on her phone. "I'll time you. Three minutes at top speed. If we don't see them we head back to that canyon we just passed. Go!"

Trey stomped on the accelerator and sped over a rolling hill dotted with saguaro and around a long bend of sand banks cut by small arroyos. No sign of Sweetgrass. He powered around another curve and blasted past the entrance to a ranch, the barns and outbuildings flying by in a blur. When they rounded the second bend after the ranch gate, Trey had to slam on the brakes to avoid crashing into a green tractor lumbering in their lane.

He exhaled and pushed his glasses up his nose. "That was close. We almost had that guy for lunch." The road stretched flat and clear well ahead of the tractor through broken red rock country. There was no sign of the car.

"Your three minutes are up. Let's go back."

Trey pulled off, turned around and raced back up the road.

Soon they saw the right turn for Aravaipa. Trey drove in the mouth of the canyon under towering shade trees and past homes on both sides. No Sweetgrass.

"Oh Christ, if we've lost Gloria," Susan said.

They passed a sign for Swift's Trading Post advertising ice cream one mile ahead. The canyon narrowed and twisted as the road hugged a rushing stream. It occurred to Susan that anything they encountered in this maze they would invariably come up on blind.

After a few more tight turns that is exactly what happened when they rounded a curve into an open bottomland and were suddenly ninety feet from the Toyota parked in front of Swift's Store. Trey slowed. Sweet-grass's glasses flashed as he walked to his car licking at a cone with a newly purchased bottle of water in his other hand. He saw Susan, froze, dropped the frozen confection and leapt into his vehicle. Gloria was asleep or more likely, Susan thought, drugged in the seat beside him. He spun out of the parking lot and charged up the road with the Nissan on his heels.

"Don't come any closer, sir. What do you want?" The taller of the two highway patrolmen demanded. They stood, Glocks holstered, over their four captives now sitting up with their hands behind their backs.

"I'm a private investigator. I'm holding my badge here in my right hand and I'm not armed."

"Quickly state your business, sir, and go back to your car, or risk an interfering charge," the stouter officer said.

Jake slowly lowered his arms. "I've been pursuing these four men. Just yesterday, one of them tried to drown me, and another knifed me." His hand went to his wounded side. The men stared at the ground, not acknowledging Jake. "Take them in for speeding and resisting and give me twenty minutes at the department and I'll prove you just arrested a band of murderers and arsonists who fit the profile of a jihadi terrorist cell based here in Phoenix."

Jake's assertion caused a momentary distraction. The driver of the truck jerked his upper body, sprang up and bolted toward Jake with his hands still tied behind his back. He was obviously gambling the officers would not shoot with a civilian standing in the line of fire.

The burly man closed the gap, bearing down on Jake with the taller officer, gun again drawn, in pursuit. The smart choice would have been to simply step out of the way. Instead, as the charging man neared, Jake dropped into a tackling stance and slammed a shoulder into his abdomen. The felon's pumping knee cracked into the middle of Jake's forehead. He felt his side rip open. Jake had felled the fugitive like a chain-sawed tree, but he lay on the ground stunned, blood soaking his shirt, and watched the lights in his head flicker twice and go out.

The Toyota bucketed up the canyon at breakneck speed, swinging dangerously wide on curves. Trey was doing an admirable job tailing. They passed side canyons alive with trees and shrubs, and bursting with green and gold vegetation. Roadside buildings tucked up on benches flashed by.

Susan encouraged Trey to keep the car in sight but, at the same time, was torn about what course of action would place Gloria in the least amount of danger. If only Susan could be certain the canyon would eventually dead-end. She suspected it didn't, and that backcountry access to the more inaccessible Apache lands to the north might have been what had motivated Sweetgrass to head up it. She worried most about what would happen to Gloria if they lost her.

The only other thing she could imagine would possess Sweetgrass to drive up Aravaipa was a plan to secretly stash Gloria in a cabin. And if that were the case—oh well—the best laid plans of mice and men, Susan thought. Sucks for you, Mickey.

The Toyota crossed the double yellow on an ascending curve and narrowly missed colliding with an oncoming UPS truck. Trey pulled back in his lane just in time to avoid sideswiping the truck himself.

The next few curves passed without incident until Susan noticed a sign indicating a blind driveway on the right and in the same instant heard a car's horn blaring as the Corolla veered onto the shoulder and narrowly missed a minivan turning out to descend the canyon. Trey braked hard and narrowly avoided rear-ending the Toyota. After clearing the van, Sweetgrass swerved back on the road and sped up again.

This all compounded Susan's worry. They were conducting an unofficial, extremely dangerous, high-speed-for-conditions chase in the worst of all possible places. Susan worked at her phone as she rocked back and forth in the car. Unfortunately, because of the high canyon walls, her GPS was no help in determining where the road led. She wasn't certain what to do. She wished she could confer with Jake, but there again her phone was showing no service.

Her concern about dangerous speed was at least momentarily answered in what some would call a providential intervention. They rounded a curve and came right up on the Toyota, brake lights flaring and traveling less than thirty miles an hour behind an old school bus painted white. It was full of singing kids. An arc of green letters on the back door spelled out, AC Bible Camp. Passing the bus, for now at least, was out of the question.

And that's pretty much how it went for twenty minutes or so. A bizarre and surreal convoy crawling up the winding road consisting of a school bus full of happy campers high on Jesus followed by a crazed Islamic jihadist half-Apache and his hostage, the Apache Chief, with the blonde PI and her driver/sidekick—the bespectacled pathologist—right behind.

And it would have made a for a serene and peaceful scenario deep in this gorgeous stream-cut gorge if the Toyota hadn't been constantly swinging out and maniacally looking for a place to pass on the canyon's scenic but suicidal road.

He finally got his chance. Or thought he had. As the canyon topped out in barren rolling terrain and the walls pulled well back, the road went from asphalt to gravel and Sweetgrass made his move. He blasted out to pass the bus, engine screaming, only to be looking into the grill of a black pickup truck hauling a silver horse trailer and barreling right at him. He wrenched the wheel to the right, overcompensating and causing the car to fishtail and slide on the gravel in front of the Nissan. It shot off the right side of the road, bucked across a sand shoulder and bounced down an embankment.

The pickup passed and the bus never slowed, not that it could much. The driver seemed to not notice. That was a good thing with the safety of children at stake, Susan thought, briefly picturing Amy.

Trey pulled off on the shoulder. Susan jumped out and ran to the edge, phone in one hand and Glock in the other. She could see the Toyota fifty yards below at the bottom of the ramped bank. It was upright but hung up in some large riprap rocks. Sweetgrass was out of the car, apparently unharmed. Susan stood in the swirling bus dust and checked for a cell signal while watching him yank an apparently groggy Gloria out of the passenger side and position her between him and Susan, his pistol in his right hand. She saw she had one bar. A text to Jake was the best option.

Sweetgrass dragged his captive toward a horse trail that crossed above them and wound up a draw to the top of the canyon. Gloria staggered to keep her feet. Trey was waiting in the car for Susan's orders, door open. She holstered her Glock and typed hastily: *WS on foot with hostage horse trail top of AV Canyon. Pursuing.* And hit send.

She slipped her phone in her front pocket and ran back to the car and opened her door.

"We're going after him. You up for it?"

"Could use some exercise, Batwoman."

"We might be out awhile. Grab some of those crap snacks. I'll take these Red Bulls."

She pulled her phone out, placed it on the seat and jammed two cans from off the floor into her front pockets.

"Let's go. He's already got several hundred yards on us. Number one priority, Gloria's safety. Number too—ours." She slammed her car door and started down the hill to the now abandoned Toyota.

Susan arrived at the car first. Trey slid down the last thirty feet to join her. The doors were closed and the windows were cracked, as if the passengers were on a short hike and planned on returning soon. Both beards and heavy tunics were in the back seat. The water bottle was missing. Susan looked up and saw Sweetgrass now approximately one half-mile ahead up the draw. She did not want to take any chances.

"Do you know how to disable a car?"

"Do I know how to disable a car? Is a bear Catholic? I misspent my youth disabling things."

"Looks like this one's not going anywhere, but I want to be absolutely certain he can't circle back and drive out the access." She pointed down the slope to a parking area at the end of a two-track descending from the main road. The trail originated at the empty parking lot.

"I'm on it."

She headed upslope to intersect with the trail. "Be quick and catch up. I need my wingman."

He called after her. "Don't go bat-shit without me. I don't want to miss it."

Susan half ran up the tight dusty switchbacks. The trail wound around boulders, through Palo Verde trees and past short round cacti and spiky cholla. She felt sweat dampening the center of her tank and wished she had a little better sun cover for her arms—and that she had her running shoes. Sandals, even close-toed sandals, were not the best choice for jogging in the desert. She occasionally sidestepped dried horse droppings. Her breath was coming hard but even. Her running regimen and high country hikes were serving her well. She squinted up into the sun, glad for her Ray-Bans and Goddard ball cap. She worried about Gloria and Trey exerting in this heat without hats and plentiful water, but at least the sun would be behind the western rim of the canyon in a few hours.

The pair above dropped out of view periodically, but it was usually just minutes before she would climb a switchback and see them again. She was definitely closing the gap, although not entirely certain what she would do once she did. Start by negotiating, she thought, and trying to convince Sweetgrass of the futility.

She stopped to check on Trey and saw that he was already working his way up the draw below. The deeper narrow portion of Aravaipa Canyon dropped to her left, and on the right tableland rolled off to distant forests and peaks. She was pleased with her vertical gain in what had been less than twenty minutes and reached for her phone to see if she had enough bars to call Jake. Her hand hit a hard round object in the front pocket where she had last stored her cell. She slapped her back pockets. Great! In her haste she had left the phone in the car. She had traded a Red Bull for what might have been Gloria's lifeline—and that after lecturing Trey. Shit! At least her Glock was snug in its holster in the middle of her back.

Tracking Trey's progress was fairly easy from her vantage point. He was slow and steady and, so far, not really gaining. It worked for the tortoise when he went head-to-head with the hare. We'll see if it works for Trey, she thought. Sweetgrass and Gloria had also slowed considerably and were now not that far ahead.

A few switchbacks up she noticed the trail zigzag through a barren patch of rock and dirt with no cover. That concerned her for two reasons. She would be exposed while crossing, and it would alert Sweetgrass to exactly how close she was to them.

Susan climbed to the edge of the open stretch. She paused to collect herself with several deep inhales. Sweetgrass was out of sight. She made a dash up the trail, reached the first switch, crossed the open ground, gained the next switchback to the right and was almost in the shelter of the boulders and bushes when a shot whizzed above her and a second ricocheted off a rock by her feet. The sound echoed down the draw laying her out flat in the dirt and scrambling for cover.

She sat in the protection of a boulder, pulled out her pistol and called out, "This has to end, William. You are placing your leader in grave danger. Put down your gun and come down and let's talk this out." She brushed at the dirt on the front of her violet tank and adjusted a black bra strap that had shifted onto her shoulder. There was no response. There was a chance that he had fired randomly to slow her down and buy time in order to regain the advantage.

While she waited in the shade of the boulder, Trey got to the last cover just below the open patch. Susan called to him. "Trey, wait. I'm concerned about your safety crossing that open stretch."

"You okay, Susan?"

"Yup. Those potshots were meant to intimidate. Close, but no stogie. Can you see him?"

"No. I think they went on up. They were already pretty close to the top. I can't help you pinned down here. I'm coming across, Susan."

Before she could protest, Trey broke from his cover and started up the exposed switches. His lumbering big-man's pace was not an advantage. Before he made the first turn a shot echoed from above and he was down holding his right calf.

"Christ. I'm hit."

Before she could think, Susan, waving her pistol blindly up the hill, sprinted and skidded straight over the switches to where Trey sat. She grabbed his arm and they butt-slid together back to the protection of the bushes and boulders.

She holstered her Glock. "How you doing?"

"Fuck this hurts." He rocked back and forth blowing out breaths.

She pulled up his pant leg up and examined his calf. "Got a knife?"

Trey gritted his teeth. "Front right pocket."

"You're going to be okay. I promise. Bullet did some damage and burrowed a trench of Flesh's flesh, but it basically grazed you. Lucky shot at a fast-moving target. Guaranteed sexy scar to accompany a good story."

He let out a burst of laughter, groaned, and leaned back so she could reach in his pocket. She fished out a crushed bag of pretzels and then dug out his Western brand, black-handled, four inch, single-bladed knife, opened it and carefully sliced his pant leg up and his sock down. Blood was streaming into his hiking shoe. She grabbed a folded blue bandana out of her back pocket.

"Fortunately for you, I haven't needed to blow my nose today." She wrapped the bandana around his wounded calf and knotted it tight.

She slid a Red Bull out of her right pocket and placed it beside him. "Keep pressure on the wound. You're benched, champ. Officially on picnic duty. Don't move up or down until I get back, okay?"

"What's that on the back of your arm?" She glanced back and saw and felt for the first time a segment of bristling cactus stuck to her flesh. She started to reach for it.

"No, Susan. That's teddy bear cholla. The spines are hollow and can hook under your skin. Don't touch it. Get my comb out of my back pocket."

He leaned forward while she yanked a well-used rag out of his hip pocket that might have once had a discernible pattern. She held it by the tip of her fingers.

"Sorry, I have had to blow my nose today."

"Today and every day for the last, what three months?" She removed his plastic comb.

"Give them here. Sit in front of me." He folded the bandana several times to increase thickness and wrapped the bottom of the comb with it.

Susan did as she was told. She grimaced as her skin pinched and pulled while Trey worked the blob free. Then she felt several individual pricks as he combed out the remaining spines. He patted her back when satisfied he had removed them all.

"How can anything so nasty to touch be so beautiful to look at?" Susan asked while standing.

"That's kind of what I like about cacti." Trey checked his fingers for spines. Determining they were all stuck in the bandana and comb, he placed his hands back on his calf. "You can't go back across that shooting gallery."

"Don't really have a choice. I could care less that he's acting suicidal but I can't let him take Gloria with him." She pulled the other can of Red Bull out of her pocket, ripped off the top and chugged it.

"This'd make a great ad for Red Bull," Trey said, grinning through sweat, dirt and pain.

Susan pushed his glasses up his nose, kissed his forehead and hugged him. She got up in a crouch, pulled out her gun, charged out of the bushes, sprinted up the trail and made the first switchback without a problem. But she thought that might be due to the element of surprise. Her heart was slamming. She barreled toward the second switch and the longest stretch of exposure. No shot. She sprinted the last ten yards and slid down behind the same boulder to let her heart slow and catch her breath. She checked her hands and knees. They were showing various degrees of abrasion. She listened. There was no sound from above. Sweetgrass might have already dragged Gloria over the top.

In the shade of the boulder, she took time to think. WWJD. What would Jake do? Sweetgrass was obviously going to put up a fight and appeared to have bullets to burn. He had two advantages, the high ground and a hostage. Gloria slowed him down, for sure, but Susan didn't dare fire even a random shot in his direction for fear of hitting her.

Jake always said to get inside their heads. What's Sweetgrass thinking? Where's he going? What's his weakness? One thing to consider is that Gloria is his leader and he is indebted to her. Also, he has water from the store so that's not an issue.

She studied the high terrain opposite her across the broad expanse of canyon. She guessed that the ground above her was probably identical to what she could see on the other side. It appeared to be flat, open, and dotted with sparse vegetation. Once on top she would be for all intents and purposes unarmed as long as Sweetgrass stayed close to Gloria, and she could anticipate no cover if/when he fired at her. She pounded the dirt beside her hip. I cannot let this son-of-a-bitch win. She put her back against the boulder, closed her eyes and tried to ignore her thirst. A small plane droned in the distance. Think!

First thought, no one in this merry band of jihadi has had the cojones, at least so far, to murder a healthy individual. What was it Jake had said? It was like cutting but not mortally stabbing. They were playing at something, trying to send a message, but were not totally committed, he said. Maybe that could work to her advantage. She wondered how Jake had fared with the other four. The unknown of course, was what any of them would do when cornered. She made her decision and headed cautiously up the trail with her Glock at the ready, ready, that is to surrender it, as soon as she got near the top. She yanked her tank top up to just under her bra.

It had been several hours since they left the car. The trail was in the shade now and topped out with one last switchback. She saw that it fed onto a plateau similar to the one she had observed across the canyon and was brilliantly lit by the slanting evening sun. The air was calm, only a slight breeze stirred the grass. She took the final steps and peered over the top, shocked to see that it was a virtual teddy bear cholla picnic. Before her spread acres of the spiky little tree-like cacti bristling with golden spines, emanating yellow light from the sun and appearing as soft as velvet.

Susan walked slowly up into the open with her hands up and her midriff exposed. Even with shades on, she had to squint into the glare. Sweetgrass was sitting thirty yards away behind Gloria, silhouetted on a boulder at the edge of a wide spot in the trail. Susan heard the small plane getting closer now but dared not look up. Sweetgrass aimed his Sig Sauer over Gloria's shoulder at Susan. The barrel glinted with the light.

"Whoa, whoa, William. Look, you wounded my friend. He's down. I'm alone and I'm surrendering. I'm going to eject my clip and put my gun down and turn around so you can see I'm not armed. I just want to talk."

She removed the clip, slowly placed her Glock on the ground, straightened and eased forward five yards. Then she rotated so he could see the empty holster and waistband. She faced him again and carefully lowered her tank. She started to walk forward.

Sweetgrass stood, took two steps away from Gloria and swung his pistol back and forth between Gloria and Susan. "Stop right there, don't come any closer, or you both die. Throw the clip in the cactus."

Susan underhanded the magazine into the cholla and then raised her hands to mid-chest, palms out.

"What do you want? Why can't you leave us alone?" Sweetgrass demanded.

Gloria looked exhausted and dirty but there was stoicism in her posture and demeanor that touched Susan's heart. The sound of the plane overhead was fading away.

"I work for your Chief, and she's here against her will. I want to take her home."

"This is none of your business and that is not happening. Leave here immediately."

"I'm not going anywhere until we talk this out, or you shoot one or both of us. I know you don't like me, but I can't believe you would murder your tribal leader. I really don't think you would do that. Gloria is like an aunt to you."

"I'm following a higher leader now. A different and more righteous path and I just need time to convince Gloria of the glory of serving Allah." His voice became more strident. "And you keep hounding me and obstructing me in my duty to my God."

"Gloria doesn't seem convinced, William."

"That's because you and your infidel partner are preventing us from opening her eyes and directing her influence to our divine cause."

Susan took two steps forward.

"I said stop," he shouted, and aimed his gun at her. "You're right that I don't wish to harm Gloria, but killing you and *kafir* like you who are the enemies of Islam avenges Allah as well as my native people's history." He gripped the pistol with both hands and took dead aim at Susan.

She froze. Gloria leapt up toward his arm. A giant, rapidly expanding, birdlike shadow driving a tremendous rush of wind and culminating in

288 • GREGORY ZEIGLER

a withering impact hammered Sweetgrass face-first into the dirt of the trail. Gloria was startled but continued her charge, leaped onto his arm with all her weight and grabbed the wrist of the hand holding the pistol. Still face down, Sweetgrass, dazed and disoriented, weakly wrestled Gloria for the pistol and groped at his face with his right hand. His glasses were shattered and had cut his face in several places. He struggled to get up. Susan bolted up the trail fumbling at her pocket, spun above him, rammed her knees into the middle of his back, pulled his head up by the hair and pushed the blade of Trey's knife against his throat. She roared in his ear. "Give up the gun *now* or I cut your fucking throat!"

His grip relaxed and Gloria pried out the pistol and handed it to Susan. She rolled him over so he could see what had hit him. He slowly sat up and stared in dull-eyed disbelief.

Jen walked up, gathering her canopy. "Hey Bill. Long time no jump." She pulled parachute cord from her utility belt and while Susan held the gun on him, hogtied his hands and feet.

August 9
Saturday

The three met in the foyer of the Phoenix restaurant Gloria had recommended. "You said to bring along the person from the tribe who shadowed William for you, Jake. That was easy. When you sent me the number, even though it was a Tucson area code, I recognized it immediately."

Gloria put her arm around the shoulder of a lovely young American Indian woman in a tailored burgundy skirt and white silk blouse. "Lenna, this is Jake Goddard, Jake, meet my daughter, Lenna Fox."

Jake grabbed the young woman's hand in both of his. "So this is the genius who cracked the case. I thought you were in France."

"I'm going as soon as I finish my master's thesis at UA."

"I can't thank you enough. You're a gutsy woman."

"I'm just glad to see Mom safe and Sweetgrass and his Islamic extremist buddies in custody with the Feds. I never liked him or trusted him." She raised her eyebrows at her mother. "But somebody wouldn't listen to me."

"Well, that's not entirely true." She turned to Jake. "I brought you and Susan on because something about William always worried me, especially after Lenna, whose instincts I have the deepest respect for, told me I had made a huge mistake making him police chief."

"So Lenna, you followed him to the mosque. And later Gloria you sent your coded text. That's when it all came together. I see where your daughter gets her brains. Superb mother-daughter investigative team. Where's Uncle Victorio?"

"He picked up my car which had been towed from the Walmart where my shopping trip got cut short and is finishing up the buying for Bina's ceremony. He said to say hello and thanks to the professor."

"Glad to see you survived your hospital stay. That can kill you," Lenna said.

"Which, knife wounds or being knocked unconscious?"

"Hospitals." She flashed a brilliant smile at Jake. He could barely take his eyes off this Indian princess. "Where's Susan?" she asked. "I want to meet her and thank her."

"And vice versa, believe me. She drove up to Flag to pick up Jennifer, the woman who falls from the sky and pile-drives bad guys. Wait until you two hear the story of how she happened to be there to save the day."

"I'd really love to. Couldn't comprehend much at the time," Gloria said. "I was kind of in shock and still a little druggy from whatever William put in my water."

"Mom and I have started referring to her as the Great God Jenerator Bird."

"She is that. Amazing woman with amazing skills."

"And your friend, Trey?" Gloria asked.

"Back at the room packing up. Has to head back to Salt Lake first thing tomorrow. But he'll be here soon; no way he'd miss a free dinner. Ladies?"

They walked arm-in-arm, Jake in the middle, into the main part of the restaurant and toward their private room.

After dessert had been served and cleared, Jake stood at the head of the table. "Can I ask for a moment of silence for the families of Andrew Millar, Brenda Petersen and Skip Denton and for the forests that were destroyed needlessly around them?"

Everyone got quiet; Susan, Jen and Trey bowed their heads. After a minute, Jake said, "Thank you. I can report the families are all grateful to have closure on their loved-ones." He reached for his water, drank and put the glass back on the table. "Well folks," holding up his wineglass. "As you know, this here dinner in this here fancy bordello-like cowboy steakhouse is on Gloria and me." He grinned at Gloria. "We had a bet and we were both right and we were both wrong, so we're paying up fair and square." His expression turned serious again for a moment. "Everyone present went above and beyond to solve these crimes and bring Gloria safely home to her people."

"Amen, brother," Trey, sitting on Jake's right between Gloria and her daughter, called out rather too loudly.

Jake continued. "But I would be remiss if I didn't make special mention of the remarkable timing and precision of the amazing person Gloria refers to as the Great God Jenerator bird." Jen, sitting beside Susan, beamed. "I want to toast you Jen, and ask you to relay how you knew Gloria and Susan were in trouble." He thrust his glass up. "To the Great God Jenerator Bird." He drank and sat.

A chorus of "cheers" and "bravos" ringed the table. Trey reached for the wine bottle.

Jen stood looking sharp in her taupe blouse with a long tail cut on the bias over white linen slacks. "It was simple, really." She looked down at her wine glass, twirled the stem with her fingers, and then turned to Susan with liquid in her eyes. "My best friend—ever—was in danger and needed me." She paused to collect herself. "I was flying alone to a jump near Flag with Bud at the controls of his Cessna 182 RG. Bud is my Flagstaff pilot friend. While approaching the jump site, I got a text from Susan with the details of where she was. It mentioned WS had a hostage. I have history with William Sweetgrass and I just knew Susan was in serious trouble."

"Susan, want to jump in here to clarify?" Jake asked.

"Yup." Susan got up and put her arm around Jen. "You know how sometimes you accidently send a text to the wrong person? I was kind of in a hurry after I saw Gloria dragged out of the car at gunpoint. I thought I was texting Jake but Jen was the last person who had texted me, and so it went to her. Thank God, because Jake was flat on his back in the ambulance after getting his bell rung on a goal line stand." Susan gave Jen a hug. "Then of course, I left my phone in the car and missed all of Jen's replies. The real question is, will Trey ever let me forget that I forgot my phone?"

"Never!" Trey yelled and yucked. Susan blew Trey a kiss and sat.

Gloria said. "But Jen, how did you find us?"

"Susan's initial text was pretty specific. Skydivers and smokejumpers have to be familiar with just about every little airstrip in the west. I knew Susan was in the Phoenix area and when her text said AV canyon I was pretty sure it was Aravaipa. There is an airstrip up on the rim that belongs to AV Canyon Ranch."

"So anyhow, Bud feels he owes me for the work I've gotten him flying fires, and he is a really good buddy, so I talked him into flying south. He thought it was just for recon and said later he was a little shocked when the plane shifted and rose slightly and he looked back to see me gone."

"You sure got the drop on Sweat-ass, Jen," Trey hooted. Everyone laughed.

"How could you be sure it was Mom?" Lenna asked.

"When you jump fires, SOP is to first fly in to get the lay of the land, identify wind direction and safe zones. Then you take her up to jump altitude. When Bud came in low at my request, I was pretty sure I saw Susan near the top of the trail, but it was the flash of his signature mirrored sunglasses that made me certain it was bad ole' Bill up to no good."

She finished the wine in her glass. "If I may say so. I've done a lot of jumps, put out a lot of fires, saved property, animals and lives. Just stating facts here with all false modesty erased by alcohol." She placed her empty glass on the table. "I'm pretty good with accuracy as well as canopy piloting, won some competitions, even. But *nothing* can compare to the rush when I positioned myself between the bad guy and the sun, swooped in with my Ram-Air chute, flared above Sweetgrass and nailed his sweaty ass to the ground." Applause, whistles, foot-stomps and shouts. "But then I overshot him and he would have recovered and killed us all if it hadn't been for the fast actions taken by Gloria."

She walked around and hugged Gloria from behind, "And Susan.

Who proved you *can* take a knife to a gunfight." She walked back to Susan who stood for one more hug. Jen and Susan both sat.

"I feel sorry for William. He was pretty decent to me until he realized you and Susan were closing in at the mosque." Gloria said from her chair. "He's delusional. But I cannot believe—even with my history as an activist—with IC abusing women, selling sex slaves, and beheading innocents, he actually thought I would convert. Let alone try and enlist the White Mountain Apache Tribe in jihad, Cochise style.

"William apparently forgot what Cochise said in the end, 'we will make peace; we will keep it faithfully,'" Lenna added.

Gloria said, "These self-radicalized recruits think they're joining a noble cause. What's the disconnect here?"

"That's a question people all over the world are asking," Jake said. I recently saw on CBS News that IC is burying us in the propaganda war. They have like, ninety thousand tweet addresses and have enlisted close to two hundred Americans so far. The recruits don't see the barbarity; they are brainwashed into thinking they are building something historic and important."

"What did the Imam have to say?" Gloria asked.

"He's a devout elderly gentleman, who I believed when he told me he thought the mosque basement was being used for a young men's religious studies and fellowship group," Jake said.

"That sounds right," Gloria added. "One of the FBI agents who interviewed me said the old guy was stunned when they informed him I had been held there overnight."

"Sounds like the Imam should pay a little more attention to what's going on in his mosque. His unsupervised *young men* were playing a deadly game of Indians in the basement with William as chief," Susan said.

Jake stood again. "Okay, just to lighten the mood I'm going to share my latest country lyric." Susan and Trey groaned simultaneously. "I had plenty of time to work on it in the hospital."

He unfolded a piece of paper and read:

"Wo" in women short for woe?
"Wo" in women short for wow?

If your woman brings you woe?
Tell that woe(man) she must go.
Find a wow(man) full of wow.

Silence. "It will probably work better set to music." He shrugged and grinned. "Trey, will you please join me for this final toast?"

Trey rose unsteadily, wincing a little from the pain in his leg. He lifted his glass.

Jake said, "Here's to all the women here tonight who have wowed us." He tipped his glass to Gloria, Lenna, Jen, and Susan in turn. "Which is each and every one of you." They all drank.

"Jake, if I may say so as your former employer—and everyone knows as Chief I have to have the last word—you men did a pretty damn good job too."

"Thank you, Gloria." Jake sat.

The party went on for several more hours and several more bottles. Trey finally signaled it might be time to leave when his head started to sink slowly toward the table. Jake was grateful for his iPhone Uber app. Reinforcements were called. Gloria and Lenna went in one car to Gloria's cousin's home where they were staying. The rest of the partygoers crammed into a second car for the Marriott. Jake and Susan checked in with all three kids on cell en route to the hotel.

The partners were alone in their room at last.

"I can't wait to see those three characters," Jake said. He removed his lime tropical shirt and khakis and laid them on the bed.

"Me either. They sounded great on the phone." Susan said stripping down to her underwear.

"And Majestic. I miss Majestic too."

"That's understandable, sweetheart. You've had her longer than your kids and me combined," Susan said. "And I miss riding Cassie and I know Amy misses Cinder. I want to talk with Sara about her no pet rule when we get back."

"What did you think of my last toast?"

"Honestly?"

"Of course," Jake said.

She hung her turquoise blouse and matching skirt in the closet.

"I know you meant well, but I thought it was a little patronizing."

"What?" He looked incredulous.

"Kinda sexist."

"It's country. Kinda sexist is required."

"Don't take it personally. I just think women are at a place where they don't wish to be singled out by gender for doing the sorts of heroic things men, and women too for that matter, have been doing for ages."

"Point taken." He sat on the bed to remove his socks. "Jen really loves you, you know."

"I know. She's incredible. I love her too."

"No, I mean love, loves you. I saw how she looked at you tonight."

"Jen's as straight as the arrows we found in those bodies. We have a very special bond that just got stronger."

"I'm kind of jealous of that. I mean, not, no ... I mean ... men just don't have that."

"I've noticed that and it's sad, really. By the way, why didn't you ID Sweetgrass early on when you were running around with him by that eye scar Jen told us about?"

"You never told me about an eye scar."

"Yes I did. I reported everything she told me about Bill Something-Indian-Sounding.

"Nope. Not the scar. I never heard about the scar."

"I'm certain—"

"No, Susan."

"Okay, okay. No big deal. Ended well, right? Hey, I need a shower. Don't fall asleep."

Jake got up and stood by the window in his boxers. A tall floor lamp, the only light on in the room, illuminated the large white patch on his side.

Susan came out of the bathroom wearing nothing but her bathrobe, padded barefoot across the room, and nestled up behind him. She rested her head against the back of his neck. He could smell her shampoo and feel her cool damp hair.

"I just need contact. We don't have to make love if you're too tired. Just let me hold you for a few minutes." She moved closer, pressed her lower belly up against his butt and slid her hands down, being especially gentle with his wounded side, to his hips.

Jake turned and grabbed handfuls of her wet hair. He kissed her gently on the lips. Her bathrobe fell open and he captured an erect nipple between his thumb and forefinger. Her breath came faster. She shrugged out of her robe, slid a hand down inside the front of his boxers, adjusted him and squeezed. She whispered, "I'm just doing a little private investigation here, lover."

He exhaled a sigh. She leaned into him and bit his neck.

Jake's cell rang in his pants on the bed.

"Shit. That damn phone always rings at the worst times. I better answer it. Could be our next job."

"Yes, you better, darling," she breathed. He started to move past her. The pressure of her hand increased. "You can go answer the phone, sweetheart, but your friend, Mr. Johnson." She gave a little tug. "He stays with me."

Being no stranger to danger, Jake put his hands up by his shoulders palms out. He cautiously eased back around her. Susan tightened her grip even more. The ringing in his pants continued. She gently bit his right nipple and bent to kiss his belly and the area around his wound. Then, still hanging on tight, she slid down to her knees. The ringing in his pants went to voicemail. A shiver shot through his body. Jake carefully reached over and switched out the light.

Acknowledgments

My favorite part of the writing process, apart from the writing of course, is the research, and the part of the research I most enjoy—being a people person who doubted he would ever be able to put in the seat-time necessary to write a novel—is the one-on-one discussions with folks of great expertise.

Of particular note are Sara and Wayne Petsch who taught me about fire and how it is fought, Patrick Foley who taught me about cancer and how it is fought, and my sister Jeanne Zeigler and her husband Kipp Greene who introduced me to the magic of Boulder, Utah.

Susan Marsh and Dimmie Zeigler offered excellent editorial services and suggestions for which I am grateful.

Then there are thanks due to the usual suspects for my writing projects: Dimmis and Stuart Weller, Lindsey Gilbert, David Swift, Bruce Thompson, Pam Sanders, Andy Breffeilh, Bronywn Minton, Ed and Dianne Burts, Clint Grosse, Todd Wilkinson and Tim Sanders, and to the amazing Jane Lavino for a beautiful cover.

I'm indebted to Gail Steinbeck and Gillian Rose for their ongoing encouragement and support.

Thanks also to Lindsay Nyquist of Raven's Eye Press for a beautiful design as well as expert guidance and management throughout the publishing process.

Thank you Jameson for the inspiration.

And Dimmie, my love, thanks as always, for doing the heavy lifting.

About the Author

Gregory Zeigler resides on a hill in Jackson, Wyoming with his wife, Dimmie. He is an educator, speaker, environmentalist and writer. Greg is a former NOLS course leader and Executive Director of the Teton Science School in Jackson.

The Zeiglers' three children, Jameson, Alexander and Wilkinson are all grown and gone but not forgotten.

Greg and Dimmie enjoy a few chickens, a cat, several dogs and a red squirrel named Phil. Fortunately, except for Phil who is pretty self-sufficient, those animals all live with other good folks who reside on the hill. The Zeiglers also cherish the company of wild birds, deer, elk, moose, the occasional bear and a venerated old friend known locally as the Sleeping Indian Mountain.